REDEMPTION
THE RISE OF RESURGENCE

REDEMPTION
THE RISE OF RESURGENCE

BOOK III

Joshua W. Nelson

Book design by Maureen Cutajar
www.gopublished.com

ISBN: 978-1731407573

*From my oldest fan – Thanks Dad – to the youngest, Jack,
this book is dedicated to all those that never stopped
believing that I could tell a good story.*

*A special tribute to Jim, whom I always wished I could impress.
You are deeply missed and will always be loved.*

PROLOGUE

AltCon Headquarters – December 6, 2043

Terrence Jolston had been sitting at the head of the Board of Directors for just under two months. His promotion may have come under unusual circumstances, but he knew he had been fulfilling the Old Man's vision since the day he took the position, and even before then. Jolston also knew that, based on his access to the Old Man, he was one of the most privileged people in the company. He never wanted to disappoint the man who created AltCon.

The file he saw sitting on the large table in front of him likely matched the one in Jolston's satchel. Jolston had a day to prep for this meeting and had reread everything that AltCon had on their inside man at the Federal Bureau of Investigations, codename: Napoleon. According to the most recent report from Napoleon, the FBI had begun an independent investigation into AltCon. The why was what frustrated Jolston; there was nothing in Napoleon's information to explain what the agents had been looking for.

Jolston stood in front of the large desk and waited patiently while the Old Man perused his own file. After a couple more minutes, the Old Man made eye contact with Jolston and indicated the chair in front of him. Jolston didn't hesitate and sat.

"The Bureau appears to have been busy, Terrence. I assume that you have already read the latest?"

"Yes, sir. I was shown the report."

"Good. You have my full trust here. Make sure you keep abreast of this," the Old Man said, motioning toward the file. "Now, tell me your thoughts."

Jolston had been going over the available data for over a day. He wasn't pleased with his answer but knew the Old Man wanted honesty above everything else.

"I don't know their endgame," he began. "At first glance, the information they requested seems benign. The details that Napoleon's squad provided could have come from the internet as easily as it could have from his section. Furthermore, there have been no further inquiries of his team. This troubles me."

The Old Man nodded his head. "Continue. Why does this trouble you?"

"Why dedicate two Special Agents, who have been given the full support of Director Melanie Grissten, and then stop at asking for superficial information about the company? Is it some kind of ploy to misdirect against their true target? Or has their investigation decided to employ methods where we don't have the same kind of insight?"

"One of the reasons you are here, in front of me, is that you aren't a 'yes man,' Terrence. I can't tell you the value of the answer 'I don't know,' but I'm glad you've learned it." The Old Man flipped open the report again and pointed toward Napoleon's story. "Director Grissten is a formidable woman with a reach throughout Washington. Have no doubt that if she wanted to call on the resources of the US Government, she could do so, so your concerns certainly have validity.

"Dig deeper on this. Look at more than just Napoleon. In particular, look at what type of requests the government has been making of us. I know you don't bother with our legal department, at least not to any great degree, but as the head of the Board, they will answer any questions you have."

"Yes, sir."

"With the regulations that govern virtual reality, you can be assured that our legal team is bombarded near daily with any number of requests. Start around the time Napoleon's team was contacted and look for any abnormalities."

Jolston nodded his head. He would put this all to paper later, but now he was just listening.

The Old Man sat back in his chair and looked to be deep in thought. Finally, he sat forward and produced a piece of paper that he handed over to Jolston.

"Contact this man, as well. He heads one of our investigative teams that works independently of the company. When we need to know something, and I don't want the hand of AltCon to be involved, this is who I call. He and his people are highly competent."

Jolston took the paper and saw a number and the name "Glenn."

"Glenn and his team are not on our official payroll. However, he has a standard fee when it comes to working for us. Our head of security, Leslie, knows how to handle that portion of things. Work with her to handle his pay. But, and I emphasize this, you are the only one who will make contact with Glenn and provide his assignment."

"And his assignment, sir?"

"I want to know everything there is to know about Special Agents Annabelle Bolden, Nicodemus Colvin, and anyone else they may have met since they made contact with Napoleon."

"I won't let you down, sir," Jolston said and stood from his chair.

"Of that, Terrence, I never had any doubt."

CHAPTER 1

December 7, 2043

I t's funny the things you notice when your world gets turned upside down. I'd never spent much time really paying attention to the weather in Resurgence. I took it for granted, because it was that routine. We had seen a bit of snow in the mountains and some rain in the swamps, but in Kich's Keep, I couldn't remember a time when the sky wasn't clear blue during the day or star-filled throughout the night.

Standing in the Slums and looking up into the sky, I took a measure of comfort in seeing that nothing had changed as far as the weather went. No foreboding clouds loomed on the horizon, nor did thunder crack in the distance. There was not a cliché to be seen that would announce to the world that I—and by extension, my team—had just been handed an impossible task.

At that moment, I was absorbing the import of what I had just learned. Supreme Overlord Riff Lifestealer was likely the host of the Wanderer's malignant code. With this revelation on my mind, I really needed the predictable normalcy of the weather.

The fluffy white clouds floated against the azure backdrop, and multicolored pennants atop the high towers of the royals' keeps flapped in the wind. This scene arrested my attention for several moments. I would need to remember it to calm me whenever I had to think about broaching this topic with my friends. No one in their right minds would actively go up against a foe like Riff.

In this I was lucky. At least two of my teammates, at any given time, could be considered not in their right mind, three including myself. Only Jason remained to be our level-headed advisor. Still, it would be me who had to calmly explain why this suicidal plan was in our best interests.

But that was for another time. As a team, we were still underdeveloped in gear, spells, and levels. Hopefully, our next quest, to abscond with the leader of House Frost, would help us improve all three of those subjects.

The quest, however, was not without danger. House Frost had left the safety of Kich's Keep and relocated deep behind enemy lines. The trip alone would likely be as dangerous as anything we had attempted thus far, and that didn't even include taking on the ice mages of the House. Thinking about what dangers lurked right before us, I couldn't risk losing my focus.

The quiet walk back to the Square, where I planned to log off for the night, gave me ample time to center my thoughts and focus on what would be needed in the next two days before leaving Kich's Keep. I took a look at my character. I still had a long way to go.

Alex:					
Rogue:		Level: 33		Resistance:	
Str:	33 (+14)	Atk:	670	Fire	32
Cst:	37 (+41)	Hps:	7800	Water	32
Agi	10 (+30)	Mana:	0	Air	32
Dex:	66 (+53)	Armor	190	Earth	47
Wsd:	22 (+13)	Movement:	90	Holy	32
Int:	1 (+13)			Dark	32
Chn:	250 (+14)			Poison	32
				Disease	32

As I arrived at the Square and ran through a mental check list of sorts, crossing off the things I had already procured for the group, a very exhausted dwarf came running my way.

It wasn't so much the sight of a winded dwarf that gave me pause, but more so that I knew this dwarf quite well. And that he had no business being in the Capital when his home was miles away.

"Tibble, what are you doing here?"

"Been looking for you, Alex, or any of you boys."

"Is everything ok? Is everyone in the Clan alright? Is something wrong with the mine?"

"Slow down, lad," Tibble said while panting a bit. "The only thing wrong here is me lungs and the fact that I don't exercise enough. Need to be spending more time with the lads killing beasties and less time writin' on parchment," he said while resting his hands on his knees. "Would ya have some water, lad? I'm a bit parched."

I handed Tibble a flask and watched as he slowly drank the water and, I assumed, let his heartrate get back to normal. I was anxious to find out why he was looking for me. I knew he was an NPC, sure, but I had started thinking of the NPCs as more than code at this point. Right or wrong, I thought of NPCs like Tibble, Stan, and even Waseem, as equals in the game.

I was happy to stand idly by, and Tibble seemed to appreciate the gesture, nodding his head one good time before standing up straight. "Thank ya, Alex. Been running for far too long. I just hope I've made it in time."

"In time for what, Tibble?"

"For battle, Alex. Yer marker has been called. The King Under the Mountain is rallying his allies."

"I'm just trying to get this straight. We're not going into Loust occupied territory?"

"Nope, Allister. Not at this time," I said to Jason and my other two teammates, Dan and Wayne.

The night before, Tibble had given me all the information he had, which was fairly short on details. I was now relaying those points to my team.

"We are going to complete the House Frost quest, of course, but first we have to help the dwarves. The very fact that we are being included under their banner is a big deal. Tibble said we would likely be the only non-dwarves at the war council."

Each head nodded in my direction, and there wasn't a single look of disagreement with my thoughts. Like me, however, they wanted more of the story.

"I wish I could tell you guys more, but this was all that Tibble gave me. One, a call came from Under the Mountain—meaning Lord Steelhammer sent runners to all the Clans—rallying all of them to battle. The runner sent to our clan stated specifically that the King Under the Mountain requested our presence as allies to the dwarves. Two, the battle is to take place underground. I asked how Tibble knew that, and he said they were told not to worry about bringing horses. Apparently, that signifies being underground."

Dan, our Ranger and resident know-it-all, on account of his ridiculously good memory, nodded his head at my comments. "The horses can't be summoned in tunnels or caves. And as you know, there aren't any real horses to be had, so any that the dwarves had or we could bring would be of the summoned variety, most likely."

"And the third thing was that this was a matter of Dwarven honor, meaning only the wounded, the frail, the feeble, the elderly, or children would be excused from taking part in the battle. Otherwise, every man, woman, and adolescent would be picking up an axe and taking part."

"Holy shit, Alex! This thing sounds like it's going to be epic."

"No arguments from me, Wayne. I just hope it doesn't take weeks to complete. We have serious questing to accomplish."

Wayne didn't hear a single word that came after "take weeks to complete." To a Warrior like Wayne, who fully embodied his character Naugha while in the game and who loved the carnage of battle, a multi-week fight would be exactly what his room in heaven would look like.

"So, when do we leave? I don't imagine there is anything else we need to do here in the Keep, right?" Jason asked.

Jason wasn't voicing any objections to our change of plans, but I could see he had a bit of trepidation, though not for the same reasons that I had. Jason wasn't particularly worried that we needed to be finishing other quests to prepare for Riff, seeing as no one else knew about Riff yet.

Jason, or Allister as he insisted being called while in game, was our cleric and had been the recipient of not only one legendary dwarven item, but two. Just owning the first item, the Legendary Shoulders of Clerical Healing, had been enough to drive any dwarven smith into a tizzy. The dwarves did not yet know about Jason's second piece of legendary armor—the Boots of Clerical Healing, also from the same set that had been created by Master Smith Grumblewat TwoHammers.

"You could always put the boots into a bag and just bring them out when it is time to fight," I told him.

Jason smiled gently, appreciating that I recognized his hesitation for what it was. "That won't be necessary, Alex. Besides, I promised their smith's that I would let them examine any other items I acquired."

"Well then, I would say we should probably leave as soon as possible. I purchased Tibble a horse. Can you believe he hoofed it all the way here? No bad puns, Dan!"

Dan was about to open his mouth, then closed it again.

"Not fair, Alex. Take away the bad puns and Dan wouldn't be able to say anything ever again," Wayne said as he started summoning his horse.

"Ooh! Ooh! Can we, Alex? Can we please?" Jason said in a very excited child-from-the-back-seat-of-the-car voice.

"Dicks."

CHAPTER 2

"**Q**uiet down, you bearded gnomes! Quiet down!"
I couldn't make out all of the details of the speaker down at the head of the war council table. The table was that massive. And we were down at the very end. Between us and the King Under the Mountain sat easily sixty dwarves, thirty to each side. These represented the entirety of the Dwarven Kingdom Clans.

As the contingent of dwarves began to settle down and take their seats, I had a good opportunity to survey the room and the people within it. It was a massive hall, with fireplaces located at both ends of the room. Even with those two blazes going, it was difficult to keep a room this size comfortable. The centerpiece of the hall was the table we were all sitting at. It was six people across and forty people long. The thirty on each side were sitting quite comfortably.

Tibble claimed that the table had been cut from the center of an ancient oak that fell during some epic battle back in some time before anyone can recall. I had to admit, it did look like one piece. Then again, I couldn't even make out the speaker at the other end, so I wasn't really in a good position to judge.

The rest of the room was arrayed with thick rugs and furs taken from various animals. They looked rather comfortable for lounging. Next to many of these sat packs overflowing with goods, armor, and weapons. According to Tibble, those dwarves who had traveled great distances would lodge under the mountain. They would do so in this room, on those rugs, but not until after the discussions were done and food served. Tibble didn't mention booze, but with dwarves, it was a pretty good bet.

As for the occupants at the table, they were all dwarves, but their looks varied. The first noticeable variation was their beards. Each Clan appeared to have their own style. Some were split into multiple braids, while others had only one braid. Some had no braids, but an obscene amount of jewelry tied into their hair.

Tibble explained that the beards and their variations stemmed from necessity several generations back when dwarves were fighting each other regularly for position within the hierarchy of clans. One of Lord Steelhammer's forefathers saw that technique as the best way to determine seniority. When the number of your entire race is as small as the dwarves', I could understand why that only lasted one generation.

As to the beards, "Even though they was dwarves fightin' dwarves, their bloody armor was all coming from the same smiths. And there wasn't no variation. Naturally they could have just added things to their armor, but was easier for 'em to just braid their beards."

"That seems kind of dumb, Tibble. What would stop another dwarf from just changing his beard and infiltrating the other Clan?"

"Dwarves got honor, Alex. Ain't no dwarf gonna cheat another like that. We'll kill each other under proper code like we did then, but we ain't no thieves."

"You didn't see your King back in that cave, when he tried to steal all that Mithral," I said under my breath. The secret of the cave and the Mithral was still closely held. Tibble laughed a bit at that and nodded his head at me. "Well, he is the King. He gets some leeway. And you may be a part of the Clan, but since you aren't technically a dwarf, he gets to fudge with the code."

"Always good to know the rules and who gets to break them."

"Aye. Well after the clans stopped warring, we still kept our beards. Just another part that makes up the independence of a clan."

I nodded at Tibble's last comment and continued to look over the assembled dwarves. I noticed that their skin color—even texture—varied. And to some degrees, quite significantly.

"That depends on where they be livin', Alex. Them over there," Tibble said while pointing to a dwarf and his entourage sitting near the front of the table. The dwarf's skin was deathly pale, and his eyes were much larger than what you would normally see on a dwarf. "Dems the Dweller Clan. They live so deep under the mountain that their whole lives have changed. They never see sun and rarely use fire to see. All this light in here has gotta be killin' 'em, but they be too proud to put on their eye covers."

Another group closer to me had skin that looked like leather. That Clan lived on top of the mountain, closest to the sun, and as such their skin had taken on that rough look. All were dwarves, however, and all were from Under the Mountain at some point or another. All but us.

Tibble was the only one actually allowed to sit at the table as the head of our clan, but we were arrayed behind him like the other clans had done.

From our vantage point, being as we were all taller than the dwarves, we could see that most of the dwarves were talking amongst their own clans or looking toward the King and waiting. However, many were staring at us. They didn't look happy to see us in their hall.

"Alright, dat's enough out of you lot. Everyone shut it! The King has the floor," the same man said, banging his mead stein against the table. Finally, everyone was quiet.

Lord Steelhammer, King Under the Mountain, stood from his chair and had a very somber look on his face. "I don't take this duty lightly. I'm one that's all for smackin' a troll upside the head or pushing an ogre over a ledge. But this ain't a game, and we's not here to be havin' fun. I've called ya all here for battle. For war. And when it's done, quite a few of you won't likely be with us anymore."

The hall was deathly quiet and lacked of the bravado normally seen from dwarves. No one was slamming a mead tankard on the table or smashing their hammer against their shield. Everyone looked worried.

The King looked around the room, making contact for a moment with each person in their seat.

"The Shield of Ashtator has been found."

And just like that, the entire room went fucking nuts.

Almost to a dwarf, they were jumping out of their seats and yelling toward the King. I could only make out snippets, but in general, it sounded like they were all yelling that they would fight to the death for this shield.

Steelhammer raised his hand and slowly the room quieted down again. When the King saw that he once again had everyone's attention, he dropped the next bit of news.

"It's being held by Drakkin."

If I thought the room had gone crazy before, I was definitely not prepared for what came next. I truly believed that the dwarves would start fighting each other, they became so enraged. Hammers, shields, swords, daggers, arrows—any and all weapons were being unsheathed. I looked over at my teammates, and I could tell they were thinking that perhaps we should just leave.

For the second time, the King raised his hand. And while the group of dwarves did get quiet eventually, it took a much longer time than the first go round. Now that the dwarves had run through their anger, they seemed pensive. Everyone was content to sit and consider what the King had just said. Well, everyone but Dan.

"Dwarf fam, seriously, why don't y'all just buy the shield from this Drakkin dude?"

One of the dwarves sitting near the center of the table leaned back in his chair and spit on the ground in our general direction then looked back toward the king. "Why are these filth even allowed in our sacred halls, let alone get to speak. I should tear that one's insolent tongue out."

Before any of us could so much as pull a weapon, the offending dwarf's face met the very hard wood of the table, Sharla appearing behind him with her hand on his head. While Sharla had been working with Tibble and our Clan, she was being hired out for her cleric skills and, more importantly, her Battle Cleric skills. When not working with our clan, Sharla was one of the King's most valued warriors, and we had seen her standing behind the King when we entered. How she made it over to the spitting dwarf so fast I will never know.

With his face pressed firmly against the wood of the table, Sharla leaned in and spoke into his ear. She made sure that she could be heard from anywhere in the room.

"That one there," she said, pointing toward Jason, "is wearing two pieces of Grumblewat's sacred armor. Two, you piece of trash! You spit at them and you spit at the honor of TwoHammers. Understood?"

Jason hadn't said anything, but it was obvious that Sharla had recognized Jason's boots at some point for what they were, armor created by Sharla's ancestor, Grumblewat TwoHammers. All eyes now turned on him, and the dwarf under Sharla's hand was nodding vigorously, bouncing his own head against the wood.

"Good. Now, there should be no further discussion about why they be here. They be kin to the East Range Mountain Dwarf Clan, and they be requested by the King. 'Nuff said."

The nods of the heads continued, and the looks of anger and contempt were, by and large, replaced with curiosity. I could work with curious.

"To answer our guest," the King said, "the Drakkin ain't a he or she lad, they be a what. They're the twisted creation of dragon's blood and humanity, warped by them same type of scum comin' from the Children of Loust. Ages ago, sorcerers was hired by dragon-kind to take slaves and mix it with dragon's blood to be creatin' the Drakkin, dragon's Kin, and to have 'em be the servants of those beasts."

I saw a lot of heads nodding in agreement with the King as he continued to tell his tale. "As y'all be knowin'—hell! as all a' Tholtos be knowin'—ain't no two worst enemies in all the land than dragon and dwarf. Same, we are sworn enemies to the Drakkin. There ain't no peace to be had and no deals to be made. We want what's ours, we best to be fightin' for it."

More cheers went up in the room as the King finished, but they quickly died down as the dwarf who had earlier called for quiet stood to speak. As he wasn't yelling this time around, I could tell from the voice that the dwarf was the King's very own Master Smith, Perry.

"It appears there is a bit of a history lesson needed for our guests here, so they can be fully aware of what is at stake. Any objections?"

There were no objections. Even if there were, one look over at Sharla would have changed anyone's mind. With her arms crossed in front of her, she scanned the room looking for someone to speak out. When none did, she turned toward Master Smith Perry and nodded.

"As any child in the land of Tholtos knows, there ain't no better craftsman of metal than a dwarf."

Several tankards clanked against the wood of the table, which was expected when talking about a dwarf and how good he or she was at blacksmithing. It's like Tibble told Wayne the first time they met: the three most important things to a Dwarf are Blacksmithing, Battling, and Boozing. And usually in that order.

"The world be knowing that when a dwarf gets a piece of metal, ain't none that can mold it into the shape they need and keep all the fine quality of the metal. If there be magic in the metal, we be the best for makin' sure it don't get lost in the process of meltin' and shapin'.

"But have ya ever wondered, why is it that so many of the ancient pieces is so much better than what we have now?"

The looks on the other dwarves changed slightly as they became a bit uncomfortable with where the discussion was leading. The King noticed and stood from his chair.

"If anyone ever really thought about it, they woulda figured it out pretty easy, but few have. This is something we wouldn't want ya to be sharin' with other folk. Understood?"

I could see Dan, Jason, and Wayne nodding their heads in agreement along with me. Having taken notice, the King looked over at Perry and motioned for him to continue.

"So, where was I? Ah, yes. It's true, no one can manipulate the magic that already be in metal better than a dwarf. And to a degree, we can be puttin' our own bit of magic into the metal, too.

"But the reason the old weapons and armor is so much better was they wasn't just made by dwarves."

There was a long pause after that. It seemed like Perry was waiting for further permission from the King. When Steelhammer finally looked over to Perry, he waved his hand again and mumbled something about Perry being "a damn actor like them painted faced ladies."

Even Perry got a chuckle out of that before continuing. "In all the lands, there was no creature with more inherent magic than the dragon. And when dwarves were first creating their works, it was the dragons that lit their forges. Their very breath was imbued with magic and the simplest steel armor you know would be havin' a touch of magic to it.

"For ages, dwarves and dragons worked side by side to create the most mazin' works the world has ever known, and will ever know. The dwarves did the labor, the dragons lit the fires, and the two split the profits.

"Dwarves, as ya know, reside under the mountains. Dragons call the tops of mountains their homes. This wasn't always the case, though. Dragons moved to their mountain homes to be closer to whatever dwarves they was werkin' with."

Perry went far more somber then, as he hung his head a bit and continued the story. "No one knows how the affliction came about, or what triggered it. One day the dragons was as happy as could be, and the next they started, very slowly, to be driven by greed. It was a slow process at first, but it got steadily worse as time went on. A piece of armor here, or a weapon there would go missing. The dwarves could never find where they went. They looked for 'em in the markets, but they was nowhere to be seen.

"The dragons were hoardin' 'em, you see. They had this insatiable greed for 'things.' It didn't even matter that they never planned on sellin' 'em. They just had to have 'em or they would go insane. At least that's what we get from our texts and the tales that have passed down through the years."

Every fantasy-based book I had ever read, and every game I'd ever played, all followed this same model. Dwarves and dragons were mortal enemies. Always had been and always would be. The reason was due to exactly the explanation given by Perry. Dragons hoarded objects of value, and no one built a better weapon or armor piece than a dwarf. Made sense they would have this animosity toward each other

This was the first time, however, that I was hearing the tale told with a "before" portion. I had to admit, I definitely liked this take on it. As I pondered this unique tale, Perry kept talking.

"During the time of my grandfather's grandfather, and his grandfather before him..."

"That's a really long time, Alex."

I looked back over my shoulder to see Dan hovering mere inches from me. His face had taken on an air of mischief, like he had just told me the greatest secret ever. Only he had said it at full volume.

"Yes. Thank you, Dan. I'm aware that was a really long time ago."

"Okay. Cool. You know I got your back. Just sayin'."

The King had stood up while Dan rambled on. "If you be finished, Ranger, maybe we could end the story and get to plannin'. You know, before it's our grandchildren's grandchildren that be fixin to go to battle."

Dan stood up and looked around, seeing every Dwarven eye on him. He nodded once and then leaned back toward Jason, whispering exactly as he had to me. Or, in other words, not at all. "They sure do have great hearing, huh?"

Jason simply gave Dan one of his signature looks then proceeded to fix his attention back on Lord Steelhammer.

Dan, shrugging his shoulders as if he had no understanding as to why anyone would be put out with his behavior, also fixed his attention on the King.

I took in the whole exchange and silently laughed to myself. Sure, he was annoying at times, but he never failed to provide a bit of levity.

The King had not sat back down and was himself continuing the tale. "It was me very own ancestor, Ashtator, that holds the title of greatest Smith to have ever graced these halls under the Mountain, lads. Grumblewat was a close second, Sharla, but you can stop shakin' yer head."

It looked like Sharla hadn't even realized she was doing so, but she stopped quickly. The King wasn't upset and showed her so by offering a broad smile her way. "Don't really do no good to argue over who was better, though, Ashtator or Grumblewat. The both of 'em were more amazing than all the smiths we have now."

I though Master Smith Perry might have some objection to that, but he was nodding his head as strongly, if not more, as everyone else. I had no doubts about the skills of Grumblewat, as Jason's armor was definitely the stuff of legends. Ashtator must have been something else entirely.

"Where TwoHammers was second to none in armor, Ashtator handled the weapons. Shields and blades were what he made, and only legend now tells of their beauty and grace in battle. The last known piece, the final shield he ever made, was thought to be lost in the great wars between dragon and dwarf. Only the magic of a dragon could destroy them weapons, as it was a dragon's breath that gave them such power. To be precise, it was the dragon Vassago, 'King' of the reptiles, who forged the shield with Ashtator.

"And then the damn beast went and stole it. Claimed it was too valuable to sell, too glorious for a dwarf to keep. Ashtator, not yet knowin' the affliction that had taken over the dragons, assembled a team to mediate between himself and Vassago. Ashtator thought it nothing more than Vassago trying to renegotiate the split on profits."

I didn't need a psychic to see this wasn't going to end well. The looks of anger on the faces of the Dwarves was also a pretty damn good indication. I also could tell that every other Dwarf in the room already knew this story and that Steelhammer was telling this story just for my party. I was following closely, and one look back confirmed that my teammates were doing the same.

"The whole party wasn't slaughtered, thankfully for the rest of us dwarves. And as the tale has been told, it was Ashtator's quick thinking that saved the ones who did make it out." He paused for a moment to take a swig of his ale and then continued the story. "Ye see, the Shield of Ashtator had been set up in the middle of the dragon's cave, directly across from the small entrance that them dwarves had come through. Vassago and two of his dragons was there, too. It was when Ashtator was walkin' through the cave that he saw what had happened. The missing pieces of armor and weapons hadn't been stolen by the likes of thieves and bandits. The dragons had been stealin' em good.

"Ashtator looked up at Vassago and realized they'd been set up from the beginning. Vassago wore a dragon's grin and started suckin' air in quick. Any fool will tell ya, that's the notice to get a runnin' and a yellin'."

Several of the Dwarves banged their tankards against the tables while others laughed. Obviously, that intake of air meant that the dragon was one step away from unleashing some unholy amount of dragon's fire on the unlucky recipient.

"And yell out he did, to all them dwarves. But before he fled himself, Ashtator grabbed the shield and took it with him. Grabbin' the shield probably saved more of 'em then anything else. You can stab, slice, and dice a dragon, and ain't nuthin' gonna make him angrier than stealing what the beast thinks is his, especially if it be valuable. So when Ashtator grabbed that shield, Vassago stopped what he was doin' to scream out in utter rage at the dwarf. However, the dragon's fire rained down soon after.

"Several dwarves just weren't fast enough to get to the cave before they was engulfed in flames. The last to make it through was Ashtator, and the shield saved their lives. Instead of carrying it back to the Mountain, Ashtator wedged it in the cave, blocking the fire that was being spit down the narrow crevice. Naturally, some of the fire got through, but not enough to do the damage Vassago intended," Steelhammer continued.

"At that moment, Alex, the dwarves realized they needed to ally themselves if they could take on the might of the dragons. We'd always had Clan Leaders, and even some of our own Lords, but none had ever tried to take the mantle of King. But since we judged our kin by their skills at the forge, Ashtator was named the first, but certainly not the last, King of the Dwarves Under the Mountain.

"When the final battle between the dwarves and the dragons took place in their lairs, the Shield was said to be lost in a cave-in of epic proportions, burying the dragons and their ill-gotten gains. Only those dragons who were already outside of the lairs would go on to torment the people of Tholtos for ages past and ages to come, I'm sure. So you see lads, that shield is the birth of our Kingdom, and any dwarf would give their life to see it back in the halls of this mountain."

CHAPTER 3

Following the story from Steelhammer, there was no question that every dwarf in the hall would support their King and his call to arms. The king called a quick vote, and every dwarf raised a hand to support the call for war. So did Dan. We were not a part of the voting contingent, but Dan's raised hand did cause a bit of laughter and a big smile from Steelhammer.

Steelhammer called for every map concerning drakkin locations be brought to the hall. Within minutes, the dwarves had cleared the large table and had begun laying everything they had that noted the locations of the Drakkin.

Sharla sidled up next to us when the dwarves left to get their maps. According to her, before the ancient battles between dwarves and dragons, the Drakkin had occupied the lower levels of their former lieges. In the case of the dragons that survived those final battles, their drakkin continued to serve them. However, a drakkin without a dragon host was free to roam. These unbounded drakkin had joined together and had created their own communities, often in underground complexes, much like dwarves.

It was in one of these underground labyrinths that the Shield of Ashtator had been seen. During his announcement, Steelhammer claimed the shield had been found, and the dwarves at the table immediately believed him, without question. I didn't doubt the king, but details surrounding the how and where of its discovery could prove beneficial.

"Lord Steelhammer, if you wouldn't mind, could you tell us the particulars behind the shield's discovery?" I asked.

"Aye, lad. Maybe it will help."

As soon as the king said he would relay how the shield was discovered, every dwarf in the room started trying to surreptitiously listen in on what the king was saying. It was a bit comedic, as dwarves weren't terribly well known for being sneaky and were leaning in toward Steelhammer. The king saw the same thing I did.

"All you bearded gnomes, pay attention. I don't wanna repeat the same information repeatedly."

The dwarves immediately turned fully toward their king. The one person I needed to be paying attention was Dan, and he seemed to be entirely uninterested in what was going on.

"Dan, you think maybe you could focus over here buddy?" I asked.

"King said bearded gnomes, dude. That's not me. Don't want to be rude."

The king got a good chuckle out of that. "Appreciate that, but y'all can listen in, too," the king said and gave me a sad smile that showed he felt my pain.

"The reason I asked for every map we got is cuz we don't know exactly where the shield is."

This was met by a set of groans, which quickly died down when they remembered who was speaking and what they were talking about.

Still, Sharla wasn't one to sit on ceremony and asked the question that was likely on all our minds. It was at least on mine. "Then how do we know that this really is the Shield of Ashtator?"

"Let me tell ya me story. I think you'll be as convinced as I was."

The king took a sip of his mead and then launched into the tale.

"Three weeks back, word came through the halls that a dwarf had been found in the desolate wastes north of the mountain. Human villagers had come across a lad while they was out hunting game. The dwarf didn't have no armor and was only wearing tattered rags. Found out later that them was prison rags.

"The villagers took the dwarf back to their homes, but they couldn't do much for him since he was unconscious. He was still like that when the boys went out and brought him back under the mountain. It wouldn't be until after another week of rest and Dwarven healing that the boy finally woke up. And he woke up screaming."

Every person in the hall was now hanging on the words of the king.

"It took another ten minutes before the healers could get him to stop screaming and another thirty minutes to get him to come out of the corner he had stuck himself in. As soon as he moved to that corner, he snatched a pair of scissors off a table, and he refused to give them up. The healers tried to calm him down, but he kept saying, 'I know yer tricks' over and over again.

"Once he calmed enough to have a conversation, which took another day, the lad told of being held by the Drakkin. He had no idea how long he was held. He wasn't part of our mountain range clans, and I've got runners out to the other dwarven clans."

"Sorry to interrupt, Lord Steelhammer," I said, "but aren't you the King of the dwarves?"

Steelhammer gave me a soft smile and nodded his head before saying, "aye, Alex, that be the case. And, as such, I be the king of all dwarves. But this be politics lad, and some clans are far from our range and only swear fealty for the sake of appearances."

"So those clans won't be helping in the war?"

This time the smile left the king's face. "No. They will not. They have no claim on the Shield of Ashtator."

"Got it. Politics."

"Indeed. Now, back to the tale," the king said before taking another swallow of his mead. "Once the lad had calmed down enough to speak coherently, he explained that he had left his own clan some time ago and went out searching for adventure in the unknown wilds. What he found was an ambush set up by drakkin."

"The details of that ambush had left his mind long ago, to include any landmarks or villages he came across before he was taken. If we had those, all of this would go much easier, as we would at least have a place to start. Unfortunately, we do not."

The King then walked over to one of the maps that was on the table and pointed out a village on the map. "This is the village that found the lad."

"Lord Steelhammer, why do you keep saying 'lad?' Does the dwarf not have a name?" I asked.

"Not one that he remembers, I'm afraid."

That brought an even greater level of somberness in the hall.

"Well, damn," Dan said.

"Yes, my friend. Damn," the king echoed. "We will get back to the village, but first let's talk about what the lad encountered while he was held by the Drakkin."

The king left his spot around the table and went over to a hearth set into the wall. "The lad said that every day he was brought into a great room and dragged in front of a throne-like seat where a huge drakkin sat. The seat was just in front of a large hearth, like this one, and above that was a shield.

"Every single day, that poor dwarf was tortured in front of that seat, in front of that shield. He would lay on the ground, twitching from magic or bleeding from wounds, while the drakkin laughed and taunted him. And he would stare at that shield. He knew it was a dwarven-made shield, as nothing so beautiful could ever be made by another hand, but he did not know what it was.

"Still, it was by remembering who he was, through that shield, that he survived each day."

One of the warriors in the hall gave a light, "Huzzah." The rest raised their mugs and took a swallow for that poor dwarf who had undergone countless sessions of torture at the hands of the drakkin.

"Trying to get that dwarf to recount what happened to him would end with him shakin' uncontrollably, and he said he couldn't remember much about where they was keepin' him, despite havin' escaped from the place. What finally got him to start remembering was recountin' what the shield looked like.

"It was during one of these sessions that I had happened to check in on our patient. This had become a routine, you see. The healers would start the mornin' by having the lad talk about the shield. So, while the boy had been in our care for days, this was the first time I was hearing about the item. You see, there was something he kept talking about that no one other than me would rightly recognize."

"Of course, isn't that always the way of it. Let me guess, there was a phrase or an inscription that had never been written down and only passed from father to son?" I asked.

"Close, Alex. There was an image that sat at the bottom point of the shield. This wasn't the mark of the Master Smith Ashtator, nor of any clan. It was something that was placed on the shield and never put on another item before or after. I once asked me grandpappy why that was, and he said he thought it was bestowed to Ashtator by the gods. Meaning he didn't have any clue either."

A small chuckle followed.

"There are many who have written about the shield, or painted its likeness, but nowhere can you find the mark I just mentioned. Yet, this young lad, beaten and tortured, described it perfectly as he recounted the tale of his trials. Two daggers, crossed at the blades, laid in a circle of fire. A war hammer rising between them and out of the flames.

"As soon as I heard the description, I knew what the lad had found. I sent for my war council that very hour, and I have had the healers working with the boy to get any further information they can. The poor soul doesn't seem to remember much of anything"

"How did he escape?" I asked.

"He wasn't the only captive in the place, nor the only one they was keepin' in his cell. His cellmate died from his torture, and they threw his body in the corner of the room until someone could come get him. All the dwarves in that place looked basically the same, he said, their faces so badly scarred, bruised, and bloody that it was nearly impossible to tell one from the other. The only thing different was their rags and how they wore their beards. The lad took the rags, put the body in his own corner, and changed his beard to look like the dead dwarf's.

"When the guards came with the wheelbarrow, the dead body looked to be in the corner sleeping, and the guards left with our lad. They brought him outside and dumped him in a hole with several other bodies. He waited several hours before climbing out and walking toward the mountains, he said. Ain't no telling how long he was out there when the villagers found him."

The king walked back to the map, where he had pointed out the village, and made a circle around the town. "This is where we start. We know where they found the lad, but we don't know what direction he was traveling from when he lost consciousness. He said he headed toward the mountains," the king said as he showed our mountain range, "which means I am assuming he travelled from this direction," and pointed north of the village, "as our range was south of it."

Those of us gathered around the maps looked at the amount of land we would need to cover. Dan gave out a long whistle, to which several heads nodded, including the king's.

"Aye. There is going to be a lot of time wasted on just searching if we can't get a better idea of where the lad was."

While the dwarves stood around their maps and talked over the best way to implement a search, I pulled my team to the side.

"What do you guys think?" I asked.

"About the war? I thought we were all in?" Wayne said.

"For sure. I meant, any ideas on how we could speed up the search? I don't want to spend forever on this storyline. We do have quite a few other things going on."

"Alex, this is possibly the most unique quest anyone could ever get!"

"That isn't really true, Wayne. We haven't actually received a quest, have we?" Dan asked.

I bet the rest of the guys did the same as me and opened their quest journals immediately. And, sure enough, there was no quest to help the dwarves. However, I had no doubt that not helping them would end up with us losing our ally status and not being able to remain a part of the East Range Mountain Clan.

"You know I hate saying Dan's right, but he called this one. I still don't think it would be wise to walk away from this, even if we aren't going to get any quest rewards," Jason said.

"No one is walking away from anything, Allister. I just don't want it to eat up all our time, is what I'm saying. So, if you guys have any ideas on how we might be able to speed up the process, I'm all pointy ears."

Silence descended amongst our group as I started thinking about different ways we could help the dwarves. I imagined the others were doing the same thing.

I, too, was looking at maps, same as the dwarves, when I heard Dan speak out, "Hey King, what was he wearing? Boots? Sandles?"

The room first turned toward Dan, then they looked over toward the king. This didn't seem like a bad question, although I had no idea where Dan was going with it.

"He didn't have any shoes. Had nothing at all but rags wrapped around his feet. Frostbite was so bad it was the first thing they told the dwarves that picked him up. Healers were worried he would lose his toes, if not the whole foot on each side. By the gods, they were able to save it all."

Dan nodded his head and asked, "Do you still have the rags that his feet were wrapped in?"

The king looked over to Sharla and she nodded once, saying, "We didn't throw anything away. Kept it all, since we didn't know what might be important later."

"Excellent. It's a long shot, but maybe he walked in something that could give us a clue as to where he was before the villagers found him," Dan said. "And speaking of villagers, if there is something on the rags, we should ask them about it since they likely know the area better than any of us."

Dan then sent us a private message asking if we wanted him to take point on this, to which we all said yes. I continued to let Dan run with it. He doesn't often do the leader thing, and it was good to give him some time at command.

"If it's ok with you, Lord Steelhammer, my friends and I can start by collecting the rags and inspecting them. If there is something there, we can quickly travel to the village and be back with any updates we find."

The king thought for a moment before turning to the assembled dwarves and asking, "Are there any objections to this?"

None raised a hand or a voice, and the king nodded in our direction. "It's a good idea, and I'm happy to give you leeway to run it down."

"Happy to serve, Lord Steelhammer." Dan finished.

"Aye, and it's appreciated. Let's take a short break here. Except for our four non-dwarf friends, we won't likely be leaving this room for a long while. Go inform the parties you came with that they will have rooms provided, and collect anything you need to work through the night. We will return to the hall in thirty minutes."

The assortment of dwarves wished us good luck then headed out of the room to connect with their retinues. I slapped Dan on the back as we were leaving the room and let him know his participation was appreciated. "That was a great idea, Dan. Let's go see if it bears any fruit."

The king approached us as we started walking out and had a smile on his face as he said, "Aye, TheClaw, that was a grand idea, indeed. If you lads will head to the healers, I wish to speak one moment with Alex. Privately."

That was a weird request, and I wasn't the only one thinking that. Dan, Jason, and Wayne all had questioning looks on their faces, much like I probably did. I thought it possible that I was being singled out because I was the leader of the group. Only one way to find out though.

"Go ahead, guys. I will catch up," I said out loud, following it up with a private message that said I would tell them whatever transpired between the King and I once I rejoined them.

The three nodded their heads and headed out of the hall.

When I turned back to address the King, his smile was gone. "Alex, you are going to want to sit down. You see, I know what you are, lad, and we need to talk."

CHAPTER 4

Talk about a loaded statement. Two ideas were fighting for dominance in my head, and I was trying to think through them both. First, did the king mean he knew I was a gamer? Or was he saying that he knew I had an inherent flaw in my "character" because of my Chance score, and he knew I was a cheat? Neither of those things should be possible, but enough weird shit has happened to me in Resurgence that I didn't rule out anything at this point.

I was slowly moving away from Steelhammer and unconsciously putting the table between us as both thoughts went through my mind. The king must have realized, and a small smile replaced his scowl. "I'm not going to hurt you, lad," he said.

The king moved to the table opposite me and let out a long sigh before saying, "Honestly, I need your help." He then planted himself into one of the chairs.

If he didn't hold my curiosity before, he certainly did now. I slowly pulled one of the chairs back from the table and sat myself down. I kept myself far enough away that if I needed to, I could jump back and pull my daggers, although I held no illusions as to how that would result. The king was an ally, but I could still see that his level was more than five times mine, as his name came through in red. Not to mention, you know, he was the king.

Again, he picked up on my demeanor with that one eye of his and chuckled. "I guess you could make a run for it if I did try anything, but we both know them daggers wouldn't do you no good."

"True enough. Besides, I can't think of any reason for you to want to do me any harm, Lord Steelhammer," I said while trying to determine what would be my best avenue for departure if I did need to run for it.

"Ha! Says the lad who took me for more mithral than any other person in this kingdom," the king exclaimed, smacking his mug of mead against the hard wood table. "But I keep tellin' ya, lad, I ain't trying to harm ya. I'm needin' your help, and I'm hopin' you'll give it to me, despite my trying to trick ya in the past."

"Trick" was a nice way to say that he tried to steal a cave filled with mithral, that I had found and claimed rights to for my clan. The king tried to force Tibble to give over the property, but I had some foresight before meeting with the king at that cave and had Tibble temporarily grant me the position of Clan Head, just long enough to thwart the king's plans. I guess I could see how he would think I was mad at that.

"I don't hold any grudges. And I'm glad to see that you don't either."

"Oh, I got plenty of grudges, but I'm not gonna take em out on you here and now. But know that I'll be waitin' for the day when I can beat you at the business table as you've done to me twice now!" The King now wore a smile big enough that my tensed muscles finally relaxed a bit.

"I look forward to the opportunity, Lord Steelhammer. Now, pray tell, what did you mean when you said you 'know what I am.'"

The king placed his mead down on the table and started fiddling with his eye patch that covered the obvious scar of his right eye. "This is going to require another story, I'm afraid. And damn if this one too doesn't have a thing or two to do with dragons. I'm tellin' ya, we got too many dragons in our lives as it is."

I wasn't going to interrupt before the king even got started, so I patiently waited for him to continue.

"When yer a king's son, people expect a lot from ya. They want ya to be a warrior, a scholar, and have some airs about ya that can make ya a statesman—at least, as much as any Dwarf is ever gonna be."

"I feel like now would be the time that a bunch of Dwarves would slam their tankards on the table and yell out 'Huzzah!'"

"Indeed they would, lad!" the king said and slammed his tankard down one time. "But if we get to drinkin' this story is going to take a lot longer."

"Sorry. I'm definitely listening."

"Good. Now, the thing with being a king's son is that you aren't a king, but you want to be. I wanted to be, anyway. I did everything my pa did, trying to be as kingly as possible. I went to the Keep and met with the lords of all the houses. I went with him when he surveyed our lands and met with our clansmen. And when he went to battle or adventure, I was the first to be by his side. Sometimes, in my efforts to be as good as my pa, I took risks. There can be some great gains from taking big risks, but sometimes... well, sometimes you can lose an eye."

I focused my attention on the patch covering the king's eye and then past that to the scar itself. Part of it was peeking out half an inch or so over the top of the covering. It also looked to me that it was a singular line going from the top of the king's eye and straight down to about an inch and a half below the patch. If that cut had taken out the eye as well, it definitely went deep.

"Dragons, lad. Dragons be the bane of our existence. When me pa said we had found one's lair, I didn't hesitate to volunteer. Since the king was leading the expedition, it was already assumed that I'd be there with him. And as I told ya, that wasn't something I was gonna miss out on.

"Entering a dragon's home can always be dangerous. They got magic, as I told ya, and they was fierce about protecting their hoard of treasure. You could bet that any place they called home would be locked up tight by wards. This wasn't our first time takin' down one of the beasts, though, and we was prepared. Our own Dwarves cast the spells to break down them wards and get us through to the wyrm's cave."

Just hearing "ward" made me think back to my time with Sally, my Rogue teacher for all things traps and wards. Pain is the only word that pops up when I think of Sally. Lots and lots of pain. I let out an involuntary shudder.

The king thought the shudder was about the damage to his eye and said, "Truthfully, I didn't really feel it when it happened." He reached up and scratched the top of the scar. "I was fueled by rage more than anything, and the red I saw in me vision I thought was the red of anger, not the red of me own blood!

"You see, Alex, we had thought we covered all angles. We waited patiently for them magicians to do their spell weaving and remove them wards. They said the beasty wouldn't even know we had done it. I tended to believe them, too, because we could see into the lair. The dragon was asleep. We knocked down one ward after the next at that entrance, and the dragon didn't so much as twitch.

I could tell we were getting close to the moment where things went wrong by the way the king's shoulders slumped in on themselves.

"Yeah, we thought we fooled him good. Turns out, we was wrong. He wasn't asleep at all. He was just real good at acting like he was," the king said then started moving some of the tankards around on the table.

"Did you want another drink, Lord Steelhammer?"

"Nah, lad. I'm showing ya what happened."

And as I looked down, I could see he was arranging the tankards in such a way that one of them had to represent the dragon and the rest were the Dwarves. I was shown to be correct when the king held up his own tankard and said, "Here I was, all ready to be the first through the hole. Was gonna split that dragon good!

"Had one of them magicians cast an invisibility spell on me. Couldn't no one in the tunnel see me, but they knew I was leaving the cave and going in, as that was the plan. I thought the beast was asleep, mind you, but we wasn't foolish enough to not take precautions. Only way tiny Dwarf beats giant dragon is if the Dwarves are smarter. And we certainly thought we were."

The king continued to move his tankard toward the mug that represented the dragon. As his tankard sat directly across from the "dragon," the king paused his story to take one more drink before setting it back down. "Sorry. Was thirsty."

"No need to apologize. It's a fascinating story."

With the tankard back in place, the king continued. "You see, the dragon wasn't sleeping at all, as I said. And, as I explained earlier, dragons are the most magical beasts on Tholtos. Turns out they can see right through a magician's invisibility spell."

I winced as I thought of what had to have happened next. I knew the dragon scored a hit, as evidenced by the scar on the king's face.

The king chuckled a bit at my wince, but nodded his head as he moved the tankard back quickly from where it was next to the dragon and placed it next to the others, the representation of the other Dwarves.

"That's how far I flew from his hit. All the way back to me pa and the others. I would have died if me armor hadn't been imbued with so much magic. Still, his hit did pierce through where my armor was thinnest, here on me head, and his damn claw sliced me eye right out."

The king went on for another five to ten minutes describing the battle that ensued and how the mages were able to use mana-draining chains that negated the dragon's magic and turned it into a primarily melee fight. By continuously flanking the dragon and overcoming it with numbers, they achieved victory. None of it told me how, or why, the king needed my help, but it was a damn good story and I was glad to hear it.

When the story was done, the king moved all of the tankards aside except for his, which only had a swallow or two of mead left. The king took that moment to finish his mug.

"At the end of that fight, I walked over to that dragon and cut out one of its eyes. I brought it back here and had one of them magicians make an eyepatch out of it for me. I did it because I wanted to always remember the cost I paid for going into that lair first and assuming that monster was asleep. I also wanted a good story, and nothing beats an eyepatch made from a dragon's eye!"

I had to laugh. One, because he was right; it was a good story. But also because I could imagine Dan saying "Fuckin' A" right about then.

The king was obviously not done yet, as he still hadn't told me what any of this had to do with my aid, but the way he squared himself to the table and looked me in the eyes, I was guessing that time had come.

"There was one benefit I didn't even know would come my way. Remember, I told ya that them dragons being magic meant that they could see through my invisible? Well, didn't matter that the eyepatch was covering me empty eye, it worked for me as well. The day I put that eyepatch on, I could see through invisibility, too," the king said, leaning in towards me.

"In fact, there's only been two times in the more than one hundred years I've had this ability that it ain't worked. The first was twenty some odd years ago when a would-be assassin came to the Mountain, looking for me. And the second was with you and in that cave," the king said and leaned even further toward me, staring intently. "I got plenty of fighters, Alex, ready to run into battle and die at my call. What I need is someone unlike any Dwarf in my kingdom.

"I've heard many a whisper about your kind since that night twenty years back. The Court of Shadows is what they called you, and a Shadow is what I be needing."

I didn't say a word.

It's not that I didn't want to. It's because I couldn't.

My special Rogue skills were predicated on the fact that I kept them secret. If I told anyone about them, and I believed that meant anyone at all, I would lose those skills. And so I sat there, not saying anything.

The king continued to stare at me for several more moments before shaking his head a bit. "I honestly don't know what kind of oaths ya have to take to join a group like that, but I'm betting they're lengthy. I got no problem believin' they don't want ya admitting who or what ya are. And that's fine with me," the king said and then tapped his eyepatch. "I already know. I don't need ya to say so one way or another. All I need, Alex, is your word that you'll help me."

I felt my body relax a bit and again those muscles that I didn't know I tensed began to loosen. The whole point to why we were here was to help the Dwarves, so I had no problem addressing that issue. "Without question, Lord Steelhammer, my team is here to help in any way we can. I know Naugha in particular is looking forward to charging into battle with his dwarven brothers."

The king nodded his head and then sat back in his chair. Now that the king had openly accused me of being a "Shadow" and had my acknowledgement that we would help the Dwarves, the king was relaxing a bit too. Never mind that I didn't actually admit to being one of these Shadows. On that point, Steelhammer had already made up his mind. Before I could venture further into what the king wanted from us, he addressed my last statement.

"I'm afraid that Naugha may be a little upset, then. I was hopin' to send ya and your friends on a separate mission altogether."

That got my attention. Maybe we would get a quest out of this after all. "What did you have in mind?" I asked.

"There was a time when I would have jumped at the chance to rally the Dwarves of this Mountain against our enemies. I'da reveled in the joy of leading me brothers on a charge through the ranks of orcs, Drakkin, or what have ya. And then finish the day with a round of drinks and songs being sung about the Dwarves who gave their lives honorably for the cause.

"But I'm not that young lad anymore, Alex, and I don't feel like carrying the bodies of hundreds, if not thousands, of Dwarves back to this mountain after this fight. Because that's what's likely to happen when we take the fight to them in their own home."

The king started looking around for his tankard and then sighed after finding it and looking inside, only to remember he had already finished the drink. Luckily, there were other, near full, tankards only a few chairs down. The king wasn't one to stand on ceremony when he needed a drink.

"Don't be fooled, though. This fight will happen. Even if it means losing all them Dwarves. The Shield of Ashtator demands it. We must have that shield back in the hands of its rightful owners, the Dwarves." He took a small sip before continuing. "That being said, it don't have to get back in this hall through all-out bloodshed, not if we could find another way to get our hands on it."

He wanted me to steal the shield. The King under the Mountain wanted me to sneak into the lair of who knows how many Drakkin and steal the single most valuable dwarven item right out from under the Drakkin noses. Or snouts. I've never seen one of these Drakkin, so I really have no idea what they looked like.

I wish he would have just said this earlier. I've got no idea where the lair is, or if it's even possible, but I was sure as hell willing to give it a try.

"You are right, Lord Steelhammer. Naugha will not be pleased by this—at least, not if there is nothing but sneaking involved. However, I am imagining that there will be numerous obstacles between my team and the final task of acquiring the shield, and those obstacles will be smacked down by Naugha's hammer. Of that I am certain.

"However, there may be quite a lot of obstacles in our path. Is it possible that I can recruit an additional team to assist in our mission? They are well known to us."

"Aye, Alex. I authorize you adding an additional team to assist in your mission if you accept the task."

"I still don't know what the task will end up being, but you already have my agreement. We will attempt to retrieve the Shield of Ashtator from the Drakkin."

A golden glow surrounded me, and I opened my quest journal. There, listed under the active quests, was the mission:

Retrieve for the King under the Mountain the Shield of Ashtator from the Drakkin lair.
Refusal to undertake the task will result in a loss of ally status with the Dwarves.
Failure to succeed in this task will not result in any negative consequences.
Reward: variable.

I also saw that the mission was designated to have up to eight people involved. I still didn't know what the actual scenario would be, but I would have the option of calling on Jenny and her teammates if I needed them.

"My friends and I will set out immediately for the village to try and discover where this Drakkin lair is located. Once we have the information, we will quickly return and advise the war council on our findings."

"Excellent, Alex. Our clansmen will begin preparations for battle and will await your information. Given the distance to the village, it'll be a several day march for us Dwarves. After that, two days to set up camp and prepare for battle. All in all, we got a week from the time you find their home. That will be the same week where you can save the lives of hundreds of Dwarves."

35

CHAPTER 5

The guys were outside the hall when I exited and had a look of confusion on their faces.

"We got this quest update, Alex. I'm confused, though. I thought we already agreed to help the Dwarves, so why are we only getting the quest now, while you were inside with Steelhammer?" Jason asked.

"Turns out the old Dwarf had some sideline tasks for us that I'll explain once we get on the road."

This piqued the interest of the guys, but I didn't want to talk about Steelhammer's quest while we were still in the mountain.

"First things first. We need to find where that lair is. Dan, did you have any luck learning anything from the Dwarf they found?" I asked.

"Unfortunately, no. While you were in there with Steelhammer, I went to the Dwarf's room. And I don't like repeatedly saying 'the Dwarf,' so I'm going to call him 'Jack.' Anyhow, I went to Jack's room, but he was passed out. The healers said he had nightmares the night before and couldn't sleep. According to the healers, this is a near nightly occurrence." Dan reached into one of his bags and accessed his inventory. "I was able to retrieve the wrappings he had on his feet when he was found. I'm hoping that with these, we can find something out from the folks at that village," Dan finished while showing us the tattered bandages.

I had no desire to see Jack, at least not while he was passed out and unable to remember much, so I suggested that we depart and start our journey to the village. With no objections from the guys, we found a Dwarf to take us through the maze of tunnels that ran from the great hall to an exit that would put us closer to where the village could be found. Dan knew the way back to the entrance we had used, but that exit was on the other side of the mountain.

Once we were outside, we activated our horses, summoning them into existence, and began riding toward the spot on our maps that identified the location of the village.

"When I spoke with the healers, they told me the village we were heading to was called South Tarren. And no, there isn't a North Tarren. Or an east or west either. I'll be sure to question the logic of the name with the villagers when we get there," Dan said.

"That'll either keep you out of trouble or get you into it. Pretty much par for the course with you, Dan."

"Thanks, Alliballi," Dan said, smiling toward our cleric while using yet another nonsensical variation of Jason's in-game name, Allister. "There's nothing on our map that labels the name of the village, but we've run around this area quite a bit when we were leveling up and Alex was learning his climbing technique, so there aren't a lot of areas that we haven't seen. This village, though, was one of them."

"Did you learn anything else, Dan? Anything about the village or the villagers?" I asked.

"Not me, but Wayne handled that part."

I looked over toward our large barbarian friend and he began to run down what he had learned. "Little to no defenses. The walls have no fortifications, and there is little to speak of as far as gates go to get into the town. They have a standing army of maybe ten soldiers and another twenty part-time conscripts they can call up. The Dwarves said their weapons and armor looked cheap, and they figured the two dwarven healers and their two-man escort could have taken the entire town in a little over a day."

After Wayne gave his "report," I saw him shrug his shoulders. "Be-fore you start, yes, I asked them about all the other things we would be interested in, like, what does the village do. I asked if it was a mill, or a farming community, or a smithy."

"And their response?" I asked.

"They said, 'Definitely weren't no smithy!' Otherwise their response was, 'You know, human stuff.' Not terribly helpful I'm afraid. But, what do you expect when you ask a Dwarf for details of a town."

We got a laugh from that. "It wasn't a total waste. We know they don't worry about being overrun, so they are either good fighters or there wasn't much of a threat for them in their immediate surroundings. Tells me that this Drakkin lair is either far away or they cooperate with the Drakkin," I said.

"I agree with Alex," Jason said. "Them being human tells us something, too. If they were wood elves, with their innate relationship with the 'forests,' we likely would have been able to show these rags and probably any of the villagers could tell us where the residue on the bottom came from. Since they are humans, though, we will want to locate their best ranger or hunter."

"Damn. I didn't think I got anything," Wayne said, which was followed by more laughter.

⊰⊱

We had been riding for a couple of hours, and I had finished relaying the story from Steelhammer and was now answering the guys' questions. We could have arrived sooner if we had stuck to the main road, but we preferred to ride just inside the tree line where our horses could manage easily and where we had some cover from potential bandits on the road. We were pretty certain we could take any mobs in this region, but we didn't want to waste any time that we didn't have to with fighting. It would have been helpful if Steelhammer could have given us a map that listed where all the bad guys were, but instead, we had to make do with a generic map that showed the village and the region around it.

As far as relaying the story went, I hadn't told the guys everything, obviously, but I did relay the King's desire to avoid all-out war and bloodshed and where he saw our role coming into play. Expectedly, Wayne was upset by the news until I told him that the quest allowed us to bring along Jenny and our teammates, and there was undoubtedly going to be plenty of opportunities for him to kill some Drakkin.

"According to the location we saw on that map in the dwarven hall, the one Steelhammer gave us, and my own internal map, I'd say the village is just over the next rise," Dan said, as he had been running point along the journey.

"Well then, I think we should stop here, and I'll go ahead on foot and scout the place out," I told the guys while bringing my horse to a stop. Gone were the days of them groaning every time I suggested I use my stealth techniques to look at an area. It was certainly understandable back when I only moved at a fraction of normal speed when invisible, but those days were long behind us. "Stay in the trees until I give the ok. If I signal, then there is something wrong, and you might as well come up the main road. However, I don't plan on starting any trouble, so I should be back in about thirty minutes."

The other three also stopped their horses but stayed riding in case I yelled out for help. With my Blacksuit, I had little fear of being seen, but anything was possible.

After several minutes of climbing up the rise, I hit the crest and was able to glimpse the village for the first time. The Dwarves had been accurate in their description, at least from what I could see of the walls.

As I continued to move closer, I started taking it all in and making note of what was there. For starters, the "wall," as I called it, was nothing more than a series of planks stood up and loosely connected, encircling the town. It looked to be more of a boundary marker than any kind of defense. In fact, there were numerous places where several boards looked to have been removed or fallen off and where a full-sized human could walk through. Another indicator that the structure was simply for symbolism was the height of the planks, of which none seemed to be higher than five feet. Lastly, and the most glaring sign that the whole thing was ornamental, was the huge opening where the road branched off and entered into the village, completely absent of a gate.

Having not seen any physical defenses, I started looking for traps or magical wards. A quick pass over the area, however, confirmed there were none of these obstacles as well. From my location, I could only see one structure on the other side of the fence, which looked to be about one hundred yards from the border wall, and I was sure I was seeing the second story of whatever building it was. Not seeing any sign of notice from the building, and having inspected the area fairly thoroughly, I felt good about scouting further.

I made my way to the wall and slipped through one of the holes between the planks. As I cleared the fence, I saw several small structures on the other side. Most looked to be around the same height as the fence, only five feet high. As I inspected further, I saw that the structures were only partially above ground, as someone exited a building not far from where I was hiding. The floor of the home looked to be subterranean, maybe four feet down, with stairs leading up from what I assumed was the front door. The woman exiting the building was human and bundled in furs. This made sense, given the cold weather of the northern regions. Our group still carried the cloaks we were awarded for dispatching the pack of wolves by the mill.

I scouted for another fifteen minutes, noting several buildings that looked to be mercantile. Based on their wares in the small windows, and the signs above their doors, I believed that I had found a tanner, potter, tailor, and cobbler. I was certain I had found the tavern, as I could see tables set up through a window and people drinking out of pint mugs. The tavern was the two-story structure I had seen from the other side of the fence. A man was beating a rug that was hanging outside a window and was being yelled at from another man hanging out a second window, shouting he was still trying to sleep. My amazing powers of deduction figured out the tavern likely housed the inn as well.

The last thing I noted as I was leaving the village was the guard barracks located next to the town's entrance. It didn't look big enough to hold more than 20 people, and I didn't see any soldiers training, though there were two guards next to where a gate would normally be. The guards were not occupied, and there were no travelers coming toward the village, as far as they could tell. Dan, Jason, and Wayne were off the main road and in the trees, and even I couldn't see them from the main entry, despite knowing exactly where they were.

These guys weren't expecting any fights or aggressors, which again fit with what the Dwarves had told Wayne. So long as there wasn't any pushback with getting the guys into the town, I planned on asking the very first people we encountered, namely the guards, what they knew of our comatose Dwarf friend, Jack. The guards should also know where we could find someone to help us with the foot wrappings and the residue on them.

I left the town, and headed back to the guys, relaying what I had found. They agreed that we should take the direct approach and ride to the front gate, being up front about our presence and our reason for visiting.

The guards certainly didn't seem used to receiving visitors, at least that's what I thought by their immediate reaction. Which, as it turned out, was to scream that they were under attack.

"Guards! Guards! Man the front, we are under siege!"

Internally I was laughing, but I didn't want to start our interactions with the villagers by laughing at their guards, so I kept it in. Looking over at Wayne, I could see he wasn't being as diplomatic I was. He had a huge grin on his face that, I will admit, did look downright menacing. And it was Wayne that the guards were pointing at as we rode up. That, too, made sense. As a near seven-foot barbarian, Wayne looked to be the most threatening of us.

I needed to stop this before some dumb soldier got in their minds to launch a pre-emptive attack and shoot Wayne with an arrow. Or at least try to.

"Dismiss the horses, guys. These guards are obviously frightened. And hold your hands out to your sides, away from your weapons."

With the horses gone and our hands obviously not reaching for our associated tools of destruction, you would think that the guards would calm down a bit. But they still had their rusty pikes pointed in our direction as we continued to slowly walk up the road toward the village entrance.

It wasn't until we heard a loud voice from behind the village guards that we saw the pikes finally move a little bit in a direction that wasn't at us, but only a tiny fraction, and their intent was still pretty clear.

"What are you, morons? Put those damn things away before you hurt yourselves with them! You did the same damn thing the last time we had visitors, and those Dwarves were as nice as could be!"

A moment later a large man, who looked to be around 250 pounds and a few inches over 6 feet, passed by the guards and toward our team. He was wearing a weathered but well cared for bearskin over his shoulders that had a couple of badges attached to it that I couldn't make out from our distance, but the skin looked to be ceremonial.

The man finally looked away from the guards and toward our party and said, "Oh. A Barbarian." And then slowly started backing away while reaching for an axe he had at his side.

Wayne growled a bit and said, "You have a problem with me being a Barbarian?" as his hand moved from being stretched out away from his body and toward the handle of his hammer.

"Cool down," I said as I walked between Wayne and the man approaching us. "We aren't here to lay siege to your town. I'm Alex, a traveler and adventurer. Along with my friends behind me, I'm here to help out those Dwarves you were speaking about earlier."

"We probably should have gotten some kind of note from Steelhammer before we left," Jason said.

"Indeed. Next time I'm letting you handle the planning, Allister," I said with a chuckle, hoping to disarm the situation in front of us. No doubt we could have laid waste to the whole village, but that wasn't going to help us with our quest.

"I don't see any Dwarves. All I see is one Barbarian. And that's one more than I want to see."

"What are you, some kind of racist?" Wayne yelled out.

"I don't know what that word means. Is that some beast that you Barbarians lay with?" the man replied.

"Ok, he's a racist," Wayne said as he turned to me and started walking away from the gate. There was no fear on Wayne's face about turning his back on the town, and I had seen little reason to worry either. "I see we have two options here. The first involves my war hammer and lots and lots of scattered bodies."

"The second?"

"I'll go for a ride out into the woods. I really want to beat this guy to within an inch of his life—on general principal if nothing else—but we need to do this quest. After, however, I'm making no promises."

"Let me talk with him first."

Wayne thought for a moment then nodded his head once in agreement.

I could easily see that Wayne was near shaking with anger. This was the first time we had met anyone that was aggressive toward Barbarians. Us elves, meaning Dan, Jason, and I, had not experienced any type of racial aggressions, but we knew it was there. Like how Dwarves hated Orcs or Dragons. That was a species-to-species thing, but there was certainly hate based on a cultural and societal model of learned aggression passed down from generation to generation. Of course, it also didn't help that Orcs tended to eat some of the Dwarves they killed. Dragons probably did, too. I didn't really care about the racial aggression in the game, outside of the fact that it was impeding my quest and I didn't really want to split up the team.

Wayne stayed back, behind the group and away from the village. I walked back toward the man wearing the bearskin on his shoulders and introduced myself again while offering my hand for a shake. "Greetings, I'm Alex. I apologize for disrupting you and the people of South Tarren, but we are here to offer aid to the Dwarves Under the Mountain, and I assure you that we have no intention of laying siege to your town."

The man looked over my shoulder, in the direction of where I knew Wayne was standing, before looking back at me. He ignored my offered hand while he responded. "I'm Fonk. Leader of South Tarren, and I know you aren't here to lay siege. It takes more than four people to lay siege to a village, even one of this size. Unfortunately, the idiots behind me don't actually know anything about being soldiers. Everything to them is a siege."

I ignored the fact that he dismissed my handshake offer and lowered my hand while he talked. When he finished, I prepared to respond, thinking carefully about the words I would use. Dan, however, beat me to the punch, as I heard his voice coming from behind me and a little to my right.

"Get the Fonk out of here! That's your name?"

Fonk reached for his axe as he looked to lunge past me and toward Dan and growled, "You wanna try and move me, little elf?"

"What? No! Sorry! That came out wrong. I didn't think about what I was saying!"

"That's likely quite true, Leader Fonk," I heard Jason say in a soothing tone. "You could fill a library in Kich's Keep with all the times this fool has spoken without thinking."

"Totally not fair, Allioverreactor. You could barely fill up a single wing of one of those libraries!" Dan said to Jason, who was also behind me and slightly to my left. He then looked over to Fonk and said, "Those libraries are really big!"

The tension in Fonk's arm lessened, but it was still another moment before he released his hand from his axe. "Is it your intention to win my assistance by making me feel pity for you because of the company you keep? First a Barbarian and now an imbecile."

I was quite happy that Wayne wasn't in earshot as all this was going down, since I don't know if I would have been able to stop him from smacking the guy around at this point. Still, we needed to try and play this angle for the quest. The sooner we left, however, the better.

"I'll get right to the point, Leader Fonk. Some time ago, your villagers came across a wounded and unconscious Dwarf in your woods and offered him aid. The Dwarves that you mentioned earlier came and escorted the wounded lad back to their home under the mountain. Lord Steelhammer, King of the Dwarves and one of our allies, asked for our assistance in determining where the Dwarf had come from prior to being found by your villagers."

"Don't you think if we had known where the Dwarf had come from, we would've told the Dwarves who came to get him? He was unconscious when we found him, and he was unconscious when they left. You made a wasted trip," Fonk told me.

I looked back toward Dan and motioned him to come forward. "While he may have been unable to talk, it's possible that what he wore can tell a story. You see, we're hoping the rags around his feet might have picked up some kind of residue that might help us follow the same path he took." I then had Dan show Fonk the foot wrappings he had in his inventory.

Fonk didn't respond at first but did lean in to get a better look at the rags. After a few moments he said, "Sorry, can't help you. I don't see anything on there that I recognize."

"Perhaps one of your hunters, who travels farther out from the village than most would go, could take a look?" Dan asked.

"We don't have no hunters. We have livestock and crops."

I looked back at Dan and Jason for some help, but Dan just shrugged his shoulders. Jason was little help either, telling me, "Despite the fact that our friend here used a double negative, he doesn't seem inclined to help us, nor does there appear to be any rangers or hunters like we thought."

"I apologize for wasting your time. It's obvious you can't help."

"And I'm glad I couldn't. Traveling with the likes of that one," he said while pointing toward Wayne in the distance, "you should be ashamed of yourselves."

"And what exactly is it that you have against our friend?"

"He's a Barbarian, ain't he? Same folk that raided our village for generations and stole our crops and our women. Only reason it stopped was because of the King and the laws he passed. Everyone has heard a rumbling coming from their tribes, though. We hear the rumors that the raids have started again, now that the King is busy with Loust's army. And what did you do? You brought the beast to our doorstep so he could see we have no defenses. He'll be telling his tribe, and it'll be on your head when our women are taken!"

Fonk was near yelling that last as the spittle flew from his lips and landed at my feet. He was enraged and barely holding himself back. His fists had tightened into balls, and his face was a deep red as the veins along his forehead bulged and the tendons in his neck tightened. Fonk was downright furious.

I took a step back in case I needed to pull my blades, avoid an attack, or both. I heard the familiar rustling sound of clothing that accompanies Dan removing his bow from his shoulder. I was certain Jason was on his guard as well. The village leader, however, did not advance a single step, and we did nothing further to provoke him.

I was with Jason; this guy wasn't going to give us anything. But I also didn't want to anger any of the other villagers by getting into an argument or altercation with their leader. I chose to say my part and collect our friend from outside the village.

"I mourn your loss, and I sympathize with your plight, but our companion played no part in those raids. Did his ancestors? I don't know, and neither does he. Our friend knows nothing of his past. I can tell you, however, that he has been named an ally to the Dwarves, and once risked his own life to save the lives of a dozen Dwarves. He is a warrior, he has honor, and if your village came under attack, he would stand before you to guard you from any enemy."

Fonk spit at the dirt. "He'd only stand in front so he could open the gates. There is nothing for you here. Be gone."

And with that, Fonk turned his back on us and walked back toward the center of the village. I didn't see any use in chasing after him and trying to get any more information out of him. He had told us to leave, but he hadn't explicitly barred our entrance to the city. The guards, too, were wary of us but didn't try to push back outside the walls of the town.

Still, I wasn't about to leave Wayne outside the village for an extended period, and I motioned for Dan and Jason to follow me. We retraced our route along the road we had traveled to arrive at the town until we arrived at Wayne's side.

"Take it that didn't go too well, huh?"

"Nope. Seems he really doesn't like Barbarians," I said.

"Whatever. That guy was an asshole all around. He damn near spit on Alex, and he called me an imbecile," Dan said.

"To sum it up, he was rude but an astute observer," Jason added.

Yet again, Jason had perfect timing with his delivery. We definitely had needed a little laugh at that moment, even if it was at Dan's expense, and that did the job. Even Dan chuckled along.

Once the laughter died down, Wayne asked the question that was on all of our minds. "What do we do now?"

I was about to respond that I didn't know when I heard from behind me, "You wait for the Herbalist."

I spun around and saw one of the villagers walking toward us. He was wearing the same drab clothing that I had seen on the other villagers, and I found nothing remarkable to comment on. He had boots, cotton pants, a shirt that also looked to be cotton, and a vest over it. His face, like his clothes, was nothing to write home about. He wore a thin beard, had brown hair, and looked to be in his mid-thirties. He had a soft look to him, and I didn't see any signs of sun exposure on his face or tan on his arms, so I doubted that he worked in the fields.

"I'm Travor, the town healer," he introduced as he stepped before us. "I'm the one who took care of the Dwarf after he was found. Them other Dwarves didn't say anything about more people coming, but if you are with them, then I think we should help you. That Dwarf was hurt bad, and I want someone to find out what happened to him.

"The Herbalist, Sherrel, he'll be able to help you, if anyone can. He knows every root, plant, and flower that grows in these parts, and several that don't. Once he returns, you need to speak with him."

"Thank you, Travor. I am Alex, and these are my companions Allister, Naugha, and TheClaw."

"I know who you are. I heard your speech at the gate. Sorry about Fonk."

"What's that guy's problem?" Wayne asked.

"Twenty years back, his son was taken by Barbarians. One of the last few raids they did before this King took power. Fonk traveled to Yerkich Keep and begged for an audience with the King, begged for a party to help rescue his son, and then ended up begging for just the weapons so the village could do it themselves. No one came to help, but they did give Fonk the weapons. More than they needed, in fact. Those rusted spears and the guard's outdated armor are the same ones Fonk received all those years back."

"Well, damn. Did he try to mount a rescue?"

"Yes, Naugha. He tried. But in the end, the weapons never saw battle. The Barbarian tribes had respected the King's laws and ended their raiding, and they didn't plan on getting into a fight with the villagers who came looking for revenge. They simply packed up and left long before Fonk arrived. They didn't take any of the villagers with them, though. They left them and the bodies of the ones who came before them.

"Fonk's son was among the bodies. The story, as I've heard it, is that his son put up one hell of a fight when they took him, and then he demanded to fight for his freedom, an ancient custom among the Barbarians. They allowed it. He never yielded, and the Barbarian he fought killed him. To hear the story told by those who were rescued, the prisoners that were there during the fight said that nothing shy of death would have stopped Fonk's son. From that day, Fonk has never trusted a Barbarian."

"Guess that makes sense why the guy was not the most helpful person we've come across in Tholtos," I said. "Travor, when will this Herbalist return? And how can we get in contact with him when he does?"

"I believe he will return tomorrow morning. As our healer, I rely on many of his wares to create tonics for my patients, so I'm probably the only person who knows his schedule well, since he is away from the village more than he is here," Travor informed us. "As far as making contact, I will bring him to you. I do not wish for Leader Fonk to see you speaking with Sherrel. It could impact both he and I negatively if he were to find out we helped."

"I thank you for your help Travor, it is greatly appreciated. We do not wish to get you into any trouble, so please, return tomorrow with Sherrel and worry no more about us."

"On the morrow then."

<hr />

For all of the excitement we had the day before with Fonk, meeting Sherrel was just down right pleasant. Travor kept his word and arrived with the Herbalist the next morning. He was certain that he could help with our problem, but he said he would need some time.

"I'm sorry I wasn't here when the poor Dwarf arrived. I was out on one of my foraging trips and, as you know, just arrived this morning. If it weren't for your companion here, I'm sure news about the Dwarf would have been the first thing I heard. However, it wasn't until Travor found me and told me the tale that I learned of it. The only news anyone could speak of was how Fonk scared off a barbarian."

"Now wait a second," Jason started in before Wayne put a hand on his forearm.

"It's fine, Allister. My pride isn't the least bit wounded if people are telling stories that Fonk protected the city."

"Oh, they are," Sherrel replied, "right until Fonk hears them and then smacks them on the back of the head for telling tales. Fonk may be a right bastard, but he has a warrior's honor and isn't about to take credit where it doesn't belong."

"Hmmph. I still don't like the guy, but that gets a little bit of respect," Wayne said.

Before we got sidetracked any more, I told the story of the wayward Dwarf, the discovery of the villagers, and our role in the undertaking. Sherrel nodded throughout the story and finally asked to see the bandages we had been carrying around with us.

"There are several layers of dirt and debris on these bandages, Alex. I can certainly tell you about the ones that are on the top most layer, but I don't think that will help you, as all of those remnants can be found around this village. I need to soak the bandages some and separate the layers. It could take several hours."

"If you are willing to help, we can certainly wait. Please return when you have the information."

And like that, Sherrel departed our makeshift camp and returned to the village with the bandages and a promise to return.

"Why can't we have more interactions with NPCs like that one?" Wayne asked. "He was friendly, didn't try to run us out of town, and was very helpful."

"The usual answer is 'Dan,' whenever you ask why something went wrong. But I have to admit, in this case he had nothing to do with it."

"Aw, you're the best!" Dan said to Jason while leaning in and batting his eyelashes in Jason's direction.

Jason smiled and laughed while calling Dan a fool, and we relaxed into our normal routine as a group. Without any fighting to be done, we waited for Sherrel.

Dan went on for a bit about the party he planned on throwing for our extended team, but he said he was having troubles finding a snow machine. After Dan's pyrotechnic display at Jenny's house, we all thought having a fire-retardant system installed was the more pragmatic and immediate goal.

We ended up not having to wait for more than an hour for Sherrel. When he arrived, however, the look on his face didn't bode well. I—and likely my team—were all expecting bad news.

"I'm going to start by saying I have a pretty good idea what happened to your Dwarf."

We all glanced at each other. The looks on our faces likely seemed like bewilderment to Sherrel, but really, we were looking at each other more in shock at the fact that we might get a direct answer.

"Your Dwarf was probably captured by beasts that look like humans and lizards mixed together."

Again, we must have appeared bewildered, because Sherrel continued, "I'm sure you don't believe me, but the lizard people are real."

"Ah bloody hell, Sherrel! It's not that we don't believe you, but no one else has ever seen them!" Travor responded.

"Drakkin." I whispered.

Sherrel and Travor both stopped and looked at me.

"They are called Drakkin, Sherrel. They are the perversion of dragon and man, mixed through blood and magic. That makes quite a bit of sense with the wounds we found on the Dwarf." I made that last part up, but these guys didn't know that.

"You see, Travor! Ha! They are real!"

"Oh, they are very real. And very dangerous. I am surprised your village is left so defenseless if there are Drakkin near."

"No, not near," Sherrel said, giving Travor a bit of a smug look. When it looked like Travor had had his fill, Sherrel looked back toward our group and continued. "It is a walk of several days, and the ground is rarely flat or without hazards on the way. But in all my travels around these parts, I've only once found a type of fungus that was embedded deep into the rags of your Dwarf.

"It was during a summer harvest that I went foraging. I wasn't looking for anything in particular, just more stock of what I had and anything new I could add to my stores. During the summers, I would travel farther out from the village, as there was little worry about starving due to the cold and lack of food to gather. The wildlife was always more abundant, but I knew the signs to avoid them."

Sherrel then pulled out the rags that Dan had given to him and laid them out on the ground between our team and where Travor and Sherrel were sitting.

"As you can see here," Sherrel continued while pointing at several spots on the rags, "we have night root, gravel berry, and here is what I've named lizard's crown."

The last was the one that Sherrel focused his attention on and pushed the other rags away. "I had been foraging for several days at that point, between a week and ten days, when I came across a valley. A large portion of it was covered in darkness, as the sun did not penetrate at all, and it was there I found lizard's crown. I had no idea what it was, so I picked quite a few and continued into the valley to see what else I could find.

"The valley narrowed significantly, and with a sharp turn, became more of a canyon. I didn't see any signs of wildlife, but something about the place felt wrong. I decided to turn around and try to follow the ridge line instead. I figured I would be better positioned if I had the high ground."

"That was smart thinking. We may have a Warrior Herbalist on our hands here, Alex. I like it!" Wayne said, reaching over and patting Sherrel on the shoulder.

Sherrel blushed and thanked Wayne, muttering that he was happy to just be an Herbalist. He then continued his story. "I left the valley and double-backed on the ridgeline, moving toward where the canyon started—or at least I thought it started. Turned out, right after the canyon narrowed, it went on for only a hundred feet before becoming a huge opening in the side of the rock. Across from where the canyon stopped, I saw a half a mile of open area, and there were several tents and what looked like a market. Past the tents and market was a large cave entrance, easily large enough for forty men to stand side by side. Only, there weren't any men in that market. Just the Drakkin, as you called them, but what I've been calling 'lizard people' for years."

Sherrel then placed the rag back on the floor and sat back on his haunches. "I've traveled almost everywhere in this region, and that's the only place I've ever found Lizard's Crown. If you have a map, I can show you where the area is, but I won't be going there myself. I hope you understand."

I nodded my understanding to Sherrel and tried to look dour to match his feelings, but inside I was ecstatic. This was exactly what we needed.

I pulled out the map Steelhammer had given us and handed it over to Sherrel. He looked down at the representation before him, turned it a little this way and that, and then asked us to come around him.

"This is us," he said, pointing to the spot on the map clearly labeled "S.T." He then pointed into the distance, northwest of our position. "The area you are looking for is out there, at the fringes of this map. You will have to travel over some rough ground to get there, but there aren't any huge obstacles. There also aren't many roads. If you had horses, I'd say you could do the ride in a day and a half if you stopped to only rest and take care of your horses. Since you are walking, probably three days minimum, five days maximum."

"We have horses, and the magical kind, so we don't need to feed or water them."

Sherrel looked at us with what seemed to be newfound respect and nodded our way. "Then probably a day, especially if your ranger there is any good."

"He is." I then stood up and offered Sherrel my hand, which he took. Pulling him up, I thanked him for his generosity. "We would have searched for months, looking for some sign of our dwarven friend's passage through the woods, and still we might not have found anything. Because of you, we know where to go. Thank you."

"You may not be thanking me when you get in front of those lizards, but I'm glad I can help. If you don't mind, pick me up a bag of lizard's crown? It's hugely beneficial in helping Travor develop healing solutions. The mushrooms are soaked with magic. They are right in this area," Sherrel finished and pointed to a spot on the map. In turn, our internal maps showed the same location highlighted.

"We would be happy to help," I responded, immediately after receiving another golden glow, marking a quest being added to my list. Opening my quest journal, I saw the listing for obtaining a bag of lizard's crown mushrooms for Sherrel with a reward of experience.

I looked over at the guys, and they all had the same smile I had. It was the kind of smile you get when you get a major break in your quest and get a little something on the side—in this case, another little quest.

That was for everyone but Dan. Naturally.

"Magic mushrooms. Bonus."

"Indeed, Dan. You get to be our tester. And hey, I say you go wild. No more fun a guy in this group than you!"

The three of us groaned at Jason's horrible pun. "Fun guy? Really? That was bad, Allister. You get no points for that one," I said.

I looked at our surroundings. It didn't make much sense to head out now and ride, only to have to stop somewhere that we didn't know if it was safe or not. We'd already stayed here one night, and I figured we could do so again. There were no objections from the team, and we agreed to return early the next morning for the next phase in this quest.

Undisclosed Location

"General, sir, Emily Renart is here."

"Send her in, Colonel Thompson."

The General waited as Emily entered the conference room, stopped briefly to thank the Colonel, and then headed over to her seat. Emily had just been assigned to her new position within AltCon and had made her first trip to the unknown AltCon facility sitting in the middle of a forest. Her latest assignment for the General was to infiltrate that very same compound. Aerial photos showed the place looked akin to a fortified bunker, and the General was eager to hear her report.

Normally, the General wouldn't have met with Emily so soon after her placement in the new job, but he couldn't pass up the opportunity. She had returned to her previous apartment to finalize the move to her new home, and her presence in the area was the perfect cover for meeting without raising any suspicion. The General knew this was likely to be the last time he could have Emily provide her briefing in this location, and subsequent meetings would have to take place closer to her new residence.

"It is good to see you, Emily. I am anxious to hear what you have to say, but first I would like to know how everything is going. Have you had any problems?"

"No, General, I haven't had any issues. Everything has gone quite smoothly. The folks at AltCon are running a very tight ship over there. I don't have much to offer, though."

"Anything you have increases our current information one hundred percent," the General said with a smile. They literally knew nothing about the place.

Emily smiled back at the General then placed her hands on the table and leaned forward. "I'm ready to get started if you are."

The General nodded his head before raising a hand toward Colonel Thompson who was still standing by the door. Thompson hit a couple of buttons near the entrance and a click was heard within the room. He then walked to the table, sat down, and took out a legal pad and pen.

"There won't be any recording of this discussion, Emily. The Colonel will take notes."

Emily looked over at Thompson and smiled, saying, "Let me know if I'm going too fast or you need me to repeat something."

Thompson simply nodded and held his hand poised over the notepad.

"I was met at my new home at 0800. A non-descript, black SUV with local plates picked me up. It had no official markings. There were three occupants. The first two were two military-looking men with black uniforms and were in the driver and passenger seats. They didn't say anything to me except for 'good morning' and focused on the drive. There was no partition between the back seat and front seats, so they were able to hear the entire conversation.

"The third occupant was a man in a suit, and he carried a briefcase. He motioned for me to join him in the back of the SUV and said they would be taking me to the 'Motel.' This is what he called it and didn't explain anything about the name."

"Seems odd, but Motel it is," The General said.

"It was all pretty odd," Emily agreed and then continued. "The drive was about 30 minutes, and was entirely taken up by a series of Non-Disclosure Agreements I was told to sign before I could get onto the compound. They all focused around restrictions from me mentioning anything about what I saw or heard in and around the Motel. The third man, who never introduced himself, took them out of the briefcase I mentioned earlier. I didn't see anything else inside."

"Standard documentation, it sounds like."

"Yes, General," Emily said. She then got a big smile on her face and said, "I guess my talking here means I am breaking the contract Oops."

That got a small chuckle from the General and Thompson before Emily continued.

"After I signed the agreements, I was handed a badge similar to the one I had at AltCon Headquarters and was told it would allow me access through the main gate and into the Motel. The badge also allowed me access to those areas where I had permission to enter. I brought the badge with me." She pulled out the item.

The General motioned toward Thompson and asked him to get a tech to look at it. He exited the room and proceeded down the hall. The General didn't want to continue the discussion without Thompson and passed the time asking Emily about her new place and her story for being there. Specifically, the military had created a scenario wherein Emily was forced to move to take care of a sick mother. Getting that accomplished required scrubbing every social media site available and removing any trace of Emily's mother, while also creating a history that went back to this new woman's birth. It was extensive but necessary. Thankfully, neither Emily nor her real mother posted to online sites often. It was also a windfall that Emily was an only child and she never knew her father. That helped things dramatically.

The ruse wouldn't survive an extremely deep dive if someone decided to invest the resources to check it out. However, there wasn't a reason to suspect Emily, so the risk was worth it.

Thompson returned after ten minutes.

"We can't copy it," the colonel said. "The technicians said that any attempt to do so would flag something internally in the badge." Thompson smirked. "They also said we should get the same thing."

"Hmm. Let's not get off track, but look into it."

Thompson handed Emily the badge, which she placed back in her bag before continuing. "So, that was just the drive to the facility. We turned at an unremarkable road that you wouldn't take notice of if you were just driving past it. After about a quarter mile, the road turned almost ninety degrees and came upon a large gate and guard post. I counted six people manning the gates, all carrying automatic rifles. A set of jersey barriers blocked the gate and forced the vehicle through a series of S turns before you arrived at the guards. In front of the gate were four steel poles, each a foot thick, sticking three feet out of the ground. The poles were hydraulically lowered once the guards entered the command. The gate was also thick steel that you couldn't see beyond. It would have been impossible to ram through the gate, what with the steel poles."

"That's some serious security," Thompson said.

Emily nodded her head and said, "That was just the beginning of it. Between the gate and the building was about a mile of road. I saw three separate positions of armed guards along the road, and there could have been more I didn't see. I was trying to make it look like I wasn't looking."

"Of course, Emily. Please continue."

"Yes, General. After that, we got to the front entrance of the building where there was another posting of guards, this time four men, also armed with automatic rifles. They didn't communicate with me or the suit but nodded at the guards from the SUV who escorted us into the building.

"Once I was inside, I was taken through the entrance hall, where you had to use your ID to pass into the interior. Each turnstile was self-contained. You walked into a small cubicle, inserted your ID, and an opaque glass door slid open. The glass looked to be six to eight inches thick."

"Probably bulletproof," Thompson added.

"That's also what I thought," Emily said. "From there it was a short walk to an elevator that descended one floor. I was told that the second floor housed HR and guest suites for when senior AltCon executives visited. Once we exited the elevator, we went down another short hallway, where I was introduced to the rest of the IT team I would be working with. I spent the remainder of the day getting to know my team and going over the computer systems and my permissions.

"After that, I was met by the same suit and guards and taken back to my place in the same SUV. I was told that I would have to register my own vehicle at the gate the next time I came onto the compound. Other than that, they told me that they knew I still had to finish my move, and they weren't going to put me through a full day until I had returned."

Emily looked over and Thompson was scratching away at the pad. She waited for him to finish before asking if he wanted her to repeat anything. He signaled he was good with a thumb's up.

"I'm sorry I don't have more, General."

"Nonsense, Emily. That was an excellent report. And it tells me exactly what I need to know."

"Which is?"

"With that much security, those bastards are definitely trying to hide something."

CHAPTER 6

December 9, 2043

We rode our horses hard and fast. We didn't worry about the wildlife around us or that we could be set upon by bandits. If there was anything that looked like a road, we took it. When we didn't see any roads, we had Dan range ahead with his horse and try to find one. No matter what, though, we kept heading north and west. We didn't pass any more towns or villages, though we did once see what looked like a bridge over a river off in the distance. Who knows how many secrets and buried treasure troves we passed by in our mad flight?

The valley came upon us rather unexpectedly, as it didn't appear natural for the landscape that we were traveling in. Equally so, I had been looking around for a spot where a canyon and a cavern could be. The vegetation, including the trees, had thinned out as we continued north, but I still didn't see much in the way of mountains or hills. This had been mostly tundra.

That's why I was surprised when we came over a rise and spotted the valley. The only way to describe it is that it looked like a giant claw had ripped out a part of the ground, and that time and wind had worn down its harshness. Since we were sitting in a video game, in which there were dragons, this could have been the actual cause.

We went into the valley first. It didn't take us long to find the mush-rooms that Sherrel had called lizard's crown. Unfortunately, none of us had the skill to "harvest" the mushrooms. Not having the Skill didn't negate our ability to collect the trophies, but it did mean that Dan, as our resident naturist due to his Wood Elf status, failed a number of times when he tried to collect them. Each failure awarded him with a small bit of poison from the shrooms, that we were unable to cure. Turned out stepping on them got you the same poison, as Dan found out on accident. If we had faced a group of mobs in this field, we probably would have struggled, depending on the mob's levels, as we undoubtedly would have stepped all over the mushrooms.

In the end, we had to wait for the poison to run its course, with Jason healing Dan, but we collected enough that we would satisfy his quest.

We also found the canyon that Sherrel spoke of and followed it for a bit. Sherrel had been lucky that he didn't travel too far in and instead chose to seek the high ground, as the canyon was not without peril.

As we went a bit further into the canyon, I began to see numerous wards placed on the sides of the route. Had Sherrel not turned around, I had no doubt he would have never returned to his small town. I stopped the guys before we got near the wards, stating it would be a good spot for the Drakkin to set up an ambush. I reminded them that we were only here to recon the area, not get into any fights. Hearing that we were avoiding fights made Wayne a bit surly, but he agreed—reluctantly, of course.

We followed the same method as Sherrel and took to the higher ridge line. I wanted to get a better picture of the force that could be waiting for our dwarven allies.

It wasn't difficult to find the large encampment that Sherrel de-scribed. Laid out before us was a huge town, located in the depressed area prior to the cave entrance. We easily saw hundreds of Drakkin milling about. I could also see there was some kind of ward that covered the entire area. It wasn't the usual trap type, though. I hadn't seen anything like it in my time training with Sally, but it was clearly magical. Shaped more like a dome, it was something I would need to ask her about.

I had Dan do his best to get an idea of the layout and the placement of all the Drakkin homes, markets, and what limited military type equipment we could see. The large cave entrance looked to be well guarded, with armored Drakkin posted on both sides. Those on display only numbered twenty, but we assumed there were plenty more within the cave itself and whatever lay behind it.

"Well, we know there has to be another way in and out," Jason said as we backed away from the ridgeline. "There is no way that our tortured Dwarf Jack went through the market place, then the canyon, and then through the valley we saw to escape. There must be somewhere else that has lizard's crown growing around here."

Jason was right. Jack couldn't have made it to the mushrooms we found earlier. With that in mind, we set off to find more of the fungus.

After five hours, we had found several other places where the fungus grew. There were three small cave entrances located near those mushrooms. Of the three, two were warded by Drakkin magic. It's possible the wards were new, but I decided to assume they weren't, and that only the third entrance was a viable one for us to check. And by us, I meant me, using my Blacksuit.

Over the course of those five hours, we had also avoided three separate patrols of Drakkin. Dan was able to range out and keep us out of needing to get into any direct conflicts. As such, Dan, Jason, and Wayne went farther back from the caves to avoid any possible roving patrols while I was gone.

However, I wasn't gone long. The third cave ended up being a bust as well. I came across several wards after only making my way several meters into the cave itself. I could have disassembled them, but I was continuing to assume that whatever cave Jack had used was one that was absent any wards.

I returned to the guys and told them that there had been a gate blocking the way into the cave, and one that looked like it had been there a long time, and didn't look like it had been opened any time recently. At some point, I was certain, I was going to have to use my special rogue skills to help with this quest, and I was going to have to explain those skills to the guys.

I would tackle that problem when it came.

For now, we were left with the information that we had collected on the make-up of the Drakkin outpost in front of the cave. Of course, we were also returning with the most likely location of where the famed Shield of Ashtator was being kept. That, in itself, vindicated our efforts. We needed to get that information back to Steelhammer to help with his preparations, and we would stop by the village on our way back to give Sherrel our thanks and his mushrooms.

Lastly, while we were successful in avoiding any type of conflicts, that did not stop us from mapping out the routes the Drakkin guards used during their patrols, or the various mobs we came across as we traveled to the valley and around the Drakkin dwelling.

Knowing the location of the Drakkin, the mobs in the area, and the fastest route we could find to get there would certainly help the Dwarves prepare for war, but I had to consider our alternate mission—avoiding massive loss of dwarven lives—still a failure. We needed to come at this in another way, and I thought I had just the group to help with the problem.

⸻

Our first stop was back at the village where we turned over the requested mushrooms to Sherrel the Herbalist. He was amazed at the amount we had found, that we returned so quickly, and truthfully, that we returned at all. Sherrel thought anyone crazy enough to search out the Drakkin would end up as fungus food amongst those valleys. At least, that's what he told us when we returned, right before blushing profusely in embarrassment and begging for our forgiveness. We were laughing too hard at the comment to worry about taking any offense.

Sherrel awarded us a small amount of experience and handed each of us a small package that contained four bundles of flora and one cake made out of mushrooms, each with their own benefit. One of the bundles of flowers and roots, when eaten, would remove any poison debuff. Similarly, there was one for disease. Of the two other bundles, one was for increasing your mana regeneration 50 percent, and the other did the same for hit points. The regen ones only lasted for 30 minutes, however. Lastly, the mushroom cake was from lizard's crown itself. When eaten, the mushroom's properties would increase the resistance to all magics to their maximum for five minutes. Sherrel could make a fortune selling these to players. That is, if the players ever had any money.

With that done, we left South Tarren and rode two hours before reaching the Dwarves under the mountain, and another hour before we could get an audience with Steelhammer. He was overly apologetic when he was finally able to get to us.

"I'm sorry, me boys. I didn't think your return would be so swift. Have ya found it?" Steelhammer asked, looking at me.

I shook my head that we had not and told him, "My friends here know what we are asked to do, Lord Steelhammer: to find some way to retrieve the Shield that did not include the needless death of thousands of Dwarves. They are fully supportive of your request."

Steelhammer didn't miss a beat and agreed to exactly what I said. I hadn't told him that Dan, Jason, and Wayne didn't know about my special Rogue abilities. I hadn't admitted to having them at all, but he could see that if I did have these gifts, I was keeping their secret from my friends as well. This wasn't his tale to tell.

"However, we are quite certain that we have found where the Drakkin that have the Shield are living. If you have a cartographer, I can have TheClaw sit with him and mark everything we learned about the area, the beasts that roam it, and the avenues we checked for secret entry."

Before I could finish, Steelhammer was yelling out for a page to send a message to the head cartographer. While we waited, Steelhammer told us of the preparations that were underway and that military exercises were being held in the great halls.

Wayne was anxious to see the Dwarves in action and suggested we do that while we wait for Dan. Jason was all ready to agree until Steelhammer told us that Sharla was one of the Dwarves leading the training. Jason had no desire to fend off Sharla's fussiness and desire to make sure he was protected at all times because of the armor he wore.

In fact, Steelhammer thought he could kill two birds with one stone, having Wayne look after the training while Jason visited the master smiths.

"All them boys can talk 'bout since you four left, was how they couldn't wait to look at the second piece of armor ol' Allister is wearing. Allister should go to them while Naugha deals with Sharla. And while they doin' that, and TheClaw helps the cartographer, me and you can talk strategy, Alex. Sounds good?"

We all answered with nods of our heads. Before we knew it, pages were leading Wayne and Jason off to their respective areas, and Steelhammer was walking me back into the main hall where we first learned about the Shield of Ashtator.

"Alright, me boy. What've ya really got?"

"Well, I can't say that I know what kind of magic they got protecting 'em, but to cover something that size, it has to be powerful."

I was nodding my head at Steelhammer. I had relayed our findings to him over the course of an hour and with each piece of information he seemed to be more and more distraught. And it was understandable.

There were no large paths that we had found from the main roads to the valley. Therefore, the Army would not be able to travel quickly, and the supply chain would need to be needlessly long, which opened it up for attacks by bandits and brigands.

There was a lot of magic at play that none of us could account for. The Dwarves had their own magic users, mostly in the realms of Earth and Holy magic. They could possibly manipulate the very ground around these wards, but Steelhammer said he had never heard of anything like that being done, and I couldn't tell him what would happen if he did set off a ward. All the ones I had ever encountered would make a loud noise when tripped, but those were for my training.

Lastly, we had not found where the Dwarf Jack had exited the complex of caves. Add to that, we had no idea what the interior of the caves looked like at all.

Still, the king was thrilled with the information we were able to bring back. The Dwarves had lots of preparations left to do, true. Now, though, they were able to focus on their tasks, since they knew their destination and some of the obstacles they would face along the way.

As for the actual interior of the complex, I had an idea, but it would require me to travel back to Kich's Keep and meet up with some old friends. Before I could do that, though, there were things I needed to address with the king.

"I wanted to thank you for following along with my earlier announcements around the rest of my friends."

"Aye, Alex. I didn't think ya told them about your special ways."

"I'm pretty sure I haven't told you about any special ways, either, Lord Steelhammer. Or admitted to knowing at all what you were talking about."

Steelhammer chuckled at my comments. "That's true as well, but if ya did have some magic of yer own, I'm sure ya would have told them boys if ya could."

"That is very astute of you, Lord Steelhammer. If I were to know something—not that I'm saying I do—I would have told my friends for sure, if I could."

"Yer makin' me head hurt, lad. Just get on with whatever it is ya gots to say."

"Sorry about that," I said, smiling at the old Dwarf. "The first thing I would say is that any conversation had between you and I concerning this quest stay between us. I have not told my team about the claims you have made about me, nor do I plan to—at least not at this time."

Steelhammer nodded his head in agreement and waved for me to continue.

"The second one is going to be a bit more delicate and would involve direct subterfuge."

"Lying?"

"Sure, we can use that word, too," I answered,

Steelhammer crossed his arms over his large dwarven chest and stared at me with his one good eye. "What would you have me do? Remember, elf, that I'm a king and not one for sullying my honor."

"Shall I remind you of our cave adventure and someone's attempt to steal a mine?"

Steelhammer remained in his grumpy state for another few seconds before cracking a smirk at me. "I really did think I had ya that time, elf. I did."

I returned his smirk and continued. "I'm going to try and track down information on these Drakkin and their home. If I'm successful, I will need to explain where the information came from. The easiest way would be for you to have 'found' new information after we explained where the Drakkin home was located. In this, you would need yourself and another to play the part. If I get a book describing an entrance, I'll need the librarian to acknowledge that he found the book and gave it to you."

"Aye. And if you were to find a painting showing something similar, you would need one of our curators to say the same, if I'm following."

"Exactly."

"Why?"

"I'm sorry, Lord Steelhammer. Why what?"

"Why not just tell the lads about this?"

I tried to put as much sadness in my voice as I could. "Remember, I'm not saying that I know anything about any special skills you may think I have, or 'Courts' you think I'm a part of, but if I did have knowledge of such a thing, it would be a lonely road to travel. And it would be my burden. No, it would have to be my burden to travel that road alone. Anything else would be too dangerous for the ones I care about."

There was admiration and sympathy in Steelhammer's eye, and I knew I had hit the right chord. "It's a brave thing, lad, and one I understand. Being a king is often the loneliest job I could imagine."

Steelhammer then walked over to a table with two mugs and filled them both with mead. He brought one over to me and raised his in a toast-like gesture. Naturally, I followed suit.

But it wasn't a toast he gave. "I'll follow your lead, but don't let this come back to tarnish my honor."

We clinked mugs and drank the contents down. At least, he did. I knew that a full mug of dwarven ale would get me tipsy.

Once the king had finished his mug and set it down, he turned and asked me the next logical question. "So, what's next?"

———❧———

We had traveled back to the Keep and were standing in the main square next to Sir Arthur Chadwick, the quest giver in the capital. I had just laid out what I thought would be the best course of action for the next couple of days, focusing mostly on preparing for the war. Along those lines, I suggested that Wayne make sure that Jenny and her crew knew we would likely be calling on them to help with grabbing the Shield.

I told them we would still take part in the fight, one way or another, but that I planned to use the diversion of the main battle to sneak our way to the Shield. It might take longer for us to get into the caves, as the Dwarves and Drakkin fought it out, but it was still our best bet for limiting the length of that battle. Thankfully for me, they bought it.

I would feel much better anyway knowing that our extended team was back together. Dan was an amazing puller, but he wasn't better than Gary—or Sayhey, as he went by in the game. As a Brawler class, Gary had a special skill that allowed him to "play dead" with a simple command. This was great when he pulled more than one mob, as they would just think he was out of the fight and walk on back to their spawn point. If Gary got lucky, one would linger a bit longer and he could split them. But with Dan as his partner, Gary didn't have to worry as much about splitting the mobs, since Dan could grab aggro from a distance with arrows and bring the mob back to our Tank.

Still, even if he did get two, we had two additional options with our teammates. Jenny, who went by Serenity, could tank one while Wayne tanked the other. If we didn't want to have two tanks going, our teammates' third member, Tim, could use his enchanter magic to charm the second mob. Slovak, which is what Tim used as an in-game name, was a former Marine. He had showed me before that if you can control the flow of battle, your path to victory was more certain.

The last, but certainly not the least, member of our team was Kaitlin. Her druid, Anastasia, was capable of healing, dealing damage, and some crowd control. I found her character to be the most versatile of all of us. She was also the only other person in the game, as far as I knew, who had a pet like Dan's. Kaitlin's wolf was named Rocky, while Dan named his Broham. That's another story entirely.

Both of our groups were top of the charts in Resurgence. Well, outside of PvP, anyway, but I don't want to talk about The Dicks just now. However, as a complete team, I didn't think there was anyone that could give us a challenge.

Wayne was happy to relay the information to Jenny, as the two had been an item for some time now. There were no other relationships in our small team, despite the desires of our Ranger. Still, he couldn't expect that Kaitlin would be all warm and fuzzy after he almost burnt down Jenny's apartment building with all of us in it. Yes, the pun was intended, and yes, that one was also another story.

Wayne also hoped to take Jenny back to the Dwarves and see their military practice. Since Wayne believed what I had told him, he thought it would be good for he and Jenny to get in some exercises with the Dwarves, as naturally that's where they believed they would be fighting. I was hoping our trip to the Keep would alleviate us of having to take part in that battle.

Dan planned to take Broham out for some lower level hunting while he traveled to the secret Elven Elder tree he used to make the shafts for his arrows. Dan was the only one of us that could collect the wood necessary from the tree and fashion the shafts out of the wood. Out of all of us, Dan was the only one who kept up with any type of crafting in the game, and that was only because it was directly related to his ability to do damage.

Jason made no attempts to hide that he was going to take this time to try and find some hidden quests in the Keep. The last one he had found in Port Town had bestowed an aristocratic title on our cleric. He had been Baron Allister Cromwell since we arrived in the Keep.

Jason had originally said he wanted to try for a higher title, but he had been unable to find any similar quests in Kich's Keep. I think we were all secretly happy that Jason hadn't been successful. We quite liked "Baron." Personally, I thought it suited him quite nicely.

For my part, I told the guys that I was going to search through every vendor in the city and try to find someone who might have any old forgotten lore that could help us against the Drakkin. Old books, paintings, drawings, or whatever I could get my hands on. Since I had earned a living before Resurgence by selling in-game items and performed similar trade negotiations for our team, this seemed natural to everyone.

And, if I didn't have any other options, that's probably what I would have done. However, unbeknownst to my colleagues, I still had one more avenue to try. For that, I headed to the Stinky Pit.

———

"Alright, Alex. You got all of us here. What's the emergency?"

Sitting around me in the Pit were the most capable Rogues in all of Resurgence. The man sitting to my left was Stan, who used the moniker Dhalean in Kich's Keep and was my first mentor and a master Shadow.

It bears repeating that the special rogue skill of Shadow was not technically supposed to exist. It was originally designed by Resurgence's creator, Robert Shoal, but Altcon decided to keep it simple and nixed it. Luckily for me, Shoal thought something was suspicious and had the AI he created for the game sneak it back in. Unfortunately, it didn't help Shoal that much.

Anyway, it was Stan who had taught me how to use my Blacksuit and how to access the "shadows" around me. Stan was also a master assassin, although he had only taught me one skill from that profession. According to our other two associates, though, Stan was the most accomplished assassin in the land. He was able to use his Blacksuit to a degree that I never would, and was purportedly so good that he could hide in the middle of a white room while dressed all in black.

To my right was Sally. At first glance, there didn't appear to be anything extraordinary about her. She was not overly attractive (if gnomes are your thing), wore a simple robe, and seemed all around plain. However, her abilities to manipulate traps, wards, and the shadows to Disassemble those very creations was legendary. It was Sally that taught me how to recognize those very same wards and traps, and also how to get around them. She was also a sadist of the highest order, and I had only seen her genuinely smile when she was putting me through endless hours of pain.

Across from me was my last mentor and easily the most narcissistic computer program I had ever come across. Where Stan and Sally were demure in their appearances, Waseem was the exact opposite. Your eyes would easily pass over either Sally or Stan in a busy street, but you wouldn't be able to keep your eyes of the gaudiness that was Waseem's appearance. Bright colors and fluffy lapels made up his outfit this day. More over, it was the very fact that you would pay so much attention to him that made his skill in thievery and Lifting items from others all the more impressive. Undoubtedly, you would likely be staring at him while he did it, and you wouldn't realize it one bit. He also knew how good he was and matched his level of pompousness to his skill in stealing.

These were my teachers. From early in my adventures in Resurgence, these three had taught me all the special skills that I had not disclosed to any of my teammates. Stan taught me how to use my Blacksuit, which led to my Disembowel skill as well. Waseem taught me how to use my shadows to Scale walls and Lift items. And Sally taught me how to Disarm traps and Disassemble wards.

And now I needed their help.

"To put it simply, there is a war coming."

"Don't know if you noticed, lad, but there's already a war going," Stan said to me.

He was obviously talking about the war between the King and the Children of Loust. That storyline is what made the quest arc we first received from Sir Kenyan and then Sir Arthur possible. I obviously wasn't talking about that war.

"It's the Dwarves. They mean to take on the Drakkin. And given the fact that the Dwarves plan to invade the Drakkin home, it's going to be a bloody mess for those Dwarves."

My three teachers looked at each other, and then at me. Sally shrugged her shoulders and asked, "What does that have to do with us? I don't rightly care one way or the other about what the Dwarves and Drakkin do to each other."

"My friends and I are allied to the Dwarves. This is our fight as well now. I'm going to be involved in this one way or another."

"See. This is why I don't have any friends. No one to drag me into any stupid wars," Waseem said while leaning back in his chair and crossing his arms over his chest. To put a nice finishing touch on his look he made sure to give me a disapproving shake of his head as well.

"The list for why you don't have any friends, ya git, is a mile long," Stan said in my defense. "But still, lad, I have to agree with Sally. What's this got to do with us?"

"Steelhammer, the king of the Dwarves, would actually like to avoid killing off thousands of his people. He has come to me and asked for my aid in surreptitiously acquiring the item they are fighting over."

The statement hung in the air for the briefest of moments before Waseem started laughing out loud. "Wait! Seriously? He wants you to steal something?"

"Yes, Waseem. In order to save thousands of Dwarves, he would prefer if I could steal the item he wants."

Stan was laughing a bit too while shaking his head. Under his breath I heard him say, "I knew it was right not killin' that one."

But I had heard him.

"That was you? You're the reason he even asked me to do this!"

"What did I have to do with this? I haven't seen that Dwarf in ages."

I related the story that Steelhammer had told me about the night that Stan almost killed him. I also told them about Steelhammer's magical eyepatch and how because he couldn't see me with it, he assumed I had a Blacksuit.

"I spent a lot of days following that Dwarf around. I was learning his routine: when he slept, when he ate, what routes he used to get from one place to the next. All of it was very normal for me prior to a job. While I'm doing this, I also learn a lot about the target itself. And most times, I learn that I'm quite happy to be ending their miserable lives. Most of the time, if I'm being called in, you've really been a bad boy.

"And that's what I was led to believe with Steelhammer. I was told that he was abusing his power and damn near enslaving them Dwarves. My contact told me Steelhammer was torturing the innocent and plenty of other nonsense."

"That doesn't sound like him at all."

"Aye, Alex. That's what I was learning as well. Once I saw that he treated his people with kindness and respect, I went and looked for these dungeons where he tortured folk. Wouldn't you know, there wasn't a single tortured soul to be found? Sure, there were plenty of drunks in the tank, but you expect that of Dwarves.

"There have been less than a handful of times that I have not completed a contract. That was one. It was also the only time I told the victim of his fate and who hired me. The deal was he address the problem without raising any concerns over my actions. He kept his word, and no one has ever known the King of the Dwarves had been under my knife until now."

That jived with what Steelhammer had told me. It also made me think about the other thing he accused me of.

"What's the Court of Shadows?"

I wasn't sure what kind of response I would get, but outright laughter was definitely not one of them—and not just from one. All three. Sally started patting Waseem on the forearm and said, "This one has lots of faults, but they can all be forgiven for this simple gift: the Court of Shadows."

"You see, Alex," Waseem said as he calmed down and wiped a tear from his eye. I doubted it was going to be that funny. "There are only three of us that can do what we do. Well, four now with you. But the last thing we would ever want is for people to start blaming us for everything that went wrong and couldn't be explained."

"Somebody came up dead and they couldn't figure out who done it, they might blame the guy who always seems to get away with killing folk," Stan chimed in.

"Or someone has their favorite sword stolen from their home and they blame the same guy who stole a painting several days earlier," Waseem added.

Sally finished by saying, "Our survival meant there couldn't be the belief that there were only three of us, so Waseem created the 'Court of Shadows' to deflect attention."

I looked around at them and saw the smug looks on their faces. Truthfully, I wasn't following and said as much.

Waseem shook his head in mock disappointment again and explained further. I wished I had Wayne's war hammer right about then. I wouldn't hit him, just drop it on his foot.

"Some snobby aristocrat kills another aristocrat. In this case, the guy pays off the local authorities. As it turns out, those same local authorities work for me, and I pay more. When the aristocrat comes to them and says they should consider the case unsolvable, they say, 'Of course, this must have been the work of the Court of Shadows.'

"After only a few times, this took on a life of its own. Now, every time a murder goes unsolved, or a treasure goes missing, or a home gets burglarized, and no one is caught, what do you think the official response is?"

"They blame it on the Court."

"Exactly. And because so many things now get blamed on the 'Court,' it is impossible that it could simply be three people. The organization must be huge!"

I joined in their laughter as I realized how ridiculous it all sounded. In order to hide that there was in fact a kind of Court of Shadows between Sally, Stan, and Waseem, they had to make up a fake, sprawling, dastardly underworld organization that had its hand in everything seedy.

"Of course, every now and then one of us pulls a job and the blame rightly gets placed on the Shadows," Sally said as she smugly smiled my way.

"I'm not going to say it's brilliant, because he won't let me live it down," I said while pointing toward Waseem, "but it certainly provided a unique way to hide yourselves from the authorities."

Returning to why I had asked them all to come together, Stan wanted to know how I thought they could help Steelhammer.

I brought out the map that that marked the location of South Tarren. With it, I was able to also show, in general, the Drakkins' location.

"Well, I was hoping one of you would be able to tell me something more about the Drakkin and this place where I found them."

"I'm afraid I won't be of any help to you, Alex. The Drakkin are steeped in magic, and they have no use for my skills in putting together wards and the like. I've never had any dealings with them."

I looked over at Stan, but he shook his head. "No one's ever hired me to kill a Drakkin, lad. Sorry."

My last hope was Waseem. Words I never thought I would consider. The only bright spot was that he had a rather large smile on his face.

"Have you stolen something from the Drakkin? These Drakkin?" I asked Waseem with a bit of pleading in my voice.

He continued to smile at me but shook his head as he said, "Nope. Never stole anything from them."

He continued to sit there with that smug look and didn't add anything more. I knew if I tried to wait him out, I would lose this battle. I was the one completely in need here.

"Ok, Mr. Waseem the Magnificent, what has you smiling so big then?"

"Oh, I like that one. Can I use it from now on, Dhalean?"

"Don't count on it, jackass. Just answer the boy's question already!"

"You are always so sensitive, Dhalean," Waseem said while continuing to suck up the moment.

Finally, after what seemed like minutes, Waseem spoke.

"There's a map."

"Wait! A map? Of the Drakkin place that I just described for you?"

"Yup."

"You have a map!"

"Nope."

And just like that, I went from ecstatic to despondent in a mere moment.

"Of course you don't. You just heard of a map. Likely story."

But Waseem had not lost his smile. "Oh, the map is definitely real. I stole it—and a whole bunch of other things—some five years back.

The guy liked drawings. There were maps, and sketches, and early paintings. But I certainly remember that map."

"I see. In order to get the map, I'm going to have to steal it from this guy."

That obnoxious smile only got bigger as Waseem shook his head no again. He was down-right giddy at this point.

"Well, if I can't steal it from him, how am I supposed to get it, oh wise one?"

"Oh, you are definitely going to have to steal it. Just not from him. You see, soon after I made my delivery, he moved it to a more secure location."

I was tired of dealing with Waseem's little riddle, but I had to play along.

"Where then?"

But by this time, both Sally and Stan were paying very close attention and seemed extremely distraught by Waseem's level of giddiness.

"No, Waseem. It ain't happening," Stan said before Waseem could go any farther.

"I can't be any part of it, you know. That would be too obvious," Sally added.

My frustrations won out, and I finally blurted out, "It's fine! I'll steal it from wherever it is stored. Just tell me where the hell it's kept!"

Waseem finally lost the laughing smile and took on a much more maniacal smirk as he leaned toward me.

"My friend, it's time to rob the Bank."

CHAPTER 7

"**I** can't believe I let you fools talk me into doing this," Stan said for about the tenth time. He hadn't been happy with the situation since the moment Waseem said he wanted to do a bank job.

"Quit your grumbling, old man, or the guards will hear you," Waseem said, also for the tenth time, as we stood near a copse of trees, away from the Bank. The job required at least three people, and Sally had told us from the outset that she wouldn't be able to help.

As it turned out, Sally made quite an honest living as a security advisor. Her abilities as a Master Trap-Maker had earned her quite the reputation, and successful companies had been coming to her for years for counseling on how to protect their wares.

While Sally's abilities in the non-magical realm were well known, she had obviously hid her Rogue abilities concerning wards. This was helpful in two ways. First, that while people asked Sally for her advice as a trap expert, they rarely ever used her traps, going instead for the magical variety, thinking they would be more protective and harder for a thief to defeat. As such, the only traps we faced were magical in nature, and we could get around them without having to destroy the trap.

Secondly, the Bank had called on Sally to consult on their security. She was quite aware of the locations of the traps the Bank used and what level of mastery each trap would take to get through. But since she had helped with the security, she made it quite clear that she wouldn't be able to take any part in the actual theft and would have to make certain she was somewhere away from the scene of the crime. On top of that, she planned to be out in the open so there would be plenty of people to witness her activities. Waseem pleaded at first, but she wasn't going to hear any of it.

"We could be in and out in seconds with you there, Sally," Waseem had said.

"It would go faster, yes, but Alex is up to the task if he follows my instructions," she responded.

After that, I spent an hour with Sally as she went over the placement of wards on the outside of the building. As a passerby, I would have been able to determine where the wards had been placed, and a fairly good idea of what level of resistance I would face. It would be like being a thief in the real world, who plans on hitting a target, but first recons the outside to see the best place for entrance. At the ground level, he can see there are two-inch thick bars over the windows, but no bars over the windows on the fifth floor.

And such was the case with the Bank. Anything on the ground level was so heavily defended that we could forget that, as there was no way I could get through those wards before sunrise. Sally, for her part, said that it would have taken even her a good thirty minutes to get through.

On the fourth floor, however, there were not the same levels of protection. Again, like with most institutions in the real world, there wasn't as much threat of illegal entry from an elevated position, as it's nearly impossible to get to those points and not be seen. This was the same for the Bank. That is, if you weren't one of the people sitting at that table.

Sally made sure I knew about the ward that I would be facing on that window, and Waseem would be ready to open the window itself once the trap had been disassembled. As for the interior of the Bank, there was greater leeway as to what types of wards I would be facing, based on where the map itself was kept. There was one thing that Sally did make clear, though: by no means were we to try for the vault. If that is where the map was kept, we could forget it.

Thankfully, the map was in a different part of the Bank's holdings, and that was a part we could get through. Waseem still wanted to try for the vault, despite Sally's warnings, but Stan put an end to that with a look.

Besides the security on the inside of the building, the Bank also had roving patrols on the outside and inside of the complex. Each patrol had a magic user as part of their squad who cast a see-invisible spell on each guard at the beginning of their work day and made sure it remained in place until the end of their shift. The only person getting around that was a Rogue wearing a Blacksuit.

You would think with the Blacksuit, it wouldn't matter what type of armor I was wearing. But Stan and Waseem both insisted that I "suit-up" for this job, and that meant that I needed to have some new clothes. I was lucky that I had until nightfall to do this job, because it took me forever to find the appropriate clothing.

For starters, I couldn't just dye my clothing black, I tried suggesting that first. Waseem insisted that I had to have something that was cloth and flowed easily with my movements. I also, apparently, wasn't supposed to just dye any cheap clothes that I found, as the dye could rub off during the operation and give us away. Which meant I needed to go and find the items in the market.

This took me into the heart of the city, toward the shops. What I found totally blew me away. There were way more player merchants than there were NPCs! I was instantly thrown back to my old days of hawking my wares in similar markets to earn a living in video games.

For several hours, I forgot about everything happening around me; I didn't worry about the Shield of Ashtator, the mission for the Wanderer, or anything else. I was back in my element, and I was using every trick I had learned in years of gaming and selling to acquire the clothes I needed. Unfortunately, no one person had everything I required, and I had to shop around. Several people had one of the same item, the leggings, and I lost myself in the simple joy of playing one merchant off of another. It was time consuming, but I acquired everything I needed. The length of time came from one guy being able to make what I needed, but didn't have the materials. This required me to shop around for the resources themselves first. Again, I found it entertaining to take part in a task I had excelled at for years, but hadn't done for much of my time in Resurgence.

The joke was on me though. When I arrived at the Pit, Stan and Waseem were still in their regular clothes. They both got a good laugh at my expense, noting that I had gone through my "initiation." When I asked Stan if Waseem tried the same on him, he reminded me that Waseem was quite afraid of what Stan's blades could do to Waseem's insides. Waseem nodded along vigorously to this explanation. Still, I wasn't all that upset at Waseem. He had given me a small gift by allowing me those few hours of no worries or concerns.

We had been watching the guards for the last thirty minutes and had mapped out their routes. Waseem and I would need a sufficient window to cross an open area and reach the building itself before we started Scaling the side of the structure. Normal climbing would work, but it would leave distinct marks in the building that an astute patrol could pick up. Instead, we would use our shadows to Scale the building, leaving almost no noticeable trail. Once we reached the fourth floor, we would anchor ourselves with our shadows and Waseem would wait while I removed the obstacle.

Stan, for his part, would remain at the ground level and wait for us to enter the building. Once we were through the ward and into the Bank, he would Scale the side as well, and close the window behind him.

Once inside, Waseem and I would head for the lockboxes where the map was being stored. I would bypass any ward that we encountered, and Waseem would get us through the actual locks.

Stan was going to be either the most valuable member of the team or the least useful, depending on how things played out. If we timed everything perfectly, and the guards inside stayed to a similar routine at night as they did in the day, we wouldn't need Stan at all. Waseem had observed the activities of the guards routinely in the hopes that one day he could do what we were doing now, but he was only able to do so during hours of operation where he could walk through the open front doors wearing his Blacksuit and then leave the same way before the close of business.

If, for whatever reason, the guards didn't follow the same routines at night, meaning we would likely meet with resistance, Stan would do what he did best and remove them from the equation.

I was taken aback at first when I learned what Stan's role was and that he seemed to be fine with the task. I imagine the look on my face must have spoken volumes, since Stan chuckled a bit when he saw my expression. He alleviated my fears by explaining, "I'm just going to Incapacitate them. It's a one hit specialty for Assassins that leaves the target alive, but they won't get up anytime soon after I thwack 'em."

And that is how we got to be outside the Bank, huddled around each other, Stan complaining again, and all with our Blacksuits on.

"It's about to be time, Alex. Once this guard rounds the corner, we will have just enough time to spring across the field without the risk of too much noise alerting one of the patrols. Get ready. When it is time to go, I will tap you on the shoulder. You run. I will follow, since I can see you," Waseem said, reminding me of the magic item he showed me the last time we robbed a place together, the one that could see through a Blacksuit.

I sat and waited for the signal. I was hopped up on all kinds of adrenaline as I watched the guard making his way along his route. Part of me couldn't believe that I was actually going to rob the bank in the game with the help of two NPCs, and the other part of me was terrified about what would happen to me if I was caught. I had no idea what everyone else in the game might be doing at that moment, but I was pretty damn sure none of them were doing anything as awesome as this.

I felt the tap on my shoulder, and I took off for the point Waseem and I had decided was the best vantage point for our ascent. I was hoofing it in a full sprint, with my eyes going from the point on the wall where we would begin our climb to the window above us, which is why I almost ruined our night before we even began.

We were moving directly toward what had to be a trap. I couldn't tell you what it was, but my Disarm Traps skill was flaring up, and it was showing me an entire patch of the ground that was highlighted in green. Green meant that it would have been easy for me to disarm—or avoid. I chose to avoid. I knew Waseem was very close behind me, though, and I didn't want him to get confused by my actions or hit the trap, whatever it was. Despite all of Waseem's pompousness and assclownery, he was no novice at thieving, and I felt certain he would follow my lead. A simple vocalization would be enough, I hoped.

"Trap, move left," I barely whispered and then executed the move. Waseem didn't respond behind me, and I didn't stop to look back. My job was to get across the field and up the wall to the fourth floor.

I didn't encounter any more obstacles and methodically ascended the side of the building. I wasn't as fast as Waseem, but I was competent with my Scaling and made it up in a respectable amount of time, I thought.

As soon as I got to the window, I anchored myself in using my Shadows and started to inspect the ward that covered the opening into the building. I hadn't said anything and was waiting for Waseem to make some kind of a smart-ass comment. Instead, I was surprised by his praise.

"Really well done, Alex. You handled that pit-trap perfectly, with just the right amount of redirection. And you let me know what you were doing with the perfect level of whisper, that even someone with enhanced hearing wouldn't have caught. More so, you didn't stop to see if I made it. You continued on and focused on your part of the job, even when we got up here. You're going to make one hell of a Rogue."

I was genuinely touched. Waseem wasn't one for giving out praise. He would say a nice thing or another but always with a backhanded compliment. This seemed sincere.

"Thanks, Waseem. I just want you to know..."

"Great. Now how about you get through that ward before Stan falls asleep down there and lets everyone know where we are from his insufferable snoring. Either that, or I die from old age."

There he was.

I smiled to myself, nodded my head a few times in Waseem's general direction since I couldn't see him, and got back to the ward in front of me.

Seven minutes later, I was through the ward and had it disassembled thoroughly. I gave the thumbs up and moved to the side of the window so Waseem could do his magic with the lock. I looked down to see if I could spot any of the guards roving around.

When I looked back up, the window was open. Bloody magic indeed. Waseem got through the lock in seconds.

I went through the window and stopped just on the other side of the ledge. I saw the window close, but the latch remained undone. Stan would be coming through the same way and would need the window unlocked.

I didn't think it made much sense for us to move toward the lockboxes until after we knew Stan was with us, but Waseem explained that Stan would be doing a full tour of the Bank as soon as he got through the window. Stan hinted that he was well aware of the Bank's layout, and I'm guessing he had done his own recon on this facility, for whatever reason, sometime in his past.

As soon as I felt Waseem gently grab my shoulder, I knew it was time for us to move out and head toward the bottom floor where the lockboxes were kept. I was keeping my senses on high alert after the trap we saw, what Waseem had called a "pit-trap," and expected to see several other non-magical traps.

But it appeared that the Bank believed their external security was sufficient and that with the security on the actual safes, boxes, and the vault, they didn't need anything more inside. With that in mind, we made it to our target, only having to stop twice to allow patrols to roam past us. The real challenge would be when we would have to remain stationary for several minutes as I got through the wards and Waseem took care of the locks.

The interior of the bank looked like what you would expect of an upscale establishment that focused on providing for the needs of the wealthy and privileged. The hallways were marble, with the floors lined by rugs that ran the entire length. In the few spots where there wasn't any carpet to muffle the sound of our passage, our Blacksuits were more than capable of doing the job of keeping us quiet.

Other than the rugs, and a few pedestals that held flowers in plain looking vases, there was nothing on the floors of the hallways. There was certainly nothing large enough that we could hide behind if we needed to. There were also numerous paintings that hung on the walls, but were covered by locked shutters. It looked like the bank took their security seriously, going so far as to lock up the art on the walls at night, but it was all a lie.

Waseem and Stan had both noted this oddity before we entered the Bank. According to Waseem, the actual paintings behind those shutters were fake, and that the originals had only hung for one day when the Bank first opened. The fakes were placed the next day and the shutters installed to give the false impression that the originals still hung.

As we hurried past them, I noted that not a single one of the "art works" had a ward over the shutters, making them the easiest thing in the Bank to steal. This, by itself, led me to believe that the story from Stan and Waseem was true.

Arriving at the lockboxes was a simple affair, but the ward covering them wasn't—or should I say, wards.

I spent a good two minutes just looking at the numerous wards that covered the lockboxes and how they intertwined. Waseem, to his credit, didn't say a word during the entire time.

"Ok," I whispered, "I'm pretty sure I got it mapped out. I have no idea how long this will take me, though."

"Don't worry about time. We can step away if a patrol comes. Stan should already be in if we need him," Waseem said, all business now.

Reluctantly, I gave over my fate to the watchful eye of Waseem and Stan's blade. Stan, I was much more comfortable with.

Ignoring everything else but the wards in front of me, I used my shadows as lenses and studied their patterns. The easiest way to explain what I was seeing would be to take a Celtic knot and try and untangle it. Its structure, by design, made it impossible to achieve. The difference here, however, is that there had to be a beginning and end for any ward. I just needed to grab the right string.

On the other hand, grabbing the wrong string could possibly kill me, and that was just one thing giving me pause about taking this route. Waseem insisted that the owner of the map wouldn't sell it, that this was the only way we could acquire what I needed. Up until now, though, I had worked almost entirely on Sally's training wards. Sadist that she is, The worst they could do was cause some short-term hearing loss. These wards, however, were rigged to explode if they went off—real consequences for anyone but me, who could respawn at my bind point.

Still, I did note that Waseem hadn't tried to get through these wards himself. He claimed it was due to his lack of skill, but I told him it was due to plain old chicken-shit fear. He didn't much like that. Or the chicken noises I made after he protested. He really didn't like the chicken dance I added at the end.

To be fair, the dance was pretty bad.

I allowed a slight smile to play across my face as I recalled the scene at the Pit, with Waseem fuming over my impromptu performance, then I turned my full attention back to the wards.

Using my shadows as tools, I slowly began to peel the various wards away from each other so that I could focus on the order I needed to Disassemble them. The timing and order, like everything else with this job, would need to be perfect. Letting myself get tunnel vision, I got to work.

Sweat started to bead on my forehead, and I only noted Waseem wiping it away on my periphery as I focused solely on the task before me. I kept my movements smooth and measured, trading precision for speed.

I remembered back to a time when a girlfriend had bought me classes at a shooting range, learning how to draw and fire a gun from a concealed holster. I don't have a gun, or a concealed holster, but it was an experience that taught me this particular mantra: slow is smooth and smooth is fast. That was exactly the mentality I was utilizing now to circumvent the wards on the boxes.

I have no idea how much time passed when I finally got the last ward disassembled. The heavy breath I released, which I didn't realize I had been keeping in, was the signal Waseem was waiting for.

"If you're done, how about moving aside so we can get out of here before the guards find us," Waseem whispered in my ear.

I slid away from the wards and let him have my spot. I knew Waseem was a master thief, but I wasn't really sure what that meant when it came to getting through locks and the like.

"How long will this take you?"

After only ten seconds he said, "Done." I watched as the keyhole for the box turned on its own and opened slightly.

"Shadows, with enough mastery, can become solid enough to become a key."

And with that, I saw exactly what it meant to be a master thief.

"Grab the map, Waseem, and let's get out of here. I've got no idea what it looks like."

We had run across an open field, negotiated a pit-trap, climbed the side of a building up four stories, and circumvented both magical and mechanical security measures to get this map. And all of that went off without a hitch. So, naturally, it was the simplest of matters that caused us the most problems.

It was right as Waseem swung open the box that a guard walked into view and saw the action. He couldn't see us, but he didn't really need to, as the moving door was more than enough for him to turn and start running toward a rope that would signal the alarm.

He made it three feet in the direction of the rope before he stiffened up and then promptly fell to the ground. Stan, having performed the Incapacitation, was now visible. I looked at the guard and could see that he was still breathing. I focused more on him, actively targeting him, and saw that the vast majority of his hit points were gone. There was no blood on the marble, however.

Stan came foward. Obviously not happy, but not downright angry, he said, "Time to go boys. We've got plenty of time to get to the window and slip out. Can you lock it from outside, Waseem?"

"Wait. Dhalean, what happened to that guard? He's out, but there's no blood. And what do you mean lock from the outside?" I whispered.

"Incapacitation uses a series of pressure points and locks to cut off the flow of blood to the brain and the heart, at the same time. The result is that guy over there, but no permanent damage. It will lead to death though if you use the maneuver for too long."

"And as far as locking up," Waseem said as he closed the lockbox after removing the map and handing it to me, "Our hope was to make it seem like we were never here."

With that, I saw the lock for the box turn back to its original position, like nothing had ever happened.

"This way, it takes them longer to figure out what happened, lad," Stan continued to whisper as we made our way back to the window we entered. "The bank will probably not even report something happened if they don't see it immediately. Obviously, they want to maintain the illusion that this establishment is untouchable."

Part of that, I learned, was going out the way we came in and locking the window behind us. Our original plan was to hang out until the bank opened in a manner of hours and walk out the front door. That wasn't a possibility now. There would be an uproar when the guard was discovered.

We did not encounter any further obstacles to our crime, and we made it back to the same copse of trees without additional resistance. Once we were all there, Waseem whispered the word "Pit," and we all went our own ways back to the establishment.

After an ambling route, doubling back on myself repeatedly to make sure I wasn't being followed, I arrived at the Stinking Pit to find Waseem and Stan already present. There was no sign of Sally, but we hadn't expected her to come around for at least several days. If Stan was right, the Bank would act like nothing happened and there would be no announcement to the general populace. Given Sally's role in their security, however, she could very easily be receiving a summons as we met.

Once I entered, Stan and Waseem stood up, with Waseem handing me a mug of something likely very alcoholic. "To a night that never happened," he toasted.

Stan and I both raised our mugs and repeated the phrase, "To a night that never happened," followed by the three of us taking large gulps from our cups.

As I reflected on the night, it went almost perfectly. I had honestly believed we would meet more hardships, have to overcome more hazards, or even fight our way out. But we were two master Rogues and one damn good journeyman taking on a challenge that was designed specifically for our skills. I never expected it to go without a hitch, but if it had, that too could have been expected.

"Now," I said to the other two scoundrels in the room, "let's take a look at this map."

FBI Headquarters

Melanie Grissten, Director of the FBI, sat behind her large oak desk and reviewed the report in front of her. On the opposite side of the desk were Special Agents Annabelle Bolden and Nicodemus Colvin, the agents assigned to the special AltCon task force. The report she now perused was the latest information from the two Special Agents. It didn't have much.

"Let's hear what you have," the Director said.

Bolden sat up straighter in her seat and began, "As you can see, Madame Director, we haven't had much more luck on the front of uncovering information about AltCon. Grimes has come up empty on the facility he found, and our investigation into the heads of the company has likewise come up with little more than what can be found on the internet. Honestly, ma'am, we've been hampered by the investigative techniques we are allowed to use here. If we could issue some subpoenas, I bet we could get more."

Director Grissten could see from the looks on her two Special Agents that they were more than a little frustrated. The power of the FBI came largely from their ability to use the law to enact their investigations. Here, though, the Director had limited their techniques to what is available on the internet.

These weren't professional hackers. They were FBI Special Agents, and their frustration was understandable.

"Let's talk about this bit here. Robert Shoal."

Special Agent Colvin took over here and he said, "It looks fishy as hell, ma'am. Excuse my language."

The Director smiled and waved him on to continue.

"This guy was supposed to have wrapped his car around a tree after drinking himself into a stupor. So many things don't add up."

"Start from the beginning and walk me through it."

"Yes, ma'am. Robert Shoal was brilliant. He designed AIs that were on the cutting edge of technology. His latest, the one now powering AltCon's game, Resurgence, was rumored to be near sentient. Needless to say, with the success of the game, he was looking to be a multi-millionaire many times over.

"According to the autopsy report, Shoal died upon impact. Forensics at the scene determined his car was likely going in excess of sixty miles an hour when it hit that tree. This is based on the damage alone, since there was no skid to measure. He didn't hit the brakes at all. And here's where things just don't add up."

"Makes sense to me. Guy goes fast. Guy hits tree. Guy dies."

"Yes, ma'am," Colvin said, his frustration growing, "But it doesn't add up. For starters, he didn't have a single moving violation in his entire life, not so much as a traffic ticket for illegally parking. On top of that, the guy was a millionaire already from his initial payout from AltCon, and the guy drove a stinking Volvo!"

"Calm down, Nico."

"Sorry, Director. I get really upset when I think about this," he said. "On top of that, the guy was a Mormon, and every piece of information that came out after his 'accident' said the guy never drank a drop of alcohol in his life. Now, I'm supposed to believe that he not only drank himself to two and a half times the legal limit but also drove his car after doing so. And directly into a tree, without stopping, to boot. None of it adds up."

"An investigation was done?"

"Yeah. And they didn't find anything. In fact, a young detective who also found it all a bit fishy even checked out the car. There wasn't anything in it but Shoal and his blood. Not that there was much left of him, either, after an impact at that speed. Even in a Volvo."

"Anything else?"

"Only one small thing. Prior to getting the gig with AltCon, the guy had been turned down for a contract with the Department of Defense to provide a new AI for some project they were working on."

The Director kept her face neutral, but inside she started to seethe. She was smelling a rat, and he wore four stars on his shoulders. Still, she knew she had to hide the DoD's hand in this and only asked, "Anything else on that?"

"No, ma'am. It seemed pretty cut and dry. He applied for the project, was a finalist, but eventually was turned down. Immediately after that, he was picked up by AltCon."

Director Grissten looked down at the folder again, thinking about her next meeting with the General but trying to maintain her calm. Her agents were doing exactly as they were ordered, and she wanted to keep them going on the case.

"This news about Robert Shoal tells me there is more to this story than we are seeing. Based on your report about Shoal, Nico, I can't see this playing out the way it did. It means there is something we are missing."

Agent Bolden looked about to speak, but the Director put her hand up before she could begin, "And yes, Annabelle, I know you could do more if you had more authority, but that's not how this one is going to work."

Director Grissten watched as both of her agents deflated a bit at her words. She wasn't happy that the General had put her in this position and, in kind, had lowered the morale of her troops. She was going to get more out of the General the next time she saw him.

"Keep Grimes focused on his task. I see from your report that he has no love for the company."

That got a bit of a smile out of Bolden and Colvin.

"He'll go until we tell him to stop. He was so pissed when they didn't let him play their game. He's being careful, but I have no doubt that guy would go no-holds-barred if we let him off his leash."

"It just may come to that," the Director said and dismissed her agents.

CHAPTER 8

December 10, 2043

It didn't take us long to identify a few areas that I hoped would allow for my team to enter the drakkin's lair. For starters, I was able to determine a number of points on the stolen map that matched landmarks we'd already encountered, like the valley of mushrooms and the large depression where we noted the drakkin market. From there, Stan, Waseem, and I tried to discern just what the map was showing us. I couldn't say that we were one hundred percent sure of what we were seeing, since there wasn't a key that any of us recognized, but it looked like there were multiple layers of tunnel systems and that some were naturally deeper in the ground than others. Additionally, some of these deeper tunnels had egresses topside that were located farther away from the depression or the large cave entrance that we had explored. These looked the most promising.

I didn't want to leave the area until I had given Sally a chance to look at the map, but her arrival to the Pit was delayed. She needed to keep herself away from the likes of us and available should any authorities want to meet with her. That left just the three of us looking at the map through every lens we could imagine, but we always came back to the same conclusion. If there was an aboveground entrance, it was likely that the farther down in the ground that the tunnel was, the farther from the cave we would find that entrance, our rationale being one of simple mobility. All things being equal, it would require a greater length of tunnel to ascend back up if the traveler didn't want to have an unbearable degree of ascent that would require ropes or ladders. Therefore, deeper tunnels meant longer ascent, which translated into greater distance from the center.

A good part of assumption came into play as well. I was assuming that since our dwarf Jack was a prisoner, the area he was held in would be deep within the network of tunnels. Again, this was largely assumption based on historical knowledge. Every medieval prison I'd ever read about, and the closest correlation I could make for the time frame that Resurgence was set in was medieval, either had the prisons deep underground or in high towers. Both scenarios were utilized to thwart any attempt at escape. Since there were no mountains to speak of, I was going with the deeper tunnels. Both Stan and Waseem corroborated my deduction, noting that this was the case for the prisons in the Keep, which were deep underground for the majority of prisoners, though there were a few rooms high in the towers of the castle that were reserved for the aristocratic prisoners.

Sally further bolstered my confidence when she finally arrived at the Pit and gave her opinion on the matter, which tracked closely with our reasoning.

By the time Sally arrived, it had been several hours since we had departed the Bank, and we all wanted to know if Sally had met any trouble. She told us all was fine, but she insisted we relate the details of the "Bank Job" to her first before telling us anymore.

Stan and I allowed Waseem to tell the story, as he had a bard-like ability to tell a tale, only adding our bits when Waseem was mistaken or over exaggerating on something. In other words, we had to interrupt a lot.

As Waseem finished, he looked over at Stan and asked, "Did you see the vault as we were leaving?"

I hadn't noted the vault at all, and neither Waseem nor Stan pointed it out to me. As such, I was paying attention to what Stan and Waseem were now saying as much as Sally was.

"Aye, I did. That thing was covered in so much magic it made me eyes hurt."

"If we didn't have to run, I would have loved to have taken a go at it. You were right, though, Sally. It would have taken a day to get through all those wards. Only other time I've seen that much magic protecting something was at the tower in the Keep," Waseem said, referencing the tower I had come across when I was learning how to Scale. The entire thing was covered in wards, and to this day, they were all still red when I looked at them. Even Sally admitted she couldn't get into the tower.

After Waseem finished his story, Sally told us again that all was well on the suspicion front and that there had been no outward reaction to the break-in. When she used the word "outward," all of our eyebrows lifted.

"I had a messenger from the Bank stop by the office. They were told by my assistant that I was at a party in the Aristocracy's portion of the Keep and had been all night. Said messenger found me at the party and informed me that the Bank was due for their annual inspection of the building's Security and that my presence was requested. I shot him quite the dirty look. 'Now?' I asked. 'In the middle of the night?' His face got quite red at my question. As you can imagine, he was quite embarrassed, which caused him to fumble a bit.

"He assured me that it wasn't required for me to go to the Bank at that moment, but that the review would be taking place soon. This is what he had been instructed to inform me. He apologized profusely at his intrusion at the party but noted that the Bank management did not say that he could leave the message with an assistant. Therefore, he felt obligated to track me down. Of course, this was all malarkey. I saw the messenger speaking with several of the staff working the party before he left, likely questioning them on whether I had been there all night. Anyhow, that's the reason for my delay."

Once we all felt comfortable that we had avoided any immediate suspicion from the authorities, and there was no further insight to be gained from the map we had found, I decided to take my leave and head back to the dwarves. There was only one thing further to discuss with Sally before I departed.

"Do you have any advice on that magical shield I told you about?

"As it turns out, I do," Sally said as she walked away from me and over to one of the closets that sat off of the Pit's main sitting room. As she walked, she continued talking. "However, what I'm about to hand to you is damn near priceless. The cost of this could buy a small mansion here in the Keep. What I'm saying to you is this: tell Steelhammer that if he accepts this, he owes a debt to the 'Court of Shadows.' Understood?"

As Sally continued her explanation, she had retrieved a small box from inside the closet. She started to hand it to me but stopped until I gave her my response.

"What kind of a debt are we talking about here? If it's something that would tarnish his honor, you know he'll tell me to go take a running jump off the side of a cliff."

Sally smiled at me as she reached out with the box and handed it to me. "Oh, I don't actually want anything. I just like the idea of putting the man through some grief as he contemplates when and how the Court will come to collect. You know it's the small things like that which give me joy."

"Remind me never to get on your bad side, Sally. Even your good side can get a guy hurt."

"Very astute observation, young man," Sally said. Once the box was fully in my control, she explained its function. "The mechanism is simple but quite rare. As you know, our shadows can slice through a ward and allow us to disassemble the parts of it. This allows us to bypass the trap, but we have to be near it to do so. This little toy, however, is a box full of shadows. It uses them to pierce the ward. When delivered correctly, it will blow a nice hole in that shield, effectively destroying it."

"Holy crap, Sally! How is this even possible?" I had done lots with the shadows and had seen Waseem and Stan do even more, but at no time in all my experiences had I seen anyone remove a shadow from themselves.

"It's a part of my gift with the shadows. I've never met any other that can do it, but I can take small bits of shadow and preserve them for a time. I designed these boxes to extend their usability, and even then, they won't last forever. A box this size would take me six months to a year to create. It is, in fact, the largest of these contraptions I own." Internally I was thinking "Shadow Grenade," but that term wouldn't mean much to Sally or the others here.

In the end, this was exactly what the dwarves needed to get through that shield, but I still didn't understand Sally's altruism. That wasn't like her. Finding joy in watching someone go through pain, that was like her.

"Still, I don't understand. Why?"

"Why give this away?" She asked. I nodded my reply and she shrugged her shoulders. "Dwarves are brutes, who think more with their hammers than with their heads. They constantly run off to battle this or that beast or to dig deeper into some mountain that will just end up being filled with creatures sure to eat them up. They have little regard for their own lives or the lives of others.

"So, when you tell me that there is a dwarf out there that is in fact trying to do the exact opposite, well I want to see that guy go on living a bit more. I'm sentimental, after all."

I stayed silent for a few seconds before shaking my head at Sally.

"Nope. Not buying it," I said as I looked at Sally with empathetic eyes. "That's not you at all. I'm gonna go with you hating drakkin, more than anything. That's the only way you would give this baby up. That keeps my worldview intact where you, Sally, look sweet and innocent on the outside, but on the inside, you plot and connive better than anyone. And all for the purpose of seeing others squirm through either emotional or physical pain."

Sally could see that I didn't really mean the words I said and that I was trying to make sure she knew I would keep her soft spot for Steelhammer between the two of us.

She patted me on the side of the face and then painfully pinched my cheek before walking away. "You always say the sweetest things, Alex."

I couldn't help but smile as I watched her walk away, only for her to stop once more before exiting the room while turning toward me.

"Alex, remember to tell his lordship dwarf to be careful. When that box hits the shield, there's going to be quite a boom!"

While my teammates continued doing their own things, I returned to the dwarven city and found Steelhammer. I was exhausted from the long night and desperately needed a few hours of sleep, but I had to get the map, and at some point the shadow grenade, into the king's hands. Steelhammer had a role to play after I dropped off the map, and I wanted to give him time to get those affairs in motion.

It wasn't long after I arrived that Steelhammer was able to meet with me in the great hall where this whole thing started. The great table we had first sat around was covered by maps and drawings. There were also numerous figurines spread out over the maps. I was inspecting one of these maps when Steelhammer walked in.

"Part of the supply line, Alex. That's why it looks like a cart."

I nodded my head in understanding as I put the "cart" back onto the table. "Makes sense. I couldn't figure out what type of military element it represented, but supply lines are as important as any other part of a campaign."

"Aye, lad. Even more so if we be lookin' to lay a siege."

"A siege isn't going to be all that likely, Lord Steelhammer, especially not after you see what I brought."

I unrolled the map that we had procured from the Bank and laid it out on the table. Once all four corners had been secured, I stepped back a bit and let the king examine the document.

It wasn't long before he nodded his head in understanding. "Too many damn tunnels. And these here," he said as he pointed at the various different markings that the other rogues and I had thought were the mouths of the tunnels. "These are just the caves we see on this map. I wouldn't be surprised if there weren't a whole lot more."

"You think these are entrances to the various levels?" I asked, hoping he was on board with what we had ascertained.

"Aye, that's likely the case. But not all of 'em. I wouldn't be surprised if some of these didn't mark flue ways and air vents. Be careful that what you think is a tunnel don't end up going straight down to yer death. Rain and critters can wear away at the opening to one of them vents to the point that it looks like a natural cave, especially if enough time has passed."

I hadn't thought of that at all and was happy to have the advice of the king to fall back on. I would ask more about the layout of the tunnels and what some of the master miners thought about the map once it had officially been "given" to my group. I'd be a fool to not seek out the wisdom of the race that lived underground and intimately knew tunneling.

"What be the next steps then, lad?"

"First, we need to get this map into our hands. I know you don't like the sneakiness involved, but I will need your help in that, as I explained earlier."

Steelhammer waved his hand, shooing away my concerns. "I have that figured already. I mean about the actual tunnels."

"I plan to take my group back to the area and determine the best place for us to make our entrance into the tunnels. I'm fully on board for using subterfuge to get the Shield of Ashtator, but I have no doubt there will be more than just a little stealing involved. Like all things related to war, this will be simple and complicated at the same time."

"Couldn't have said it better meself, lad."

"I'm going to rest now," I told Steelhammer, nodding toward a cot. "When I awaken, I will have all of the guys make their way here to the mountain, and we will begin the next part of this mission. I hope to have a tunnel chosen quickly, with a plan in place by the day after tomorrow for making our attempt at sneaking into their lair. How long will it take the forces to move into position?"

"In that, we got lucky. Turned out there was an old tunnel system that runs a good distance toward that region. We will still have to move a fair bit of our gear over land that ain't kind to carts and large forces, but knowing that we ain't to be siegin' the place means I have a whole lot less equipment I need brought along on the first maneuvers."

"All this works like we hope," I said as I laid down on the cot, ready to log out, "and we won't need much more after the first maneuvers."

"From your lips to the gods' ears, lad."

December 11, 2043

I logged back into the game after only a few hours of sleep. I was exhausted but couldn't let on why that was. The guys would have no problem accepting my explanation that I simply didn't sleep well. Not every lie has to be steeped in misdirection and falsehoods.

I expected to find myself in a completely—or at least mostly—empty hall. When I sat up from the cot, however, I saw that the hall was packed full of dwarves. Near the front of the table, I also saw three very non-dwarven individuals, namely my groupmates.

Dan was the first to notice that I had logged on and started waving his hand and calling me over to the table. As I approached, I saw that Steelhammer and Sharla were both there, as well as Master Smith Perry. They were all looking down at the table. Specifically, they were looking at a map that I was quite familiar with.

I didn't have time to do anything more than raise one eyebrow toward Steelhammer before Dan grabbed me by the arm and pulled me the rest of the way toward the gathering.

"Dude! Check out what the Master Mapdude found!"

"I'm a blasted Master Cartographer, you idjit! How many times do I gotta tell ya?"

"Right! My bad, Master Mapbro. I got a terrible memory!" Dan said to the angry dwarf before winking at the three of us. "Seriously, though, check it out!"

I looked at the map, at first, with indifference, since I was not supposed to have any idea what it was. As I looked longer, I started to lean in and focus more on the outside areas, where the tunnel entrances would be. I lightly ran my hands over those spots, not quite touching the paper, and putting just a slight quiver in my hand as I really tried to sell my shock at seeing the map for the "first time."

"Is that what I think it is?"

97

"Sure is, man! MapGuyver found it as he was going through their archives. He said after the detailed description I was able to give him from our scouting, he had remembered seeing something similar. Over the course of an hour or so, we were able to piece it all together and he found this!"

"Just the two of you for an hour, huh?"

"Way more than that, dude. Me and him are besties now."

I turned toward the cartographer with a look of sympathy and said, "Such a detailed map could turn the tide of a campaign. Your king is, no doubt, deeply in your debt for such a sacrifice."

"Oh, lad, you have no idea," the King said to me as he pulled the map from the table and proceeded to roll it up.

"What do you mean, sacrifice?" Wayne asked. It was never a good idea to ask any dwarf to sacrifice anything when Wayne was around. Of course, Wayne didn't realize that I was talking about the pain the cartographer went through dealing with Dan for such an extended period of time. Thankfully, the cartographer himself had my back.

"Alex understands that, to me, maps be me life. Giving one away, even for a deed like this, is still a sacrifice on my part. I pray that you'll be able to return it when you're done."

Wayne nodded his head and clasped the dwarf on his shoulder, giving out a low "huzzah" that the rest of the dwarves echoed in the room.

With that done, I placed the map in my inventory and told the guys to get ready to ride out. As everyone got ready, I approached the king.

"Not exactly what we discussed, huh?"

"I thought it would sell better if them two 'discovered' it instead of what we talked about before. This way, no one be suspectin' you or the Court."

"The Court? Never heard of it," I said. "But I'm glad to see you have no problem being a bit sneaky yourself."

Steelhammer had quite the mischievous look on his face as I left the room, and I have no doubt he would have winked if it weren't for the lack of two working eyes.

The plan from this point was simple, and I relayed it to my groupmates without any fanfare as we rode toward our destination. "We get to the area. We check the tunnels. We plot our route. Once we have a good idea about which of these tunnels we want to use, we get the hell out of here and get our team together for the all-out assault."

"I thought the idea was to use the same tunnel that Jack used?" Jason asked.

"Yeah, at first it was. But that was when all we knew was that Jack ran through some mushrooms and those were our only clue. Now that we have this map, I want to look at all the tunnels we can. If we have to use Jack's route, so be it, but that one has me worried."

"The dungeons, right Alex?" Wayne said.

"What do dungeons have to do with anything, brocef?"

"I didn't really mean the dungeons. I meant the fact that prisoners are being kept in the dungeons, Dan. Trying to fight through an area that undoubtedly has multiple access points behind lock and key would not be easy. They aren't going to just have one door that opens to all of the prison, I'm sure."

"Good point, Naugha."

"Thanks, Allister. So, I'm also with Alex on finding a different route, if we can. That cool with you guys?"

Jason and Dan nodded their heads. The group fell silent as we continued to ride toward the drakkin home, which also gave me time to think about our situation.

I didn't doubt that we were doing the right thing. I didn't mean morally; I meant in the realm of gaining an advantage in the game. As I saw it, the problem was that I didn't know what that advantage was.

I didn't want to lose the ally status we had gained from the dwarves, especially as we were likely to see some good dividends starting to come our way in the form of Wayne's armor and our portion of the money made from the mines by our clan. To date, our positive status with the dwarves had provided us with better prices on items they made and had gotten us the unique opportunity to take on this quest. But at what cost?

For my groupmates, they didn't understand what was at stake for all of us. They had no idea about the Wanderer, the code in the game, how Supreme Overlord Riff Lifestealer was the embodiment of that code, or the fact that the creator of Resurgence had likely been killed by the very company who now owned that same game. For them, this was an epic quest line that no other group in Resurgence was getting to take part in.

There was no way I could have pulled them away from this quest. Not before, and certainly not now. And, honestly, I had to believe that a week's detour to undertake these tasks wasn't going to mean the end of the world, figuratively speaking.

I realized that a large part of me was rationalizing my own desires, but I had to believe that if the Wanderer didn't want me to keep going with this quest line, he could have stopped me at any time. I knew that he didn't like to interfere, but I felt that he would if he thought we were squandering what time we had.

And I was having fun! We were learning about new lore, and my special rogue abilities were coming into play more than they ever had in the game. I had robbed the bloody fucking Bank for heaven's sake! Since that first time I walked out of the Wanderer's underground, I was having fun without worrying about life or death matters.

Except, here I was, doing that very thing and turning over those life and death questions in my head. Consequently, this brought me back to my earlier conundrum: what advantage would we get out of this? For the moment, I had to admit to myself that I really didn't know. But having dwarves not only as an ally, but owing us one hell of a big ass favor if we pulled this off, was something I knew I could use. Time would tell what that would be. I had to trust I would recognize that opportunity when it presented itself.

"You done being all pensive and broody over there?" Dan yelled out from the front of our group's formation. "You were starting to look like Allibrooder."

"You already said brood, fool. You can't use the same word to describe both of us, ass hat. See what I did there? I used fool and ass hat to accurately describe you. Two different words. Afraid you committed a foul on that one."

"What the hell, Allireferee? Since when did you get to decide how my own nonsensical game gets played? I'm the only one who gets to choose the rules. Right, Alex?"

"I have absolutely no idea why you would even bring me into this conversation."

"Duh. You're the leader."

"For the umpteenth time, Dan, I'm not our leader. But, since you insist, I say we put it to a vote. All in favor of Allister's judgement?"

Jason, Wayne, and myself raised our hands.

"All opposed?"

"I'm not raising my hand. I know all three of you fuckers can count. Totally not fair," Dan said, brooding on his horse.

Wayne showed a bit of sympathy on Dan, and I heard him whisper, "Allireferee was a good one. Bonus points for quick wit."

Dan smiled at Wayne and gave him a fist bump as they kept riding together. "Can't believe you voted against me, man. That 'Pink Tutu' thing was months ago!"

"The affair will never die, Dan!" Jason yelled toward the both of them.

"Butt out, Allieavesdropper!" Dan yelled, followed by another fist bump from Wayne and acknowledgement by him of another "quick wit" point.

Jason and I watched as the two rode off ahead of us, and I couldn't help but laugh at the spectacle. "It never gets old. I mean, you would think, after months and months of you two taunting each other, that it would get old. But really, it doesn't."

"Oddly enough, Alex, it was old for me when he first started and has grown enjoyable only after the months have passed. At first, I didn't know if he was just being mean, only realizing later that he was just being Dan. I've also learned that 'being Dan' has more connotations than Star Wars has fanboys."

"It was a close call."

We were laughing along when Dan and Wayne came into view. They had stopped their horses at the top of a ridge and were waiting on our arrival. As we pulled up next to them, I could see the depression off in the distance where the drakkin kept their market.

"We walk from here."

CHAPTER 9

Over the course of several hours, we found three things of note. Two of them were welcome. Unfortunately, to get to the good things, we were going to have to get through the third, which turned out to be entirely unavoidable due to some very sneaky goblins that appeared to have the ability to camouflage themselves amongst the barren wasteland that housed our drakkin enemies.

It happened soon after we unsummoned our horses and left the ridge, heading toward where we believed the first set of tunnels would be located. As we traveled, we passed several large rock outcroppings. A bunch of rocks and boulders piled together was nothing to take notice of, and I passed them without giving a second thought. It wasn't until the first arrow lodged itself in my rear deltoid that I realized something was amiss.

That something was four Goblin Scouts, all colored blue to us, and all hefting some pretty hefty bows. All of them were reloading as well, as each of us, save Dan, had taken an arrow from the goblins. Dan had been too far ahead, ranging and looking for mobs for us to avoid. I would have to remember this later to use as an explanation for Dan of what irony was.

Dan quickly came running back when he noted the drop in our health and Wayne's loud "Fuck!"

Wayne hadn't missed a beat. Before I could say anything, he had already targeted one of the goblins and was moving in to engage. As I watched Wayne's trajectory unfold, one of Dan's arrows flew right past my face and lodged into the chest of one of the other goblins.

"Taking this one for a quick run while you guys figure this out!" Dan said as I saw him cast Snare on the goblin and run off over the rocky area.

"Just be careful of more scouts," I said as loudly as I thought allowable given where we were. I really didn't want to spend any more time than was necessary out here in the open, so close to the drakkin home, fighting a bunch of goblins.

With four goblins, I was going to have to handle some of the tanking duties. And, by that, I meant I approached the one goblin that wasn't already attacking Wayne, choosing to focus on Jason instead and stuck my dagger deep into its side. I landed a solid critical strike on the goblin, which was enough to get him to turn toward me and start swinging his fists at my face.

Our normal tactic for dealing with four mobs like this was to have Dan grab two and kite them while Wayne tanked the other two. However, the terrain where we were was not conducive for kiting, and Dan was having to do all he could to keep just the one goblin under control. Our fallback was to have the left-over mob beat on me, with me maintaining just enough aggro to keep it off of Jason.

While the goblin swung at me, I stabbed into the back of Wayne's target. Its thick green hide acted as another layer of armor that I had to get through, on top of the leathers it already wore. As I was driving daggers deep into the goblin, I also noted that its armor was painted to match the rocks in this area. My attacks did good damage but were slightly blunted by the goblin's armor and thick skin. No hide or leather was going to stop the concussive impacts of Wayne's war hammer though, and the goblin spent most of the time in the fight in a Stunned state, unable to move.

With the mob being stunned, the resistance to my attacks was non-existent. I was able to land more accurate and vicious blows along the goblin's back and upper spine. Before long, Wayne landed the first death blow and switched to the mob that had been attacking me for the better part of thirty seconds. Thankfully, my armor was decent enough that I hadn't required a heal and Jason hadn't pulled any agro.

Jason was a seasoned cleric and knew that healing me could wait until Wayne had a firm grip on the aggro management for both mobs. I spared a moment to look at our group member interface and saw that Dan was still doing fine and hadn't lost much in the way of hit points.

After waiting several seconds for Wayne to gain enough agro, I jumped into the mix. With the fourth mob gone, we quickly took up our old routine and mowed through the remaining mobs in a matter of minutes. The last to die was Dan's kited mob, who was riddled with arrows from our Ranger.

As the last goblin fell at our feet, we all looked around to make sure we hadn't alerted any other creatures to our presence. Seeing that we were in the clear, we paused so I could loot the goblins, who carried mostly scraps of leather and a few of the bows they had used against us. There were also a few silvers but not a significant amount to even take note of. The only other object I found was a pouch with a grayish paste labeled "Rock Dye."

I held the pouch up for the guys to see and said, "Remember when I told you about the dyes that we could use to help us camouflage in certain areas? Well, this is how it works. Pretty effective, right?"

The guys looked around the rocky area where we stood, and they noted that the goblins' armor blended in extremely well with the environment. They were all nods after that.

"This makes me feel better about using the camo trick you had been talking about, Alex. Not that I doubted, you of course."

"Of course, Allister. I never doubted your trust in me or my foolish schemes."

"Your words, buddy. Your words."

<hr />

None of us had the desire to fight more of the goblins, except for maybe Wayne, but we also didn't want to stumble on more of them while we tried to reach our next point. It ended up wasting about a half hour, but I did a thorough search of our immediate area to try and see if I could find where these goblins had come from.

I donned my Blacksuit and quickly made my way around the area. We lucked out, and I spotted a clearing in the distance from the top of some rocks. I ran toward it, relying on my Blacksuit to keep me hidden, and found the medium-sized goblin camp. There were probably twenty goblins in the area, with several tents and a cooking fire. It was the smoke from the fire that I had seen from a distance that led me to the camp. The other good news was that the camp was in the opposite direction of where we were going, and these goblins didn't look in any hurry to go out adventuring. That may change when their Scout group didn't return, but it was impossible for us to know for certain.

Instead, we decided to continue on our way and deal with any goblins we encountered but not go looking for trouble. And when I said "we decided," it really meant that Wayne begrudgingly accepted while noting he never got to have any fun.

Our next turn of good fortune came about an hour after we encountered the goblins and while we were still searching for tunnel entrances. Up to then, we had found three cave-like entrances, but one of them ended up being a vent or flue and only looked like a cave. Thankfully the king's words were fresh in my mind when we started looking at these caves, and I related Steelhammer's warnings to my friends.

Of the two that were caves to tunnels, both were blocked. One had a gate of sorts on it with weak wards surrounding it. The dirt around the bottom of the gate didn't look to have been disturbed, and there was the presence of the wards, which led me to believe this certainly wasn't the way that Jack had come. The other tunnel had a natural blockage, a cave-in of sorts. A massive pile of rocks blocked any way of going forward.

After those three, we continued on and only realized there might be a cave in the vicinity when we noticed the Lizard's Crown growing near a slight depression in the ground. As we went to examine the area, we saw that there was a path through the mushrooms from something that had disturbed the area and flattened the fungus. This looked promising for Jack's escape route, and I informed my team that I was going to check it out.

I donned my Blacksuit and walked through the same path of disrupted mushrooms. The depression continued deeper, but that had been hard to see from where we stood, as the shadows were very dark due to a natural overhang that blocked out all light the deeper you went. Thanks to my enhanced vision, however, I was still able to see. Thankfully, that meant that I didn't miss the opening to the tunnel. Without enhanced sight, or a very large bonfire going right in the depression, there is no way I would have been able to see the opening.

As soon as I entered the tunnel, I noticed the smell. It was what I always imagined a septic tank would smell like, and I was suddenly happy that I was descending through the tunnel and not going up. Otherwise, I couldn't imagine what I might be walking through. Still, I didn't want to know just what it was I was inhaling. But that wasn't the only sensation I noted after being in the tunnel for only a short time.

I could hear. And where I could keep my eyes up so I didn't see what I was walking through, I couldn't plug my ears. And so, I could hear. And the only way to describe the sounds was misery.

No wailing. No screaming. No tortured cries. The sound was that of lost hope. It was the murmur of a man who wants death but knows it can't come fast enough for him. It carried the acceptance that no matter how much they desire it, death will likely always be out of their reach.

All I could think, as I continued to climb through that tunnel, was that if Wayne were there with me, there was no way he would have gone any farther before trying to save whomever was making those noises.

While I was also moved by the sorrow I heard, I wasn't as selfless as our warrior, and our goal wasn't to rescue these people but to find a way to save many more. I promised myself that I would tell Steelhammer about what we found, though. He could send a party to release them when the campaign kicked off.

I did my best to try and ignore the sounds and continued through the tunnel. It wasn't long before I came around a bend in the tunnel and found what looked like a break area for the guards in the prison. There were four drakkin sitting around a table, very much looking like every played-out scenario you see in movies where the guards are playing some game with their weapons lying next to them. This looked exactly like that. Only I wasn't the swashbuckling savior who planned to kill them with their own weapons.

There were three additional tunnels that branched from this room, not counting the one I had used to arrive. I walked past them and tried the first tunnel to my left, hoping to find an exit that would get me away from the area and deeper into the drakkin lair. The first tunnel didn't get me what I wanted, but at least it solidified my earlier belief that I had found the prison.

I couldn't go any farther because I was blocked by a locked door made of metal bars. On the other side of the prison door was a hallway of sorts that had cells lining both sides. On each side, there were three open-air cells, followed by three stone cells where I could only see the doors that led to their interiors.

What I could see, though, were the occupants in those open-air cells. I could only guess that they were alive, whoever or whatever they were. Truly, all I could really make out were rags on the floor that moved from breathing or twitching. And the noise.

This is where the sounds of sorrow had originated.

I didn't need to see any more. I knew what was down here, and I would tell Steelhammer how to find it. I had other work that was expected of me.

With that, I went back to another of the tunnels that branched off the guards' break area. I walked several meters before I came to another cell door. It was closed, and I didn't want to give away my position by opening it, so I opted for the last tunnel that branched off of the room.

This led to a barracks and storage area. I looked around for any other tunnels that might have branched off from this room but came up empty. Wanting to see one more thing, I decided to return once more to the tunnel with the cell door.

Once I arrived, I attempted to get as close as I could to the door and see if there was anything I could see down the tunnel that ran past the door. The bars on the door did not run entirely from the top of the door down to the bottom. There was a cross member in the middle, where the other bars had been attached to the cell door. As it turned out, the bars on the bottom were a little wider spaced than the ones on top. With enough maneuvering, I could get my head through the bars and take a look around. The rest of me wouldn't likely fit through, though. I had pretty good-sized soldiers, but in this case, I had been blessed with a smaller head. I laughed to myself as I thought of all the "that's not what she said," jokes Dan would be coming up with.

It only took me a few seconds to get my head through the bars. What I saw only reaffirmed the earlier decision we had made. There was another cell-type door down at the end of this tunnel, and this one was warded. In order for us to use this route into the drakkin lair, we would need to get through multiple locked doors (although I was sure one of the guards in the room I had just passed had to have had a key for them) and get through the ward on at least one door.

Thankfully, I didn't get my head stuck between the bars and was able to extract myself from the door. I was doing a lot of making myself laugh as I also envisioned how I would get out of that specific scenario, imagining me removing my Blacksuit and yelling down the tunnel to the guards, "Hey lizards, your dad might have been a dragon, but your mom was a biyatch!" Then waiting for them to come and kill me, sending me back to my spawn point in Kich's Keep.

I didn't meet any resistance on my way out of the prison and was happy to rid myself of that smell. I relayed what I found to the group, except the part about the prisoner's misery. I promised myself again that I would tell the king what I had found.

Knowing how Jack had escaped, and from where, was a great boon. However, it still didn't provide us the entrance we needed. We took the map back out, noted where we were, and headed off to find the other tunnels that were marked on the parchment.

It was another hour and a half, and several more dead ends, before we found what we hoped was the answer to our prayers. It was an entrance that looked to have been neglected by the lizards, and one that mother nature had taken back over. I could see that it started descending almost immediately after I crossed the threshold.

After a good hundred meters, I came to a door. I couldn't tell if it was locked or not, but I could see the wards that were hung on it. They glowed green in my vision, and I knew I could slice through them, disassembling them with no problems. I also didn't see any disturbed dirt around the door, which led me to believe the door hadn't been used in a long time. Finally, I saw one non-magical trap also on the door, and this too was covered in a green hue. What made me decide to see where this door led was that I could see by the layer of dust on the trap that it had indeed been a long time since anyone had come this way.

The first thing I did was disassemble the wards. After having worked away at the magic in the Bank, these were practically child's play. I had both of them disassembled in under three minutes, and that was with one minute to double check my work. The last part was to disarm the trap.

I was still very familiar with disarming. Pain was a good way to reinforce the lessons I had learned under Sally's tutelage. And for Sally, pain was always something she had a heaping of to dish out. It was no shocker to me that I had that done in three minutes as well. However, there was a slight difference between Disassemble and Disarm.

When I Disassembled a ward, it all happened in the spectrum of magic. There was nothing for the untrained eye to see. Anyone who watched me disassemble that earlier ward would have just seen a guy standing in front of a door, waving his arms around like a moron.

But when I used the Disarm skill, I tended to break down the trap into pieces in order to negate the trap. That's what happened at the door. Which should have been no big deal since no one had used the door in who knows how long.

And I wasn't worried that anyone would see me. Even with me disarming a trap, as long as I didn't take any damage from the trap, I wouldn't lose my invisibility from my Blacksuit. So, when I finished disarming the simple trap, I wasn't concerned about being seen. And I wasn't.

But that trap sure did make a clatter when parts of it hit the ground right next to where I was standing.

It was only because I turned my head to look at the ground where the pieces hit that I even saw the claws coming my way. I didn't think and immediately jumped backward, away from the door and those claws.

Claws that belonged to a Wyvern, a big-ass Wyvern whose tag was in red with a nice dark red hue all around it. It had been nestled into a corner of the tunnel, its dark hide having matched with the rocks in the tunnel, giving yet another creature that we came across some natural camouflage. The only saving grace was that the Wyvern had swatted at the trap pieces, not at me. I had been lucky enough to avoid the attack; however, there was no way I was going to try and open that door.

And at this point, I was just tired of running around these damn tunnels. I decided then and there we were done looking for entrances. This was our way in. This Wyvern was just going to have to get the fuck on or get its ass handed to it. I was guessing it was going to have to be the second.

And that would require the rest of our group. It was officially time to bring the band back together.

CHAPTER 10

We spent the rest of the day traveling back to the mountains. Before anything else could be accomplished for our quest, we needed to update the King as to what we found and where we would attempt our intrusion of the drakkin's underground lair. I also took the opportunity to update the guys as to what awaited us in the tunnel.

After the wyvern had scared the piss out of me, I took the time to study it in more detail. One thing that jumped out at me was the fact that it wasn't a normal wyvern; the red tag over its head read Wyvern Young. And if this is what the young looked like, I really didn't want to meet the elders.

The creature itself followed the usual design for a wyvern, with a dragonesque head and reptilian-type scales on the body, along which rested furled wings. As we were in a cave, I couldn't make out what type of a wingspan it might have, nor did I have any intention of allowing it out of the cave to take flight and have that unique advantage over our band.

As for legs, it was the two-legged variant of the creature, differing from most dragons I had read about that normally had four. I could see the claws at the end of those feet, and they certainly looked capable of rending both my leather armor and flesh. I hoped Wayne and Jenny would have better luck with their steel plate.

The tail was behind its body in the corner of the cave, so I couldn't see what was at the end of the appendage. That the tail could be used in combat seemed likely, and I just hoped it didn't have some type of nasty surprise associated with it. Wyverns are often capable of producing some type of poison or venom in other games I had played, and I made sure to note that to my friends. We would want to make certain the group had their resistances buffed to the highest levels possible.

The next part of our discussion needed to wait until we had the whole group together, so we could talk the strategy for dealing with not only the wyvern, but how we would tackle the underground tunnels as a whole. I had every intention of doing as complete of a mapping as I could in the tunnels before the full group entered. If I was lucky, I would find the actual hall where the shield was kept before we started exploring as a full team. I had no doubt that we would need to fight along the way. Our best weapon, however, was the speed by which we could navigate the tunnels and steal the shield before the drakkin were any the wiser. Again, that was going to require us to encounter as few drakkin as possible. And that's why, before discussing any plans about the group's intentions, we needed to make sure the King was comfortable with his part, and I needed to gift him with Sally's shadow bomb—or as I started calling it, the "Barrier Breaker."

Our larger team was already waiting for us when we arrived at the home of the Dwarves, as our trip was longer than their journey. The four old friends looked amused.

"You know why I never get bored with this game, Gary?" Tim asked his group mate.

"This seems like a trick question. I'm just going to let you answer it," Gary said.

"Alex. Alex is the reason that I never get tired of this job. Just when the threat of endless grinding looms over our heads, Alex comes to our rescue," he replied to Gary and then came over to me with a hand out. "What crazy mess have you gotten us into this time?"

"I want to say it's all Wayne's fault, but this time it's definitely me," I said and shook the offered hand. "Turns out we have to go kill a dragon."

That stopped the laughter and smiles all at once. "How the fuck did you find a dragon?"

Wayne walked over and took Tim's hand out of mine. He had forgotten to release it after I said the word "dragon," and I liked seeing this real-world warrior be a bit out of sorts. "He didn't find a dragon. Stop playing with our friends, Alex," Wayne said, and then whispered to Tim and I, "besides, Jenny would kick my ass if I didn't tell her we had found a dragon!"

I finally relented and shared that we had found what amounted to the most basic of baby dragons, a wyvern. Since it was a mob that none of us had ever seen before, my earlier antics were forgiven. I made sure to greet the rest of the group, share hugs and fist bumps, and then motioned everyone to enter the mountain. We also sent a runner to ask the King to join us in the great hall.

Having Dan with us, there wasn't any need for a guide back to the room, but we allowed one of the dwarves to do us the honor, as he put it, anyhow. It turned out the young dwarf was great for gossip, and we discovered that, since there was no need for large siege engines, the preparations for war were almost finished. Still, I hoped the King had some catapults, as they were integral to my plan.

The King was already in place by the time we arrived. He looked tired but brightened up slightly when he saw the eight of us walk in. "Tell me you have good news, Alex."

"Well, I have both good and bad. Which one do you want first?"

"Never easy with this one," Steelhammer said, looking around at the other dwarves in the room. "Let's start with the bad news."

"Big ass wyvern!"

Naturally, the statement didn't come from me, but everyone's favorite ranger.

"Care to be a bit more specific, TheClaw?"

"Umm. No."

All the dwarven heads in the room turned towards Dan. It sounded exactly like he had just disrespected the King. Given the stress everyone was under, verbal faux pas by Dan needed to be avoided at all costs. Heads could roll.

"Sheath your blades," I called out. "He can't give any more clarity because he didn't actually see the beast. Our ranger simply spoke out of turn."

"I do that a lot," Dan whispered to the dwarf next to him, who just happened to be Sharla.

"Oh, I'm well aware of your tendencies, elf," Sharla said while waggling her very bushy eyebrows at Dan.

I would have been sad to the end of my days if I hadn't been watching at that moment to see the reactions that crossed Dan's face. First, he turned a bright red that went all the way to the tips of his pointy elven ears. Second, Dan looked over at our team and realized that he was in the same room with Kaitlin and a bearded dwarf he may have slept with, making his face go from red to deathly white in a matter of seconds. Thirdly, and a scene no one from that room will likely ever forget, Dan let out a small shriek as he ran from the room.

"I just missed something, didn't I?" Kaitlin asked.

"A lady never tells," Sharla replied.

Before things got out of hand, and any chance Dan had with Kaitlin disappeared, Wayne interrupted. "How about we return to the matter at hand, and Alex describes what he saw in the tunnels."

I nodded my head toward Wayne for the assist—for both me and Dan—and described what I had found. The dwarves despised the dragons in all forms, and the wyverns were no different. When we explained that the beast was likely too powerful for my small group of four, the dwarves nodded their heads in understanding. No one questioned our judgement of leaving and returning to join up with allies.

"What be the good news then, Alex?"

"Before the wyvern made itself known, I found a door that will give us access to the underground tunnels. As soon as that wyvern is dispatched, we will begin our part of the mission."

Steelhammer nodded his head in our direction and then waved his arm to indicate the contingent of dwarves in the room, which numbered about 15-20 dwarves. "These lads here have been informed of your goals."

I looked at the dwarves and studied them a bit more closely than I had before. We hadn't received much love when we were first invited to the hall and war council. That had changed over time, however, as we showed our value. All of the dwarves who had been let in on our secret mission were looking at us with respect. They realized how dangerous of a mission we were undertaking. Or, at least, they thought they did. My plans were to reduce that danger quite a bit.

"Well, the next steps, then, are to talk about how we are going to attack. I have some ideas I think you will like."

—————

Standing around the large table were my team, still minus Dan, and a handful of the dwarves that were previously in the room, including Sharla. That could explain Dan still being absent—and why Wayne was obviously standing between Sharla and Kaitlin. Say what you want about Wayne, but you can't deny that he always had his buddy's back.

Opening my inventory, I removed the map that I stole from the Bank—though almost everyone else in the room thought came from the dwarven archives—and placed it on the table. Once they were all in a position to see the map, I pointed out where we had found the entrance to the underground tunnels. I added, probably unnecessarily, that this is where the wyvern was located, too. However, this reminded Jason of our earlier encounter with the goblins, and he added his information on where the camp was located, pointing it out on the map.

I then proceeded to go through my plan. Or, at least, the basis for a plan. There were two things I was keeping to myself, namely the Barrier Breaker and the location where we found the prisoners. Both of those I would relay to the king only. I couldn't rightly pass over Sally's gift in front of everyone without going into the details of how I got it. As for the prisoners, I had promised myself I would tell the King, and I had every intention of doing so.

As I laid out the plan to my teammates and the other dwarves, I could see they were tracking with what my goal was: to distract, not win. As such, the initial actions taken by the dwarves had to be swift and had to catch the drakkin off guard. Again, surprise was going to be our best weapon here.

I also pointed out the canyon entrance where the herbalist from South Tarren first found the Lizard's Crown mushrooms. I suggested a small team use this entrance as a means of advancing from multiple angles. I wanted the dwarves to attack, but not to a degree that it made the drakkin flee. Their pace had to be slow enough that the drakkin chose to fortify the front entrance to the cave with bodies and not magic or any other means of blocking the entrance. That meant that the dwarves would have to go slowly.

The first move would be to shoot rocks from multiple catapults into the marketplace, causing a panic. I believed there only needed to be one volley to be successful at this, mostly because when the drakkin looked up to the ridge to see where the rocks had come from, they would see a line of dwarves, ready to descend against them. And descend they would.

For this purpose, I wanted the King to make sure they had ladders they could drop into the depression. It needed to be as far back from the cave entrance as they could get it without being in the canyon itself. There was still the issue of the magical wards in the canyon, but I was going to address that matter with Steelhammer once everyone had left.

With the dwarves descending far from the cave and taking their time to form up at the bottom, I hoped the rallying call would come to dispatch the dwarven enemy and not allow them to lay siege, despite our complete lack of intention to make this a prolonged campaign.

With the drakkin moving to the market area to combat the dwarves, the way to the Shield of Ashtator should be relatively clear. This was my hope, at least. The boom from the Barrier Breaker was going to help in our plans, but again, this would be in addition to everything else we covered.

It all made sense to the dwarves, but it would require them to do some creative explaining to their squads. Dwarves weren't known for "holding back" when it came to fighting, and the lack of any kind of siege equipment with us would tip them off that it wasn't meant to be a drawn-out affair. I couldn't come up with every answer, though, and they were left on their own to manage their squads.

After explaining the plan, including the timing of when everything needed to happen, the dwarves broke up to go speak with their clans. The timing itself was going to be one of the most crucial elements of this whole thing. I would make certain that Steelhammer understood that in greater detail when I provided him the additional information. The troops in the canyon would need to go in earlier than the rest, and obviously the Barrier Breaker would need to be launched prior to the catapults launching their payloads.

When the meeting broke up, Jenny and Wayne headed to the practice fields to watch the dwarves at play, while Jason headed back to the master smiths to allow them to inspect his legendary armor again. I think he did it just to stay away from Sharla. Dan, as it turned out, had gone off to see Jack the dwarf and find out if he remembered any more about his confinement. I was betting he was also doing so to avoid Sharla.

The rest of the team, Gary, Kaitlin, and Tim, took advantage of the dwarven hospitality being offered and proceeded to the marketplace to see if there were any upgrades they could acquire. That left just me and the King.

"Anything else I need to be knowing before we get this whole thing started, lad?"

"As a matter of fact, there is. Three things," I said, making my way over to the table where I placed the Barrier Breaker. "This is the first. A gift from the Court."

Steelhammer came over and was about to grab the box before I stopped him. "Let me explain what this is for before you pick it up. I need you to understand just how carefully this needs to be handled."

I proceeded to explain how this singular item would eradicate the barrier over the marketplace in one fell swoop. The reaction, however, would be a very loud bang. I had planned on that bang as part of my diversion. Steelhammer easily understood the value of the item sitting in front of him, and he looked very hesitant to accept it, especially given where it came from.

"What will this cost me?"

"I told you, it's a gift."

"Ain't nothin' free in this world, lad. Especially nothin' coming from the Court of Shadows. So, I'll ask ya again. What's this gonna cost me?"

I wanted to play the scenario out a bit because it was fun to see Steelhammer a bit off kilter. There wasn't much that likely scared this old dwarf, but Stan's blade to his throat was definitely one of them. In the end, I couldn't let him suffer much and told him he wouldn't need to worry. I sold him a tale, but the truth would have been harder to believe. No one ever believes people are selfless.

"Turns out the drakkin don't only steal from dwarves," I explained. "They have their own debt to pay, and stealing the single greatest dwarven artifact from under their noses will go some way towards repaying that debt. Any drakkin we can kill along the way will help too."

Steelhammer took the box in his hands and gingerly placed it in a bag at his side. Likely the game's version of an NPC's inventory. "I take it gladly, then. Anything else?"

I informed Steelhammer about the wards guarding the canyon entrance. I told him that he should still send a party through, probably just a bit before they launched the Barrier Breaker at the shield. The wards were either going to be destructive, and would bring down the canyon itself, or they would be an early alarm system to let someone know of intruders. In either case, I suggested having the team for the canyon have some way of sending a device that could trip the wards. Steelhammer said the dwarves had just the thing but didn't go into further details.

Finally, I told him about the prisoners being held in the underground tunnels and what I had found and heard. I honestly didn't know if there were any more dwarves being held in the prison, as I didn't see any faces, and told him so. But I thought he would want to release them while we had this opportunity.

Steelhammer lived up to his reputation and promised that a squad of dwarves would be sent to the location I showed him. While the full might of the dwarven army surprised the drakkin into responding, a small group would liberate the prison while we liberated the Shield of Ashtator.

"I've got nothing else to add. How soon can the dwarves be on the move?"

"We plan to begin our march this evening. We've got a magic man that will spell us with the sight of you elves for the night. Since we don't need a full contingent, and we ain't sieging, we gonna move fast through the darkness."

"What about the catapults?"

"Don't need many of 'em, and dwarves been setting up catapults since before elves was playing in trees. We got mobile parts, and we set them up on location. There may be a bit of magic involved, too."

"Excellent. My friends and I will leave as soon as possible and be at the caves before you arrive at your location. Our plan is to dispatch the wyvern this evening before making camp for the morning. Should we fail in our endeavor, I will let you know, and we can plan for a contingency then."

"Aye lad, the contingency will be more people attacking the same damn wyvern."

"My thoughts exactly, Lord Steelhammer. If you don't hear from me, then assume we were successful and launch your attack according to schedule."

"Be careful out there," Steelhammer said before clasping my forearm in his. He held it a little longer than necessary and looked me in the eyes before finally saying, "This is a great thing you do for my people, Alex. You and your friends. Whether we win or lose, this will not be forgotten by any dwarf. Ever."

I didn't need to say anything. I simply nodded, released the king's forearm, and left the room. Our next stop would be the caves.

⏤⏤⏤

The group traveled at an accelerated clip, trying to get to the cave as quickly as possible. Now that we knew exactly where we wanted to go, navigating the route was much easier and less time consuming. Still, if we wanted to use our horses, we needed to stay on trails. The only problem was that a trail could lead to an ambush, which it did in our case.

The obvious giveaway was the tree that had mysteriously fallen across the path. And the fact that the tree looked to have been recently cut down. Either way, it would require us to navigate around the obstacle, as it was too high for our horses to jump over.

For those without magical mounts, this could be a serious problem. Not only would they need to worry about protecting themselves from an ambush, but they would also need to make sure their horses didn't run off in the middle of a fight. We didn't have that problem.

As soon as we dismounted from our horses, we banished them entirely. Getting them back was a simple matter of casting the ten-second spell. A ten-second cast in a fight would likely be impossible, but in the normal pace of the game, ten seconds was no big deal.

We wouldn't get the chance to summon those horses back immediately, though, since we were attacked as soon as we dismounted. There was no fanfare beforehand, telling us about how we would need to pay a tax or something as silly. These bandits simply came out of the woods and attacked us without a word.

They didn't have much time to regret that decision, either. There were four of them, and they were blue to all of us. My group, by itself, could likely take four mobs if we had room to kite them. With the two groups together, it certainly wasn't a fair fight at all.

Jenny and Wayne each took one, while Tim casted Enchantment on a third and Dan cast Snare on the last and kited him around the small area. Gary and I joined up on Wayne's bandit and dispatched it rather quickly. Jenny wasn't taking much damage, so Kaitlin was able to add her direct damage spells to our fight. As soon as we finished with our bandit, we switched and killed Jenny's.

Dan ran his mob over to us, and with the full complement of the group, the mob lasted a matter of seconds. That left only Tim's mob, who was still enchanted.

It can sometimes be eerie to see a mob—that you know would try to take your head off with his sword if he could—standing right next to you.

This, of course, was the beauty of the enchantment spell and why it was the king of crowd control. That mob would remain standing there until Tim's spell wore off or we attacked it. We opted for the latter.

The only downfall to Enchantment was the aggro the Enchanter incurred. In this case, there was no doubt the bandit would go after Tim first. However, any team that has played with an Enchanter for as long as we have already knew how to handle that situation. Stuns, Taunts, and Bashes, coupled with good old-fashioned melee attacks, were the quickest way to grow on the aggro list for our tanks. This is exactly what they did to the last mob, while the rest of us also added our damage. The poor bastard didn't even last long enough to target one of us with all the damage we were putting on it.

We looted the mobs, collecting the few coins that they dropped, and continued on our way past the fallen tree. Once clear, we summoned our mounts and continued down the trail.

It wasn't long before we arrived at our destination, although the time seemed to pass much slower as we tried to stay as quiet as we could. Granted, running down the trail with horses wasn't all that stealthy, but adding our raised voices would only increase the likelihood of us encountering more mobs. The lack of banter from everyone, even our Ranger, just made the time drag on.

Still, we weren't tired when we finally reached the cave. Instead, everyone was amped up to see and fight an entirely new mob. We had no idea just how much damage this thing was going to do, or if we could even beat it. On top of that, once we cleared this beast, we were facing an entirely new scenario that no other players were getting a shot at, and that only increased our adrenaline. At this point, I couldn't get these guys to log off even if I wanted them to.

As soon as we entered the mouth of the cave and were away from any wandering mobs that could cross by, I went to the back and found the Wyvern Young again. Once I had it targeted, I returned to the group, where everyone was receiving their buffs. Tim was casting a spell to increase everyone's attack speed, and the healers were buffing our resistances. Kaitlin also had a spell that would increase our Strength and Dexterity. Every little bit helped.

We didn't see anything out of the ordinary about the mob, or how we planned to pull it. With us in a single team setting, any one of them could target the same mob that I had. Accordingly, the plan was for Gary to run toward the mob until it chased him down. When he got about half way back to us, he would use his Play Dead skill, allowing him to lose the aggro. As soon as he knew the mob wasn't going to attack him any longer, Dan would shoot an arrow from a distance and continue the pull.

As the mob moved past Gary and on to Dan, Wayne would enter the fray and engage it. Our plan was to fight it around the middle point between the cave entrance and the door to the tunnels. We didn't want to risk any wandering mobs, and we had no idea what was on the other side of the door to the tunnels, so a halfway point seemed like a good idea.

For all intents and purposes, this was the easy part. If we couldn't successfully pull a single mob, fifty meters from its starting position, and make sure it attacked our Tank first, then we needed to pack up our shit and go. There wouldn't be any point in bothering with the rest.

Once all the buffs were passed out and our casters had full mana, Gary ran off to pull the wyvern. It wasn't but a few seconds before Gary announced he was on his way back. Dan was already in place and just waiting on Gary's call that it was clear to keep pulling.

At the appropriate location, Gary activated Play Dead and hit the floor like a sack of flour. It looked like it hurt, but Gary assured us he didn't feel anything when he landed. From a distance, we could see the mob turn its back, a sure signal that the skill worked and Gary had lost his aggro. For anyone who couldn't see in the dark, however, Gary announced that he was free of aggro and Dan was clear to fire. An arrow flew from our Ranger and hit the wyvern in the back.

The wyvern let out a screech and continued up the tunnel toward Dan. Wayne, already in line to take over tanking duties, ran up to meet the beast with a blow from his war hammer.

Like clockwork, we all fell into our roles and started attacking the mob. It had a very high armor class and looked to have a crap-ton of hit points as well. In other words, we weren't doing much damage. We were definitely whittling it down, though.

Wayne also had a fairly high armor class, and he wasn't taking much in the way of damage, either. Our healers were more than capable of keeping him alive at this pace, and it would be just a matter of attrition, of which we looked to be the clear winners.

Naturally, it was right after I had that thought that Wayne shattered the illusion I had so comfortably cradled in my mind.

"I just got hit with a Wyvern Poison."

No one else seemed to have been hit with the same debuff. Or, at least, I hadn't. However, in the short time that I looked away from the fight to check and make sure I wasn't poisoned as well, I saw a noticeable dip in Wayne's hit points.

"Wayne, buddy, are you getting smacked around, or is that the poison?"

There was a brief pause before Wayne responded. "Shit! I hadn't even noticed. This poison is kicking my ass, Allister. I'm gonna need you to speed up the heals."

"I'll help out, Allister. We can do our usual rotation if you want," Kaitlin said. We had fought alongside our teammates on numerous occasions now, and it was no surprise to me that Jason and Kaitlin had created a rotation.

"Sounds good, Anastasia. You grab the next one."

The wyvern didn't appear to be any kind of boss, as we noted a lack of special skill when it hit 75 percent. But it had a ton of hit points and a wicked poison from the sound of it. The battle of attrition was still ours to lose, but the race had gotten a whole lot closer.

And again, just like with the poison, my own thoughts were proceeded by catastrophe.

The wyvern was at 63 percent health when it let out a mighty screech that reverberated through our bodies and the tunnel. I also noted an icon appear in my periphery that let me know I had received a debuff of some kind. However, at first glance, I didn't notice any change to my damage output, my health, or my movement, so it didn't appear to have much of an effect on me. Still, as a good player always does, I focused on the icon in my heads-up display for a brief second and read the name of the spell.

I had been hit by something called Wyvern Sap. There was nothing further for me to gather from the description, and no one else seemed to be bothered by it, so we kept on attacking. It wasn't until a couple more rounds of healing occurred that we learned what the debuff was.

"Shit! I'm not regenerating mana!" Jason yelled out.

"Dammit, neither am I, Allister! Do you have this stupid Wyvern Sap on you?" Kaitlin asked.

"I think we all do," I said. "It obviously had no effect on me, but if I also have it, it must have been an area of effect spell."

"I'm moving to healing," Jenny called out, as she had some limited healing abilities with her Paladin class.

"I'm going to keep on shooting arrows," Dan yelled from farther away. "I can heal, but it's pretty worthless. I'm doing more good with DPS."

I liked that I didn't have to do anything and everyone knew how to complement the role of the other players. Tim was the only one of us that was not as active in the battle. He had cast a spell on the mob early in the fight that slowed its ability to attack and occasionally cast a direct damage spell, but he stopped after the wyvern resisted the first three in a row.

What really worried me was that same battle for time. Jason and Kaitlin were tearing through their heals because of that damn poison on Wayne, and no one was regening their mana because of the debuff. The wyvern was slowly dying, but so was Wayne. And if Wayne fell, there was little to no chance that any of us would survive the rest of the fight, except for Gary. Gary, after all, could still Play Dead if he needed to.

I saw no other option but to keep swinging my daggers at the beast. I was intently listening to the calls from Jason and Kaitlin on how much mana they had, thinking that I could try and use my Force Multiplier ring to finish this off. Even then, though, I didn't know how much more damage I would do to this thing, and if that would be enough to save everyone. With the type of hits that Wayne was taking, even with his high armor class, I imagined that I wouldn't get a chance to use the five minutes on the ring.

"Ah, hell! Naugha, eat the cake!" Jason yelled out.

"Don't get Dan started on eating cake again, Allister!"

"Shit, Alligoodidea is right, Wayne! The cake from Sherrel. How the hell did I forget about that?"

We had received five items from Sherrel, the herbalist in South Tarren, as part of our quest completion. One of those removed any poison debuff.

"It worked!" Wayne yelled and the rate by which his hit points continued to go down looked to slow a bit. "I'm just taking melee damage now. I can last for a bit like this."

"Well, I hope it's more than a bit, because that was my last heal. I'm tapped," Kaitlin said.

"Shit! I'm out too," Jenny added.

All eyes looked over at Jason, and he only shook his head. "I've got one more heal in me."

There wasn't any more that we could do, other than me using the ring, which I had been hoping to avoid. I had no idea what awaited us when we finally got to the shield room, and I wanted to save every advantage I could. Still, I also had no intention of wiping here if we could avoid it.

And we were close. I mean truly, we were so damn close that I could barely see any hit points left on the Wyvern Young, but with Jason yelling that he was out, I didn't see a choice.

And then I heard Jenny.

"Three massages and dishes for the week," she said.

"Deal!" Wayne yelled back.

With that, I saw Jenny jump to Wayne and put her hands on his back. A glow surrounded her hands, and I saw Wayne's hit points go from almost 0 to 75 percent. Then I remembered that Jenny, as a Paladin, had received the skill Divine Heal at level 20. At the first level, the skill would heal half of a player's hit points. At 35, it increased to 75 percent, and at level 47, she would be able to heal a player for 100 percent of their hit points. The drawback was that the skill could only be used once every 24 hours.

But Wayne at 75 percent health meant one thing. We were going to win.

After another minute, and one last mighty swing of Wayne's war hammer, the Wyvern Young's head met the tunnel floor with a re-sounding thwack that I felt in my feet. The system notification that I had received experience clinched the fact that we had won.

Everyone looked frazzled, and we understood how close we had come to a wipe there. Jenny had definitely saved our asses.

I looted the wyvern and found nothing but crafting materials. There were close to thirty High Quality Wyvern Scales that could be used in Smithing. I also found three High Quality Wyvern Claws that could likely be used to make weapons but also just said Smithing. Finally, I found several Glands of Wyvern Venom that I guessed could be used as a poison for one of my blades.

I had given up on the whole poison making for Rogues soon after the AltCon quest that forced us to take up a craft. With the number of glands looted, I might try my hand at seeing if I could make one of them for my daggers. Otherwise, I'd likely sell them to a vendor.

With the Wyvern Young dead at our feet, it was finally time for me to go through the door and see just what we had in store for us. Besides, no one was in any hurry to go anywhere until the Wyvern Sap had expired and our casters were able to replenish their mana. It was a perfect time for me to don my Blacksuit and get back to why we were here.

I approached the door, checked it one more time for wards and traps, and reached toward the handle. Just before grabbing it, I turned toward my friends and whispered to the group in a cheesy Austrian accent, "I'll be back."

I was met by groans but also smiles and waves as I turned back toward the door. There was no more reason to delay.

It was time to find where these lizards were keeping the Shield of Ashtator.

CHAPTER 11

It was impossible for me, or anyone else in my party, to determine if there was anyone on the other side of the door or, for that matter, if there were traps that I couldn't see on the other side of it. Therefore, I made sure to go very slowly as I turned the handle and gently pushed the door away from me. As soon as the door was open a smidge, I concentrated on the areas around the doorjambs, looking for the telltale signs of a trap or ward.

I was thankful that I didn't find anything to slow me down. Continuing to move slowly, I opened the door the rest of the way. I continued to check for any obstacles, always keeping my eye out for both the magical and mechanical traps. I got the door open enough that I could squeeze through and did so after determining there weren't any pit traps on the other side of the portal.

Once I was fully through, and I could see there were no mobs in my immediate vicinity, I closed the door behind me. Only then, after releasing the breath I didn't realize I had been holding, did I look farther from the door and take in my surroundings.

The door I had come through was at the end of a long tunnel and was the end of this particular passage. I could see, up ahead of me, that the tunnel ended at a T junction. Moving with purpose, but still ever wary of the possible wards that could be in this underground city, I made my way to the end of my first hallway. It wasn't until I had made it to the junction that I saw my first drakkin—two of them, in fact. They looked to be some kind of a patrol. The names above their heads, that of Drakkin Guard, greatly added to my deduction. The fact that they were armored, carrying weapons, and were simply standing in one location and talking when I spotted them only added to my assessment. Like any good gamer, the first thing I did after seeing them was check to see their difficulty level, which turned out to be higher than my group, but not terribly so. The yellow of their names told me that the Drakkin Guards were 3–4 levels higher than us.

Up until this point, we had only seen the creatures from a distance. This was my first real chance to get a look at the beasts, and I wasn't going to miss my chance to gather as much information as I could. The first thing that stood out were the creatures themselves.

They looked to be closer to a lizard than a dragon, but that could have been the effect of human and dragon features blending. The face lacked the elongated dragon snout, though their noses did protrude farther than a human's would. At the end of the protrusion were two slits that added to the lizard look. The mouth was also larger than most humans', and it looked like it could likely open wider as well, with the jaw hinged further back along the skull of the drakkin. And I could see that the teeth were pointed, pure carnivore in their characteristics, when the two guards spoke. Their eyes, yellow in color, were set deep in their faces. There were also two horn-like appendages rising from the back of their heads. They were small, and I couldn't tell if they were decorative only or could also be used in combat.

The last things I noticed about their faces, and truly all the exposed parts I could see around the armor, was the color and texture of their skin. The skin itself was gray, and there were noticeable scales that ran along the face and the arms that I could see. They were nothing like the scales that we collected from the Wyvern Young, but they undoubtedly owed their lineage to their dragon creators. As I continued to assess the bodies and clothing of the beasts, I also noticed their hands only consisted of four digits each, but that one looked to be opposable in nature, allowing them to wield and grip the swords at their sides. Their feet were wrapped in leathers, creating a sandal of sorts, which also allowed the claws at the end of their feet to protrude slightly.

The armor they wore was a mixture of well-made leathers and some chain mesh parts covering larger body parts and adding another layer of protection. It looked like they would be able to move easily within their clothing. The pieces also looked worn, with deep, well-worn and developed creases that showed where the material had bent naturally over the course of its life. I saw that each carried two weapons: a spear they were holding and a sword in a sheath. The weapons looked to be well maintained. The last item of note was a small shield that rode on the forearm and didn't look like it could hold off anything bigger than a knife. Even the swords in their sheaths looked far too big for the small shield. I did note, however, a complex set of etchings on each shield. Since I had little to no idea how magic could work with this race, I was going to assume that the shields were more than they appeared and warn the team appropriately.

The lack of a helm made me think they either didn't truly expect to be attacked here in their home or they simply didn't wear helmets. Either way, I hoped the lack of protection on their arms and head would lower their armor class enough that we could do some serious damage on them, because I had no doubt we would have to fight these creatures, and probably lots of them, before we got to the Shield of Ashtator.

Probably most important of all for my part of this mission, the drakkin didn't appear capable of seeing through my Blacksuit. There was always the slim chance, given their propensity for magic, that the drakkin would have a better chance at seeing through my invisible shroud of shadows. That would have made my task here impossible and would have completely negated our role as the sneaky ones.

Following my one-sided introduction to the drakkin, and waiting a bit to note that they never left their spot in the tunnel, I set off to complete my task. Continuing to move slowly, always checking for wards and traps, I began to map out the tunnels around our entrance. There were several times that I came upon dead ends, and I was forced to retrace my steps. Other times, I found junctions and crossroads that caused me to backtrack on myself. I stopped frequently when I came upon a patrol. The goal was to determine if these were stationary guards or roving security. I came across twenty separate patrols, and it was a pretty even split on which ones were stationary and which ones roamed. Additionally, there were three instances where wandering patrols overlapped with stationary guards. The last thing we wanted to deal with were four yellow mobs.

I didn't worry about how much time it was taking, as this was not one of those tasks that you would want to screw up at all. It also appeared my group wasn't in a hurry to leave, as they were all still online and chatting amongst themselves. I would have loved to be a part of that camaraderie, but I couldn't spare the focus. I kept my attention on finding the shield and getting back to my team.

There were only two occasions where I encountered more than two drakkin together. The first occurred when I found myself in what I assumed was a barracks of sorts, with row after row of beds and way too many drakkin. I estimated there were between thirty and forty in the room. I also saw numerous swords, spears, and sets of armor throughout the hall. No one saw me, and I left there as fast as I could.

The second instance was an even larger gathering of the beasts. I found a dining hall, where easily a hundred drakkin were eating. It was not only terribly frightening, given the amount of them that were there, but it was also unbelievably disgusting to see. Where I assumed they were carnivore before by their teeth, it was confirmed when I saw them eat.

Their meals consisted of small animals, still alive, that they grabbed out of pens located on each table. While the animal still lived, the drakkin would tuck in and blood would splatter everywhere. If I didn't know it was a meal by seeing them eating, I would have thought a massacre had happened in the room. I guess, to some degree, that was in fact what was happening.

I left the dining area as fast as I could and resumed my search. The benefit of mapping out all the tunnels was that I could see on my map where I had been. To this point, the barracks and the dining hall were the only two large rooms I had come across, and as such, it should be easier to avoid them.

It was after another thirty minutes of slowly mapping out the underground warren that I finally came across the room I had been searching for. I had turned a corner and come upon a long tunnel that ended in a set of large doors, a drakkin guard posted on each side. The guards, I noted, were dressed in finer armor than their patrolling counterparts and were appropriately named Drakkin Elite Guards. Also, they were red to me, meaning that they were at least five levels higher than me. I hoped that we would avoid any red mobs, but I also had to consider myself lucky that I had only encountered these two up to this point.

The doors, thankfully, were open. Had they been closed, I would have had to make an assumption on whether or not I had found the right spot. And as the saying goes, I've had plenty of opportunities to make an ass out of myself up to this point, so I was glad this wouldn't be another time. I crept past the two guards, checking the threshold of the doorway for any magical or mechanical traps, and made my way into a grand hall.

The room I entered closely resembled the description given by the amnesiac dwarf we had named Jack. The doorway sat on the side of the room, and it only took one glance to my left to see where the dwarf had been forced to kneel so many times. The room itself was empty at that moment, but I made certain to look for any traps as I walked in.

The throne Jack described, or a close approximation to one, sat against the far wall, though I only gave it the slightest glance. My eyes quickly caught on the prize we had come for. Sitting above the throne had to be the Shield of Ashtator. Even from a distance, it looked amazing, and I crept ever closer to get a better look.

Seeing there weren't any obstacles between me and the shield, I made my way forward. This gave me an opportunity to look at the throne area more closely as well. There was a section of the floor, located about ten feet from the seat, that was a darker color than the rest of the floor. More so, that discoloration drew me to get a better look at the floor as a whole.

My first belief that the floor was simply smooth and worn bedrock turned out to be false. All around the throne, the ground was covered in meticulous etchings that radiated out 20 feet from the seat. In particular, the area that showed discoloration had even more complex runic work, with a circle marked in the ground and various markings in the center. I was making a guess, but I assumed it was some kind of holding circle for the prisoners that were brought in, and the red discoloration I saw in that circle had to have been from blood.

Again, I was making assumptions, but at this point I couldn't avoid it. I certainly didn't want to step on the runes and "figure it out" from there. What gave me further pause, though, was that the etchings on the ground swept back past the throne and went all the way up to the wall behind the seat where the shield was hanging. Bottom line, walking up to the wall directly under the shield was out of the question unless I wanted to test those carvings.

I scouted out the area around the throne and the wall some more and found what would likely be my route for getting to the shield. I would have to start on a different part of the wall and climb over to the shield, moving both sideways and up along the cavern wall. The indicators that popped into my view told me that this would be a difficult, but not impossible feat. Add in my Shadows, and I should be able to not only make the climb, using my Scaling, but do so quickly enough to make short work of removing the shield. That was, of course, dependent on how complex the warding was over the shield. Given enough time, I could Disassemble most wards. Time, however, was not going to be on our side, and our goal was speed and stealth.

Now that I had found what I believed was the Shield of Ashtator, it was time to get back to my group and wait for the pre-arranged time to launch our part of the operation. I would take the most direct route back to where our team was waiting and decide if there were any detours from that route we would need to take based on the patrols. This would be difficult, but we should be able to manage it.

Those were my thoughts, at least, until I turned away from the wall I was looking at and saw a new drakkin enter the room. Not only was it wearing better armor than the patrols I had seen, it was even better than that of the Elites outside the door. In fact, with the exception of Jason's legendary gear, I had never seen better looking armor. The creature wearing it, the Guardian of the Drakkin, moved as if it weighed nothing, and he was definitely red to me when I looked at him. The sword at his side also looked to be of the grandest quality I had ever seen.

This was a boss mob if I had ever seen one. I had no idea what type of skills this mob had, whether it was pure melee or a hybrid melee/caster, but I knew that it would be a challenge. And, honestly, depending on what level it was and what fighting style it used, it could very well be above our abilities.

This didn't change our plan, but it would make speed and stealth a lot more difficult if this mob was in the throne room when we got here. The only thing I could hope for was that when the attack by the dwarves started, the Guardian went to defend his people.

I slipped out of the room, past the Guardian and the Elite guards, and made my way back to the team. I found that there were two spots that we would need to detour around to avoid patrols and stationary guards that overlapped too often. Other than those two spots, I did not find any other hazardous areas, though all of that could change the first time we attacked a guard.

Also, unless they all decided to abandon their posts when the dwarves came, we would have to fight. I counted twenty likely encounters that we would have to face—forty mobs total. This was within our capabilities, and more importantly, within our timeframe. Steelhammer was preparing to fight, in case we failed, and had agreed to give us three hours to complete our task. Even then, it went against everything he knew about warfare. Giving the enemy that much time to prepare was anathema to winning a campaign quickly and completely negated his surprise.

And that surprise would be the signal to begin our task. I really wish I could have been there to see the looks on the drakkins' faces when their shield popped like a balloon, courtesy of Sally's generous gift of the Barrier Breaker. Of course, Steelhammer probably wished he could be there to witness their ire when they figured out we had robbed them of the shield.

—◄◄◄◄◅◅)̶(◅◅►►►►—

December 12, 2043

"I've got full mana. Let's get the next two," Jason said.

We were moving up on our fourth set of mobs. This would be the first time that we had to worry about a roving patrol, a situation negated slightly by my ability to scout ahead and say when the optimal time to engage was upon us. The potential for secondary mobs was why we had waited for Jason to fully regen his mana.

When we would traditionally pull two mobs, we would have Dan kite one of them, but that was impossible with these mobs. In fact, it was a whole new experience for us. If you didn't actively engage the mob in a fight, they would attempt to flee and, we assumed, warn the others. The only thing that saved us on that first pull was that Jason already had his Stun spell loaded up and was able to cast before one of the guards turned the corner and announced our arrival. So for that reason, we engaged the two mobs at the same time. Wayne would lead with enough taunting and bashing to keep the aggro on the mob and to keep its attention. For the second mob, Jenny would lead with a Bash from her shield, which had a modifier to her Bash skill and so far, had landed successfully each time. Following her Bash, Kaitlin would root the drakkin in place, then Tim would cast Enchant until the mob had been placated. We had been relatively successful so far. Overall, except for that first experience that almost gave us heart attacks, we had been doing well since the drakkin had taken off in the tunnels toward the dwarves.

I couldn't help but smile when I thought about that scene. After I returned to my group and gave them a full account of what I found, we decided that I should be in the tunnels when Steelhammer launched his assault. More specifically, I should be somewhere that I could check to make sure the tunnels emptied out the way we wanted them to when the time came. I knew just the spot to start.

I reached the barracks a few minutes before Steelhammer was due to announce his presence. The first indication I saw of something happening was from a drakkin running into the barracks, yelling something I couldn't understand. I peeked around the corner of the barracks door and saw numerous drakkin grabbing their armor and weapons. I figured someone had finally spotted our dwarven friends.

I next ran over to the mess hall. Where the barracks was in disarray, and drakkin were running around trying to get their gear together, the lizard folk in the mess were still focused on their slaughter of little animals. It wasn't until the earth shook that they stopped their meal.

And boy did the ground move. I had no idea what kind of an effect the Barrier Breaker would have, but the result from taking out the magic shield that protected the entrance to the drakkin home could be felt all the way down below the surface. First was the violent movement of the earth at our feet, akin to an earthquake but much faster. Soon after was the sound that made it to our ears, which sounded like the popping of a balloon. A really large balloon.

The effect on the lizards in the mess hall was immediate. As soon as the ground moved below their feet, they all stopped eating and sat perfectly still. Almost as one, their heads turned toward the open door of the hall when the explosive sound ripped through the air. I had, thankfully, removed myself from the doorway when they all looked that way, or I may have been trampled by the very same guard who had already informed the barracks about what was happening.

I saw him as he turned into the mess hall, screamed out a few words, and then ran on to some new place. I didn't follow him to his next port of call. Instead, I took a quick look into the dining area and saw the pandemonium that followed whatever the guard had yelled, probably something about being under attack, as every drakkin moved to grab their equipment and make their way toward the door.

I saw that I had a few seconds to get out of there, as their equipment was stacked against walls and they looked to be falling over each other to get to their goods. While seeing a few of them trip over themselves was funny, I didn't want to get caught up in a trampling session. Once I had moved down the hall enough that I could observe the doorway and not get smothered, I started to see the drakkin filing out and heading toward what I could only assume was the surface.

I made a roundabout return to my group to check that the barracks had cleared out as well, noting that all the patrols were still in place. This was the best-case scenario we could have hoped for. As soon as I returned to the group, we buffed up fully and began our part of the operation.

Now on our fourth group, things were going smoothly, and we had cleared out enough of the mobs behind us to try an experiment with Tim's ability to Charm a mob, and in essence become one of our team. I had no doubt my teammates would bitch and moan about this being one of my all too famous experiments. However, I also knew that Tim would be up for the challenge and always looked for an opportunity to be more involved in the offensive part of the fighting. No matter how much he denied it, as a former recon Marine, there was no way Tim would pass up an opportunity to be a part of the damage equation and not just crowd control.

Our tactic for controlling the two mobs worked as before, and we slowly cut through the two guards in front of us. That was the other part we had to factor in when dealing with a potential roving patrol coming upon us—these drakkin had an insane amount of hitpoints and putting them down was slow going. Our engagement of the two in front of us started when the rovers were far enough away so as not to join their compatriots when we began, but still on the outbound portion of their patrol. We should, theoretically, have had enough time to get through both mobs before the patrol looped back to us.

I would have loved to have just pulled the mobs back farther, but with them attempting to flee and likely sounding an alarm, we couldn't take that chance. We had to Enchant the one mob right where it was. Although, if that mob did break free from being under Tim's spell, there is little doubt it would first rush Tim and kill him before running off to sound an alarm. Unfortunately, as a caster, Tim had almost no hitpoints and no armor, so one or two punches from the guard and he would probably go down.

What we had now was working, but it would be more difficult further on where the timing between when the roving patrols crossed paths with the stationary guards was closer together. An additional fighter, *i.e.* a Charmed mob, would make a huge difference.

We downed the second guard we were fighting a minute or so before the roving pair would arrive. Just enough time for me to put my plan in motion but not enough time for anyone to bitch about it.

"We've got a patrol coming down the hall. I suggest we go back around this corner and hit them when they arrive. I got to tell you, though, this is going to get trickier as we move in, because the timing between patrols will be much shorter. We could definitely use another damage dealer. You up for it, Timmy?" I said.

"Hell yeah, Alex! Let's just do it the same way we are now. Bash, Root, and then let me try a Charm. I'm going to try to land it on the mob before I cast a Magic debuff to lower his resistances. If the Charm doesn't land, then I should still have enough time to cast the debuff and try again."

"Wait, did you just suggest you do an experiment on yourself?" Dan asked.

"Proof! Right there is proof! I didn't ask him, he volunteered," I said

"No one believes that you didn't secretly manipulate him, Alex."

I smiled and shook my head at Wayne who had uttered the last comment. "Man, I can't win with you guys for nothing!"

"Enough chatter, boys. We got incoming," Kaitlin reminded us.

The Charm Tim casted landed on his first attempt. I knew that Tim had some gear that gave him a bonus to his Enchanter-only spells, and it seemed that they were definitely helpful here. He was still wearing the Smoking Jacket we picked up for him fighting the undead oh so long ago. The item may have been of a low level, but you couldn't pass up the 10 percent modifier to Spells.

The additional damage of Tim's new friend also helped immensely in whittling down the hitpoints on the second mob. With Tim's new pet in tow, we should be able to move even quicker. He would still need to Enchant the secondary mob from here on out, but our ability to remove a stationary patrol before the roving patrols returned was now much more plausible.

And that's pretty much how it all played out. There were a few occasions where Kaitlin had to join in and help with healing Wayne, and another instance where we got to see just how many strikes from one of the drakkin Tim could take when he was unable to reestablish Charm on his pet and the guard attacked him. Thankfully, Jason's Stun was quick enough to stop the guard, allowing Kaitlin's root to land. With that, we were able to keep the guard stationary long enough for Jenny to establish aggro on it.

The good news was that incident occurred near the end of our journey and we could take all the time we needed to dispatch the three guards we were now dealing with. The bad news was that it was, in fact, the end of our journey and it was the two red Elite Guards that we had to face next. I really wished we had Tim's Charmed pet for those.

Surprisingly, though, Tim was quite happy to be rid of his pet.

"I'ma Charm one of these assholes." Tim could only have one pet at a time, after all.

"You sure that's a good idea, buddy?" Gary asked. "You miss, and I'm going to have to scrape you off the floor."

"If Kaitlin can land a Root and keep him stationary, then yeah, I'm going to give it a try. I mean, I haven't had to use my Magic debuff on these guys yet, right? So, it should be doable! I'll lead with my debuff here, then hit the Charm. If we can get one of these bad boys as a pet, we will be golden."

"Oh, it's sound logic, sure. But that's usually what preempts most of the ass whoopings you end up getting."

"Shut up, Gary."

Tim and Gary were our Jason and Dan, only neither of them were the same level of special that Dan was. Also, neither of them had almost burned down Jenny's apartment.

There was definitely merit in having one of these mobs as a pet, especially with the possibility that the Guardian was in the very next room after we faced the Elites. Still, landing a spell like Charm on a red mob—even with Tim's buffs to Enchanter spells and Magic debuff— was going to be a long shot.

"It's not much, but I have a Magic debuff as well," Jenny said.

"That's right, Jenny! I forgot about that. Let me try mine first, and then if it doesn't land, you can try yours as well?"

Jenny nodded her head and looked over at Kaitlin. "You ok with this? If your Root doesn't land, it's you he will come after first."

"These guys may live underground, but they don't seem to have any resistance to my Earth magic. I haven't had a single resist on Root. I should be good. If I'm not, well, we're all fucked."

Most of us had spoken up at this point, and I figured we should get the rest of the crew's thoughts.

"I'll have Stun ready," was all Jason said. Wayne simply looked at me like I was a moron for asking if he was ok trying to take two red mobs if it came to that.

Finally, there was Dan, and even I couldn't believe the next words that came out of my mouth.

"You've been awfully quiet, Dan. Any thoughts?"

Dan didn't say anything at first and just shook his head then, after a beat, said, "If Kaitlin's Root doesn't land, I'll have a Snare ready and will stand between the mob and her. No way she dies down here." And with that, he turned away from the group and stared off toward the next mobs.

Ever since the aforementioned incident involving the almost burned down apartment, and the subsequent smothering of Kaitlin with a fire extinguisher, Dan had worried his chances with Kaitlin had disappeared entirely. The look in her eyes said he still had a shot, at least if he kept making comments like that.

A smile that Dan couldn't see escaped more than just my lips, and I nodded my head in his direction.

With that, we were ready to turn the corner and take on a couple of red mobs.

As we rounded the corner, I saw that the door to the grand hall was closed now, but the two Elite Guards were still standing on either side of the doorway. Despite the fact that we could see them, they did not leave their posts. And even as we got closer, they did not move. Once we were on the limits of our spellcasting range, I saw Kaitlin start to cast her spell. That was Wayne's cue to run at the mobs, and he took off at a sprint for the guard on the right.

Kaitlin's root landed just as Wayne took to the air with his hammer above his head. Wayne's strike landed with a resounding crack against the shield of the Elite Guard but didn't budge him a bit. Instead, he swung his spear around, trying to trip Wayne up.

I looked over to the other guard. I had maintained my Conceal/Stealth invisibility, so I could drag the bodies if everything went bad. Tim had just finished casting his Charm spell, and I heard him mumble "shit" under his breath.

"No good?"

"Nope, no good," he said in a low voice. Then, in a louder one, he announced "Charm didn't stick! Casting, debuff!"

The Root spell continued to hold, and Tim's debuff spell was quickly finished and applied to his Elite mob. As Tim continued to Charm, I looked back over to Wayne and his mob. Despite being a red mob, Wayne was holding his own and Jason was efficiently maintaining his heals.

"Landed!" Tim yelled out, as I looked back toward him and what was now his new pet.

Tim wouldn't be able to do anything with the pet until the Root spell wore off, not wanting to risk any negative feedback to Kaitlin if she dropped her spell. Kaitlin had informed us that the chances of her receiving feedback, which amounted to damage to her, were about 1 percent if she dropped the spell. If a mob broke her spell, it was closer to 10 percent. This was the same for Tim.

Dan's Snare was slightly different than Kaitlin's Root, although they were both Earth-based spells, in that it only limited the movement speed of the mob and didn't fully arrest its movement. As such, Dan had never had any mob break his spell. It either landed, or it didn't.

With Tim's new friend fully under his control, I felt comfortable joining the fight. I took my place behind the Drakkin Elite Guard, standing near Gary, and let loose with my daggers. Within a few moments, Kaitlin's Root faded, and Tim was able to direct his new pet into the mix.

It became obvious there was a new hitter in the mix, as the Elite's hitpoints started dropping noticeably faster. I had tensed up a bit when the mob's health got closer to 75 percent, in case this was some sort of a boss fight. Thankfully, nothing happened at either 75 or 50 percent, and I assessed this was just a hard-ass mob.

With just a bit more time, we were able to kill the Elite. I looted the corpse and found several gold coins but no other items. This had been the case for all the guards. None of their armor or weapons had dropped, but each had several gold coins.

With our way clear to the final room, I made sure everyone buffed up. With little else to do, I told the group that I planned to backtrack our route a bit and make certain our way out remained clear. I also took the opportunity to activate my Blacksuit and gather the shadows around me. I did, in fact, make sure our way out was clear, and did not see any wandering mobs around our part of the underground complex.

With that done, I had everyone retreat down the hall, away from the double doors, as I prepared to open them up. If I died for some reason, Gary would be able to retrieve my body and Play Dead if anything came after him.

Despite being a good ten feet tall and three feet wide per door, the hinges didn't protest a bit, and the door moved smoothly inward. Opening the doors did not appear to be enough of a trigger to aggro the Guardian who remained standing in the middle of the room. The Shield of Ashtator remained in the same location, and I could clearly see my route highlighted along the wall for my impending thievery. All that was required was to kill the Guardian and take the shield.

I returned to the group and saw Wayne ready to go. There had already been a bit of discussion about how, exactly, the group should engage the Guardian. Wayne was arguing for a one-man approach, and I was leaning toward his logic.

"We have no idea what this guy's level is, or really anything about him. It was relatively safe to think the Elites were two or three levels above the regular guards. But if this guy follows that same logic, then he could be six levels higher than us.

"And while I think we can handle almost anything as a full team, anything over six levels higher than us and we could be looking at a full-blown wipe. I'd rather know that beforehand, is all I'm saying."

"So what, Wayne? You go in there and get yourself killed? And you think we are going to be ok with that?" Jenny asked with her arms crossed over her chest.

"Yes. That's exactly what I'm thinking. Alex can drag me out, and Allister can give me a resurrection, if it comes to that. You don't really think that I would do something that would end up putting everyone at risk, do you?" Wayne asked.

"It's the experience you will lose, brother. No one wants to lose that much experience if it can be helped." Gary added.

"Sure, but that's the risk we take. I'm cool with it. I know my role."

There wasn't going to be much in the way of arguing with Wayne once he had made up his mind on this, and honestly, his logic was sound. I kept out of the argument and simply waited for everyone to come to the same conclusion. I would be ready to drag Wayne's body out if it came to that.

After the group came to agree with Wayne's idea, I placed myself near the open doorway. This way I would be able to view the fight and be near enough to drag Wayne's body out if something went wrong.

"If you start getting pummeled, try to die near the doorway. That way, when I drag your overly large ass out of the room, I won't have to go inside the room."

"Thanks for that vote of confidence." Wayne said, but smiled in the direction that my voice had come from. I hadn't yet dropped my Blacksuit and didn't plan to until that shield was in my hand.

Without any additional fanfare, Wayne rushed into the room and engaged the Guardian.

Immediately, we knew this wasn't going to end well. The very first hit that the Guardian landed removed almost ten percent of Wayne's health. That was a mountain of hitpoints for a player.

The next series of hits removed another ten percent. I turned back toward the team and saw Jenny starting to come down the hall. Thankfully, Kaitlin grabbed her arm and it stopped Jenny from going forward.

"I know you want to, Jenny, but we can't save him."

"I know, Alex. And my Lay on Hands won't be active anytime soon, since I used it in the fight with the Wyvern."

In that short time, Wayne's hitpoints dropped another 40 percent, and I could see he was slowly inching his way back toward the door.

"Just don't cross the threshold, brother."

"Got ya, I'll die just on the other side of the door."

It wasn't but another 10 seconds before Wayne's body crumpled to the floor and he was lying dead in front of me.

Maybe, at the most, a minute. That's how long Wayne was able to last. There was no way we were going to be able to take this guy, even as a team. With a raid group, and a rotating team of at least three healers, we could have done it. As it was, our team wasn't big enough.

I received a notification in the game that I had permission to drag Wayne's body and pulled his corpse over to Jason. His resurrection would come momentarily, and he would get half his experience back. The loss of experience definitely sucked, wiping out anything that Wayne had earned down here in the tunnels. More devastatingly, our morale took a severe hit as well. Everyone looked despondent.

So often, my group and our larger team overcame crazy odds. Like when we defeated the Wyvern outside these halls, we did so by the skin of our teeth. Honestly, we weren't used to losing. When it happened, it hit us pretty hard.

But, I remembered that this mission had nothing to do with killing a Guardian, it had to do with getting a shield. I was asked to accomplish this task, not because of my martial abilities, but for my thieving ones, and I had an idea how I could make that work.

"That definitely sucked, huh Wayne?"

"Yeah, Alex, you could say that. Dude hits too hard man. Not to mention, I spent most of the time stunned. I'd be shocked if I hit him at all."

I had been close enough to see how the fight played out. Wayne definitely made contact, but he was right about his efforts being negligible. Wayne didn't have the hitpoints to stay in there long enough, not if I wanted to get over to that shield and get it off the wall. So, we needed another tank, and one that had a whole lot more hitpoints.

Like a Drakkin Elite Guard.

An idea started to form in my mind.

"Hey Tim, you still have that amulet from the raid?"

"Sure do, Alex. The Master's Amulet of Earth. It's only level 10, but I haven't come across anything better."

"What was the effect on it?"

"Weight of the Earth. Area of Effect: 40 percent slow."

"Get it ready. I have a plan."

"We are so going to die," I heard Jason mumble.

"Oh ye of little faith, Alli.... umm... Allifaithless," Dan said.

"For the record, that one sucked, Dan."

Dan hung his head low and shook it back and forth. "It did. It really, really did."

With a bit of the tension having been broken by Dan and Jason's banter, I returned back to the topic at hand.

"I really don't like the amount of assuming we are having to do down here, but that's the way of it. Given this guy's likely level, and the fact that your spells had a problem landing on the Elite without a debuff, I'm going to assume the Guardian has an even higher resistance to magic. Which, given their heritage, makes perfect sense.

"But their resistance to Earth-based spells doesn't seem to be there at all. So, we use what we have." I said then turned toward Kaitlin. "Start by throwing a Root at the mob. I want you to be just inside the doorway when you do. If it doesn't land, you'll likely be dead in two or three swings, but it won't wipe the team."

"Got it." Kaitlin said.

"Next up will be you, Tim. Once that Root lands, I want you to send in your pet. At the same time, cast your magic debuff and then Slow spell. If the debuff doesn't take, or the Slow doesn't stick, I want you to activate your amulet. What's the cast time on it?"

"Instant."

"Perfect. Again, I'm assuming, but since it's the Master's Amulet of Earth, I'm going to say the spell checks against Earth resistances and not the magic resistance you usually cast against."

I thought about it a bit more and then added, "If we can get that Slow to land, either of them really, then we need to simply stop him from attacking as often as he does. Jenny and Allister, you guys will be responsible for casting Stuns on the Guardian, keeping it from attacking.

Kaitlin, you'll keep a Root on it as well. The Elite pet of Tim's should have enough time to maintain aggro, but in case one of those Stuns really pisses it off, the Root will keep it in place long enough for the pet to get back to the top of the aggro list."

"And the rest of us?" Gary asked.

"Nothing. Stay out of the room. We aren't here to kill the Guardian, we're here to steal a shield. To do that, I just need some time."

I could see them thinking through the idea. It wasn't a normal method for completing a quest, but our team also knew there was little chance of us actually beating the Guardian, even with it slowed. Those Stuns that would be keeping it out of commission, and unable to attack, wouldn't be available if Jason, and likely Jenny, had to heal Wayne.

"Final thing," I said. "Dan, when I give you the signal, I want you to cast Snare on the Guardian. Kaitlin, I'll need you to drop your Root, as well. I know it could cause feedback but we need to take that risk. Snare lasts longer than Root, and we are going to want to run out of this place and delay that thing for as long as we can. If we are lucky, and we put enough distance between us, maybe it will lose the aggro."

The plan was completely unorthodox, but so was this whole quest. I was happy to switch it up if we could make it work.

Once everyone's mana was full, Kaitlin led the way with her Root spell.

A breath I didn't even realize I had been holding came out in a sigh of relief when Kaitlin yelled out, "Landed!"

I immediately saw Tim's pet run past me and into the room, toward the Guardian. At the same time, I saw Tim finish his casting of his debuff.

"No good, Alex. Didn't land. Triggering the amulet!" Tim yelled out as he brought the necklace from around his neck up, stepped fully into the room, and pointed it toward the Guardian.

Another sigh of relief escaped my lips as I saw a noticeable drop in the speed of the Guardian's attacks as Tim's Slow spell landed. And if I had any doubt before, Tim put all question to rest.

"Take that, you ugly lizard fuck! Slow landed!"

"Heading to the shield," I said and ran for the wall. As soon as I was close enough, I reached out with my hands, and Shadows, and Scaled the side of the wall toward the shield.

"I'm not going to be able to follow what's going on down there. You call it how you see it, guys."

"I'm on it, Alex," Wayne said. I knew it grated on him to be neutered like this; our Warrior always wanted to be the one in the thick of the fight. This would give him something to do, and Wayne was a solid leader in his own right. It was another worry I could let slip away as I made my way toward the prize. I knew I would need all my concentration when I could finally see how the shield was secured to the wall.

There was a moderately simple trap that tied into the latching mechanism that held the shield against the surface of the wall. I could, in my assessment, disarm the trap in a matter of seconds, if not a minute, but getting to that trap was going to be the problem.

The ward that surrounded that trap was yellow in color, which meant it was one of the hardest wards around but still within my abilities. The only Rogue I knew who could have gotten through that obstacle with any speed was Sally, and she wasn't anywhere around. I could do it, but it wasn't going to be fast. Not if I wanted to do it without getting myself killed or announcing myself to the whole place.

"How long you think we got before the Guardian tears through your pet, Tim?"

"If Allister and Jenny can keep landing these Stuns, we might get five minutes."

"There's something keeping this shield in place. I'll try to figure it out."

Five minutes was not a lot of time, certainly way less than it's ever taken me to get through a ward this difficult. Still, I didn't have a choice. I tried to block out the rest of my senses and focused exclusively on the ward and how to Disassemble it. I wasn't terribly worried that anyone figured out what I did, but the only way I knew how to get through these wards was to do it the Rogue way, and that meant to make it look like we were never here.

Focusing my Shadows into the tools I would need to take apart the ward, I tucked in to the project. The problem, I noted, wasn't how complex the ward was. Instead, it was the amount of magic itself that was poured into the ward.

The wards at the bank were thinly layered over each other to create a knotwork that required precision to get through. There was no finesse in the magical obstacle facing me now. This was pure, brute force magic at work, and the level of difficulty was set according to how tough it would be to slice through the cords of magic holding the ward in place with just Shadows. I wasn't a novice with the Shadows, but I wasn't a master either. I was a journeyman, through and through.

Reviewing the obstruction again, I realized that its design lacked any real complexity and that Sally could have gotten through it in seconds. That gave me hope, since it would be a matter of strength vice finesse that would win the day, and I could move much quicker with only strength to consider.

Still, it wasn't a simple matter of slice and done. I had to get through a layer to peel it back and that meant sawing through with my smaller Shadows. The timing of the whole affair started to worry my teammates a bit, and they made their concerns known to me.

"We ain't got much time left here, Alex. I don't know what the fuck you are doing up there, but you got about another minute before my pet eats shit and we all wipe."

"Copy," I said to the group, and Tim in particular. "It's going to be close. Dan, listen for my call."

I didn't bother to look and see what Dan's response was and leaned back into my task. It looked like I had only one layer left of this ward and then the mechanical trap to be rid of. At the rate I had been going, I'd finish with maybe 15 seconds to spare. If there had been any craftsmanship to the ward, I'd have failed.

As I quickly Disarmed the mechanical trap, I pulled the shield from the wall. As soon as I touched it, I was greeted with a notification that it was, in fact, the Shield of Ashtator. However, there was no box that also populated to show me what the stats of the shield were. I couldn't, apparently, loot this item for the purposes of using it in the game. All the better, since temptation could have reared its ugly head if the properties had been overpowering. Jenny would look good with the greatest shield ever made. Since there was no chance of that, it would go in my inventory as the quest item that it was.

"I've got it! Heading for the door now. Hit the Snare, Dan."

"Dropping Root in 5, 4, 3, 2, 1." Kaitlin counted out.

"Snare landed!" Dan chimed in.

"Elite has maybe 25 to 30 seconds left in him."

"Thanks, Tim. Let's beat feet for our exit," I said, bee lining for the doorway.

I noticed the runes just shy of the threshold of the door and on the floor for the first time, right as they flared up to life, and glowing red. This was another ward, and I wasn't going to be able to stop myself before I triggered it.

The only reasonable explanation for the ward had to be that it was tied into the proximity of the Shield of Ashtator. The result of my crossing that doorway was immediate. The first thing you couldn't avoid was the ear-splitting siren that went off all around us. It was loud enough to honestly qualify as deafening.

The second thing was a pulse of red light that pushed out from the runes on the ground and toward the Guardian. The pulse ended at the Guardian and his whole body glowed red for a second. After both of those happened, the Guardian let out a roar that was almost as load as the siren we were hearing.

The pulse of magic had a secondary effect: it negated my Blacksuit, and I was as visible as anyone else. Not great, since the Guardian was now looking directly at me. That is, until the Elite guard that was Tim's pet raked his claws against the Guardian's face. This caused the Guardian to look back toward his aggressor, and I saw our opportunity to escape.

"Now, while he's preoccupied with the Elite! The more distance we can put between us the better!"

I was about to start running when I heard Tim mutter, "Oh, shit!" in something like amazement.

The smart move was to put my head down and make for the exit, but the awe in Tim's voice drew my attention against my better judgement.

One look at the scene explained Tim's response. The Elite was dead, slumped against the far wall. Tim looked at me and said, "One-shotted him. Single punch took off the rest of his life and launched him into the wall. We're fucked."

"Not if we move! He's still got the Snare on him. We just gotta get outta here, so go!"

I didn't wait to see if anyone followed me and ran as fast as my legs could take me. If we could get outside, and had enough time to do so, we could summon our horses and then outrun the Guardian all the way back to the Dwarves. The Guardian may be a beast, but a full dwarven army would put him down in no time.

I wound through the tunnels, following my map to our exit. There were no other mobs in the tunnels. They had either gone to the surface to prepare for the fight against Steelhammer or we had killed them all. This was starting to look doable.

Naturally, that's when things got bad.

"Snares down," Dan whispered.

And if that wasn't enough to put the fear in us, we could hear the scream of the Guardian get closer as his speed increased and the distance between us diminished.

It's a simple matter of game mechanics, and it's been this way in every game I've ever played: if you try to run from a monster, the monster will be faster than you. The monster itself does not matter. Bears were faster than us, wolves were faster than us, and hell, even bunnies were faster if they were chasing us. And those didn't have a hit of magical steroids like our friend the Guardian had. We were ahead of him, but he would catch up if given enough time.

The second rule that seemed to be universal was that mounts were slightly faster than whatever was chasing you. If we could get to a place that we could summon our horses, we still had a chance. But those horses took 10 seconds to summon, and I didn't know if we were going to get those 10 seconds.

We came upon our entrance to the tunnels and threw open the door to the outside world.

As soon as we were through the door I tried to summon my horse;

however, the notification said there wasn't enough room and was impossible at that time. I needed to get to where the blue skies were above me. And I could see them at the end of the long tunnel. I didn't waste any time and ran for all I was worth.

I could hear the Guardian in the tunnels as he raged—but I could also hear something else. A lot of something elses.

Right before we approached the entrance to the tunnel, two things happened. The first was I saw what looked like two platoons of dwarves and a dozen prisoners. The second was the Guardian coming through the same doorway we had just passed by.

"Root it, Kaitlin!"

"Resisted, Alex!"

"Dan!" I yelled.

"Snare landed! But it's going to catch up to us if we stop to do these horses. And that's not counting our friends ahead!"

"Where the hell did these guys come from?" Wayne asked.

"Looks like the dwarves that Steelhammer sent to liberate the prison I found the first time we came through here."

"Wait. What prison? You didn't say you found the prison."

"No time for that now, Wayne!"

The dwarves recognized us as allies to their people and stopped. They looked apprehensive, but I guessed it was because of the roaring coming out of the tunnel courtesy of the Guardian. That look of apprehension didn't stop me from running up to the first dwarf I could and trying to give him the shield to get it to Steelhammer.

But the stupid game wouldn't allow me to make the trade.

"Shit! I've got the Shield of Ashtator, but I can't give it to you. I'm being told I can only give it to Steelhammer!"

I don't know if the dwarf understood that I had been given a notification that said this item could only be given to King Steelhammer, but he didn't seem to care. His eyes had fired up when I said the name of the shield.

"Ya have it, lad? Truly?"

I was able to take it out of my inventory and show him, and that was all it took to get every dwarf around me, over twenty, riled up.

"Get that to Steelhammer," he said to me. Then he turned to another of the dwarves and pointed to the prisoners. "You and yer three boys take the prisoners away from here and back to Steelhammer. Me and my lads will stop whatever is coming through that tunnel."

The thing coming through that tunnel was a death sentence for those dwarves, but it would give us the time we needed to get on our horses and get away from here.

The plan was perfectly sound. Which of course was the reason Wayne wouldn't have it.

"We fight together! I'll not let you dwarves die for us."

"And risk the lives of thousands, boy? Don't be daft. Get with yer folk and get that shield to Steelhammer."

Wayne was about to object again when he heard the roar of the Guardian almost upon the gathering. Even knowing it was the right call, Wayne's resistance was strong.

Finally, the dwarf pushed him away with his shield, and Wayne took the hint. As he was about to join us the same dwarf called out his name, "Naugha!"

Wayne looked back, and the dwarf said, "Remember our names, lad, and be singing our praises tonight!"

"*Huzzah!*" echoed from every dwarf in that small clearing.

"Huzzah," Wayne said as he lifted his hammer in salute before running to our group.

We stood in the clearing and summoned our horses, just as I saw the Guardian crest the rise out of the tunnel with the dwarves turning to meet him. "Smack him with your shields! If you can Stun him, it'll give us and the prisoners even more time to get out of here," I said,

"Bah! Was gonna do that anyway!" the dwarf replied.

With five seconds remaining on our summons, I saw twenty dwarves swarm over the Guardian.

It was just enough time.

Those twenty dwarves that stood against the Guardian were the only dwarven casualties in the Great Shield War, as it would come to be known. Bards had already begun working up songs to describe the feats of valor that the dwarves would undertake and were already composing their first piece around the destruction of the drakkins' magical shield. The fact that Steelhammer was able to destroy the shield in one fell swoop was to be something of legend.

Of course, there was no war in the end, and Steelhammer was happy to pick up and go back to his mountain as soon as the shield was in his possession. The only thing we waited for were the prisoners being escorted back, which Steelhammer sent out additional troops to find and assist with the escort. That and the Guardian.

Despite having traveled a great distance, the Guardian never stopped chasing the shield. However, he found an army of dwarves and not just twenty when he arrived. The dwarven men and women made quick work of him.

My team and I, save for Wayne and Jenny, lounged in a corner, away from the revelry. Our tanking couple, however, were mostly responsible for that revelry. Wayne was helping to fete the brave dwarves that sacrificed their lives so that the Shield of Ashtator could be returned to its rightful place, namely above the throne of King Steelhammer.

For tonight, anyhow. When I reminded the king of how easy it would be for me to steal it, he noted he was going to put it in their vault. He also made note that his vault would rival the one in the Bank, so I shouldn't get any ideas.

He said all of this with a smile, though. Not a big smile, but a smile all the same. He was a bit untrusting.

I was not asked to reveal the particulars behind our mission. That was partly done to hide my abilities and partly done to celebrate the king for his wise judgement in asymmetrical warfare. In other words, he gets a party for cheating.

The king himself was walking around and thanking all his generals for a job well done. He was wearing his politician hat now, and he was doing a fine job of being the king. His rounds were taking him near my team, and he walked over when I made eye contact with him.

"None of these clans here will ever know the debt they owe to you and yers, but I do. That shield has been missing for a long time, and no words will ever describe the gratitude I be feeling toward ya," he said as he raised his tankard of mead to me and my team. We returned the gesture and all took a swig. I thought that would be the end of it, but Steelhammer lowered his tankard and leaned in a bit more.

"Know this, if ever you should need the Dwarves Under the Mountains, for anything, all you needs do is ask, and the weight of this kingdom will answer your call. For anything."

And with that, we received a notification:

You have completed the Quest: Retrieve the Shield of Ashtator
Reward: Your team may call upon the Dwarves Under the Mountain one time.

Undisclosed Location

Sitting atop the General's desk were two files. One he had requested himself. The other he had requested from the Joint Special Operations Command. To his left was the redacted file for one Honorably Discharged Marine Corps Staff Sergeant Timothy Slokavitch. The contents were 50 percent blacked out.

To his right sat the same file, without redaction.

The General began to review the contents.

It wasn't fifteen minutes before he stopped and called in Colonel Thompson. The new information he saw impressed the hell out of the General, and he was a bit upset that this Marine wasn't still in the field, instead playing a damn video game. His record was exemplary.

What few knew in this command was that Colonel Thompson had come over from the Army Rangers, an elite team of soldiers who were renowned for their ability to infiltrate enemy lines and decimate their foes. If there was anyone who would know what to do with "Slovak," as his teammates called him, it was the Colonel.

Thompson came into the General's office and picked up the file he was handed. Without waiting, he opened up the thick missive and began to pour over the contents. Thompson was the silent type, so the General knew he was impressed by the number of grunts coming from Thompson as he read.

It took thirty minutes, but the General was comfortable letting Thompson get through the entire file. When he was done, he closed the folder and put it back on the General's desk, sliding it back across the wooden surface.

"The guy is a damn lucky rabbit's foot. Did you see how many attacks they survived?"

The General nodded. He had seen what the Colonel was talking about. Slovak's company had been involved in numerous firefights and had been the victims of several improvised explosive devices. Whenever Slovak was with them, though, they never lost a man. That being said, Slovak himself had received three Purple Hearts and was restricted from returning to armed combat. The rest of his career would require him to ride a desk, and for that, he separated from the service.

"I know you saw the footage from Mr. Hamson's escapades and subsequent fire show. You saw Mr. Slokavitch's response to the whole affair. He hasn't lost a step."

"Nope, I don't think he has. His report says he did private security before taking this gig with AltCon, so I have to assume he has kept his skills up, as best he can."

"The real question here, Colonel, is how we can use this man to our benefit? I don't need another person reporting on what's happening in game. Despite Mr. Hamson's flaws, you can't discount his amazing memory, not to mention he was the first to figure out what AltCon was doing to the players."

"No, I don't need another player in the game. I need a player outside of the game. Can we get a meeting set up with Mr. Slokavitch?"

Thompson thought about it for a few moments and nodded his head in the affirmative. "With his past association in private security, I can set something up that looks too good to pass up but still believable, and on a flexible timeline. Meaning, it is something he could take after this AltCon job is done. It should be enough to hook him in."

The General agreed. Still, it wasn't clear what Slovak's role could be. "And how can we use him?"

"Honestly, I think I have just the thing. I've been having some concerns about the civilians. Dan and his teammates. If this thing goes sideways, those guys are going to be the first targets I would go after."

"I've had the same thoughts, Colonel. What are you thinking?"

"Making Mr. Slokavitch aware of our concerns, for starters. It would mean including another person in this show."

"I wouldn't be asking for your thoughts if I hadn't already considered that and came to that same conclusion. What then?"

"Start small. Looking at his own set-up and determining how he could safeguard his own family. What steps he would take. What contingencies he has already set up. Then find out what, if anything, we can do to help him with that. He'll be able to accomplish far more within his own home than he can with any of the other players. After that, expand that to the rest of Dan's team."

"To what end?"

"To save their lives, obviously."

CHAPTER 12

It had been almost a week since Tibble ran up to me in the courtyard of Kich's Keep, completely out of breath, and told me of the summons he received from King Steelhammer—a week that found us running all over the lands of Tholtos, helping the dwarves in their quest, and completing an epic adventure. In the end, we earned little in the way of experience or loot, but we gained the favor of the entire Dwarven Kingdom. That was no small reward.

Still, we had a multitude of challenges in front of us, which began with the quest to abscond with the leader of House Frost, or his head, and return him to the Keep. As challenging as it was to get the Shield of Ashtator, this mission was likely to be just as difficult and dangerous, if not more so. Thankfully, this last quest had shown the guys the benefits of subterfuge and general sneakiness, which I knew we would need to bypass much of Loust's army on our way to House Frost's hideout.

I waited in the courtyard near Sir Chadwick for the rest of my team to arrive and mentally reviewed our next steps. Getting to the front lines wouldn't be difficult with our horses, but getting beyond those lines would require us to travel largely by foot. Going only off the maps we were inherently gifted by the game's interface and the intelligence gathered by the turncoat Captain, I estimated the journey on foot would take us three days. House Frost was deep in Loust's region.

Specifically, there was a fortified keep located in what used to be a far-off Barony for the king, but it was now deep behind those enemy lines. And once the Captain's information was deemed accurate, the chance to capture the rogue House had already passed, so we had been asked to infiltrate and relieve that family of their head. Literally.

Those three days were contingent on us not meeting much resistance. I had little faith this would be the case.

I was happy to have my contemplation interrupted by the arrival of my teammates, who arrived almost simultaneously. There had been much revelry the night before during the dwarven celebration, and much libations were consumed. That was obvious on the faces of Dan and Wayne, and Jason to a lesser extent, who partied the hardest the night before. Hangovers were a real thing in Resurgence, and they were likely feeling more than a little sluggish this day.

"Hi guys!" I yelled, unnecessarily loudly.

"Just because you don't drink with us, doesn't mean you have to be a complete and total ass, Alex. You know these things suck."

"Dan, you're certainly correct that I don't have to. But I would never miss out on the opportunity."

"Dick," Wayne simply added.

I looked over to Jason, but he only raised his hands in my direction before saying, "Don't look at me. I might be mildly dehydrated, but I wasn't going at it anywhere near as much as these two. Well, four if you count Jenny and Gary. I've no doubt they are hating life this morning too."

Wayne continued to communicate through single syllables and grunts. I knew from experience this would last for another hour or two before he became more pleasant. His hand movements and head nods led me to believe that Jason was correct, though, and that Jenny also felt like crap. None of us could speak for Gary.

"Good news: we don't have anything to do today but travel to the front lines. I figure it will take us most of the day to get there. Once we arrive, and we get the latest intelligence from the officers there, we can decide our next steps."

"That ride isn't going to be pleasant," Dan said.

"Nope. Make sure you and Wayne stay to the outside in case you need to hurl."

"I don't like the term 'hurl,' Alex. It doesn't sound anything like 'hurl.' Let's go with 'Ralph,' ok?"

"Not even a hangover can stop Dan from being Dan."

"You got that right, Allitoodamnsober."

"I told you not to get into a drinking contest with Sharla."

At the mention of Sharla, Dan turned an unnatural shade of white. He was already sporting the classic hangover complexion, but this went to deathly white.

"I didn't? Did I? Again? Please tell me I didn't!"

Wayne wasn't in his right mind, what with the hangover. That's the only reason he would miss out on the chance of harassing our Ranger and his past—possible—escapade with Sharla the dwarf. That is why we were visibly disappointed with him when he said, "Nah, Dan. I made sure you stayed away from that."

"Well, that was a perfectly good opportunity wasted."

I looked at Jason and nodded in agreement.

Wayne looked a bit confused with us, and then I saw the lightbulb go when he realized that he missed a great opportunity.

"Damn, my bad."

Dan chose to ignore the rest of our banter and was simply excited to know that he had not, again, possibly slept with Sharla. Truth be told, Dan claimed to have no memory of that evening, and Sharla never said one way or another if it did happen or not. All I know, is she always twirled her beard a little more often when Dan was around.

We left the courtyard and walked toward the front of Kich's Keep and the main road that would lead us toward the war. Until we had the latest information on the war effort, we weren't going to make any plans, other than those we had already crafted. We would enter through stealth and execute with as much subterfuge as possible. The multiple packets of dye for our clothing would help with both the stealth and subterfuge, so long as the Camouflage spell I acquired worked as well in the forests near the Frost household as they did in the woods by the Keep. That spell could only be cast once per day, though it did last for several hours. That would give us ample time to traverse the woods, without having to engage any mobs. We hoped.

"That's a pleasant surprise," Wayne said as we approached the last known location for the King's army. The surprise was that the front had moved, and in the King's favor. We weren't able to see the camp-fire smoke from where we were, and we assumed the new fortified position had moved significantly. Any time we could spend traveling on the road, and not moving slowly through the dense forests, was time well spent.

We had already been traveling for several hours, and since we couldn't see any smoke, it looked like we would be traveling for another couple of hours, at least.

I nodded in Wayne's direction, kicked my horse into gear, and con-tinued along the road. Not another word was spoken, and I heard the beating of hooves against the ground as the rest of the horses took off behind mine. The closer we got to the keep of House Frost, the more I thought of contingency plans we could use if being sneaky didn't pay off.

As the hours passed, Wayne and Dan became less like zombies and more sociable. Where we were all riding in silence for the first couple of hours, there was now more chatter between the group. We spoke at length about the quest to steal the Shield of Ashtator and how crazy that Guardian had been.

Wayne continued to be quite sad about the loss of the twenty dwa-rves that sacrificed themselves to buy us the time to summon our horses and get both the shield and the rescued prisoners to Steelhammer before the Guardian had a chance to catch us all. It did little good to remind Wayne about the number of dwarves whose lives were saved because of those twenty; that's just not how Wayne was made. To our Warrior, the sacrifice of himself was worth it to save them. I wasn't quite that selfless, but I did decide against reminding him that he would not have succeeded.

We also talked about the reward we had been given by Steelhammer for completing the quest. I wasn't the only one that was a little upset that we didn't get any experience—or loot—for what was a mission that mostly put our group in danger, and me more than anyone. It was certainly unique to be able to call on the dwarves one time, but I doubted we would ever be in a position to call on such a favor.

Wayne was also a bit upset that the war preparations slowed down the production of his new armor, as every dwarf was gearing up for war, not making specialty armor sets. Wayne was likely more upset that the actual war didn't happen and he didn't get to slaughter hundreds of drakkin.

As we continued our ride down the road, the moment I had been dreading since we left the throne room where the Shield of Ashtator was held finally came to pass. I knew, at some point, the guys would have to ask what I was doing while they were fighting and I was going for the shield. I also couldn't lie too much, since Jason had an amulet that could see through a Blacksuit.

"What the hell were you doing up on that wall while we were trying to keep the Guardian busy, anyhow Alex? We know you can climb with no problems, so it couldn't have taken you long to get up there," Wayne said.

"You mean, while everyone else was trying to keep the Guardian busy," I said, trying to deflect a bit but putting enough of a teasing tone in my words to let Wayne know I wasn't giving him too much shit.

"Whatever. You told me not to engage," he harrumphed a bit.

"I know, buddy. I was just fooling. One death was enough."

The guys were silent for a bit as we all thought about how much it sucked for Wayne to lose that experience and also how quickly the Guardian ate through his hit points. I was hoping the distraction would last, but I would find no such luck.

"You still didn't answer the question, Alex," Dan noted.

I shrugged my shoulders and said, "There was a trap on it. I had to get rid of it."

I was in the front of the group so I had no idea how they physically reacted to what I said, or my shrug, but Wayne's voice sure sounded like there was a fair bit of incredulity when he said, "What do you mean, 'get rid of it,' exactly?"

"I have a skill. Disarm Traps. I used that," I said, trying to sound as innocent as possible. "It's not something I'm very good at, so it took me a while for it to work."

There was more silence as we continued to ride. I fought hard not to look behind me.

"So, let me get this straight," Dan said. "You have a skill that Disarms Traps, and this is something that we've never heard of before?"

I was skirting very dangerous ground here. Disarm Trap was, in fact, a skill that a Rogue could purchase from a trainer and learn. But I had never done so because I learned the hard and painful way from Sally. And because of that, I had never told the guys about it.

"It's not something that had ever come up before. I learned it and trained it up to what I could with the Rogue Trainer, but this was the first time that I've come across a trap in all our time together. That's why it took me so damn long to defeat the trap."

More silence followed, and I was worried there was going to be more badgering and questions about when exactly I got the skill, but I was saved by the army. Or, more accurately, from the three scouts who came out on to the road. Two of them had their bows out and arrows drawn tight along their cheeks. The third spoke for the group.

"Who goes there?"

"Adventurers on a mission for His Majesty. We are traveling to the front," I responded, as I was our group leader.

"Do you have papers?"

Shit. We didn't have any papers and didn't think to get any before we left. I looked at the other guys, and they shrugged in my direction.

"I'm afraid we don't. We were sent by Sir Chadwick to undertake an assignment for His Majesty, an assignment that is of the highest importance," I said, hoping that would work.

"When the latrine is full, the guy cleaning it has an assignment that is of the highest importance as well. Are you here to clean the shitter?"

"Seriously, what is it with these guys and toilets?" Dan asked.

I fought to keep any laughter inside but couldn't hide the smirk that crossed my lips.

"We've fought on the same side multiple times, and you may know us for our success eradicating the troll menace," I said, hoping that noting an earlier quest might help.

The guy talking didn't budge, but I noticed one of the archers let his arrow hang and looked at us closer. He then walked over to the speaker and whispered in his ear. The soldier listened, asked a couple of questions, and nodded his head a few times. He then looked back at us and crossed his arms.

"This soldier knows you," he said, pointing at the archer who still hadn't put his arrow back to his bow. The other archer had unnotched his arrow as well. "He says he was there when you returned to the camp and spoke with our captain. What be his name?"

"You mean old Treeswain? That guy can talk strategy for hours," I replied.

The man speaking let out a small smirk of his own and nodded his head, "Aye. That be Captain Treeswain. You may pass," he said and approached my horse. "Take this note with you. It will inform any other scouts that you are reporting to the captain. Safe travels," he concluded, walking back into the forest after handing me the note.

Our earlier discussion concerning my Disarming skills had been forgotten for the moment, and we continued down the well-traveled road toward Treeswain's camp. As we continued to move, there were obvious markers to show that an army had indeed been through here. On several occasions, we saw large areas of trees completely removed and what looked like the remnants of camps. That the cleared areas weren't simply a matter of having been commercially logged was given away by the ample amounts filled in trenches. These were the ubiquitous latrines the scout spoke of.

We hadn't traveled this particular stretch of road before, but we saw evidence that it had been traveled by a large contingent. The ruts in the ground were deep and fresh, and you could see numerous examples that the ground on the road had been trampled flat. The growth to the sides of the roads had also been flattened by many feet. Mother nature—or the Resurgence equivalent, I presumed—would eventually retake these patches of land, but it would be a long time coming before that happened.

We passed the next couple of hours speculating about what the army had been up to in our last week away from the main game. There hadn't been any announcements about the progress of the king's army within the game, but we couldn't help guessing at the situation. It was also hard to talk to each other, as I was pushing the horses as fast as they would go. I wanted to have plenty of light left when we reached the camp, just in case we decided to immediately start our foray into the forest.

Another thirty minutes of travel and we were able to see the first smoke trails wafting into the air from what we assumed to be the army campfires, based on the pattern and separation between the plumes of smoke. If they were clumped together and less orderly, I might think it was the aftermath of a battle. However, the symmetry of the fires was too orderly to likely be the result of a battle.

It only took us several more minutes before we came upon a rise in the road and we were able to see the camp itself. Not only did we see no evidence of any attacks, but the base camp for the King's army looked to have grown substantially since our last time venturing out toward the army. That made sense, of course, since it had been quite some time since our last visit to Captain Treeswain during our quest to capture the turncoat captain.

We made straight for the first guards we could find on the outskirts of the camp and produced our note. They took one look at it and ushered us through their barricade. They also sent a runner ahead to notify the captain of our approach.

We only had to wait a moment after arriving at Captain Treeswain's main tent. It was, naturally, the largest tent in the compound, and it had a healthy amount of traffic going in and out. Treeswain himself came out to greet us. He looked over the four of us and nodded his head once, before gesturing at us to join him in his tent.

The four of us disembarked from our horses, unsummoned the mounts, and entered the tent. Treeswain was dismissing the rest of the officers in the tent as we came in.

"Everyone out. I'll call for you when you are needed again," he told the assembled flock of soldiers. There were more than a few looks of skepticism at us, a bunch of adventurers, especially given Dan's Furry Bunny Britches.

Once the tent was cleared, Treeswain called us over to the large map that was laid out on his center table. We knew from experience that the captain had extremely detailed maps, and we hurried over to see what new additions had been added to the large parchment.

"I'll be honest," Treeswain said while looking down at the map, "I was not entirely supportive of this idea when I received word that the King planned an incursion behind enemy lines. I rescind my hesitations now that I see he has chosen you for this expedition and not regular forces."

He then looked up and made eye contact with me. "You were the ones to capture the turncoat to begin with, so it is only right that you should be the ones to undertake this task." He then shook his head slightly and had a downtrodden look upon his face as he continued. "Don't let our position fool you. We have made progress, but the news that one of our own Houses has turned traitor has demolished morale. And that it was not only such a noble house, but also one full of powerful mages, has only made that hit to our morale that much worse. The army needs a victory here, my friends, and not one that our knights or archers can give us."

He then gestured toward the large map on his table and pointed to what I assumed was the location of the keep. From what I could make out on the parchment, the keep was surrounded by forest on all sides except where it butted up against a cliff's edge. There was no way that an army could come at it from behind given that cliff, and any force trying to get to the keep from the front would be staggered by the forest. Only one small road approached the keep's main gates.

"I can see by the looks on your faces that you see our dilemma," Treeswain said. "There is no way that a traditional force could attack the keep with any stealth. Our forces would be picked off, either by the creatures in the surrounding forest or by the mages from their perches high on the keep's walls. With their ice magic, our soldiers would be sitting ducks. For what it's worth, you'll have these teleportation scrolls for when you finish the job. They won't be useable until you succeed in taking the head from the traitor."

Dan was actively soaking up all the information that was presented on the map. There were several annotations on the representation that Treeswain was happy to explain. I let Dan do his thing while I looked at the various routes we could take. It was still our plan to go through the forest and camouflage our approach. It sounded like the forest was full of all kinds of nasties, based just on what Treeswain was explaining, and I doubted we would be able to get through without several fights, even with our plan.

I had begun to think that our best bet was to travel by night. We could all see just fine in the dark, since Wayne had his amulet. This would also give us the added benefit of having the cover of dark as well as our camouflage. However, while we could see fine at night, we couldn't see as far. This could mean that we missed several opportunities to better our position. I also didn't want to leave that night, mostly because I was tired from our long day of travel.

Finally, I had an idea that no one was going to like, and I wanted to be fully rested when I had to argue for my position.

December 14, 2043

Having seen the captain's map and received a full explanation of the demarcations, we added Treeswain's survey to our own in-game map. This made it easier for me to lay out my new plan. The only problem was that Treeswain had almost no information on the particular route I wanted to take.

"Let's start with the obvious hurdles we are going to face," I said. "The first one, as I see it, is the terrain around the keep. I see plenty of ways for us to travel to the keep, but there is that large clearing around the keep's wall. It's going to make us easy targets as we approach.

"The second problem is the paths through the forest that lead us to the keep. Each of them sports a rather large grouping of baddies that we will likely have to face, no matter what. Alone, I bet I could get around them, but even with camouflage, I doubt we could avoid those particular mobs. They are the ones that are native to those areas—like the Forest Cobras, Spike Spiders, and Timber Rats. And we know how much Dan loves rats."

Dan visually shuddered at the thought of the rats.

"Third, the patrols that will likely be around the keep itself, originating from House Frost. These I am the least worried about with our camo. Still, who knows what kind of traps they may have set up around the place."

"You can see those, right?" Wayne asked.

I realized my mistake after I said it, as I really didn't want to bring this conversational topic up again. Still, it was the truth, and I wanted to make the best argument for my plan as I could.

"Yeah, I can see them, but we saw how long it took me to get rid of that trap with the shield. And even if I do get it apart, someone could hear it or see it happening."

"What do you suggest, Alex?" Jason asked.

"The route no one would expect. We climb the cliff."

"I know you are our fearless leader, and really smart, but did you bump your head or something? You know none of us can climb, right?" Wayne asked.

"Once again, I'm not our leader. And, do you guys remember when I had Steelhammer join me in that new mine?"

They all nodded their heads.

"Do you remember the rope that he used to climb up and join me?"

Again, nods all around.

Now I was ready to play my trump card.

"Specifically, this rope right here, the one that gives a bonus that makes anyone an expert climber?" I pulled out the same rope I had used with the King Under the Mountain that had cost me 10 Platinum. Here, I was hoping, it would pay for itself again.

The guys all got huge smiles on their faces and looked again at the map. I detailed the route I hoped we could take, showing where we could likely use our camo to get around where I thought the House Frost patrols would likely be, and what beasties we would still have to fight. I specifically made certain that we avoided any of the Timber Rats for Dan's sake. I saw that he noticed and gave a small sign of thanks toward me for doing so.

The biggest question, for all of us, was what would be at the bottom of the ravine we would travel through before climbing up the side of the cliff. Treeswain did not have any information about what might potentially lay at the bottom of that crevice, since no one in their right mind would go down there.

My group had never been accused of being anywhere near right-minded.

———◁▯▯◁ ◁▯▯▷———

"Get this fuckin' thing off me!" Dan whispered, albeit quite emphatically, not wanting to make too much noise.

We had been fighting one of the Forest Cobras, a snake that could grow to eight feet long in the real world and was even bigger in Resurgence. Forget the fact that the Forest Cobra was native to central Africa. Dan provided that bit of knowledge, explaining that he once binge watched hours of a National Geographic special on the denizens of the deepest, darkest jungles of Africa. The developers for Resurgence decided that it made for a perfectly good mob here in this forest, and they had added a good four feet on the damn thing. I also think it was much thicker here in the game world and doubted that the real world one had the ability to squeeze the life out of a person, akin to a python, as this one was currently doing to Dan.

Wayne had engaged the first cobra we came across when it ignored our camo and came right at him. Without waiting for any direction from me, our group dropped into our usual combat modes, and Dan started to pepper the mob with arrows from a distance. Unfortunately, that put him under a branch that had another cobra, and Dan aggro'ed him almost as soon as he started shooting his arrows.

Thankfully, with Wayne's high armor class and massive amount of hit points, he wasn't taking too much damage. He did get hit by a poison DoT, also known as a Damage over Time spell, but it was doing minimal damage. The main point of the DoT was that it also snared him. If he had tried to run, the snake would have just bore down on him and attempted to crush him like the second one was doing to Dan.

Another saving grace was that the Forest Cobra was a lower level than us, but that wasn't helping Dan in the slightest. With his arms tied to his side, he was unable to cast or shoot his bow. Dan had a dagger, as he was able to melee as well, but he never used that skill, so his ability was terribly low. Not that it mattered, since the constricting snake was also keeping him from reaching his blade. He currently had a DoT on him, called Crush, that was slowly taking off his hit points.

Jason looked from Dan to Wayne a couple of times and then called out, "Changing from heal to stun. Wayne will survive long enough to make it through this fight if you stay on his target, Alex."

"You got it, Allister!"

With that, Jason ran closer to Dan and launched his Stun spell on the Cobra. As soon as it hit, the Crush DoT disappeared.

"If this thing comes at me, you need to be ready to try and aggro, Naugha. Just don't turn your back on the one you are fighting now, or it might try to Crush you too."

"On it, Allister."

Thankfully, Dan had lost enough hit points that the AI registered that he was still the weakest target, maintaining aggro on him. Jason was able to land two more Stuns before the Cobra released Dan and came at Jason. At that point, we were almost done with the first snake, and Dan's addition of arrows to Wayne's mob put it down quickly.

Jason only suffered from a bit of snake cuddles before Wayne was able to acquire aggro and tank the second serpent.

"I'm not going to make any jokes, Dan. I could barely breathe when that thing got around me, and you were handling that like a champ."

"Thanks, Allisympathizer. That sucked almost as much as rats."

"We could still do the rats instead, Dan."

"Fuck you, Alex."

"Thought so."

"Let's be a little more careful as we keep walking," Wayne said. "Dan, you keep your eyes peeled above us to make sure we don't get ambushed again."

"Now that I know what to look for, it shouldn't be a problem."

"Tell me again how you missed the 12-foot snake?" I asked

"I was thinking about Kaitlin," Dan answered, with no shame.

"Well at least that's an honest answer," Jason replied, laughing a bit.

Once the group was all healed up, we continued toward the ravine. We had avoided two patrols that we came across, surprised that House Frost had set up scouts this far out. That was the other reason we tried to stay quiet while fighting the snakes, as we didn't know if one of those patrols might cross our path while we were in the middle of a fight.

Additionally, the two patrols we saw were three people each, with two fighters and one mage per patrol. Each patrol was made up of mobs that were higher level than us with all three mobs being yellow. We might have been able to take two, but three would be a challenge, especially with a caster.

We had also come across one cluster of Spike Spiders. Those we dispatched relatively quickly, as their method for victory was overwhelming numbers. Fortunately for us, the tiny spiderlings were of a low enough level that we could almost one-shot them, and the larger "momma" spider was weak to blunt force trauma. That was something Wayne could dish out in spades.

Our path was now almost clear to the entrance of the ravine. There was a bit more of forest, but we hoped to avoid any more confrontations with the mobs in the forest and the patrols. It was also getting late, and we wanted to log off for the night. However, no one was eager to do so in the middle of the forest.

We had a lucky break when we came out of the forest and approached the ravine. It appeared to be a clear area, devoid of any mobs, and had a slight bend as soon as you entered the crevice that blocked any view from the forest. I assumed my role of invisible scout and ventured a little farther into the ravine to make sure we were alone before I returned to the guys and let them know we had found the likeliest place to camp for the night. No one was overly happy with the location, but it was better than being back in the forest. We waited another twenty minutes before logging, just to make sure we were really alone. It was impossible to say for sure if we still would be when we logged back in, but we took our chances. With more than just a little trepidation, we left Resurgence.

Undisclosed Location

Gone were the trappings of the General's office. Nor was there the constant traffic of a well-run military command. Emily Renart was simply in a room. It didn't have any windows and only had one door that connected directly to the garage she had just come from.

"I'm sorry for the dramatics, Emily."

"I totally get it, General. Lying about being somewhere is a lot easier if I have no idea where I am. And the best lies are always shrouded in the truth. You taught me that."

The General had sent a vehicle to pick up Emily in an underground parking structure connected to a busy shopping area. The spot was away from any cameras, and the windows into the vehicle were completely blacked out. Completely. Emily hadn't been able to see either in or out. She hadn't known where they took her, but the General was there when she entered the room.

Also in attendance was Colonel Thompson, pen and paper ready to go. He smiled at Emily, shared a short greeting, and showed he was ready to get started.

Over the course of the next two hours, Emily mapped out her daily routine, and in so doing, diagramed everything she saw in the course of that routine. She started with the route she took from her home to the nondescript road that housed the main gate for the Motel. She then noted where she saw each of the patrols on the road, starting from the gate, and ending with the main building.

"I set my cruise control to 30 mph, the speed limit posted on the road, and then counted as I drove. The patrols were pretty evenly spaced at about every 20 seconds. I counted five before I got to the main building. I'm sorry, General, but I never saw them rotate the guards out."

"No need to apologize, Emily. Setting your cruise and counting was a brilliant idea. We received more aerial photos, but those patrols are under cover and we can't see them from above. Requisitioning a military satellite to take thermal images would be far too alerting, so you just dramatically added to our knowledge of their positioning."

Emily smiled her thanks to the General's compliment and continued her report. She detailed her interactions within the building, the people that she met and worked with, and the type of systems that were being used at the Motel. She said that the computers and software were identical to the ones she used at AltCon's headquarters, so there was no learning curve there and she was able to get straight to work.

Her transfer to the Motel had come with a glowing review, explaining how Emily had been extremely efficient in clearing the overwhelming back orders for the IT department at the headquarters. This was the task given to her almost immediately upon starting her new position.

Unfortunately, there wasn't anything that stood out as an abnormality, and all of the work orders were routine. None of her work had yet taken her from the IT room she shared with her coworkers, and she was unable to comment on what the remainder of the compound looked like. However, she did have a general idea of the structure.

She was able to go back to the earliest requests for IT support, which began some two years previous, when AltCon was establishing the complex network. Most of those orders were in support of setting up an extensive server farm at the Motel. After that, the orders focused mostly on fixing connectivity problems between workstations and the information being provided by the servers. She hadn't seen anything that said when the facility was actually built, though.

"The servers are located on four of the bottom floors of the building, sub floors six through nine. There is likely also a large command center type set up on sub floor five. The orders for this floor were for consoles configured to examine the server data, but there were no server requests for this floor. The sheer number of computers leads me to believe this is where the majority of technicians do their work.

"The third and fourth sub floors are where the guards and on-site technicians live. I learned I was a bit of an anomaly for the Motel, as almost everyone who worked there also lived on site. There's a cafeteria on one of those floors as well. The guys in my office raved about their cooks. I seemed to be the only person in the IT office that lived off-site. There was more than a little jealousy at that."

The General nodded and thought about the information Emily had supplied. It was sounding more and more like AltCon was hiding something if they were controlling the movement of their people to that degree. Emily also had done an excellent job at an initial recon of the facility, without actually having traveled through any of it. But she had left out one sub floor.

"And what of the most subterranean floor? Number ten?"

"That one is more of a mystery. I mean, I know what's down there, but it's shrouded in a lot of mystery," she said.

That got the attention of the General and Colonel Thompson, and they both leaned a bit forward in their chairs.

"I wish I could give you more information, but it was only a passing comment that piqued my interest. One of the techs mentioned that the fiber line in sub ten was having an issue and they needed to get someone out there to work on it. This led to one of the other technicians saying, 'Who the hell is going to come? We designed the damn thing. Not like there is anyone we can call.' So, I assumed there was a fiber optic line running into the building and that it was housed in the tenth sub floor."

"Makes sense. Was that it?" the General asked.

"No, sir. Being the inquisitive type," she said with a smirk, "I asked why not just get a replacement for the broken part. The guys in the room laughed at me. I think they wanted to show how much smarter they were than me, and I was happy to let them. I was playing the dumb girl card, after all."

The General turned to Thompson and said with a laugh, "This one is far more dangerous than we give her credit for!"

The three chuckled at the General's comment, and Emily continued, "The one technician who sees himself as the boss said, 'This is next-level tech, Emily. We're not bouncing the information. We're twisting it. It removes the drag of bouncing off the walls. We've got the delay almost completely removed. We're talking near speed of light."

The General sat up straighter at that and said, "Are you sure that's what he said. Twisting? And near speed of light?"

"Yes, General, those were his exact words. Does that mean something to you?"

"Son of a bitch, it certainly does! And it could be something we can exploit. I don't want to tell you anything more, though. If you don't show the right amount of lack of understanding if it should come up again, it could tip our hand," he said. Then he added, "But know that this was a great find."

Emily smiled at the General's praise. She didn't know how successful she had been, but so far, the General had been very happy with her work. And in such a short time. But she wasn't done.

"Sir, there was one other thing that was kind of weird."

"Continue."

"Two network guys were visiting, chatting with some of our IT people, and they were complaining about a problem they were having. They said they were having a bitch of a time, their words, maintaining connectivity at the Tower with the volume of data. They had put a leaky bucket algorithm in place to manage the information slipping through. When they said 'Tower,' it was emphasized, like it was a place. But there aren't any towers on the premises or any of the surrounding areas. It just seemed odd."

"Noted. And again, excellent job, Emily. Keep up the good work, follow our meeting schedule, and we will meet again."

At that, Emily stood up, shook the hands of both the General and Colonel Thompson, and exited the room to the garage. The General could hear the vehicle start and the garage door open and close.

With that done, the General turned to Thompson. "There is something I need to check, and then I need to get to Washington, Colonel. I think we may have gotten a break, but I don't want to speak too soon. I'll brief you when I get back."

The Colonel nodded his head and watched as the General quickly left the room for his car in the garage.

CHAPTER 13

December 15, 2043

had thought about logging in before everyone else, with the idea that I could don my Blacksuit quickly and be available to drag dead bodies if things went bad when we came back into the game. It was only a fleeting moment. If I pulled aggro from anything, I wouldn't be able to kill it. Worse, I wouldn't be able to help my friends, as I would be dead.

In the end, it didn't matter. Our area remained free of any mobs when we rejoined the game. As soon as we were all present and grouped up, I put my Blacksuit to work and started venturing into the ravine. It had been night when we arrived, so I was able to see, just not with the same clarity as I could during the day.

Elven night vision was like looking through those old night vision goggles but with a more purplish tint, as opposed to the traditional green you see in the old movies. The big difference, though, was that with Elven night vision, I could still see depth and distance. Still, nothing beat a good old burning star in the sky to provide optimal lighting.

The interior of the ravine remained darker than it was above, but the daylight illuminated a few sights that I hadn't seen the night before.

The first was a river that was cutting through the ravine and seemed to travel the length of the crevice. Treeswain's map did not indicate how long this small canyon went, but I could already see that it traveled a great distance. It was also moving rather slowly. The source that fed into the river appeared to come from an underground location, with only a small cave granting access. It was large enough to allow the water out, but not large enough for even our small Wood Elf Ranger to go through.

The second thing I saw was that the water spanned almost the entirety of the ravine floor, which was only twenty feet wide or so at our location. There were ledges, of sorts, that ran along the sides of the water. These would likely offer us purchase to travel alongside the slow-moving stream. I approached the water's edge and tried to see if any creatures were inside, but my eyes didn't spot any movement and nothing popped up on my interface.

I returned to the party and explained to them what I had found and asked for their thoughts. We hadn't traveled any distance into the canyon yet, so we still had the option of going back through the woods. My vote was to explore the river's side for a bit, since I already knew what awaited us through the forest and our chances weren't good in that direction.

My groupmates shared my thoughts and all opted to try the ravine for now. We could always change our mind if we found the path unpassable. Neither I nor my friends brought up the possibility that we could try and ford the river as well. I've always been one to stay out of water at all costs. Fighting in water was far tougher. We didn't have any skills that would allow us to breathe underwater, and our main strategy for crowd control—namely kiting the mobs—would be completely negated. Hell, I didn't even know if Dan's Snare would work in the water.

The space we had available to us to walk by the water was only big enough for one person at a time. This gave us a quick pause to discuss our strategy for party order, as I didn't know if we wanted to have Dan in front, like normal. My first thought was to have me lead the way, with my Blacksuit on, so I could pass any potential mobs. If Wayne led, and we had to get in a fight, we likely wouldn't be able to maneuver past the creature. As such, I wouldn't get any bonuses from fighting from behind, wouldn't be able to use my Backstab skill, and I would be subject to any Riposte damage the mob dished out. Our damage would lessen significantly. With me in the lead, I could pass the mob—hopefully—and Wayne could engage after I passed.

Wayne naturally wanted to be in front but saw my point. Unfortunately, we were also not likely to get a lot of damage from Dan, unless he could find an angle to shoot his arrows without interference from us. None of this was ideal, but it still felt like a better option than trying to go the direct approach through the woods.

"Do we want to at least try and see how deep the water is next to us?" Jason asked.

"It's not a bad idea. Other than jumping in, or having Wayne dip his hammer into the water, I don't see any other way to do so," I replied.

"I would rather not," Wayne said.

"Yeah, Wayne really shouldn't be dipping his shaft into anything. Jenny would get super pissed," Dan added. He likely thought it was helpful.

Wayne was one moment from replying to Dan's comment when Jason put a hand on his forearm and said, "If you don't say anything, he'll just stop there, Naugha."

I leaned in and whispered, "But think of all the ways this could go horribly wrong if you do reply. It could be epic."

Wayne gave me a look that showed he was not supportive of my idea and said, "You are not right in the head, Alex."

"And yet all of you insist on saying I'm the leader," I said while laughing.

"Alex does have a point, Naugha," Jason responded.

"You can't think that was a good idea, Allister!"

"What Alex said? No. But that maybe we should get a new leader? Yes."

Everyone but Dan was laughing. Dan had walked away toward the entrance of the ravine when Jason stopped Wayne from responding to his comment. I could still see him when he walked away, and now saw him coming back with a good size rock in his hand.

"You got that rope handy, Alex?"

I was a bit suspicious when Dan asked for anything, but I nodded my head slowly all the same.

"Cool. Give it to me really quick. I have an idea."

I was still hesitant, but I shrugged my shoulders, handed over the rope, and said, "Ok. What's the worst that could happen?"

"We could all die."

"Wrong answer, Dan. Give it back."

"What? I'm not saying we are going to die. I'm just saying that whenever someone uses that phrase, I always think that. Like, 'Sure. Here's the flaming sword. What's the worst that could happen?' The answer is, usually, 'We could all die.' It's a really dumb question."

While he was talking, Dan took the rope and tied it around the rock. Then, as he finished, he tossed the rock into the water. It sank to the bottom and we saw that the rope only descended a foot.

"See, no problems."

"Dan, if there had been a monster in that water, you would have definitely just aggro'ed it!" Jason hissed.

"Oh. Yeah, sorry. Didn't think of that," Dan said as he dragged the rock and rope out of the water. "Well, then I guess we could have died!"

I stopped Dan from handing the rope and rock back to me. "That's actually a great way to check, Dan. How about in the future you just gently lower the rock into the water instead of throwing it in?"

"Can do!"

"Also, for the future, you probably should avoid references to anything that has to do with flaming anything. Still too soon."

Dan's face got really red, and he muttered something I couldn't hear under his breath as he turned away. Ever since Dan lit Jenny's house on fire while trying to impress Kaitlin, we hadn't missed an opportunity to rib him about it.

We were all friends. Good friends. But we were still a bit of assholes at heart.

Jason and Wayne had noticeable smirks on their faces, and I knew I would have gotten at least one fist bump if Dan wasn't standing right there looking more than a little angry. Still, totally worth it.

"Let's get started, guys. I'll call out anything I see," I said and headed off after activating my Blacksuit skill.

—⦿—

We had taken the right side of the ravine, since that was the side we would need to climb up. The way ahead had been clear of any mobs. There were two or three spots where the footing was tricky and we had to jump a bit to get to the next part of the ledge. I had no problems, since I could just jump at the wall and hold on with my climbing skill. Wayne was a little clumsier, and I had to grab him and steady the warrior a bit. Jason had even less Agility, and he basically stumbled toward us, only staying upright thanks to both Wayne and me. Dan's agility was so high, it looked like he ran right across the water as he crossed.

We had traveled about a third of the way down the ravine when we encountered our first mob. I didn't even see it.

I had passed yet another part of wall that looked to be entirely nondescript—just another patch of rock—when a creature sprung from off the side directly toward Wayne's face. Our warrior's constant attentiveness, and the fact that he had kept his war hammer up in defensive position, were the only thing that stopped the creature from latching onto his torso.

As soon as I heard the screech of the creature, I turned back around. All I could see from my vantage point was what looked like a big chunk of rock bouncing off of Wayne's war hammer. The move did not do any damage to our tank, but the resulting impact almost knocked him off the narrow ledge and into the water. The area was not conducive to any type of traditional battle.

The creature hit the ground and bounced back to its feet in a second. In that short time, I was able to see that it was covered by rocky armor all around its body; however, its back was more covered than the front. It was this grouping of rocks that allowed it to blend in with the wall so thoroughly. It was like the rock goblins that we had fought in the drakkins' area.

181

Now that it was back on its feet, a name appeared over the mob, colored blue. It was called a Crag Scavenger. As soon as I saw the name, I immediately looked around for more mobs. Scavengers rarely traveled alone. We had lucked out here, however. This one appeared to be solo, since no further beasts joined in the battle. Once I had given Wayne a few moments to establish satisfactory aggro, I engaged the beast with a backstab. I knew that there was always a chance that I could land a Disembowel when launching my Backstab skill while wearing my Blacksuit. If that landed, Wayne would need to have plenty of aggro to negate the hate I would accrue.

Having already used his Taunt and Bash skills, and landing a couple of hammer strikes, I had little fear that the Scavenger would turn on me, even if my Disembowel landed.

I had little reason to worry. The rocks on the Scavenger's back were for more than just camouflage, and I did minimal damage with my daggers. The mob was losing some hit points from Wayne's attacks, but it was going to take us longer than I would like if we had to rely on just Wayne and my neutered damage.

The battle was loud in the canyon, and while I worried about attracting more mobs, the possibly of also alerting anyone who could be patrolling the edge of the ravine above worried me more. We needed to end this quickly, and our damage was stunted due to its armor and Dan's inability to get a good shot off.

"I got a Snare off, for what it's worth," Dan said.

At least we could run from the creature if we had to, so there was that.

Wayne took a solid hit at the Scavenger and it turned slightly to take the shot on its armored side, where the rock overlapped toward the front. It did minimal damage, and Wayne said, "This guy must be heavy as shit. He barely moved when I hit him full force, and he knocked me back a ton when he jumped at me."

I was still facing the Scavenger's back and had the water to my right. I got a crazy idea, and just hoped that it would work.

"Wayne, are any of your Bashes landing a Stun on him?"

"Not a one, Alex."

"Shit. Ok. You have Stun loaded Allister?"

"Always, brother."

"Then give it a shot. Even if it lands, it shouldn't be enough to pull aggro. I hope."

"I hear a whole lot of 'ifs' in there, buddy."

"Yeah, I know, but we need to finish this before we get company from more mobs or a wandering patrol up top. This might work. Probably. Maybe."

Jason laughed and launched his Stun. While the Scavenger was able to negate all the physical Bash Stuns, he wasn't able to stop the magic one, and he stopped fighting for a moment after Jason cast his spell.

"We're good, but he does have some innate protection. The Stun is only half as long."

"Should be enough, Allister," I said and then looked over toward Wayne. "The next time Allister lands a Stun, get in the best position that you can and swing your hammer horizontal. Toward the water."

I saw a huge smile form on the faces of Dan, Jason, and Wayne. They saw exactly what I had in mind.

As soon as the second Stun landed, Wayne stepped back, pivoted his hips, and swung his hammer like a baseball bat. The hammer landed true, although the damage was blunted some by the rock armor hanging over the Scavenger's side, and the mob moved just like I wanted it to. Right toward the water.

With the damage having been lessened, the Crag beast didn't leave his feet and fly off, but it did stumble toward the river's edge. And then, as if in slow motion, it tipped over the side and disappeared into the water.

"I really hope that fucker can't swim," Dan muttered.

We were all thinking the same, I was sure. I watched the mob's health bar in my interface and waited. All of a sudden, the bar started to go down and after several seconds it was empty. A message appeared that the Scavenger had died, and I let go of the breath I had been holding.

We didn't get any experience for the death, but I wasn't going to complain. We had found a quick way to remove the threat, and that was more important. We weren't in that ravine to grind for experience.

"Sorry, guys, but I'm not likely to see these mobs before they attack."

"At least we know what to do. And, if we get more than one, we just do the usual. Naugha will have to get aggro on them all, and then I'll Stun one at a time. If we can't get it to work that way, we figure another way," Jason added.

Everyone agreed to what was really our only strategy. Once we were back in position, I reactivated my Blacksuit.

Throughout our trek down in the ravine, Dan had continued to check the depth of the water using the rock and rope method. There were areas where the water got up to ten feet deep, but mostly it was a maximum of five to six feet deep. I wasn't a fan of having to move into the water, but if it were five feet, we could all keep our head above water and the Scavenger we fought was shorter than that.

Over the course of the next twenty minutes, we were attacked by two more Scavengers, and we used the same technique to dispatch them. They both attacked as singles, and they were gone quick, lessening the amount of noise we made.

"You know what would be cool?" Jason asked.

"I'm afraid to ask," I said.

"If we could see this thing before it launched off the wall. Then I could have my Stun ready to go as soon as it jumped," Jason said before looking to Wayne. "Then, with the Stun on, Naugha could take batting practice for real!"

"That's a great idea, Allister!" Wayne said. "That's way better than any and all of the ideas that Alex has come up with for his 'experiments' on us."

"What the fuck? I came up with the strategy of hitting them into the water, dude!"

"But that was out of desperation. Allister's idea is for pure enjoyment. So, way better."

"Cold blooded, bro," I said, but smiled all the same.

I was just getting ready to continue down the path when I heard Dan from behind us.

"Um, guys. I, umm, I think I found a really deep part."

I stopped what I was doing and looked over toward where Dan was standing with the rope in his hand. It was continuing to move through his grip and was nearly half way through the 100 feet rope.

"Stop it there, Dan. We don't know how far down all the way is. It's enough to know it's really deep."

Dan grabbed the rope tightly and it stopped in his hands. Then, almost imperceptibly, I saw the rope start to move again. It was just a small jerk in his hand.

And then I saw his hands tighten on the rope hard.

"Oh, shit," Dan said right before I saw him almost go into the water.

We had moved back toward Dan when he said he had found the deep water. That was the only thing that kept Dan from flying into the water as Wayne grabbed him around the waist and held him tight.

"I think I got the big one!"

"That's... ugh... what your mom said!" I heard Wayne grunt out as he tried to hold Dan and lower his center of gravity.

That rope was the only way up the side of the ravine for our team.

"Don't let go, Dan!"

"Hell no, I'm not letting go! I'm going to mount this bitch over my fireplace. Right next to Wayne's mom's giant panties!"

Wayne was holding on tight to Dan but was finding it difficult with how much he was laughing. If it wasn't so damn dire a situation I would have been on the floor laughing, myself. I even heard Jason guffaw behind me.

Everyone stopped laughing, though, when the "big one" surfaced from the water and we saw a giant maw, rope hanging from it, come toward us. We moved from where it approached the ledge and watched as it smacked into the side of the wall. The movement loosened its jaw and the rope fell free, which Dan reeled in quickly and put in his inventory.

Unfortunately, we were all now staring at a much aggro'ed mob, and it didn't look like it was going to dip back under the water until we had been removed from this ravine.

The size of it was huge. Easily twenty feet, it looked like a combination of a water dragon and a python. As it rose from the water, I could see that the sides of the mob had small fins that likely helped it move through the water. It was easily six to eight feet around. It also had a longer snout than a snake, but its mouth did not sport the usual sharpened fangs you would think to find in a dragon-type mob. More so, it did not sport scales like a dragon, but rather a smooth skin like a snake. Its color was also more akin to a python.

As it hovered above the water, a name finally appeared.

It was an Enlarged Crag Snake, and its name shone with a yellow color.

This meant it was definitely a higher level than we were, but it also meant that we could kill it. If we could find its weakness.

The first thing I was certain of was that there was no way we could fight it where we were. With our current setup, all standing in a line, we had no strategy to fall back to. Additionally, trying to get in the water here would mean suicide. We weren't swimmers at all, and the size of this thing meant the water had to be deep.

But that hadn't always been the case.

"Dan, take the rope and rock and run back the way we came. Find a spot where the water was shallowest. If you come in contact with a Scavenger, just Snare it and keep running," I ordered. "Wayne, do your thing and keep aggro on it until Dan finds a spot."

Dan didn't hesitate and took off back the way we came, and I saw the rope come out in his hand, the rock still tied to the end. With his agility, Dan could run along the ledge without any concerns.

Wayne took a few swings at the mob, but with its mobility in the water, he wasn't making any decent contact. The limited damage he did inflict had no noticeable impact on the snake's hit points.

The snake made another attempt to strike Wayne, and its head flew toward the warrior again. Wayne wasn't able to fully dodge, and he took a hit from the snake's head. The resulting hit took almost 10 percent of Wayne's hit points. However, the snake's maw also smacked into the wall again.

This time, since Wayne was actively engaged in combat with the beast, he was able to see that the contact with the side of the ravine caused the snake to get Stunned for a brief moment. It wasn't long enough for us to capitalize on the action, and again, our positioning was of little help.

"I got the spot! It's only a foot and a half deep in the center!"

According to our map, Dan wasn't all that far from us, but I couldn't see him past our large warrior. I wasn't going to question his find and called for us to run, with Jason landing a Stun on it the next time it hit the wall after attacking Wayne, hopefully lengthening the amount of time it would be out of commission.

As soon as the compounded Stuns were on the mob, we raced toward Dan's location.

It wasn't long before we heard the mob behind us, rushing through the river in our direction. We got to Dan's spot just before the snake, and we got ready to do battle.

Because of the depth, or lack thereof, the snake had to raise a significant amount of its body out of the water to strike at us. This gave all of us options for placement around the mob. Dan was off on its right side, prepared to fire off arrows, and I was to its left. I was hoping to get enough of an angle to avoid any return damage.

Wayne adjusted his stance and took a swing at the beast as it descended. It was still extremely quick, and Wayne's hits weren't having much effect. Plus, each hit from the snake was eating away at our warrior's hit points. Finally, the damage from Dan's arrows were lighting the snake up, and it caused him to take aggro for a moment. The snake lunged at Dan.

But with Dan's high agility, it wasn't hard for him to dodge out of the way of such a large target and take no damage at all. Also, because Dan was so much shorter than Wayne, the angle the snake had to use to attack brought its head much closer to the ground. He was so close, in fact, that the snake's mouth smacked into the ground. And it was stunned again.

Once more, we didn't have enough time to seriously capitalize on this action, but it did give Wayne the few moments he needed to reacquire aggro.

It also gave me an idea. One that might possibly be the worst idea I've ever come up with.

It was a true testament to the faith my teammates had in my abilities as a strategist that they only screamed "What?!" one time when I said the words, "Dan, get to the middle and tank!" But they did all scream it at the same time.

"When he attacks, dodge! When his head hits the ground, Wayne, you hit him with a Bash and Allister use your Stun. Dan, jump back far enough to fire your arrows. As soon as he's back to attacking, get back in the middle. Now go!"

It was crazy enough that it might work. It might also get us all killed. For the love of all the gods I really hoped that fortune really did favor the bold.

"I'm a tank!" Dan screamed as he jumped closer to the middle and started launching arrows at the snake. Just to help build aggro, Dan also fired off one of his damage spells and his Snare. It wasn't likely that the Snare would do anything, but it would put Dan higher on the aggro list.

After a few arrows, the snake did exactly what I wanted. Its mouth dropped down onto Dan—or it would have if Dan hadn't jumped at the last second and rolled out of the way. The snake's head impacted the bottom of the river, and I saw that it worked. Both Wayne's Bash and Jason's Stun spells also landed. While he was immobilized, all of us were able to take turns at hitting him. Because Wayne wasn't using any of his additional aggro-building skills like Taunt and Kick, combined with the pure damage of Dan's arrows and spells, Dan never lost the aggro.

It wasn't a fast battle. The tactic meant that I couldn't do too much damage, or else I'd pull aggro. I had a decent Agility, but I didn't know if it would be enough to dodge an attack and I wasn't really willing to risk it. We slowly whittled away at the snake's hit points.

But we won. Amazingly enough, we won. Moreover, we took almost no damage. Jason only had to heal Dan once when he only half dodged out of the way of the snake. Thankfully, the snake was stunned again after hitting Dan, because he wouldn't have survived another two hits. Dan's hit points fell that much with a single hit.

The experience bar moved a few percentage points. Definitely a mob worth fighting again, if only for the experience we got from it. The loot from the mob consisted of an Enlarged Snake skin, several

Enlarged Snake teeth, and several pieces of Enlarged Snake meat. I hoped all of these would sell well at a vendor, since none of us had the crafting skills to use any of the items. Hell, we didn't have any crafting skills at all, save for Dan's fletching ability.

"I don't want you to think I'm going to take your job, Wayne. You can still be our tank. I may have to talk to Jenny, though, about taking over secondary duties when we are in a bigger group."

Jason and I laughed at Dan, and even Wayne smirked. "Sure thing, buddy. I'll let her know first chance I get."

"Kidding! I was kidding!"

That really had Wayne laughing. Dan was a bit afraid of Jenny. Not her avatar in the game, but the real Jenny. Especially after he almost burned down her apartment.

I broke up the laughter and reminded the guys that we still had a mission to finish and needed to get back to traveling down the ravine toward the spot where I would ascend to the keep.

⟞⟝

We didn't encounter any further resistance and only once had a scare when Wayne fell into the river. His left foot slipped off the side of the ledge and tumbled into the water.

We hadn't been checking the depth of the water any more, as we didn't want to risk another fishing mishap. So, we were more than a little happy when Wayne popped up from out of the water, standing on solid ground and only about half of his body in the river. Still, he moved very quickly to extract himself, since we had no idea what could be lurking below the depths.

We gave him a fair amount of ribbing but nothing he wasn't used to. The most important thing was that nothing came after us and we were able to continue toward the spot I figured we could climb.

After another ten minutes, we were there. I looked up from our position and focused on the rocks. I instantly saw the hand- and footholds I would be able to use to make my ascent. The climb was not going to be difficult at all.

I had worried about this part of the trip. If the route had been red in my view, I would have had to use my Shadows to help with Scaling the side of the wall. With Jason's amulet, and his ability to see through my Blacksuit, I didn't know if he would also be able to see me use the Shadows to aid in my climbing. With the route I was seeing, I could do the whole thing with just my Climbing Skill. Still, without the rope, it would have been impossible for my friends.

I didn't hesitate in the slightest and launched myself onto the wall to begin my way up. Jason was giving the team a play-by-play of my progress. I had the rope tied around my waist and was letting it spool out from behind me. It wouldn't do any good if we needed to travel 150 feet up, and I only had 100 feet of rope.

Thankfully, after the first few minutes of my voyage, I judged the top to be 80 or 90 feet from the ravine floor, and I would have enough rope to tie off at the top somewhere. I just needed to find a place to do so.

Upon reaching the top of the ravine, and what was likely the bottom of the keep, I found a number of windows along the keep's side. I climbed along the side of the building and looked into each of the windows. Several of them had people inside, but there was one that was attached to a small room, with no current occupant. Also, there was a support column built into the corner of the room, and I could use that as a place to anchor the rope. There weren't any wards on the windows, and this window was not locked. I figured no one worried about locking a window that opened out to an almost 100-foot fall into the ravine.

I climbed through the now open window and noted first that the door locked from the inside and was currently not barred. Additionally, the door opened inward to the room, so I could hide in the corner, behind the open door if someone were to come. For that reason, I kept the window closed until I was ready to drop the rope down. Even after the rope was in the ravine, I would keep the window closed as much as possible. Those first few moments might be the edge I needed to get a jump on whomever came through.

Considering how lucky we had been so far, I was surprised that it continued to hold until all three of the guys had climbed up the rope and made their way into the room. Dan came up first, then Jason, followed lastly by Wayne, in case we had to use our own weight to help keep the rope in place. It was not a large space and only had a single bed with a small chest at the foot of it.

Once I had taken the rope and placed it back in my inventory, then closed the window, I looked back toward my friends. It was time to discuss our next steps. My vote was for me to solo scout the halls and try to find where the head of the family was sleeping.

I never got the chance to ask, though, as the door to the room rattled slightly and looked like it was about to open. Everyone looked at each other quickly and then moved to the corner I had identified as the only spot I could hide. The only problem was that it wasn't anywhere near big enough for all four of us!

Instead, I activated my Blacksuit and stepped away. The other three moved to the wall behind the door, and from my vantage point, it looked quite comical. The spot was barely big enough for just Wayne, never mind all three.

The person that walked into the room was a green mob that sported the name House Frost Guard, and he wasn't paying the least bit of attention to anyone who might have been in what I assumed was his room. The guard turned his back on me and closed the door behind him. That's when I struck.

From my position, I was going to land a backstab. However, my luck continued to hold out, and I hit him with a Disembowel as well. His hit points dropped more than half, and I realized he wasn't just a green mob, but that we were likely twice his level.

Wayne didn't hesitate either and hit him with a hammer strike and Bash that stunned the guard. His armor was non-existent, and he was only wearing the colors of House Frost as his uniform. Mere seconds later, the Guard was dead.

He fell face up, and I saw he wasn't likely older than 20. He was just a kid. The other guys must have seen the same thing I did.

"Damn," Dan whispered. "That sucks!"

I nodded my head in agreement, as did Wayne. Jason, however, kept us in perspective.

"The King would burn this whole place to the ground, including this guy and probably any children that were here. We gotta remember that."

"I'm not killing kids," Wayne said.

"Nope, me neither," I agreed.

Jason put his hands up to calm us down. "Me neither. I'm saying that we are probably likely to save any kids that are here if we do this right."

There was silence between us—until Dan spoke, that is.

"Wait. Was burning the place down an option? You know I'm good at torching places!"

We all had hands over our mouths as we tried to stifle the laughter we were struggling to hold in!

CHAPTER 14

I looked around the room again and was reminded that there was little in the small space that was going to help us out. At Dan's suggestion, I opened the footlocker at the end of the dead guard's bed, but there wasn't anything in there but another uniform and some trinkets. Nothing that would help us.

"Well, could we take the guard's clothes and sneak through the place?" Jason asked.

"I think I'm the only one who would fit in this guy's uniform, and I have no need for it, since I can go invisible through the place. It's too big for Dan, and it would only kind of fit you, Allister. I obviously don't need to say how much that wouldn't work for Wayne."

The others nodded their heads in agreement, and we considered our options again. It was our hope that we could avoid any direct confrontation with the guards and family members of House Frost. The guard may have been way below us in level, but the Frosts were renowned for their abilities with ice magic. I didn't want to go up against all of them if we didn't have to. I honestly didn't think we would win.

"Well, we need to come up with something pretty quick. We have no idea how long this guy was supposed to be gone for," Wayne said, pointing to the corpse on the floor of the room.

That reminded me that we needed to loot the body if we wanted it to disappear, and I knelt next to the corpse and laid my hands against it, providing me with the loot. All the guard carried was a regular sword and a small coin purse. I took both, and his body vanished after a few more seconds. I also closed the footlocker. If anyone were to peek into the room, they wouldn't find the guard or his room in disarray. That is, as long as the other three got behind the door quickly enough.

"Going out this door is also kind of a bad idea," I said. "If there is someone out in that hall and they see the door open and close with no one coming out, that could draw their attention."

I was realizing that coming in here wasn't the best idea, but we needed to get the guys up from the ravine floor before we ran out of rope. I looked out the window and got an idea.

"Why don't we try going up the same way, then? I'll go back out the window and climb farther up the side of the keep. I can look through any other windows I find, and then if there is a suitable spot to go back in, I'll let you guys know. We can keep the end of the rope in here, hanging through the window, and still tied to this column, and I'll make my climb. It's only a few floors and definitely not 100 feet. If I find something suitable, I'll anchor off the rope and pull all the slack until it goes taught. Then you guys untie it from this end and climb up to the next spot," I said.

It wasn't a great idea, as it split the party again, something that is never a great idea. However, the guys seemed to agree that this was the best option we had at the moment.

Without any further delay, I tied the end of the rope back around me and headed for the window. I would have to make sure that I only exposed the upper half of my body, the part above the tied rope, if I peeked into any rooms. I would be invisible, but the rope wouldn't. This wasn't something I had to consider climbing up the ravine, but it would be a crazy rookie mistake to forget about now.

With everything set, I opened the window and headed back out to the side of the keep. The way the place was designed, with blocks as the building material, there were more than enough handholds for my climb, and any route I decided to take was going to be easy.

As I began my climb, I realized the Shield of Ashtator quest had really set us up well for dealing with this sneaky mission. I doubt the guys would have given me any pushback on avoiding a frontal assault, but they may have balked at the amount of experience we were leaving on the table by not going through the forest.

Above me, I could see several more floors and even more windows to look through. My first task was to find a room that was more secure than the one the guys were in now, or at least one that was a bit bigger and didn't have as much risk of having someone walk in and find my team.

The first window I approached was out of the question, as it was another bedroom, larger than the guard's, and currently occupied by a number of women working on sewing or crocheting. More importantly, the door to the room was open, and a guard was standing in the hallway outside the room. This was the window almost directly above us, and I didn't have to worry about the rope being seen by anyone.

I planned on checking the next room above the one with the women. I was lucky, and it was slightly to the right of the one I had just looked through. Otherwise, the guys would have to climb the rope and pass directly in front of the portal. If the next window didn't work, it was going to be a bit more challenging.

I traveled the next portion and hit pay dirt. The room didn't look into a bedroom or a hallway. In fact, it looked to be a storage room of some kind, filled with large pieces of furniture on one side and footlockers on the other. If I had to guess, I would say this room had the overflow of beds, chairs, and other furnishings that had to be removed when all of House Frost arrived at the keep. No way this place had enough space for a family that size, and an abundance of the large pieces had to be removed to make room for all the people.

This would be our windfall, and I started by Disassembling the small ward on the window, before opening it. This window wasn't locked, either, and I entered the room, still in my Blacksuit. I closed the window behind me, leaving just enough room for the rope to come through, and inspected the rest of the interior.

Quickly, I found several pieces that would likely be heavy enough to support the weight of my friends, except for maybe Wayne. He would need to come last again, the three of us bracing the rope if necessary. Without further delay, I began slowly moving the furniture around to suit our needs, being careful to make as little noise as possible. Just because I couldn't be seen didn't mean I couldn't be heard.

Once I had the rope secured around the leg of a large bed and two quite heavy footlockers sitting on the rope, I pulled the whole thing very taught, so the guys could see it was ready. After several moments, I saw the rope start to move slightly, and only a couple of minutes after that, I saw Dan come through the window. I had dropped my Blacksuit so he could see me when he came through the portal, and my finger up to my lips to remind him to be quiet.

Next was Jason, and then Wayne after the three of us sat on top of the two footlockers. Wayne cleared the window, which was a tight fit for our warrior, and stood in the room with the rest of us. Once all were present, we quietly discussed our next options.

"There is another floor above us and numerous windows I can still look through on this floor. If nothing else, I need to make sure that no one is waiting for us in the hallway."

Everyone nodded in my direction.

"I'm going to head back out and see what it looks like on this floor. If the hallway looks empty, I'm going to go through the window and then come back to this door. If it's clear, I'll open the door."

I didn't remove the rope from the bed, or from beneath the lockers, since we may need it again, and I could simply go inside the room and get it before we entered the hall.

The next step was to scout the rest of the outside windows. I didn't have the rope to worry about, so I could move as freely as I wanted and as quickly as was safe. I wouldn't have the safety of the rope around my waist if I fell, which would undoubtedly result in my death. There would not be any chance of resurrection.

I left our new hiding spot and went upwards first. I checked the three windows I could see on the floor above us, but each one had curtains covering the window, preventing me from seeing inside. That was not an option.

I returned to the floor we were on and started checking the windows around our hidey hole. I didn't have far to go. The first window I came to looked into the hallway, and it appeared completely clear of any foot traffic. I waited several minutes then decided to go through the opening. As before, there was a small ward that needed to be Disassembled, and the window was unlocked.

I opened the window and climbed through, closing the window behind me. The path remained clear, and I moved to the door and depressed the latch to it.

It was locked.

"Shit," I whispered, not worrying about anyone around us.

I heard shuffling on the other side of the barrier and heard Jason whisper back, "What?"

"It's locked! I forgot to check when we got in there."

"Well damn. Are you coming back then?" Jason responded.

I looked around the hallway a bit and then decided to explore some more. If the keys were on a ring or something, maybe I could still make this work.

I whispered again, "I want to search a bit and see if we have any other options first. Just stay put, and if you hear a key rattle in the door without hearing me first, then hide and get ready for a fight."

"Got it," Jason responded, and I left the side of the door, intent on finding something to help me.

I quickly made my way down the hall and came upon a corner. From the representation that Treeswain had on his map, the keep was set up as a rectangle, and the hallway I was in seemed to go the full distance of this side. In both directions, I could see a corner for me to go around. I chose the closest corner and went around to the next portion.

The path traveled about half the distance of the previous hallway to another corner. There weren't any doors or windows on this portion. I continued down the same way and turned the next corner.

This passage only traveled half as far as its opposite side and ended in an open portal with a staircase winding down. There was also one door that led to the interior of the building. The door was open, so I sneaked a peek inside.

The room looked to have been some kind of grand sitting room, or some kind of parlor for entertaining guests, but that wasn't what it was now. Instead, there were a dozen members of House Frost in the room, and it had been converted into a mini hostel-type location. There could have been even more people in there, but the dozen were the first ones I saw. This way was out of the question.

I retraced my steps. My next goal was the other side of the passage I originally entered. Hopefully I could find something that could help us.

All of the rooms that lined the long hallway led to rooms set up on the exterior of the wall, like our storage room. All of the doors were closed, though, and I wasn't going to risk opening them and alerting someone inside.

I came upon the next corner and made my way around the right angle. Halfway down the hall, I saw one lone guard standing his watch. He was another of the House Frost Guards, and he was green in color just like the last one. Where the last short hallway that mirrored this one had no doors, this one had one. It led to the interior and sat open.

I moved around the standing guard and took a better look at him. I had to hold back the laugh that almost escaped from my mouth.

Where it originally looked like he was simply standing with his back to the wall, he was actually sleeping while standing up. I imagined this must be a skill that all guards learn at some time.

I moved around the slumbering mob and looked into the room. It was a small enclave, with a couple of desks and some weapons leaning against a wall. There was no sign on the wall saying this was where the guards kept their stuff, but it certainly looked like it. I risked a quick trip inside to examine the interior and see if there was anything useful.

The room was quite small and one fast pass was enough to determine that nothing was lying around on the desks or hanging on the walls. The desks had drawers, but opening those could alert the guard sleeping outside.

I left the small alcove and continued down the hallway. I turned the corner and found a similar scene as on the other side of the stronghold. There was an archway, with stairs leading up this time, and another one of the doors that opened into the interior of the keep. As this one also stood ajar, I took a peek inside.

This was the library, or, like the previous room, had been used for that purpose. Now, the shelves of books had been moved to the sides of the room to make space for another camp-like scene. There were at least another dozen House Frost family members in the library's spaces.

I had completed my search and had really found nothing. I only had one more idea, and I was a bit nervous to try it.

One of the first things I learned from Waseem upon arriving at Kich's Keep was how to Lift an item. Using a mixture of my own skills at stealing, or Lifting, and my Shadows, I could rob a target without them knowing what happened. Thankfully, Lifting was a skill that all Rogues obtained, and it wouldn't be suspicious for me to have this skill. Using the Shadows, however, was something only a few people in Resurgence could do, and I was the only non-NPC who could do it. Using the Shadows to increase my Lifting skill, in essence "numbing" the area around the item I wanted to take, I could take from both players and NPCs.

The problem, as I saw it, was that I wasn't all that great at it. I had trained up to a very low skill level, and then had moved on to other skills in my Rogue tool box. But I thought it was worth a try now. Otherwise, we might have to go back to the guard's room and try to make our way up to this floor.

I focused on the sleeping guard with the intention of seeing if he had anything I could steal. Two areas, both on his belt, lit up. One was green, and one was blue. This meant that the green one would be an easy theft for me. The blue one meant it was more of a challenge but doable.

I went for the green one first. After several seconds, and the manipulation of my Shadows and his clothing, I had his coin purse in my hands. I figured one of the two items had to have been his money.

The other item wasn't a sword, as he carried a stave of sorts. But it could be any number of things. I was without any other good options. I moved to the side where the blue outline was and moved my hands toward his belt.

It was slower this time. Partly because I was so damn nervous, and also because he was still asleep. I was going to take advantage of that fact.

I almost exclaimed in pleasure when the item popped into my inventory, and I saw it was a set of keys. I didn't take the time to inspect them, instead running back to where my team was still hiding. It had been several minutes since I left them, and I knew they had to be worried.

Before opening the door, I ran around the first corner I had traversed, making certain there was still no one down that hall. Seeing the area was clear, I went back to the door, whispered, "It's me," and began trying the keys to the door. I eventually found the one I needed, after the third attempt, and I silently slipped into the room. Thankfully, the door opened smoothly, and no noise originated from the door's movement.

Once the door was closed behind me, I dropped my Blacksuit, with the keys dangling from my hand.

"Nic..mmphm!" Dan exclaimed rather loudly before Wayne put his hand over Dan's mouth.

We stood still and listened. It would really suck if all our sneaking around was thwarted now.

After several seconds of us not hearing anything, we all released the breaths we knew we were holding in. Wayne removed his hand from Dan's mouth, and our Ranger mouthed the word, "Sorry."

Jason gave Dan his signature look then whispered to me, "Where did those come from?"

I walked over and unhooked the rope, putting it back in my inventory. "I stole them from a guard in the hallway. He's sleeping. While standing. That alone is crazy impressive."

Wayne chuckled under his breath and said, "I've seen guys do that when I was a bouncer. I tried it once and fell down. That was enough for me."

"You can steal, too?" Dan asked.

"Sure. It's a lower-level Rogue skill. I'm just lucky that it worked, since I haven't practiced it in a long time. I've never been one for stealing from people," I whispered back.

Keeping my voice as low as I could, I explained to the guys what I had found. It was obvious that our target wasn't on this floor and we needed to get up to the next one. That meant getting past the guard and up those stairs, all without alerting the room of mages holed up in the library.

The first step was getting past the guard. I saw two ways of going about that.

"We either wait for him to wake up, make his rounds, and walk past this room, making a run for it when he turns the corner, or we just kill him where he stands, while he is sleeping, loot the body, and then go for the stairs. Both obviously have risks."

"We need a shield bomb like the King had," Dan said.

"There isn't any shield," Wayne responded.

"I think our Ranger means we need a distraction," Jason said. Dan nodded at Jason's words.

"I also hate that I was able to understand what he meant," our cleric added.

That got smiles out of all of us.

"So, what do you think, Alex? Can you make a distraction?" Wayne asked.

I thought about it for a moment, and then I smiled real big.

⊸⫘⫘⊷

Taking out the guard was a matter of seconds. Like one second. Turns out, my Disembowel does even more damage if the target is unconscious. Being asleep counted, and I one-shotted the guard with my knife. One second he was sleeping on his feet, the next he was crumpled on the ground.

I quickly looted the corpse, of which there was nothing left since I took his coin purse and keys already, and we entered the guard's room. I reapplied my Blacksuit and told the guys to wait just around the corner until I made my distraction. I told them they would know it when it happened.

I was more than a little nervous again when I entered the library.

The room was full of House Frost mages, and a good number of them were blue to me. I wouldn't survive if they saw me at any point while I was in the room.

I had noted earlier that the bookshelves had been moved around to make room for all of the people in the room. There were numerous spots set up for sleeping, and several of the mages were walking around the library. More than a few were by the shelves and looking at the books.

I was waiting for that right moment when one of them put a book back into its slot with just the right amount of force.

If anyone took the time to really think about it, putting a book back into a shelf wouldn't be nearly enough to make the book case move. However, I was gambling that the moving of the shelves would make the habitants think it was their own fault.

I had opened enough doors while in my Blacksuit to know that moving an object wouldn't negate my Blacksuit, so I didn't have any fear that my pushing would make me visible. On the other hand, if one of the books—or one of the mages—bumped into me, that could be enough to cancel out my skill. I had to be careful.

It only took me a moment to find my victim. He was a younger lad, wearing the mage's robes of his House. He was going through a stack of books on a table next to him. Each time, he opened a book, quickly flipped through it, then closed it with more force than was necessary. Then he tossed the book back on the table. Based on the stack in front of him, he was almost done with the pile there. I patiently observed what he would do next.

When you are standing in the middle of a room, surrounded by people who would kill you without thought, every second seems like an eternity. It was only another two minutes of waiting, but to me it seemed like forever. The short wait paid off, though, and I saw the young mage get up and stalk over to the shelves. If he just grabbed books, this wouldn't work. Also, if he was gentle with their placement, this wouldn't work either. I needed him to be as forceful with the books at the shelves as he had been with the ones at the table.

Another selling point was that the occupants of the library were already showing their annoyance with the guy. Every time he closed a book forcefully and tossed it on the table, a number of the other mages in the room shot him dirty looks.

When he approached the shelves, I placed myself away from him, at the far end. He continued in his previous manner and grabbed a book and opened it. He flipped through quickly and slammed it shut.

But before he could place it back, one of the other casters in the room addressed him. "Your father may be an elder, Shand, but you are not! Take care with our knowledge!"

At that, the name of the man went from House Frost Mage to Shand Frost. I guessed he was related to the head of the house. The fact that the man sneered at the speaker led me to believe his father was someone quite high in the hierarchy.

Despite the sneer, Shand said, "My apologies," making a show of gently putting the book back.

The other mage harrumphed and turned back to the other mages he had been talking with. Shand had made a show of slowly placing that last book back in its spot, but I knew men like him. He likely believed his birth made him better than the others in the room and didn't like being told what to do.

I got ready.

He pulled another tome, opened it quickly, barely looked inside, and then loudly closed it. His actions garnered the attention of all the mages in the room. He said, "These offer nothing," and then slammed the book back in its spot.

And then the shelf started to fall.

I timed my push at exactly the time he rammed the book back, and the shift looked perfectly natural. Before he could react, the shelf had tipped too far, and his efforts to right it were failing.

"Help!" he yelled.

"Don't let it fall, you fool!" I heard from another mage, and several others joined in yelling at Shand. The other mages in the room ran over to try and keep the shelf upright.

As soon as I had the shelf going, I ran back to the entry door, turned right, and headed for the stairs leading up. When I turned around, I saw my teammates running past the library's door. Wayne was the last to cross the open entryway. There was plenty of noise coming from within the large room, but none of it was directed toward the four of us. I didn't hear a crash from the shelf, so I guessed they saved it from falling.

Without a word, we ascended toward the fourth floor. I whispered for the three to remain halfway between the third and fourth floor, out of sight, while I quickly scanned whether it was clear above.

Once I got out of the stairway, I saw that this floor was well appointed, with only one hallway that ran from our stairway going up. There was no doorway at the other end of the hall. Instead, there were three doors that led into the interior of the building. This was, undoubtedly, where the heads of the house would reside.

The first door I came to was open, and a look inside showed me a regal stateroom, fully furnished, and currently unoccupied.

The second door was closed.

The third door, like the first, was also open, but this one looked to be a magic user's laboratory. In every fantasy I had ever read, there was always some room where the wizard or whatever practiced their art. All I cared about was that the room was currently empty.

That left only the second room, which I hoped was the location of our target.

I ran back and grabbed the guys. I told them that I would stay in my invisible status, since I had a possibility to get a bonus on my first backstab if I was in Conceal/Stealth. Wayne would enter first, followed by Dan and Jason. I would close the door behind me.

We approached the door, and I grabbed the handle. To our delight, the door was not locked. Wayne entered, and the rest of the team followed. As we discussed, I closed the door behind me.

Once we were inside, I saw that there were two men standing next to a large table with what looked like a map sitting on it. Both men continued to look at the map and hadn't seen us yet.

I saw both men's names. One was Shantus Frost, and he was white to us. The other was Dastin Frost, and he was yellow. He must have been the Head of the House Frost.

Continuing to ignore us, Shantus said, "What do you want? We said we were not to be disturbed."

Wayne had given the room a quick onceover when we came in and likely saw the same thing I did. We were alone. He also must have seen the large slab of wood that lay next to the door we entered through, which acted as a way to bar any entrance from outside.

Wayne grabbed the piece of wood and slammed it into place. That got their attention.

As one, the two turned from the table and looked at my friends. Their eyes passed over me as I made my way around to their backs. I got into position to attack.

Not a word was spoken between either side. The silence continued for another several moments until Dastin Frost began laughing, quite loudly.

Shantus joined him in his laughter, although I had no clue if he knew what he was laughing about or not. Dastin's mirth finally abated and he shook his head at my friends.

"I have no idea how you made it into this room, but I will certainly find out. Now, however, I only care about how painful your death would be. I would normally consider letting you live long enough to torture you for whatever information you have, but you can't be too smart. After all, you chose to lock yourself in here, with my brother and I, two of the most powerful Ice Mages in this land."

"This guy sure does like to monologue," Dan said.

Wayne and Jason laughed at Dan's comments, and I saw Dastin's face become red.

"Silence, worm!" Shantus yelled at our Ranger.

"You don't get it, Frosty," Wayne said, which only made the mage's face even redder. "Now you can't leave," he said. And then Wayne rushed him.

We had no idea what we would face in this room, so there had not been any discussion on strategy. But it didn't matter which of the mages Wayne decided to attack first, the priority was taking down the weaker of the two so we could put all of our attention on the stronger mob without worrying about the adds. Or, in this case, the singular add.

Wayne's first attack was a Bash that temporarily stunned the higher-level mob and interrupted his casting. I chose that moment to let my presence be known. And I backstabbed Shantus as he was in the middle of his own cast.

Shantus yelled out in pain, and his spell was interrupted by my damage.

"What treachery is this?" Dastin looked over to where his brother was. Once he saw me, he opened his eyes wide. In the next moment, he cast a near instant spell that froze Wayne where he stood and put up a shield of ice between himself and any of Dan's arrows that might have come his direction. His brother stumbled away from me and also got behind the screen. His hit points had dropped significantly.

"Since when did the Court work directly with mercenaries?" He hissed at me.

"I don't know about 'the Court,' but the King has passed judgement on you. I would say this court is definitely in session. Get ready for justice," I said.

I was worried about what the mage had said about the Court, and how my friends would react, but when I looked their way, they were shaking their heads in disappointment.

"You don't get to do catchphrases anymore, Alex. That was just horrible," Dan said.

"Embarrassment, really," Jason added.

"You too, Wayne?" I asked

"Sucked, dude. Like, bad. I'm with them."

"Oh, shut up, and just hit that fucker!" I mock yelled at them. I was happy to be changing the topic.

But the stupid mage wouldn't shut up.

"You can't hide your nature from me! I know well of your kind, and none other could have hid from my eyes!" He yelled at me and then growled out, "I say again: know your place! Do you have no honor? Do you take a job one day, only to betray on the next?"

"In answer to that last one, probably. But, dude, seriously, we don't care," Dan said as he moved around the edge of the ice shield and shot a triple shot arrow at the mage.

Dastin ducked behind his shield and growled again. He was definitely not happy. I didn't know if it was because of us or because he thought I was with the Court.

In the end, it didn't really matter. This asshole had to die, regardless, and that started with his weaker brother.

Mages were famous for being crazy powerful, but they were also weak when it came to total hit points. If we could get enough sustained damage on Shantus, I hoped it would be enough to interrupt his casting.

"Wayne and Allister, focus on Dastin! Go for Stuns only. Dan, you're with me. Get Broham out if you can, and go full damage on Shantus," I ordered.

Jason didn't hesitate and launched a Stun at the Head of the Frost family. I bet that asshat was surprised when it landed, too. Jason's magic wasn't your traditional kind, since he was a cleric, and common magic resistances, meaning those of an elemental nature, didn't work as well against his spells.

Wayne was close behind and threw a Bash at him as well, followed by a Kick. I was happy with anything that would keep him off balance and cancel any type of casting he could throw our way.

I went to Shantus and started swinging my daggers at him. I was way out of my element in this position, having taken the place of a Tank, but this was about sustained damage, not where it was coming from. Several seconds later, I realized that Dan was able to summon his four-legged friend, as his Dire Wolf, Broham, leaped past me and onto Shantus.

The mage raised his hands in fright and yelled out when Broham attacked. He cast an almost instant spell that froze the wolf in place, much as Dastin had done to Wayne earlier. It took Broham out of the damage equation temporarily. Between us, however, Broham did the least amount of damage, and if I could have picked someone to be the recipient of that spell, it would have been Dan's pet.

My daggers never stopped swinging, and I was doing damage from both my blades and from my Blood Blade's proc, which took a chunk of hit points from the target every time it cycled. That proc also worked to interrupt his casting. Finally, my Dagger of Jagged Rock's proc, which dropped the target's armor rating by 40 percent, had already gone off and it was as if Shantus had no armor on at all.

I could see in my interface that Dastin was full into his fight with Wayne and Jason. Wayne's health was down to 60 percent. Their Stuns were landing, but Jason's only worked every ten seconds, and Wayne's Bash refreshed every five seconds. In the interim, Dastin was able to land a few high-powered spells that had begun chipping away at Wayne's health. The secondary effect of Dastin's ice magic caused Wayne's attacks to slow down. It was freezing Wayne's body and making it harder for him to swing his war hammer.

Shantis was having none of his brother's luck. Another thirty seconds and the caster folded in on himself and laid dead at our feet.

Dantis noticed immediately, and screamed out in anger, "I will mount your heads over this keep!"

We ignored his threats and immediately transitioned into our usual fighting stance. Wayne was in front, I was behind, Dan was off to the side to fire arrows and deal with any extra mobs that spawned. Jason stood far enough away to heal Wayne but not be hit by any small radius AoE spells. Wayne had also turned Dastin so that Broham was with me, behind the mage's back.

We lit into the mob for reals, and his hit points started dropping quickly. We were also more successful at interrupting his attempts at casting. However, that dynamic only lasted for another 30 seconds.

At least that's when I heard the beating against the door. What sounded like many people were out in the hall and trying to get in. That was also the moment that Dastin hit 50 percent health, and he unleashed a massive AoE spell in the room that caught all of us in its range.

I was immediately frozen in place, unable to move. I saw Broham was in the same condition, as were Wayne and Jason. None of us could cast or attack.

Except for our Ranger.

Dan had won the Amulet of Troll Resistances when we completed the Eradicate the Troll Menace quest. That item gave him a +15 to all resistances. In more than one instance, that amulet had kept our Ranger in the game when the rest of us were knocked out, and it worked again here.

As soon as we all froze in place, the mage made a dash for the door. I had little doubt he was going to try and let whoever was in the hall into his chambers. Unfortunately for him, his dash only lasted a moment, as Dan's ever-trusty spell, Snare, landed on the caster. He went from a run to a crawl in a second.

"Blast you and your wretched Nature Magic!" he yelled. Then he screamed, "Get an axe and break the door down!"

If that door came open, we would undoubtedly have the entire House Frost on our asses. We were now on a no-shit timer.

Dan kept firing arrows at near point-blank range on the mage as he continued to slowly move to the door. After fifteen seconds from when it landed, an eternity in a fight like this, the AoE effect finally faded, and we could all move.

That's when I heard the first thunk of an axe against the door.

"I was hoping we would have time to finish this guy and search this room, but that just went out the window," I said. "I wanted to save this until it was necessary, but I'm gonna say that's now!"

With that, I activated the ability on my Force Multiplier ring. The effect, Unstoppable, multiplied all of my base stats by a factor of four and lasted five minutes. With my already high Dexterity and decent Strength, the result was a flurry of blades and procs that tore through almost any enemy. With each activation of my Blood Blade, I took 200 hit points. And since activation was based largely on my level of Dexterity, it was near constant. My damage was also increased dramatically, as Strength played an integral part of how damage was calculated.

I got Dastin down to 25 percent, and another instant cast went off around us. This time, however, the effect was on the mage and not us. He was now surrounded by a shield of ice. He wasn't able to cast, but we also couldn't do any damage on him until that shield was gone.

And the sound of the axe was getting louder.

If this were a normal fight, we might not have made it. But I was amped up on magical steroids, and what should have taken long enough for the rest of the Frost family to get through that door was reduced dramatically.

And even then, we just made it.

While my ring was still active, I drilled into that shield until it shattered around us. The shield being obliterated also sent a shot of magical feedback into Dastin, and he staggered from the impact. He was then completely vulnerable, and we wasted no time in slaying him.

But the bastard wouldn't die without at least one last parting monologue.

"You think this is a victory for your precious King? The Children of Loust have already infested this land with their people, and you are the ones who are fighting on the side of the damned! Killing me solves nothing!"

"It'll get you to at least shut the hell up," I said as I plunged my dagger into him one last time.

I was bending over the corpse to loot when part of the door finally shattered. We only had seconds to go. I did a quick look at the loot, saw the head we needed, and several other items on the body. Other than our quest item were two rings, a robe, several spells, and a book of some kind. The robe, rings, and spells were all tradeable items, so I didn't even bother to look at their stats. I simply looted everything, including the book and the head.

"Got it. Go!" I yelled.

As soon as I had started standing, and before I even had time to yell, I saw the rest of my team had triggered their teleportation scrolls. We then had a ten second wait before they would activate.

With three seconds to go, Dan yelled out, "Shit! Broham!" And then I saw our Ranger's companion vanish.

If Dan hadn't remembered to unsummon his pet, he would have been left behind and would have been killed in the room, losing valuable experience.

I saw a blast of ice coming through the door, and right at my face, as the teleportation scroll finally activated and the interior of the room vanished from my view.

A second later, we were back in the tent with Captain Treeswain and a large number of his officers. Everyone in the room turned toward us when we appeared and began pulling blades, likely thinking we were intruders there to attack the Captain. Treeswain, however, recognized us immediately and held out his hands, yelling, "Hold!"

After a few tense moments, the others calmed down. Treeswain walked over, and I pulled the head out of my bag to show him. It was the first time I had ever seen Treeswain smile.

He called over one of the officers and told him, "Get a runner prepped to send a message to the King." He then turned to the rest of the assembled staff and said, "Get the camp ready. Tonight, we feast!"

CHAPTER 15

Treeswain clapped all of us on the back. He then informed us he was going to make sure both the runner and the feast were being handled. Treeswain was a bit of a micromanager.

Once he left the tent, we celebrated amongst ourselves. We hadn't received a notification that the quest was over and would likely have to wait for the head being turned in before we could get our reward. Still, we knew we had won, and it felt great.

The next task was to look through the loot I had taken from Dastin Frost. When I looked in my bag, I saw the robe and two rings in addition to the book and head. Thankfully, it wasn't bleeding everywhere, because that would just be nasty.

The rings and robe were for users of the Ice discipline only. I didn't even realize that specializing in a particular element was possible, but it made perfect sense. It wasn't "Ice" exactly, but the element of Water. Unfortunately, we didn't have anyone in our group who used that particular discipline. Neither did Jenny or Tyke's groups, who were our go to for a raid—Jenny's, usually, if it was an eight-man party, Tyke's for twelve.

As I noted before, however, they were all tradeable, and given the effects of the rings, I knew I could get a lot for them.

During our fight with Dastin, he instant casted a massive AoE freeze spell at 50 percent health that knocked out all of us except Dan, who had the highest resistances. At 25 percent, he instant casted that massive shield. I had thought these were the result of him being a boss of some kind, but that wasn't the case.

Instead, the rings were the culprits. The first one gave a +5 to Intelligence and a +5 percent to the effect of Water spells. That was nothing special. The real value came from the effect, Frozen Tundra. According to the text, Frozen Tundra did the following:

When the wearer loses half their health, an area effect spell is instantly cast to freeze the surrounding enemies for twenty seconds. This effect can be triggered once every 24 hours. Water specialists only.

The second ring was even more badass. Again, the ring only gave a small bonus to stats— also +5 to Intelligence and +5 percent to the effects of Water spells. But this time, the spell associated was called Wall of Frozen Shields.

When the wearer falls to critical health, a shield of ice will encapsulate them, protecting the wearer for 10 times the amount of their normal, undamaged health. The wearer cannot cast or be healed while protected by the Wall of Frozen Shields. This effect can be triggered once every 24 hours. Water Specialists only.

This would, in effect, protect the wearer from two potentially killing blows immediately, and in the case of the shield, it would keep them alive for a whole lot longer. It was definitely enough time for a tank to reacquire aggro if the mage was careless.

The robe was marginally better, adding bonuses to Intelligence and Wisdom and adding a +20 percent to Water spells. There was no additional effect associated with the robe.

The head was self-explanatory, so I didn't bother taking it out of my inventory. Not to mention, I didn't really like looking at decapitated heads.

That only left the book.

I took it out and examined the cover. It was leather-bound and lacked any title or indication as to what was inside. I opened it and the disappointment on my face must have been obvious.

"Empty?"

"No. Not empty, Allister. Just not helpful. It's an inventory list at the keep. Looks like how much food they have and other supplies. No doubt valuable to a group of rogue citizens of the Kingdom looking to wait out a war, but it's not going to do anything for us."

"Let me see it, Alex," Dan said, and I handed the book over.

Dan flipped through the pages, first quickly, and then again, slower.

"Boom!" Dan yelled.

That got all of our attention, and we waited for him to continue. Naturally, he didn't.

"Assclown, don't just say 'Boom,' and then stop. Why must you make us ask?" Wayne said.

"I thought it would make it more dramatic if I made you wait."

"Annoying, Dan. The word you are looking for is 'annoying.' It's not synonymous with 'dramatic,'" Jason said.

"I don't know, Allister. It's a tough one for him to wrap his head around, since burning down Jenny's place was both dramatic and annoying. I can see where he could be confused."

Dan looked hurt and said, "That was just mean, Alex."

"Better than my catch-phrasing, huh?" I asked

"Oh, good one! I didn't see that coming back to bite me so quickly!" Dan exclaimed, followed by a fist bump to me and a smile.

We continued to wait until Wayne said, "And..."

"Oh, right, Sorry," Dan said again and then held up the book. "It's not a book on inventory. I mean, it is, but it isn't. It's code," he said and then flipped the book open.

He pointed to a particular entry that looked like a representation of how much grain they had stockpiled.

"Looks normal to me," I said.

"Yup, that's what makes it a code. But I can tell you that based on the size of that keep, they couldn't have had this much grain in there. Even if the place went down three levels underground, they couldn't have had this much grain, let alone the rest of it. So, either this is a record of some other location or it's code. I'm gonna go with code."

"What does it mean, though?" Jason asked.

"I got no idea. All I know, Allidramatic—or was it Alliannoying? I get confused—is that it's something someone will care about and, therefore, valuable."

It was that moment that Treeswain returned with the runner for the King and we stopped our bickering and bantering to formulate the message back to his Majesty.

"I can't tell you the last time the men looked this happy!" Treeswain said in my ear as we sat at the head of the feast. Treeswain may be a micromanager, but I wasn't going to complain right then. The feast was epic and would have made any dwarf jealous at just the amount of alcohol that was flowing, not to mention the food. The only thing missing was the near constant yelling of "Huzzah!"

Always ones to partake at a party, I had to tell Dan and Wayne to imbibe slowly, reminding them how much it sucked the last time they had hangovers. Still, we were forced to drink with every toast in our direction.

The feast was in full swing and had been going for about an hour. We were desperate to get back to the Kingdom, but that would require a long day's ride. And honestly, we felt we deserved the break. We knew our next task, discovering the unknown monastery, would have us riding into the Globi desert, and none of us knew how long that would take or how treacherous the trip would be.

Treeswain was not one to shy away from mixing business and pleasure and hounded us extensively about what we saw at the keep, where we saw patrols, and what we could expect from its occupants.

I put Dan on the task, as he had the best memory for these things, and I listened along. I added my input where I thought it was helpful. One thing I noticed, and passed along, was that the Frosts had placed their strongest fighters and mages outside of the keep as patrols. That made a good bit of sense, since they would be the most likely to survive an initial incursion by scouts and return to warn the keep. That left the keep filled with weaker guards and mages, which we were able to exploit.

I noted, however, that the dynamic could have changed following the death of their family patriarch, and it was impossible to gauge what, if any, effect that would have on the makeup of the patrols.

To his credit, Treeswain abandoned any line of questioning about mimicking our successful tactic when he learned that we climbed the cliff and snuck in through a window. His was an army, and he knew he couldn't repurpose our strategy.

Treeswain also asked about the creatures we had faced in the forest. Dan was in the middle of recounting our battle with the Forest Cobras when a sentry came running up to the table.

He dashed up to the captain before popping to attention, saluting, and saying, "Sir!"

"Report," Treeswain ordered.

"Sir," the sentry said before looking a bit nervous as he continued, "horses approach."

"How many?" Treeswain asked.

"Um, sir. I think all of them."

It was then that we started to hear the sound of hooves. As it grew louder, it sounded like hundreds of horses were coming our way. From our vantage point of the high table, we were able to stand on our chairs and see a great distance. The sentry was right. The sea of horse flesh stretched as far as I could see. It did look like all the horses in Tholtos.

It was then we heard, even over the sound of the hooves, a booming voice.

"Rise for the King!"

At that moment, every soldier at every table dropped their utensils, food, mugs, or whatever else they may have in their hands.

Treeswain didn't miss a beat and yelled out, "Atten–*tion*!"

Every soldier snapped to position, arms pinned to their sides, and their heads held high.

Before this feast, I don't know if the looks on those soldiers would have been so proud, but morale was soaring now, and even more so that their king was here. This also looked great for us.

My group also stood in respect for the King.

His Majesty, King Kameron, looked regal. I definitely had to give him that. His armor looked impressive, and he moved in it like someone who was used to doing battle, the weight of his plate not impeding him at all. And instead of a solid piece of plate, the suit looked to be made of interlocking pieces that overlapped each other. This led to more pieces, but also more flexibility. The chest piece shone like it had just been polished, and gleamed with the color of Mithral. Undoubtedly, the King of the land would have a full suit of the best armor, and without question it would be made of the best material available. The greaves, boots, vambraces, and gloves were also made of the same overlapping pieces, and also had the same color. The sigil of Kameron's family, a flaming eagle, sat proudly on the chest of the King as well as on his shield that stayed on his horse as he dismounted from his steed.

He could have ridden forward and stopped at the head table, but instead, he left his mount at the perimeter of the feast, took off his helmet, and then walked toward us. Being all military, no one bowed, but everyone stayed at attention. I didn't want to piss the guy off from the outset, so I got down on one knee, and motioned for the others to do the same. Knowing the king had killed off Lady Tessa's family for his own benefit reminded me that this guy wasn't to be messed with, and the knee couldn't hurt.

The king looked around at his men as he traveled the distance, and he had a large smile on his face. It was infectious, and I saw a number of the men put smiles on their own faces once the king had passed. They were loving him.

Once he reached the head table, he stepped between me and Treeswain, turned to the assembled men, and yelled out, "At rest!"

Every man snapped to a position of "rest," which still looked a lot like attention, since they were staying rigid in their stance. The king then turned to me and said, "The head."

I reached into my pack and handed over our trophy.

The king took it from me, grabbed it by the hair, and lifted it over his head.

"Witness the fate of betrayal! The head of House Frost is dead!"

Everyone knew why the feast was being held, but this was the first sign they had seen of the result. The effect was immediate.

Order and discipline be damned, every man in that camp cheered as loud as possible!

The king let it go on for several seconds before he lowered the head. With that, the cheering died down. The king then looked over the assembled crowd for several more moments before continuing, "The House of Frost is in disarray. They are, undoubtedly, promoting a new head as we speak, likely his despicable brother, Shantus Frost," he called out loudly to the crowd.

"Nah, we killed that bum, too," Dan said, rather loudly.

I cringed at Dan's timing. But since it was Dan, cringing at his timing had become almost normal. Right now, though, I was worried how the king might react to his interruption.

I needn't have worried. The cheers that erupted from the surrounding army were even louder than when the king lifted the head.

I looked over questioningly at the king, and he smiled at us before speaking again. "Dastin may have been the patriarch of his vile family, but Shantus was a man who knew no equal when it came to brutality and torture. My only regret is that I couldn't be the one to slay him myself!"

This resulted in another round of cheers. But the king was not done.

"House Frost may think they are safe behind their walls, but they are not. Nor will they have time to regroup, or ask for reinforcements, for I have not traveled here alone!"

At that moment, the remaining group of riders began entering the campground. There were numerous knights and soldiers, but also a huge number of what looked like civilians.

"I bring with me every noble house in the kingdom! Tomorrow, House Frost becomes an example of what happens to the enemies of this land, and their blight will be wiped from this world!"

The men let out the loudest cheer yet, and I saw all the house leaders speaking with the men in the camp, slapping them on the back, and congratulating them. We were told that killing the head of the family would boost morale, but this could be the moment that truly turned the tide of the campaign.

When the king was finished with his speech, he turned to my group and Treeswain and said, "I would have you attend me in your tent," then walked off.

After the king left, we waited a few moments before moving to the tent. We let Treeswain proceed us as well. I had a few words for my friends.

"Let's not forget this is the bastard that condemned all of Lady Tessa's family to death. He may look like a good guy, but he can be just as vicious as any other person we've encountered."

The guys nodded their heads and we started walking before Wayne arrested our progress. He turned to us and said, "Can we try and save the kids?"

Confused, I looked at him a bit, and he continued, "We didn't see any kids when we were there, but there might be some in that keep. I don't like the idea of killing kids."

"You softy. I'm going to tell Jenny that you changed your mind about wanting to wait for children," Dan said.

"I'll tell Kaitlin about a certain bearded female dwarf."

"Kids are horrible."

"That's what I thought," Wayne finished and looked at me.

"We can ask, Wayne, but I don't know that he'll listen."

"We do have the book," Dan said.

"Thanks, Dan. There goes any chance I had of using that book for anything else."

Wayne's visage hardened, and he had an edge in his voice when he said, "Use the book."

There was no arguing with our warrior when he got like that, and I simply nodded.

Wayne walked off toward the tent, and I gave Dan my best impression of a Jason look. He mouthed, "Sorry," before we continued.

Dan then whispered my way and said, "Sorry, man, I don't like the kid thing either."

I just nodded. I would have at least liked to try to get the concession without the book, but now Wayne would butt in if I didn't immediately lead with it. Even if he agreed not to. I couldn't be mad at him for that. He cared about the "people" of Resurgence just like I cared about Sally, Stan, and even Waseem.

We entered the tent and saw the king talking to Treeswain. He stopped when we arrived and addressed our group. "I am in your debt more than you could know. Today you did far more than just kill a traitor. Please, everyone, sit." Once we were all seated, the king continued, "There were questions around my leadership. The other houses were beginning to speculate about my ability to lead and saw House Frost as an example of my faults. There was no talk of rebellion, but getting direct support was becoming more difficult.

"With the death of Dastin, I saw my opportunity. Once the news spread, which I let happen quite quickly, every house was offering their congratulations and their support. No one wanted to be on the same receiving end. When they came and offered their aid, I took it. I told each one that I planned to remove House Frost entirely, and that I needed their assistance. They accepted without thinking twice, likely thinking they were the only ones being offered this opportunity, and the aid I required would be in soldiers, supplies, or money.

"It wasn't until I had every House's pledge that I announced my intention to travel here, to the front, and deal with the traitors myself, and that each house would bring not just soldiers, but their mages and heads as well. Their fear was palpable at first. That was, until they saw the force we had mustered when we worked together."

I raised my hand, and the king laughed. "You don't need to raise your hand, Alex. Please, speak freely."

"Thank you, Your Majesty. I'm just a bit confused. How did this information get to you so quickly? And how did you get here so quickly? We didn't complete this task all that long ago."

"If I may, Highness?" Treeswain said, and the King nodded. "Our runner didn't actually run. He had a teleportation scroll that took him to Kich's Keep."

"Ok, that makes sense. But what about this army?"

"That's a bit of a secret, Alex, that I hope you can keep to yourselves," the King said.

My group nodded, and I said, "Of course, Your Majesty."

"The kingdom has a teleportation portal that can be used to move large groups from Kich's Keep to anywhere in the kingdom I control. It is very costly, though," he said, then added, "I admit that I could have arrived much closer to the camp, but I wanted the impact of a dramatic entrance."

Dan looked immediately over at Jason and raised his eyebrows.

"No, Dan. That's an accurate use of the word 'dramatic.'"

The king rightly looked confused but accepted when I said, "Think nothing of it. An internal argument."

The king nodded his head. "I would normally not use the portal, save for responding to an invasion, but I need this victory to bring the kingdom together before we push on Loust."

"Makes sense to me," I said.

The king then stood. My group and Treeswain followed suit. The king took on a regal look and said, "You have completed your mission and delivered the Head of House Frost, both figuratively and literally. The kingdom thanks you."

With that, we were surrounded by a golden glow, and we were informed that we had gained experience and had leveled up! Additionally, we saw a scrawling text that announced our achievements.

The Children of Loust may continue in their desire to subjugate the Kingdom of Tholtos, but let it be known to all that they will not be victorious! Their attempt at betraying our lands from within have failed and the House of Frost will cease to exist forever more. The Head of House Frost has been delivered to King Kameron by the honorable adventurers Alex, Allister, Naugha, and TheClaw! Forevermore, these adventurers will be known as The Heroes of Tholtos!

We also received a second notification that announced:

As the first to defeat the Head of House Frost in the lands controlled by the Children of Loust, you have been given the title of Hero of Tholtos. This title bestows upon the wearer a bonus to the player. All stats are +5 and all resistances +20

Do you wish to display your title? Failure to display the title will negate the bonus, but you will still maintain the title in your archive. Any additional bonuses from previous titles will be added to the highest title of the player.

I didn't hesitate for a moment and indicated yes.

The other guys were quick to accept as well, and I saw their new titles displayed over their heads. "That looks so awesome," I said.

Wayne nodded his head and said, "Alex, Hero of Tholtos. That does look awesome."

We all had the same change to our characters. Now, whenever anyone saw us walking the street, they would see the name and title.

"It is entirely deserved," the king said and then sat back down. We followed suit and he continued to speak. "I have more to ask of you, but I hesitate to burden you further."

I was about to tell him to burden away when I saw I had received a personal message from Tyke. "Jesus, man! Another one?!? I hate you guys so much! But really, congratulations from all of us. Let us know when our next raid is!"

"Everyone get a message from Tyke?" Dan asked.

"Yup. I'll talk with King Kameron if you could handle that, Dan. Tell him we'll let him know first raid we come to."

"You got it, Alex. I'll also tell him Naugha wants nudes of Lug," he answered.

"What are 'nudes,' Alex?" the king asked.

If I had been drinking anything at that moment, it would have ended up all over the king's face. Thankfully, all I did was cough and say, "They are a... um... type of painting, Your Majesty."

"Ah, and Naugha wants them of the warrior Lug? I see," he said then turned to Wayne and continued, "I hold no animosity for he who would share his bed with another man. Your choice of love holds no sway over my esteem for you as a warrior, my friend."

Wayne was almost shaking. Dan, Jason, and I were forcing our mouths closed so hard, we all looked super constipated. It was all we could do to keep the laughter in.

But I had to give Wayne his due. He nodded and growled out a thank you.

He did turn to Dan, however, and mouthed the words, "dead man."

I was a bit surprised to hear the king call Lug by his class. "You are aware of Lug, our warrior friend?"

"I know of all my subjects, Alex," the king said. It sounded a little creepy the way he said it, too. Then he continued, "On to my previous request."

We nodded our heads, and I said, "Apologies."

The king simply raised his hand to halt any further need to ask forgiveness. "This next battle with House Frost will not include adventurers. It is nothing personal. I would be honored to fight alongside any of you. However, this is as much a political ploy as anything else. It must remain that way.

"That being said, I will undoubtedly need you and your friends in the campaign to come. Am I able to call on you and your fellow adventurers for future tasks?"

"I can't speak for all the other adventurers in your lands, but I can tell you that my friends and I are here when you need us."

"Good!" the king said before standing and looked to be ready to depart the tent.

"Alex," Wayne growled out and I sighed.

"There is another thing, Your Majesty."

"Oh?" The king said and sat back down.

"We found various items on Dastin Frost's body," I said.

The king nodded and said, "Those are yours to keep and do with what you will. They are the legitimate spoils of this war."

"Well, you see, one of them is a book. And our Ranger believes the contents are actually a code."

"For what, TheClaw?"

It still sounded weird whenever an NPC said Dan's game name. Partly because it was a ridiculous name, and also because it sounded funny coming out without a pause between The and Claw.

"I got no idea, Your Worship. I just know it's not what it seems. Um, Your Greatness."

The king laughed and said, "Your Majesty or Highness are all the honorifics I can take. Thank you, TheClaw, I always appreciate the opportunity to truly laugh." Then he said, "May I see the book?"

"Well, see, that's the thing. We were hoping to trade it," I said.

The king leaned back in his chair and his face changed from that of a smiling and laughing man to the look of a merchant ready to haggle over a single copper. It's a look I was used to seeing on King Steelhammer of the dwarves.

"I see. What do you request?"

I never got a chance to respond. Wayne beat me to the punch and said, "The kids."

The king's face changed again, and this time he looked legitimately confused. "I don't understand."

I put my hand up, but this time toward Wayne, who was about to keep talking, and said, "We didn't see any children at the keep, but we assume that when House Frost fled, they took their children with them. Our warrior is asking that you spare the lives of the young. You did say that you planned to 'Wipe out the blight that was the entirety of House Frost.'"

The king regained his merchant-like pose and said, "May I see the book?"

I handed it over, and Kameron began flipping through it. At one point, he stopped and turned the book around and pointed at the entry for grain. "Is this what gave it away?"

Dan looked and nodded. "Way too much," he said.

"I agree. Compounded with all the other goods, I would be inclined to agree that this must be code, and well concealed," he said and then closed the book.

Then he looked at Wayne and said, "You need not fear, Naugha. There are already families selected to take the children of House Frost and raise them as their own. They will not be shown any hostility for the actions of their parents."

Wayne let out a huge sigh.

"We are not the Children of Loust, and I do not kill children," he said sternly. After a pause, his visage softened, and he followed with, "But I am even more impressed by a man who can never have children, given his choice in life partners, who would have such caring in his heart. There is no offense taken at your question."

"I'm so dead," I heard Dan whisper behind me.

"Thank you for the book. Take these scrolls, which will teleport you back to Kich's Keep. When the time comes, Sir Arthur will have your next assignment. I now leave you so I may plan our attack on the remnants of House Frost," King Kameron finished and walked out of the tent.

I turned to the guys as soon as the king left and tried to get in front of whatever Wayne was about to dish out to Dan. "Let's not waste any time here, guys. Hit the scrolls and let's get back to Kich's Keep. It's been a crazy long day, and I, for one, am ready to call it done."

"Sounds good," Dan said and immediately hit his scroll. The rest of us followed suit.

Seconds later, we were back in the square, next to Sir Arthur. Dan was beside me, and then Jason and Wayne popped into view. I tried to position myself between Dan and Wayne, but it was a vain attempt. Wayne simply walked through me, moving my body with his own bulk.

He stood in front of our Ranger, who was now shaking.

Wayne held an angry stare at Dan for several seconds—before he broke out in a huge smile and picked up Dan in a hug then putting him down.

"That worked out awesome, Dan! I know you didn't plan it, but I don't know how the king might have reacted if you hadn't made him think I was Lug's lover!" he laughed.

"You aren't mad?" Dan asked, looking bewildered.

"Of that? Hell no! What do I care that an NPC thinks Lugs and I are getting it on?" he asked. "Besides, one of my best friends is married to another man," he said, putting his hand on Jason's shoulder and laughing. "I've obviously got no hang-ups about it!"

Dan's shoulders slumped in obvious relief.

"Of course, I'm not going to let it go that you got me good. Oh, no. That I'll definitely be paying back at some point!"

The look of fear returned to Dan's face again, and that got laughs out of the rest of us.

Undisclosed Location

The General was coming into the conference room at the tail end of Dan Hamson's most recent debrief. He had listened in from his office, and there hadn't been any new information that Dan had learned from his escapades inside the game, Resurgence. He had spent a good ten minutes explaining to Colonel Thompson about some drawn out quest he and his team had completed with dwarves and dragons. Dan had just finished complaining about a lack of "sweet loots" at the end of the mission.

"Well it certainly sounds like you're having a good time, Mr. Hamson," the General said as he entered.

Dan must have learned his lesson about talking about the game with the General and responded, "It's progressing along, sir, but I haven't learned anything of value, I'm afraid. AltCon has been pretty hands-off since they hosted their Resurgence appreciation day. There haven't been any special offers or events. We've been playing as if there's nothing going on."

The General nodded his head and appreciated Dan not sprinkling in any of his catch phrases from his character in the game. Still, it wasn't only Dan that interested the General.

"And what news of your teammates?"

Dan paused long enough to look like he was thinking of his answer. "Nothing really new to report there. Personally, they all seemed to have benefited from the 'Family Day' that AltCon hosted, especially those with spouses. Without looking at their brain scans we can't know if AltCon tried to manipulate their thoughts, though."

The General paused a moment and asked, "Mr. Hamson, are you ok? That was two coherent reports without a single odd statement?"

Dan looked flabbergasted for a moment but then saw the General smile. "Sorry, Dan. I couldn't resist."

"Damn, I'm getting it from you and Jason."

"Apologies. Please continue."

"Nah, no need to apologize. I like when you throw out the zingers. Unfortunately, I don't have anything more to add. Wayne and Jenny are still an item. Jason continues to impress me with his wit, and Alex is still the luckiest bastard alive."

"Tell me about that."

"I was telling the Colonel about a quest we did, one that involved our dwarven allies in the game. It's not that anything crazy happened, it's that we got the quest at all and that we ended up doing it in such an unorthodox manner."

"Meaning what?"

"So, in these games, you usually get a quest to do something, and then you fight lots of stuff, and then you get a reward. But in this case, we weren't asked to fight. We were asked to steal. And the only one who could have done that was Alex. And, on top of that, I think he was having his own side convos with the main NPC," Dan explained, then he added, "The real shitty part was that in the end, we didn't even get a real reward."

"No sweet loots?"

Dan's face got really red and in an embarrassed tone he said, "Shit. I should have known you were listening."

"Not to worry, Dan. Even if I hadn't heard it before, I listen to all these conversations later. And don't be disheartened if there isn't anything to report, especially if nothing is happening. Continue to do your job, and we will see you at your next report."

The General was about to dismiss Dan when Colonel Thompson said, "Sir, what about that tower?"

The General thought about it for a moment and nodded his head. If the tower Emily mentioned wasn't on the grounds of the Motel, maybe it was in the game.

"What tower?" Dan asked.

"In all of your time in the game, have you ever come across a tower?"

"Yeah. Plenty. But I don't think you mean some guard tower or something."

"I don't really know. All I know is that there is a 'tower' of some kind that is of interest to the AltCon people outside of the game. We couldn't find anything that qualified except maybe the AltCon headquarters building, but it's never been called by that name."

This time it definitely looked like Dan really was thinking about what the General asked and must have been going through his memory. "Well, there is one thing."

"Go on."

"I can't say this is anything for sure, especially since we haven't been to every part of the game, but there is a singular tower in the main city, a place called Kich's Keep. That's the city, not the tower. I have no idea what the tower is called.

"Anyway," Dan said as he saw the General wave for him to continue, "the tower is probably five stories tall and sits in the middle of the town. Strangely, though, it doesn't have any doors, and no one ever approaches it. I've walked past it lots of times, and I always avoid it because it just feels odd. I've also seen the other players and NPCs do the same. I mean, no one ever goes near it. That's weird now that I think about it."

The General looked over at Colonel Thompson who simply shrugged his shoulders. "It's worth checking out, if nothing else."

"Agreed." The General said. "I would also like to learn what your friend Alex thinks about this tower. If he does have some unique connection to the game, maybe he knows more than he has told you."

"I'll see what I can find out, sir."

"That's all I can ask. Dismissed."

CHAPTER 16

December 16, 2043

I logged back into Resurgence at our usual time of ten in the morning. Dan and Jason were already in the square, and Wayne showed up just a minute later. This was to be a big day for our group. Where others in our position would start grinding to get the levels for the next story quest, we were turning back to Lady Tessa's missions and the next monastery on our list. The only problem was that we didn't know where the monastery was, how to get to it, or even what it was called. All we knew was that Aaron Lancaster had been given another of these monastery quests, but even he didn't know what he was looking for. All he knew, like us, was that the monastery was located somewhere in the Globi desert and that the Jalusi tribe were the key to the quest.

Based on the information that had been found in Constance Lancaster's journal, we knew that Aaron had been unhappy about the task. I had also been given a little help from the Wanderer, but I couldn't tell the guys about that. There wasn't any reason to delay, and I said as much to the group.

"Let's get our heads wrapped around this next monastery and start thinking about our strategy. I've got my own ideas, but I want to know what you guys think."

"We need to stock up on supplies, regardless," Jason said. "Probably smart to get plenty of food and drink, since we are going to a desert."

"Agreed, Allister. How are you for arrows, Dan?"

"I'm fine. I barely used any in our fights."

"Good. And if we need to go stealthy, I've got plenty of dyes to use Camouflage on all of us," I said.

"I'm also good, Alex," Wayne said.

"Let's look at that passage from the Journal again," I said and read out the text:

As it turned out, I didn't need to trick Aaron at all to get him to open up about his letter. He was so angry that he was just waiting for someone to tell. He threw the letter in my face and told me to see the garbage he had been delivered.

The only instruction was that Aaron was to travel to the Monastery of... located in the Globi Desert, confirming my earlier suspicions that something was tying these Monasteries together. The location of the Monastery was unknown to the King and his people. Instead, Aaron was to find a wandering tribe in the Globi – the Jalusi tribe, who were said to be the only group who traded with the Monastery and knew its location. I was no help to him, as I had never heard of the tribe, either. I envy his circumstance less than even my own.

"Yeah, that's not really any help at all. The Globi desert has to be huge," Wayne noted.

"It is a start, though. We won't know what we are facing until we get there, I guess," Jason added.

"Well," I said, with a pause. That got everyone to focus on me. "We could always ask Della from the swamp. She does owe us a favor."

That got the guys thinking. Della had been extremely helpful in getting us to the Monastery of Might, although that was likely because she wanted something from us.

What they didn't know was that I had already spoken to the Wanderer about this, and he had told me that I should speak with Della about our desire to travel into the desert to find this monastery. Doing so would get her to tell us about a settlement just inside the Globi Desert. The people at the settlement would make sure we had the necessary protection to get us through the desert as well as provide opportunities to learn more. Even the Wanderer didn't know exactly what they would say, though. He believed our relationship to Della would help us, though. Still, this was supposed to be a hard quest, so I wasn't expecting much.

"Definitely worth a try," Jason agreed.

"I don't have any better idea, Alex, so I'm game," Wayne added.

That looked to be the end of the conversation. At least, it would have been, but Dan held up his hand.

"Totally off topic here, but do you guys have any idea what that tower over there is all about?" Dan said, pointing at the warded tower Waseem had warned me against.

While I had been leveling my skill in Scaling, I had come across the tower. It wasn't hard to find, as it sat in the middle of the town. When I had looked at it through my magically aided sight, the building was all red, top to bottom. There wasn't a single place that I could have climbed.

Waseem had told me that the "Tower," and he said it with a capital T, was from the earliest days of Kich's Keep, back during the time of Loust, not his so-called "Children."

According to Waseem, the Tower housed the entire collection of Loust artifacts, going back hundreds of years. The wards that were placed on the Tower were designed to keep people away. Even those that weren't attuned to magic, like Warriors, would feel the magic that saturated the area and would stay far away.

But all that information came from my relationship with an NPC that I shouldn't know, so I didn't offer any information. I did feel like there was some I could say, though.

"I wanted to try climbing it once," I said, "but it registers as being impossible to navigate. When I got closer, I felt kind of sick. I just kept away from it after that."

Jason and Wayne nodded their heads. "I've had that same feeling when I've walked past it," Wayne said.

"Me too," Jason agreed.

Dan sat for a second in thought then headed over to the center of the square where Sir Arthur Chadwick stood. He then left the group.

"What are you doing, Dan?" I asked.

"I'm going to ask about the Tower, but Sir Arthur won't answer me if I'm not the leader."

"Well then, just be the leader. If you get a quest, I want it too!" I said with excitement in my voice that I didn't really feel.

"That'll work!" Dan said, and we regrouped with Dan as the leader.

Dan finished his walk to Sir Arthur and said, "Oh glorious and mighty Sir Arthur, what can you tell us poor adventurers about the tower off in the distance," he said, pointing toward the structure.

"And that's why we would never make him the leader," Jason said, chuckling.

Sir Arthur actually looked to where Dan was pointing. After a moment, he began speaking. "Ah. I see you have noticed the Tower. That is a structure you should not trouble yourself with, young adventurer. There is nothing in there of value, and the wards would keep you out, regardless. But since you have asked, I will tell you that this is not the first time Loust and his minions have risen up against the forces of good. His villainy was well known, and his tools for enslaving our people were many and fierce. A place was needed to house those vile items. That tower was the answer."

"In the middle of the city?" Dan asked, incredulously.

Surprisingly, Sir Arthur answered Dan. "The time of Loust was long past, and this keep was not the grand city you see around you now. Kich's Keep has grown around the Tower, but no one would ever try to move it, or its contents. I doubt there is anyone today who could. No person, or thing, can enter. Or even go near, for that matter. I again suggest you forget it, TheClaw."

"A tower in the middle of the city that no one can get near or enter. That sounds about right," Dan said.

"Right for what?" Jason asked.

Dan looked at us like he had just realized he spoke that last sentence out loud.

"Um, for this game. Give us something tempting and then keep us away from it. I bet that it becomes live in the official game, though," he said before disbanding our group. "Time for you to go back to being leader, Alex. I'm good."

Dan's behavior was odd, but Dan's antics were always a little odd. I wasn't going to spend too much time thinking about it, especially with us having other priorities.

"Let's go get our supplies, then, and head out to the swamp. I hope Della is happy to see us."

"Alex!" Della yelled when she saw me and the group. She was wearing a flowing dress that hung off her shoulders and ended around her calves. She had been walking through a glade of healthy grass when we approached. It was the only part of the swamp that could be considered healthy, and the flourishing part of the swamp moved with her.

When we had quested to conquer the Monastery of Might, we had needed Della's help. Although, back then, she was known as the Witch, and she had made us swear to help her in kind. We learned then that swearing an oath bound you to the task and trying to abandon it carried a very harsh penalty.

In return for her help, we were to deliver an item, the Vivre Stone, which had the power of ancient magic. It, in turn, was able to change a small area of the swamp into a beautiful and thriving patch of forest, pushing back the plague that had cursed this swamp. Since Della wore it as an amulet, that patch followed wherever she went.

We had navigated through the swamp to find her, killing off creatures as we traveled. Having seen Della's map, Dan had memorized the locations of all the mobs, so we were able to avoid any of the difficult areas that could still challenge us, even at our levels.

Della ran up to me and gave me a big hug. She then did the same to my teammates.

"I'm just glad to see you wearing something, this time," I said. This elicited a large blush from Della. She had been naked the first two times we encountered her, using an illusion of a breathtakingly naked woman to lure wayward travelers to her, where she in turn would attack them. That was when she was the Witch, though. Now, she was Della of the Glade, and she looked more motherly than alluring. I didn't have any desire to see her without her clothes.

"To what do I owe this welcome interruption?"

"We are continuing our search for the monasteries," I said. "We have good information that Constance Lancaster wasn't the only one in his family looking for these institutions. His brother Aaron had been sent into the Globi Desert to look for another, only he didn't know where in the desert it was or even what it was called."

"Ahh, I should have thought of this already. Have you searched for other monasteries before?"

"Yes. We found the Monastery of Calm before coming here."

"Did those in that hallowed place meet the same fate as my darling monks?"

"I'm afraid so, Della. The monasteries appear to have been targeted by vile forces. We are on a quest to uncover what happened to the men of the Lancaster family, and each seem to have been sent to a monastery of some kind," I said.

"Hmm. How many men were there in the family?"

"Five—four young men and their father."

"Then not all of them were sent to monasteries. There were only four of those in Tholtos. You have already been to the Monasteries of Calm and Might. The Globi Desert was the home to the Monastery of the Swift, and the lands far to the east housed the Monastery of Momentum. These were the four Monasteries."

Even if we got nothing more from Della, this was a win. Being able to tell the Jalusi tribe that we were searching for the Monastery of the Swift was a boon, although it did make me wonder what the fifth task could have been.

"We've also uncovered that the Jalusi Tribe of the Globi Desert were the key to its location. It is said that they were the only ones to trade with this monastery."

Della nodded her head. "The Jalusi have been around since as long as I can remember. They are the original inhabitants of that desert. If anyone were to know, it would be them. But they are a nomadic people, and finding them could be as difficult as finding the monastery.

"However, there is a small village on the border of the desert that may be able to help you. They routinely trade with the Jalusi when their wandering takes them to the edges of the vast sand, so that would be your best place to start."

"Can you give us directions to the settlement?" Since the swamp butted up against the desert, it should be somewhere Della was familiar with.

"I can indeed. If you come back to my home, I can show you on my map. I have traveled there twice since you delivered the stone to me, and I have made friends with the people there. My knowledge of the plants that surround their outpost has aided them in creating remedies for several ailments that had befallen their citizens. I believe a note from me could help you. They are not normally the trusting type, having lived between an unforgiving desert and a deadly swamp."

We traveled back to Della's home, where she used her map to show Dan where the settlement was, automatically updating his map. With all the other information Dan saw there, he would be able to lead us to the settlement without encountering any deadly obstacles.

"Thank you, Della. You have done us a great service and have repaid any debt you may think you owed us. Truly, seeing your happiness and the life that follows you was always more than enough."

Della blushed at my words and nodded her head in thanks. "My power continues to grow, although slowly. Every day, the strength of the stone increases, and a larger part of the plague recedes. I pray that one day the curse will be lifted forever, but that will be many, many years from now."

Della's countenance then went from one of contentedness to a more serious one. "Be wary of the Jalusi, Alex. They have survived in the harshness of the desert for hundreds of years by being ruthless, both to the creatures that inhabit the sands and the people they meet along the way. They may not want to part with the information you desire." She handed over the note she had promised.

"I guess we will just have to be extra nice then."

"You could start by not shooting them with an arrow when first you meet, like you did me," she said while smiling and pushing us out of her home.

———

The trip to the outskirts of the swamp and the edges of the desert would have gone much faster if we could have had Della accompany us along the way. The effect of the Vivre Stone not only beat back the plague, but it also turned all the animals in its range into non-aggressive fauna. As it was, we had to undertake a few fights and avoid even more.

Still, with an hour to go before we logged off, we arrived at the settlement that Della had told us about. It was a small village with high walls. The guards on duty outside the village were far more attentive than even the ones that we had encountered near Port Town or Kich's Keep. Long before we saw them, they were already aware of us, and their weapons were at the ready.

We had kept our blades and bows stowed and approached with our hands out to our sides. The guards didn't put their weapons down, though, and they called for us to halt when we were fifty meters from the front gate.

"State your business."

"We are adventures heading into the desert. We have a note from Della of the Glade vouching for us," I said.

The guards looked at each other and then said, "Send over the tiny one with the note."

I could hear Wayne giggle under his helmet and I had to stifle my own smile. "I think they mean you, Dan."

"I'll show them tiny," Dan said, with a bit of anger in his voice.

"I knew that's what you called it! You owe me a gold, Naugha."

"Shit," Dan said, and kicked the ground. "Walked right into that one."

I laughed and passed the note to Dan. He went forward, keeping his bow on his back, and passed the note to the guards.

Wayne's body had tensed as soon as Dan was past us. If a fight started, Wayne would rush those guards without a thought. They were blue to us, so it was a winnable fight, but Dan may not survive if they decided to land some cheap shots.

We needn't have worried, though, as the guards called us forward after looking over the note. When we approached, one of the guards ran through the gate and inside the village.

"We are summoning the council. We've not had adventurers through here, so you must understand our hesitancy," the other guard said.

We nodded and joined Dan just outside the village as the council was gathered. Wayne had relaxed some, but only a small bit. He still remembered the welcome we received at the last village we visited.

The council was made up of two women and a man, with the older of the two women leading the way. She spoke for all three.

"Welcome to Sand's Edge. We've not seen your type before in these parts. What is your reason for coming here?"

I decided to play it slow and started with a general explanation. "Our adventures have taken us to this desert, and we wish to venture forth into the Globi Desert. We fear, however, that our preparations may be lacking, and we seek your guidance and an opportunity to trade."

"Trade is something we can certainly do," the old women said. "Information and supplies, if your goods are right. Please, come to our hall."

We followed the council through the gate and saw that the village had turned out for our arrival. Given the lack of visitors they received, this wasn't a surprise. The hall she mentioned was a building located near the center of the village. The council entered, along with some guards, and some merchants, but the rest of the town stayed outside.

Everyone spread out around the inside of the building, with our group being led to where the three council members were seated. The building wasn't overly large, and everyone could easily hear each other and talk without having to raise their voices. I took the time to get a good look at the citizens of Sand's Edge.

The council wore long robes, with the hoods down. They were a light brown that would have blended in with the desert outside. Contrasting the plainness of the robes, each were adorned with several trappings that I presumed symbolized their rank. The older woman wore a very elaborate necklace that included pieces of what looked like obsidian, maybe agate, and several pieces of gold. The other two also wore necklaces of similar design, but the rocks and gold pieces were much smaller. They also had elaborate woven belts that cinched their robes around their bodies.

The merchants also wore robes, although theirs seemed to be of a better quality and didn't have hoods, nor did they sport the necklaces that the council members had. The merchants also wore belts, but where the council had very elaborate patterns in the weave of theirs, the merchants had more simple affairs. The difference was that each merchant had various items hanging from their belts that I was unable to discern from our seated position. The guards wore armor, a mixture of leather and chain.

The council leader had been watching me as I took in the room and nodded her head at me when I returned my attention to her. "We would hear of your adventures, if you don't mind. We get little information this far from the larger settlements."

I smiled and nodded my head, "I am happy to share our tales." At that, I began to tell the assembled group of the current struggle between the King and the Children of Loust. I kept out our specific parts but spoke as if we were a part of the ordeal. I glossed over much, but I went into a bit more detail as I narrated the tale of House Frost, their betrayal, and their ultimate downfall. It's possible I was embellishing a bit there, since we weren't actually involved or had heard an update about how the fight went. I wasn't surprised to see them pay particular attention to the House Frost tale; everyone loves a good story of intrigue.

"Why do you now come here and not continue with your king?" the council woman asked.

"Wars take time. It's impossible to know just when the next battle will begin. Mostly, though, we aren't soldiers. We are adventurers, and we are always looking for something new to discover. As you've said, we are the first of our kind you have seen. I do not doubt you will see more as time goes on, but for now, we wish to be the first to experience the desert."

"It is not a forgiving land, young man. This first piece of information I will share with you freely. You are not prepared for what lies ahead," she said, pointing at our clothing. "You have two who wear heavy steel, a burden that will arrest your progress from the first step. Your armor and that of TheClaw are far more suitable, but they, too, will dry out quickly in the sands. I can offer a tincture that will protect your leathers, but I have nothing for the metal." She then turned to the assembled merchants. "What have you?"

They looked amongst each other, and finally one stood up to speak. I saw that he had bits of chain hanging from his belt. "We have a solution that can be rubbed over the metal. It will protect your goods from rust and the damage of the desert. I must say, though, that we've only used it on the chain of our fighters, and I don't know how it will work on your plate."

"Thank you," I said. I then asked, "Do the pieces on your belt symbolize the materials you specialize in selling?"

"Very good eye, sir. That is exactly what they symbolize." He motioned for the other three merchants to stand. One had herbs and flowers hanging from his belt, another woman had the feet of small birds, and the last had two knives hanging from her belt.

"As you can see, I focus on armor, and the others are our head merchants in herbalism, husbandry, and weapons."

"In regard to travel, how would horses fare in the desert?" I asked.

"If you had them, they would be able to maneuver through the land, with proper training. However, we don't have any to sell," said the woman whose specialty was husbandry.

"We have magical horses. I believe they could be suitable, as they come with innate abilities to navigate the land, so I believe. They haven't encountered a terrain they couldn't overcome yet."

The council woman lifted an eyebrow and asked, "Magical horses? You can summon them?"

"Yes, but not in here," I finished, laughing.

The rest chuckled as well.

"No. I would not want you to do that! But I can see how you could earn the favor of Della if you are powerful enough to have a collection of magical steeds."

I decided to take a chance and gambled on what information I should offer.

"Our favor comes from the Vivre Stone that Della wears around her neck. We traded it to her in exchange for her aid."

This stopped any further conversation in the hall, and the villagers looked at each other. One of the other councilwomen leaned in to say something before the leader put a hand up to stop her. The first woman looked upset but sat back in her position.

"Securing that stone could not have been an easy task," she said.

"You can say that again," Dan chimed in. "I still have nightmares of those rats."

The boss of the monastery had sent an army of dead rats to gnaw away at Dan's lower half. Compounded with Dan's phobia of rats, and it was a true horror show for him.

The council woman scrunched up her weather-beaten wrinkled face and exclaimed, "I hate rats!"

Dan leaned toward me and said, "I like her!"

Since Dan only has one volume, loud, everyone heard him. It got more laughter in the hall.

I smiled at Dan's good timing and continued. "It was difficult, but worth the effort. We were able to rid this land of a vile beast loyal to the villain Loust *and* help our friend Della. Her happiness was almost enough of a reward for the effort."

One of the merchants chuckled and said, "I like how he said, 'almost enough of a reward.' Watch this one."

There was more laughter, and the mood in the hall turned jovial. We were in a good spot.

"So, you have the means to travel the desert, and we can certainly help to keep your equipment in the best condition possible. You will need to consume water at a faster rate, but we can assist there if you have not brought enough. What else could you need from us? Certainly not our aid in a fight, as someone who could conquer a foe outside the skill of Della would definitely be above us."

"We wish to find the Jalusi Tribe."

The laughter, unfortunately, left the room. The mention of the Jalusi had brought a sober mood quite quickly. I hoped I hadn't over played our hand too soon.

"What would you want with the nomads?"

"We've learned that they have traveled these deserts for longer than anyone can remember them not being here. Like now, we search for the knowledge they may possess about the secrets of the Globi," I said.

"Della would certainly know of the Jalusi, although I don't know why she would point you to them. They are not a hospitable type."

I didn't say that our information about the Jalusi did not come from Della, as I was happy to let them believe that variation of the story.

"And yet... they are traders, yes? Perhaps we could trade with them as well."

The councilwoman nodded her head, but then shook it slightly. "They are traders and have traded with Sand's Edge for generations, but a tale of treachery and laughter will not move them as it has us. I'm afraid you will need to have far more than that."

We still had the rings and robe from House Frost, and I was thinking we could trade those. I wanted to try trading money before anything else, though. First, I needed the help of the people of Sand's Edge.

"I've noticed you haven't said 'no,'" I said with a smile. "Is there anything we can do, perhaps, to earn your assistance?"

The old woman leaned back and smiled at us and then to the other councilwoman sitting next to her. That was the moment I realized that the older, craftier woman had just maneuvered us into offering aid instead of them asking for it. Her smile was one of triumph, and the younger councilmember had an easily recognizable look of respect on her face.

She then leaned forward and said, "As it turns out, Alex. We do."

"A bloody gathering quest. I can't believe it!" Dan said from on top of his mount. We were out in the desert, beyond the walls of Sand's Edge, sitting astride our horses. The older woman had kept her word, and we were outfitted with the tincture and solution that protected our armor. She also provided ample water.

The summoning of our horses was another thing the townsfolk had come out for. Everyone in the town wanted to touch at least one of the animals before they would let us leave. They stood atop the walls to watch us leave, waving as we went.

It wasn't but a few minutes after I made our offer that the councilwoman offered us a trade. We were to gather twenty of the stones she wore around her neck, the ones that looked like obsidian but were called "desert glass" here. The only catch, as we learned, was that the rocks came from just one place—the belly of giant Bore Worms. As their name implied, they lived beneath the deserts and likely bored through the ground, producing the desert glass as a byproduct.

Dan asked the obvious question before we left: "Do they poop them out?"

Of course, Dan asked in the center of the village, which led to unending laughter from the populace. Even the children were on the floor laughing.

"I'll take that as a no, then."

"We haven't laughed this often in a long time, Alex. Thank you for that," the councilman said.

The younger councilwoman was laughing, too, but she at least answered the question. "No, they do not! We think they use them to make it easier to eat whatever they find in the desert. Only from their bellies can you find them."

"So, we just find a few worms and open them up. Easy enough."

"Just avoid the teeth, which are many. They could devour a small person. It also doesn't help that they can grow to be almost as large as one of your magical horses. And, of course, they usually travel in packs."

"Right," Dan said. "So, not easy at all."

We received the golden glow of a quest and were informed that we would finish when we had collected twenty desert glass.

It wasn't long before we had crested one of the large dunes in the desert and were out of sight of the village. Ten minutes of traveling in the direction the townsfolk had indicated, we got to see our first Bore Worm.

It popped out of the desert just in front of our horses, and we quickly unsummoned the beasts. From ground level, we were eye to eye with the mob—or in this case, eye to teeth.

When it came to fighting mobs, our group was well practiced, and we fell into our usual formation. Wayne stepped up to the worm and led with a strike of his war hammer before executing a Kick. I hadn't been in my Blacksuit, so I was only able to do a normal backstab from behind the creature, my usual location. Dan had set up to the side of Wayne and was firing arrows from a distance. Jason, as our Cleric, stood several paces behind Wayne and was ready to heal as necessary. This was familiar ground.

The beast was blue to us, and it looked like its hide offered a level of natural armor. Our weapons were strong though, and the amount of armor only negated a small portion of our potential damage. Wayne needed one heal during the fight, but that was a pittance to the amount of mana Jason had at his disposal. With a final arrow from Dan, the Bore Worm died. I quickly looted the creature and found one piece of desert glass.

Over the last week and a half, we had spent so much time sneaking around and avoiding fights, that it was nice to think we would only have a simple grind to complete this quest. We chose to stay on foot for now, traveling along the sand a short distance and hoping we could aggro other worms. We quickly learned that the desert had its own limitations.

"I'm moving at half speed, at best," Wayne said.

"Me, too," I said.

"Let me look at my character," Jason said. "I'm moving even slower than that."

After a few moments, Jason confirmed what he thought.

"My movement speed has been reduced to only 20 percent of its original."

"That's weird, mine is perfectly fine," Dan said.

"Then it has to be based on Agility," Jason said. "Dan has the highest in that stat and mine is definitely the lowest. There's no way we can do this without the horses."

That was going to put quite a damper on things, at least for me. If I had to keep summoning my horse, I wasn't going to be able to use my Blacksuit at all. That meant I wasn't going to get any bonuses for my first backstab. But, more importantly, it meant I wasn't going to be able to do any scouting at all.

Seeing as we couldn't move effectively with Jason's movement speed almost completely wiped out, we summoned our horses again and continued our journey into the desert.

Over the course of the next hour, we encountered another five worms, dispatching them in the same efficient manner as before. Four of the five had the desert glass, which brought our total up to five. We had traveled throughout most of the day, had dealt with Della and the citizens of Sand's Edge, and were a quarter of the way through this quest. I saw it as a good time to call it a night and begin again in the morning.

I didn't receive any argument from the guys, and we made our way back to the settlement. We hoped to spend the next day completing the quest for the people of Sand's Edge and start our journey to the Jalusi Tribe. I knew if we got lucky, by the end of the next day we could be on our way to the Monastery of the Swift.

The guards of Sand's Edge welcomed us and offered refuge for the night. Once we banished our horses, we agreed to meet at ten in the morning the next day and logged out.

FBI Headquarters

The General had shown up to the meeting with Director Grissten ready to share some good news. It was quite obvious, however, that the Director was not in a good mood. Deciding to wait instead of leading the conversation, the General sat until the Director spoke.

"Keeping information from me does no one any good, General," Director Grissten said with more than a little ice in her tone.

The General was aware he had been keeping lots of things from the Director but wasn't going to take the bait that easily. He continued to wait.

Finally, Director Grissten said, "Why in the hell did you keep it from me that Robert Shoal was working for you?"

Now that the General knew the issue, he felt more poised to engage. "He didn't work for me. He applied for a position with me. He didn't get it."

"And you didn't think that was relevant?"

"No, Melanie, I did not."

"Don't you 'Melanie' me! You kept valuable information from me, information that I could have given my team," she almost yelled. "Now, what haven't you told me?"

"Honestly, Director, very little. I told you initially to look at Shoal and that I didn't want to bias your judgement. Did you find something?"

"Yes, dammit. The guy was murdered!"

"Wait, you have proof of that?" the General said, leaning forward.

Director Grissten calmed down a bit, and said, "No. We don't. But it sure does look like it. And this whole time I've had my people scouring the internet looking at banal information when they could have been investigating a murder!" she finished raising her voice again.

The General held his hands up to try and calm the Director. If the FBI had proof that AltCon had murdered Robert Shoal, he would have pulled all his people off this project and let the Bureau action its warrant. He wouldn't risk his people if he didn't have to.

"But you could make a case, Director? I'll leave this entirely in your lane if you can prove Robert Shoal was killed by AltCon."

Again, the Director had to calm down. She had reviewed the Shoal case herself, and there weren't any new angles to take. Robert Shoal had purchased a bottle of alcohol at a liquor store near where he died and did so with a credit card. The clerk couldn't remember anything about the purchase, and there weren't any cameras anywhere near the establishment or inside the store. Nor was there any footage from when Shoal made the purchase and his untimely end with his car wrapped around that tree.

"No. We can't make a case, and we don't even have grounds to reopen the investigation," she said. "But my people are losing their confidence, and they're at the end of their rope. I don't know what more they can do."

"That's why I'm here, Director. I've got a lead."

Director Grissten went from angry to interested in a moment. "It better be good."

"It's damn good," the General said. He removed a folder from his folio. "About three years ago, the Department of Defense began designing a next-generation fiber optic line. As you know, it's often information and the ability to get it quickly that wins wars. This was going to be a huge boon to the military.

"Eventually, like all things developed by the military, it would be released to the world and would drastically enrich the lives of the everyday citizen. I don't know if you know this, but it was the Military Industrial Complex that first invented Velcro. We used it for years before sharing it with the rest of humanity. That invention had a huge impact."

The Director had to smile. "Yes, General. You've told me that same story on several occasions. I'm well aware of it."

"And I'm damn proud of what our military has done to better our fellow man. But I'm getting off topic." He opened the folder, passing it over to Grissten. "The project faltered when the lead engineer left after his one-year contract was finished. The remaining engineers were unable to complete the project. However, all of them signed non-disclosure agreements and statements that their work remained the property of the US Government."

The Director was looking at the contents and saw numerous diagrams and blueprints for what looked like a tube, with the interior in a DNA-type double helix. She didn't understand it and told the General as such.

"Honestly, neither do I. It's far more complex than I can get my old brain around. What I do know, though, is that the lead engineer, Dr. Travis Weiss, had made his pitch around the hypothesis that if the photons of light that carried the information were twisted, as opposed to bouncing off the walls of the line, the speed of information could be 'near the speed of light.' And here is where it gets interesting.

"I don't have any information to suggest that the same engineer is now working for AltCon; I don't have access to that kind of information. But I can tell you that AltCon has designed a fiber optic line that matches this description exactly."

"Oh, that's good," the Director said, looking at the diagram in front of her again. After a brief pause she said, "I can work with this. We've got theft of intellectual property here. Or maybe even corporate espionage. Lots of angles. Yeah, I can definitely work with this."

She closed the folder and started to hand it back to the General, but he held his hand up. "Give that to your Special Agents and explain to them what it means."

The military wasn't one for giving up their secrets and Grissten hesitated. "Are you certain? This won't bite you in the ass?"

"Make sure the agents know it can't go past you and them, and I'm fine with it."

"There is one other member of the team, but I can guarantee his secrecy," she said, meaning Grimes.

"Agreed, but no more," the General said and stood up. "I'm not sorry I didn't tell you about Shoal. I wanted you to come to that conclusion, but I didn't want to cloud your thoughts. I am sorry, however, that your agents have felt unproductive. This could be the break we need, Director, and it's your team that will give it to us."

She held the folder up, smiled, and said, "We're back to Melanie. But just barely."

With that, the General left the Director's office.

Several minutes later, Special Agents Bolden and Colvin entered the Director's office and took the two chairs in front of the Director's desk. Grissten had relayed word through her assistant that she wanted to see the two and to send them in as soon as they arrived. They had already been in the building, which was fortuitous.

"I've got something for you," she said.

"Please let it be good," Colvin said, skipping the practice of usually letting Bolden speak first, given her rank as lead agent.

Bolden ignored his breach of protocol as the Director continued. "Oh, it is. I need you to review this file in its entirety. It's highly technical, but get as familiar with it as you can. I don't need you to understand how the tech works, just what's here."

She then handed over the file to Bolden, who opened it immediately and started reading. "Once you have become completely versed in the material, I need you to go to Grimes with the data. The folder, unfortunately, has to remain here; however, you can explain to Grimes what it contains.

"What you are looking at is the prototype of a next-gen fiber optic line designed by the Department of Defense. It never got off the ground, because the lead engineer left after his one-year contract expired. AltCon is now in possession of the exact same tech."

Bolden looked up from the report and raised her eyebrows. "No way. Didn't he sign NDAs to stop that from happening?"

"He most certainly did. Now, we don't have any proof or indication that this guy is working for AltCon, but that tech is so revolutionary that it could drastically change how data moves in the world. Almost as revolutionary as this new game that AltCon is making."

"I see where you are going with this, but without the ability to subpoena information, how can we work with this?" Colvin asked.

Bolden beat the Director to the punch and said, "Patents."

"Exactly what I was thinking, Annabelle. Start with this new Virtual Reality system that AltCon is designing. Patent applications are public material. Get Grimes to see what their patents look like, then start searching for fiber optics. If we get lucky, the language will be similar. Then Grimes can do his thing and scour the public record for a trail."

"If they stole this information from the military, ma'am, we could be looking at real warrants."

"Exactly, Nico. It's time we took the fight to them."

CHAPTER 17

The sun was already beating down on the square of Sand's Edge when I logged in. There was no recourse from the blazing heat, as Sand's Edge was removed from the swamp's canopy. I wouldn't want to have any of those branches hanging over my wall, either. Without the Vivre Stone, anything that came off those branches was likely to be deadly.

Dan, Jason, and Wayne were already logged in when I arrived, and we didn't waste any time getting our party together and heading for the town's gates. Once we had left the confines of the walls, we summoned our horses and started riding out again for the desert.

"I don't want to bring this up, but I feel like we should be prepared," Dan said once we cleared the first dune.

I nodded for Dan to continue, not ever being sure of what might come next with our Ranger.

"It's something one of the council said, that the worms travel in packs. So far they've all been singles."

I nodded my head again. I had thought about that as well. It wasn't that the levels of the worms were such that we couldn't handle multiples. No, the problem was that we couldn't move on the sand all that well. Except for Dan.

"Your high Agility may be our savior in that regard, Dan. You can still run around normally in the sand, so you should still be able to Snare and kite the mobs."

"And if the Snare doesn't land?"

"Then we have Wayne take two. If we get three, or more, we will probably die. So, at least, we have that going for us."

It would be a very long trip back to our bodies, too. Since we weren't a part of the Sand's Edge community, we couldn't change our respawn points to the town. That meant we were still bound to the square at Kich's Keep. As it was, the only other places we could use to change our respawn point were Port Town and the camp of the East Range Mountain Dwarf Clan, as we were kin to the dwarves.

Either of those would have been an even longer trek to here.

"You do realize, now that you've mentioned it, we're sure to get multiples."

Dan grimaced but defended himself admirably. "Still needed to be asked, Allibadattitude!"

I laughed but supported Dan. "If we get a single on the next one, Dan, feel free to try your Snare. If it doesn't land, at least we will know where we stand."

"Will do, Alex. Should have tried it out already, but we had a long day and I just didn't think of it."

We didn't have long to wait. After traveling over another dune, we had one of the Bore Worms pop out of the sand in front of us. We dismounted and immediately engaged. Our luck held, and it was only a single.

Once Wayne had fully established his aggro, Dan cast his Snare.

"Well, that sucks."

"Didn't land, Dan?"

"Nope. And it wasn't just a resist. Message says this creature is immune to this spell."

"Well then, things just got a whole lot more interesting."

We finished off the worm and collected our sixth piece of the Desert Glass. We mounted our horses again and went off searching for more of the worms, hoping our luck would hold out.

We had been searching in a general back and forth pattern from Sand's Edge. We would venture out away from the town and then travel parallel to the village, once we had traveled a good distance, we would go out a bit farther and repeat. This way, we didn't travel terribly far from the town in case we did need to make a run back to our bodies at some point, and still covered a significant amount of ground.

Unfortunately, that tactic seemed to have run its course, and for thirty minutes since killing the last mob, we hadn't encountered any more. We were going to have to travel deeper into the desert.

Turning our mounts away from Sand's Edge, we went deeper into the unhospitable desert.

It was about ten minutes later when we encountered our next mob. This one was still blue, but was called a Large Bore Worm, and it was slightly larger than the earlier version. It popped out of the desert like the rest and we went to work. We had the mob down to 75 percent when it did something new.

Instead of lunging at Wayne as it had previously, it rose out of the sand to its almost full height of seven feet and then screeched. We didn't receive any system messages telling us what the scream meant. It also didn't have any noticeable effect on us, and I thought it was just another part of the game. I realized that wasn't the case at all when we saw another worm come tunneling toward us at top speed.

It popped up right next to the first one and was about to attack me when Wayne hit it with a Bash and a Kick. That got its attention, and it turned from me to Wayne and started attacking our tank.

After several seconds, Wayne said, "Try another Snare on the add, Dan. I've got Taunt ready."

I saw Dan stop firing arrows and cast his Snare.

The second worm immediately turned like it was going to attack Dan but turned back on Wayne after only a moment.

Dan and Wayne spoke at the same time, saying, "Immune to Snare." And "Taunt landed."

It looked like our chances for running from a fight were about nil.

The worm had called for reinforcements at 75 percent, and I was all kinds of worried that it would do the same at 50 percent.

Two we could take. Three, I wasn't so sure about. Four was impossible. And if this mob called for aid at 75, 50, and 25 percent, that's exactly what we would get.

I didn't see that we had many options, and I kept stabbing into the tough hide of the Bore Worm. If we did get sent to our respawn, I would have lots of time to think about how we could do this differently. The trip back would take us hours.

At 50 percent, just like I feared, the Bore Worm rose up again. It opened its giant maw. But, before it could get its call out, I saw it hit with a powerful magic blast that knocked it back. It then smacked onto the surface of the sand, shaking the ground around us.

"Stun landed!" I heard Jason yell. The Stun had interrupted the Bore Worm's "spell."

We didn't hesitate and got right back into hacking, hitting, and shooting the mob.

It dropped below the 50 percent threshold and didn't pop back up to call for more reinforcements. Instead, it went back to fighting in its normal style.

At 25 percent, it followed the same path and rose, and Jason didn't need to be told what to do. The Stun landed, and it flopped back to the ground. Jason's mana was in safe territory, and I wasn't worried about the second mob, which Wayne continued to control with his Bash and Kick.

Once the first one was dead, Wayne turned on the second mob and got to work. The call for reinforcements gave me a great idea.

"How would you guys like to really speed this quest up?"

"Why do I get the feeling this could go horribly wrong?" Jason asked.

"Because it's Alex's idea!"

"Thanks for the confidence, Wayne!"

"I believe in you, Alex," Dan said.

"That's not helping his case at all, Dan!" Jason said, laughing. He then said, "Ok, let's hear it."

"Stun this one at 75 and 50 percent, but let him make his call at 25 percent. That way we get our next mob without having to go search for it. Then we just repeat until we are done!"

"And what if the 25 percent call brings more than one mob?" Wayne asked.

Shit. I hadn't thought of that. "Well, then Jason would be right, and this goes horribly wrong. But if only one comes, it would make it so Jason can keep a high mana count in case something goes bad."

"Let's try this one at 50 percent. If two come, then we know we have to let it call at 75 percent and stop the other two. Otherwise, I like the plan!" Wayne said.

I thought about that. But wasn't sure if we could take three and said as much.

"I've got the mana to do that one time," Jason said.

"It'll take a lot longer, but I can control all three," Wayne added.

I knew the guys wouldn't overstate their abilities in a situation like this. If they said they could do it, then I had faith in them. I was all in. "Let's do it!"

Jason landed his Stun at 75 percent but let the worm make his call at 50 percent. Luck was on our side and we only saw one more worm come racing toward us through the desert. It popped out of the ground and Wayne immediately gained aggro.

"Score!" Jason yelled.

It was agreed that the next one we would let get its scream out at 25 percent and again held our breath. Favor continued to shine on us, and the third mob we were fighting again only called one more worm.

For the next hour, we grinded out in that same location. At 25 percent, the Large Bore Worm would make its call, and we would have our next mob. Each of the worms had a piece of desert glass, and we were finished after only 14 more mobs total. That was a long time to continuously be fighting, and we were ecstatic when we collected the last piece of glass.

With the last mob dead, and one extra piece of desert glass in our inventory, we summoned our horses and rode back to Sand's Edge.

"But, how?" The young councilwoman asked as she looked at the assorted pieces of desert glass sitting on the table in front of her.

That seemed like an odd question.

"What do you mean, how? Didn't you think we would accomplish the quest? I mean, I figured that's why you gave it to us."

"Finish? Maybe! But we figured if you could do it, the task would take you a week or more. It's almost impossible to catch one of those Bore Worms alone, and I can't believe even you could take the mass of worms that come as you hurt them!"

"Our tactics were sound. The worms were challenging, but we were able to handle them. Now, may we speak about your end of the bargain?"

The councilwoman continued to stare at the Desert Glass for several moments before she focused back on us. "I didn't fully believe your boast that you had delivered the Vivre Stone to Della, but I see that I was wrong. I will get our leader," she said, making her way to the exit of the hall. She looked back briefly before leaving and smiled. "We should have asked for more!"

Several minutes later, the older of the councilwomen arrived and looked at the Desert Glass strewn across the tabletop. "Impressive," she said. "I didn't fully believe it and thought maybe this was some trick, but this is undoubtedly desert glass. You have fulfilled your end of our deal."

With that, we received the golden glow that symbolized we had finished the quest.

"I agreed to help you find the Jalusi Tribe, but that task is not mine. Come with me."

We followed her outside the hall and walked with her to one of the smaller huts. She opened the curtain that hung over the door and motioned us inside. Once we cleared the threshold, we saw a man sitting in a chair. He was human, but that was where the similarities to the residents of Sand's Edge ended.

For starters, he skin was much darker, almost black. His hair was long and coarse, looking almost like dreadlocks, and his face was covered in tattoos and scars. He was wearing a flowing robe, made of much finer material than the cloth the villagers wore. Only his arms showed, and these were covered in tattoos as well. Both of his ears were pierced in multiple places. A large scimitar sat near his feet.

"Allow me to introduce Chakib, formerly of the Jalusi tribe."

The man stood up and shook our hands. The many and rough calluses that adorned his palms were evident with the handshake, and his grip was extremely strong. "Be welcomed in my home," he said.

He motioned for me to sit and poured me tea. He also handed me a small piece of bread. He took a sip of his tea and took a small nibble from the bread. I had no idea what the proper protocol was here, so I mimicked his actions. Once I swallowed the bread and sipped the tea, Chakib smiled.

"Amongst my people, traditions are sacred. The sharing of bread and tea means you are under my protection and no harm may come upon you while you are in my dwelling. If I were the chief and offered the same, you would be protected by the entire tribe," he explained. "But be wary; the addition of salt would negate the gesture. Salt makes one thirsty, and in the desert, water is not something we can spare."

"Thank you for the lesson, Mr. Chakib," I said.

"Just Chakib, adventurer. And it would take more than a year to teach all the traditions that govern my people. Those traditions are one of the reasons I am no longer with the tribe."

I could tell there was a story coming, and I leaned into it, saying, "Why did you leave?"

"Leave? I guess that's what it looks like. I know the council woman said I was a 'former' member of the tribe, but there is truly no leaving. Once a member, always a member," he said. "In truth, I fled.

"The only way for my people to thrive is to grow the tribe. However, none come willingly to the Jalusi. We take them. Then there is a great tournament to determine who will take our prisoners for wives. We only take women. There are already too many men."

This was some messed up shit. I was going to comment, but Chakib wasn't finished.

"I fought like all my brothers, and I won. I was gifted the right to select my bride. I never questioned the ways of my people, and I was delighted to have the honor of furthering the tribe through my off-spring."

At that moment, the young councilwoman came into the hut. I thought she was there to watch and listen, but she walked up to Chakib and kissed him on his cheek. Then she sat next to him and held his scarred hand. It all came together.

"I see the understanding in your eyes, young adventurer. This," he said pointing to the woman, "was my salvation. It wasn't long before I was shown the error of my ways. My love for this woman transcended any tradition. In the dead of night, we fled. I would be killed on sight by any in my tribe."

I turned to the older councilwoman and asked, "If the Jalusi kidnap your people, then why do you trade with them?"

"We couldn't possibly defeat them, Alex. They number in the hundreds. So, we trade, and hope our trading is enough to subdue their greed. There is only one way to ensure they don't take our people. Desert Glass.

"They are forbidden from hunting the worms of the desert themselves. Another tradition. They can trade for it, however, and they are able to use it to form powerful artifacts that provide an immeasurable boon to them in the desert: the ability to conjure water. So long as we provide one piece of the glass, they vow to not raid near our home. To the Jalusi, their word is sacred."

"And how often do they come through here?" I asked.

"Once every six moons."

"Damn," I heard Dan say from behind me. "We just saved these people from ten years of raiding."

The council woman nodded and said, "More than that. We usually lose at least one or two of our people on every worm fight. We will have time to grow our village now without fear." She then rested her hand on her belly.

I caught the gesture and asked, "How long?"

She beamed. "Three months now."

We all gave our congratulations. The father, Chakib, was grinning at his wife. He then turned back to me and continued.

"Many would say that my tribe is barbaric, and I would have trouble arguing in their favor. But they are honorable and will keep their word should they give it. Just make certain to share tea and bread. And avoid the salt," he finished before pulling out a crude map of the desert. "Now let me show you where they should be on their travels through the sands."

"Wait," Dan said. "If you're a part of the tribe, shouldn't you be able to tell us where the monastery is located?"

"I'm afraid not. I was never a part of the trading parties that traveled to the Monastery of the Swift. Besides, it has been many years since our people traveled to that place. Our last trading venture was met with a devastating end. Our chief led the group to discover what happened and returned claiming the trade lost. There was never another word of the monastery or the party that disappeared."

"So, the chief knows where it is?" I asked.

"He does."

That was enough for me.

—⟨⟩—

The trip out required us to fight several more of the Large Bore Worms. With our tactics, we were able to stop them from calling for any more worms, and we could take each one down as a single mob. A couple of them ended up being equal level to us, which made for a longer fight, but the Stuns kept working and we never had to worry about more than one at a time. Additionally, each one rewarded us with a piece of Desert Glass.

Our saving grace, as I saw it, was that we didn't encounter any more mobs of a higher level than the Large Bore Worms. Those were a small challenge, and their ability to call reinforcements would have made them impossible without our Stuns. I worried, though, that a higher-level worm mob might resist the Stun, and then we would be looking at a minimum of at least one more high-level fight. Then that pattern would just keep repeating until we were messy patches in the sand.

The directions Chakib gave us weren't fantastic, as his crude map was as basic as they came. Still, he was able to give us a direction to travel, something we wouldn't have had without the escaped tribal member.

Several more worm fights later, we crested a dune like all the others. We had been traveling for over an hour and a half, and our water supply was taking a small hit. If we hadn't overloaded at Sand's Edge, we would have been in trouble quickly. With the extra supplies, we weren't in any immediate danger. That extra piece of Desert Glass we collected from the first worms paid for the supply of water, and I knew we were getting shafted on the deal but didn't complain.

It was good to know that single item would keep the town safe for another six months.

Additionally, our resupply of Desert Glass was going fine from our trip out here. It was to be my main leverage in our negotiations with the Jalusi.

As we crested the dune, we finally saw the camp of the Jalusi Tribe. It was huge. There were easily more than a hundred tents, set up in concentric circles that radiated out from an extremely large tent in the center. Undoubtedly, that was the chief's tent and our ultimate destination.

But first we would need to get into the camp. That meant getting past the two men riding toward us on horses from the camp. They didn't look to be wearing any armor, and they didn't have spears or shields. As they got closer, I could see that they carried scimitars similar to the one Chakib had resting near him back at Sand's Edge. They also had the same dark skin as Chakib.

We slowed our mounts as they approached and waited to greet them.

"Well met," said the one on my left. "You are very much not from around here," he ended with a smile that showed off two gold teeth. Like Chakib, his face and arms were covered with tattoos and scars, and his ears held more jewelry than Chakib's ears.

"That is a true statement, and well met," I answered. "We are adventurers from Yerkich's Keep. We have ventured to the Globi desert searching for new foes and new challenges. We have not been disappointed!"

The two looked at each other briefly and then the one on my right spoke, "It isn't many that could cross such a stretch of our domain and survive. You must be fierce warriors."

Wayne was about to answer, but I put my hand on his leg and shook my head. Every single thing said with the Jalusi had to be considered. I didn't know if claiming to be warriors would be stating our status as challengers to their tribe. Wayne stopped before uttering a word.

"We are nothing more than we have said. We are adventurers. In our travels, we have defended ourselves against the harsh desert, but our goal is to explore, not fight. We seek to continue our journey and possibly meet with your people. We like to trade as well as explore. Both offer the opportunity to learn."

"Well phrased, my friend," said the one on the right. "I am Mahmut of the Jalusi Tribe. This is my brother Kalil," he said, pointing to the other rider.

"I am Alex, and this is Allister, Naugha, and TheClaw," I said, pointing to each of my teammates. "Adventurers are not a part of a formal Tribe, but we are as close as family."

"Then be welcomed as a guest in our camp. If you have items to trade, I can assure you at least a pleasant experience, but I can't promise it will be completely profitable. Our merchants are the fiercest in the land!" Mahmut exclaimed.

He smiled at us and his brother when he made the claim, and the smile was infectious. I found myself smiling back along with my teammates.

We followed the two riders into their camp and made our way to a hitching post for the horses. Mahmut and Kalil dismounted and tied their animals to the wood. My team and I followed suit, but simply unsummoned our horses.

Like in Sand's Edge, our arrival had drawn a large crowd. And again, like in the small village, the people of the Jalusi camp exclaimed in shock when our horses simply disappeared. The two riders stared at us in shock. "What magic is this?"

"We have the ability to summon steeds to our sides."

"Try to say that five times fast," Dan said and then tried to accomplish the task. "Summon steeds to our sides. Summon steeds to our sides."

"That's good, Dan! Thanks," I said, stopping him.

"Sun sickness?" Mahmut asked pointing at Dan.

"Nah. Just regular sickness. Pay him no mind," Jason replied.

That got a laugh from the two Jalusi, and they started walking toward the center of the camp.

I gave Dan a withering look, and he held his hands up in defense of his actions. "What? It's hard! You give it a try!"

"Dan," I whispered, "we've got to be careful about everything we say here! Please, for the love of everything that revolves around Kaitlin, just keep it to yourself."

"Damn. Ok. Now I know you're serious."

I shook my head toward Jason and Wayne, and they simply shrugged their shoulders. Dan was always our wildcard.

The brothers continued their course directly toward the main tent, and we followed. We had a large group of people following us, all wide-eyed at our appearance. I was certain they didn't see people from outside of their tribe, or the people they traded with, very often. No one spoke to us, but some of the kids did run up and try to touch Wayne. He towered over everyone in the camp.

The brothers waited at the flap of the tent and then pulled it apart, gesturing us forward. This would have been the perfect time for an ambush, and I saw the guys tense a bit. I tried to show a look of calm, hoping to put them at ease. If the Jalusi wanted us dead, they had more than enough people here to do so without an ambush.

I went through first, and it only took my eyes a moment to adjust to the lower light within the tent. There were torches burning inside, which provided some light, but there were numerous corners of deep shadows where anyone could hide.

Sitting in the middle of the tent was the oldest human I had ever seen. His face was so covered in tattoos and scars that I could barely make out his features. On top of that, his face was a mass of wrinkles.

His arms looked emaciated and were covered in the same markings as his face. His hands, however, were covered in rings, and his ears carried more jewelry than anyone I had ever seen. Sitting to each side of him was a young woman. I assumed they were concubines.

We stopped before the man, and Mahmut walked over to his side. He leaned down and whispered in the man's ear. Then after a nod from the old man, Mahmut spoke.

"I welcome you in the name of the Jalusi. My father, Majid Jalusi, Chief of the Jalusi Tribes offers you respite."

I waited for Mahmut to continue, and when he didn't, I replied. "Thank you for your hospitality, Chief Majid Jalusi of the Jalusi Tribe. We accept your offer of respite."

Mahmut nodded his head and then moved before his father, placing a small table between the chief and us. From the side of the tent, a woman approached carrying a jar, a basket of bread, two glasses, and a small bowl.

Without saying a word, she set the tray down on the table and poured out tea into each of the glasses. She then stood, turned toward the chief, nodded once, and walked away.

The chief lifted his hand and pointed for Mahmut to move forward toward the table. Mahmut gave him a sideways glance that didn't look happy but approached the table all the same. I imagined, in this way, the chief could claim he had nothing to do with any treachery that was about to befall us, and Mahmut didn't look happy about it.

Thankfully, Chakib had prepared us for this very moment.

"Please, Alex. Share with me our nourishment. In the way of our people, sharing drink and food shows our acknowledgement of you as a guest amongst us."

I walked forward and kneeled before the table. Mahmut matched my movements. It was deathly quiet inside the tent.

I grasped the cup of tea but waited for Mahmut to make the next move. He saw my actions and continued, grabbing his own cup. He took a sip of the tea, and I matched his movement.

He then took the bread and tore off a small chunk. I grabbed mine and did the same.

Mahmut then said, "We find that a touch of salt brings out the flavor of the bread and cancels out the tea's bitterness. Please," he said, motioning toward the clay jar that held salt.

But his eyes were looking into mine, and if I hadn't already known what the salt meant, I might have been able to figure it out on that look. And his words that the salt "cancels out" the tea, solidified for me that he was trying to keep me from being betrayed. I just didn't know why.

"I find the tea to be savory. Salt would only spoil the flavor. I would take the bread without, if that is permissible?" I asked.

Mahmut's eyes shone, and he nodded for me to continue. "In the house of Jalusi, we would be remiss to not honor the request of our guest," he said and took a bite of his bread. Without any salt.

It was then that the chief spoke. I was surprised to find he had a deep baritone voice. I didn't think a man that looked so frail could produce so much power.

"You are now protected under the hand of the Jalusi. You may roam freely amongst my people for this day and the next. I would hear what brings you to our home."

I nodded my thanks to the chief and then Mahmut. I waited for Mahmut to get up from the floor, and I followed suit, standing next to my team.

"We are grateful for your hospitality. The word of the Jalusi is known far and wide, and we know no harm could befall us within your home. Thank you."

"You speak truly. The Jalusi are honorable," was all the chief said. I didn't respond that he had just tried to stab us in the back a moment ago, what with us still being in the middle of their encampment. And truly, he had only tried to do so within his own traditions. It was only our own knowledge that kept us from being the victims of that tradition.

Since he didn't look like he was going to speak any further, I continued. "Our journeys through this land have uncovered stories of mystery and wonder that are hidden by the sands of the Globi Desert. It is our quest, as adventurers, to uncover those mysteries and increase our status in this land," I was laying it on thick.

"The Globi Desert is vast, but I doubt you will find much in it. The Jalusi have traveled over every dune, and we have claimed every mystery there is to find."

Knowing how Resurgence worked, I doubted that very much, but I wasn't interested in the vast mysteries of the desert. I was interested in only one.

"Then I have to believe that you have the knowledge we seek, esteemed Chief Majid. Our exploration has uncovered a story of a lost monastery, home to a group focused on the advancement of their people. The location couldn't be found in any of the libraries we searched, and we came here hoping to find knowledge." This wasn't entirely untrue. We didn't find anything in the libraries we searched since we didn't search any.

"The monastery is no more," Chief Majid said.

"It was destroyed?" I asked.

"No. I did not say that. I said it was no more."

I thought about his words, and how I should phrase my next statement. It was obvious to me that the chief was particular about how we asked for his aid.

"By your words, I understand the place that housed the monastery still exists, but that those who once called it home are no more?"

The Chief gave me a long, hard stare. At least, I think that's what he was doing. With all those damn wrinkles, and the low light, I couldn't see his eyes. He could be sleeping for all I knew.

Finally, he spoke. "That's it, exactly, adventurer. It makes me think you aren't telling me everything you know."

I decided to gamble with a bit more information.

"It's not the first monastery to fall."

This got everyone's attention. All of the inhabitants of the great tent were now leaning forward and looking at us closely. Some looked between us and the chief, likely wondering what he would say next. They didn't have to wait long.

"And you have seen these others?"

"Other, Chief Majid," I corrected, not about to give away that we had been to two of the monasteries. "We have been to another monastery and saw the devastation wrought upon its people."

"And you survived?" He asked, with a sound of disbelief in his voice.

"No, Chief Majid," I answered. This led to confused looks on everyone, including the chief.

"No?"

"No. We didn't survive. We conquered," I said. "That monastery has been liberated from the evil within."

That did the trick. Now there was an audible amount of banter between everyone in the tent. Those assembled looked older, and they may have remembered the people they had lost to the monastery in the desert.

The chief leaned back and put a hand under his face, rubbing at his chin. He was in thought again.

"And you believe you could do the same here?"

"It is our intention to try. The worst that could happen is that we fail, and you are unburdened of us as guests. But I believe we will be successful, yes."

The chief then went on to relay the same story as Chakib had told us, but he added more detail about how there was only a single member of the tribe found that was sent to trade with the monastery. His body was found at the entrance of the building, and he had been ripped apart.

"It is our tradition to avenge those killed by the hands of others, and I would see this done!" he exclaimed with a surprising amount of force. But he wasn't done.

"It was in my time that those who died traveled to the monastery, and their lives are mine to avenge. It is uncommon for one such as the Chief of this Tribe to give this task on another, and the honor of such a gift would require tribute."

He wanted to trade.

My first offer of gold, and even platinum, were waved off. "We have no need for useless metals in the desert," he said.

I then produced the rings that I had taken from the head of House Frost and showed their properties to the Chief. Unfortunately, he was not moved.

266

"Powerful items, indeed. But we have none amongst us who could wield such items. Water is not a resource we have in abundance. Wasting it to use as a weapon would be looked down upon our people. Water is life."

Which left me with my trump card. I produced one of the pieces of desert glass.

This led to a few "oohs" from the crowd, which led to the chief scowling at those people. They had given away their hand.

"Yes, that is a bounty in our land, but a single piece of desert glass would not bring a sufficient tribute. It would take ten pieces to equal what you are asking."

This produced a few more gasps. I knew how valuable the glass was, since a single piece would grant the people of Sand's Edge an entire half year of freedom. The chief's smile was evident, even between all the wrinkles. He was pleased with his people's reaction this time. He must have figured it was an amount that couldn't be achieved, much like the people of the village.

I dumped the remaining nine pieces from my inventory, with two left over in my inventory.

The gasps this time weren't in the chief's favor.

"So, where's that monastery?"

CHAPTER 18

It didn't take long for us to get the details on the monastery and the location of the building. The chief had a map of the desert that looked large enough to encompass the entire thing. However, Chief Majid wasn't as giving with his information as Della had been, and he only showed us the route from the current location of the camp to the Monastery of the Swift. That route updated on our maps.

The chief said there would be other Bore Worms that patrolled the area but that there weren't any other mobs that we would encounter. Since it was his ass on the line by giving us this chance to enact his revenge, he was free with that information. If we failed, it would cost him some of his reputation amongst his people. Unfortunately, it wasn't accompanied by a secondary quest.

Once we had all the information we were going to get from the chief, we left the central tent. We made our way back toward the outskirts of the encampment, heading in a line for where our journey would begin. Mahmut and Kalil joined us for the walk. There were no other members of the tribe that came with us.

At the edge of their camp, I turned to the brothers and thanked them for their hospitality.

"The honor and hospitality of the Jalusi are known, and we were pleased to see those tales spoke true. We will do our part to rid the monastery of the blight that killed your tribesmen."

Mahmut bowed his head in acknowledgement. Then, rather conspiratorially, he looked around from our group, to his brother, and then the area around us. Apparently satisfied with what he saw, or didn't see, Mahmut turned back to us.

"I must know, Alex. Did you know about the salt, or did my warning help?"

I was now on my guard. Chakib had told us that his tribe would not forgive him for his betrayal, and I was not about to give away his existence. However, before I could answer, Mahmut continued.

"I swear on the honor of my people: no harm will come to you or any other for the information you know. Not now, while you are guests of this camp, or any time after."

I looked at my team, but they had nothing to offer. They shrugged their shoulders and left the decision up to me. Once again, I chose my words carefully.

"There are numerous ways for one to gain knowledge in this world, Mahmut. It can come from the stories passed from father to son, from the tomes filling our libraries, or from the blessings of individuals. The knowledge of the salt was known to us," I said, then followed with, "but your warning was noted and appreciated. I am curious. Why did you do so?"

Mahmut ignored my question at first and looked over at Kalil and smiled, saying, "Perhaps our brother yet lives."

This threw me off, and I asked, "Your brother?"

Mahmut's smile faded as he turned back to me and looked to be in thought for a moment. He then said, "Our eldest brother, Chakib, was lost to the tribe when he fled our camp with his wife. He had wanted to end her bondage, but our father would hear nothing of it. He believed that if one woman was freed, more would follow, and it would destroy our traditions.

"It is a tradition I have abhorred for most of my life."

"You don't want your own wife?"

"Of course, I do." The smile returned. "But I would have her choose me freely. And there are many I think I could have courted. But in our tribe, one is granted a wife only through battle."

"And how does one become chief? Is that also through battle?"

Both Mahmut and Kalil laughed at that. "No, Alex," Kalil said. "Only he who could make the tribe prosper is given that right."

"What about a she?" Asked Dan.

"I do not understand," Kalil said.

"What if a woman could make the tribe prosperous? Would she then get the right to be chief?"

Kalil and Mahmut looked at Dan like he had three heads. So, the brothers were a bit progressive but not quite there yet.

Still, I had an idea.

"How is it decided if the tribe is prosperous?" I asked.

"There is a ceremony every year, and those who wish to challenge for the head of the Jalusi must show what they have brought to our people. My father may look frail, but his ability to barter for our people is second to none. Besides, those we trade with will only deal with our father. And I'm afraid that the ten pieces of desert glass we have been granted from you and your friends will solidify my father's place again this year."

"And who decides what counts as prosperous?" Jason asked.

"The elders of the tribe. The men you saw inside my father's tent."

"And you would take the place of your father?" I asked.

"That would have been Chakib, before he left. But now, I am the eldest and the most likely to succeed."

Yup, I definitely had an idea.

"I hope your brother one day returns to you and your tribe, Mahmut."

"Thank you, Alex. May the sun ever shine on you and yours."

After we spoke with Mahmut, we summoned our horses and rode out toward the monastery.

We didn't speak for several minutes as we crested several dunes and kept our eyes open for any potential mobs. We still hadn't seen what triggered one of the worms, so we knew it would pop up on us in a single moment.

Finally, after several more dunes, Wayne spoke up. "I didn't really like them."

I knew what he meant. I wasn't too fond of the tribe we had just left either and said so. "Pretty backward if you ask me. But I did find the part about Chakib to be interesting."

The others nodded at that. Jason said, "It's too bad we can't get him placed as the head of the tribe. I bet they would be more progressive in no time. Mostly because I think his wife would make him."

We were laughing at that when our moment of levity was disrupted by one of the Large Bore Worms popping out of the sand and advancing on our group.

With the laughter done, we jumped off our horses and engaged the beast. With our strategy firmly in place, we defeated the worm without any adds. We got another piece of desert glass for our trouble.

We encountered another ten of the Large Bore Worms, with only one instance that we had to deal with two at a time. Jason's Stun spell failed as he was casting it, and the worm was able to get his scream off. With Jason's level of spells, he rarely ever failed an attempt to cast, but it could still happen. It was probably tied somehow to Chance, and Jason only had a base Chance of 1. He did have several modifiers, though, which is probably why I could never remember him failing before.

Jason confirmed my thoughts and said that it happened but was so rare that he never commented on it before.

Our journey continued, and it wasn't long before we could see the monastery in the distance. It rose from out of the desert as a triangular shape. It didn't take us much longer to realize it was a pyramid of sorts.

Unlike the pyramids of ancient Egypt, though, this one didn't end in a point. It looked more like those the ancient Mayan built, having a flat top.

It also became quite evident after several more minutes that the structure we saw was still far in the distance. What we were seeing must have been huge.

We encountered one more of the Large Bore Worms before we reached the edge of the pyramid, and we dispatched that one as easily as the others. The loot was the same as before, and I pocketed yet another piece of the desert glass.

Once we had passed by the worm's corpse, our path was clear to the pyramid's base. We could see, as we rode up, that the outside of the building had once housed a small settlement of sorts. There were areas that looked to be dwellings, and another that looked to be a market-place.

All of it was in rubble. Clearly, there had been a battle here and everything had been destroyed. There was also no sign of any bodies. The entire area was just a big, open ruin. It looked foreboding but not as desolate as the wide-opening maw that represented the entrance of the monastery. There was no gate to be seen. We couldn't see beyond the threshold, and the darkness within seemed to suck the light from the bright sun beating down around us.

"Well, it doesn't take a rocket scientist to know where we gotta go next. I'll scout the interior and tell you what I find."

"Bro, rocket science is so overrated! How hard is it to say that if you make big explosions and direct them outward that the thing in front of the explosion will go really fast?" Dan asked.

"You think that's all there is?"

"Of course not, Allirocketscientist. You also gotta point it up!"

I couldn't help but laugh as I moved past the entrance of the pyramid and walked down a long hallway. It went on for quite a distance and would have been completely black if not for the small bit of light coming in from the entrance and my inherent ability to see better in the dark. I couldn't see in complete blackness, and I was thankful for the small bit of light. After a couple more minutes, I started seeing another bit of light coming from the other side of the tunnel. I made my way for that light.

I kept a keen eye out for any side passages or doors, but the hallway was just a singular passage from the outside to the interior. This would have been a good place to set up defenses against an invading force, blocking the progress of the invaders and making a long choke point.

I finally reached the light on the other side of the tunnel, and it illuminated an open area. The room I entered stretched up for several stories and was completely empty of enemies or furniture. On the far side of the room, maybe one hundred meters away, were two staircases that rose to another level of the pyramid and met at another open archway. This one, like the doorway outside, was filled with darkness and I couldn't see anything past the opening.

The room was about fifty meters wide, and I walked its entirety. My investigation yielded one small discovery: there were several torches that lined the sides of the walls, and they were all extinguished. If we could light them, we would have a lot more light by which to explore.

The small bit of light that I had noticed from within the hallway came from a hole in the ceiling many, many floors above. The sunlight penetrated through that hole and provided the scant amount of illumination that I had now. The lack of sunlight wouldn't be a problem in this room, what with Dan and Jason being Elves and Wayne possessing his necklace that allowed to him to see in the dark.

With my inspection complete, I returned to the group and told them what I had found. As a group, we reentered the pyramid and made our way to the central room. I figured we had to be in the right place, and my assumptions were proven correct when the last of my group finally stood in the center of the monastery.

From all around us, we heard a voice that said, "What do we have here? Another sacrifice for the Master? It has been too long since we have had a worthy challenge. I hope you last longer than the last!"

With that, we received a new message prompt.

Restoration of House Lancaster IV: Cleanse the Monastery of the Swift

Immediately, all the torches surrounding us flared to life, and we could suddenly see.

"Come in, my sacrifices. Feed our Master!"

"Why do they always have to be so damn creepy? Why can't they just say that it's time to fight? But nope, always got to go to feeding or some other nasty crap!" Jason said.

I had to nod at our Cleric. Our boss fights in the monasteries have had far too much creepiness associated with them. This one probably wasn't going to be much different.

It didn't look like we had any options outside of the stairs and the next dark portal. We had already been logged on for four hours, and we could play for another four with no concerns. However, I doubted we would finish that quickly. So, we either had to finish in less than eight hours, the amount of time we could play before having to take a break, or we needed to find a place to camp. I was all for trying to run this thing for as long as we could.

We walked through the large room and ascended the stairs to the second level. We were entirely on our guard from the first steps we took. In cases like this, I often wished the enemy would just present itself and fight. If my teammates were anything like me, then our imaginations came up with all kinds of dastardly evil that waited around every corner.

The room and the stairs remained clear, and we crossed through the blackness of the door. But that lack of light didn't last long, and as soon as we entered the next room, the torches lining the interior flared to life again. It was a small, square room, maybe fifteen feet long and across. There was only one exit, other than the one we came through, and that was on the other side of the room, but we wouldn't be crossing to that door.

We were facing our foe.

Another of the Death Priests stood in front of us. The first one of these we faced in the Monastery of Calm was cloaked in a robe, with a hood that hung over his face. It was common garb for a casting class. The second one we faced, in the Monastery of Might, was a Death Mage, and he too wore robes, like most mages. This one, however, was quite different. This one looked like a fighter.

He wore what looked like light chain mail, although it looked to only cover about fifty percent of his body. His chest and shoulders were covered, as was his groin area. The area to the sides of his chest, and his arms, were left bare. He looked a bit emaciated, and his gray skin could be seen clearly. His legs were mostly bare as well, but he did have what looked like thick leather boots. His face was uncovered, and he was a sight to behold.

His eyes were sunken into his skull and they glowed green. His scalp was entirely devoid of hair, and his skin was stretched tight against his skull, pulling his face taught so we could see every bone jutting from his face. The gray of his skin was more pronounced on his head, illuminated by the glowing eyes. He was smiling, and his teeth were protruding from his mouth in sharp points.

He carried a blade in each hand, and they looked quite similar to the scimitars we noted when we were in the camp of the Jalusi tribe. These glowed with the same sickly green as his eyes. He also wore two daggers at his waist.

The Death Priest was Red to me and my team. And the ugly bastard was smiling.

"I hoped for more of a challenge," he said. "I wouldn't need but one of my weapons to defeat such a sad group. I'm afraid my fun will be all too short."

"It sure will be!" Wayne yelled and then launched himself toward the Death Priest.

I would have loved to have had my Blacksuit on before the fight, but I hadn't had time to do so before we entered the room, and now that Wayne had launched his attack, it wouldn't give me the bonuses for a backstab. I would just need to rely on regular DPS and no initial bonus damage.

Or, at least, I thought I would. That changed dramatically when Wayne's first hit landed. What should have been a direct hit, simply bounced off some kind of shield that covered the Death Priest. He laughed at us.

"Oh no, young one. You have not earned the right to fight me yet. I shall await your challenge, if you can make it that far!" he said and then simply walked out of the room. Dan tried to fire a few arrows at him, but they all bounced off the shield. In a matter of seconds, the Death Priest had left the room through the exit on the other side.

"Well that was anticlimactic," Jason said.

But before I could answer his comment, we saw our real fight. Through the same door that the Priest had left, three mobs appeared. They had the same gray skin and light green, glowing eyes as the Death Priest, but that was where the resemblance ended. These creatures were wearing full leather armor, and they moved with grace as they fanned out from the entrance. They looked almost human, despite the skin and eyes, with full heads of black hair and normal features to their faces. The tags above their heads read Moroi Fighter, and they were blue to us.

"Any idea what a 'Moroi' is, Dan?" I asked our encyclopedia of just about everything. But it wasn't Dan that answered.

"It's like a vampire, Alex. They feed on blood and 'life energy.' They're from Eastern Europe originally, or something like that. Fierce fighters," Jason said.

I looked over at our Cleric, questioningly.

He just shrugged his shoulders and said, "What? I have a thing for vampires. I got hooked on that old movie with Brad Pitt. He was hot."

I had no idea what he was talking about, but at least I now had an idea of what these guys were. They probably did some kind of "life tap" to take our blood. That meant it would take more of our mana to get through a fight if they kept healing themselves.

But vampires were undead, so we should have an advantage with Jason's Holy spells.

"Usual formation!" I yelled out. "Dan, try to Kite one around the edges. We don't have a lot of room in here, so be careful. Wayne, pick a guy and go. Jason, hold off on anything but heals until we have some decent aggro."

The guys didn't hesitate, and Wayne brought down his war hammer on one of the beasts. As soon as he hit, it turned on him and began swinging its blade at his midsection.

"Damn. It's dodging like crazy, and I'm not hitting for much. Bash and Kick are hitting for normal, though," our warrior said.

In the meantime, Dan's Snare had landed, and he was kiting one of the Moroi.

"Let Broham loose if you think you can use him in here. If it's too cramped, just wait until later."

"I'll hold off, Alex."

While I was saying all of this, I was trying to stab the Moroi in front of me. Unfortunately, his dodges were insane, even with me behind him.

"Fuck. He keeps hitting me with some kind of debuff and a life tap. And he's landing more and more strikes."

With me at his back, I wasn't getting any of the life taps or the debuffs, but my hits were landing less and less, and the Moroi's dodges became even more frequent. I had a bad feeling about this.

This was the Monastery of the Swift. And if these were remnants of the temple, like the previous two monasteries had been, then these guys were spawned from some kind of NPC that was a student of a "swift" discipline.

"I hate to say this, but check your character Wayne. Specifically, your Agility."

A second later I heard Wayne groan. "It's almost gone man. And I didn't have much to begin with. No wonder I'm not dodging."

"And that's why the mob is! It's not a debuff, he's stealing your 'energy.' In this case, that's your Agility." I yelled.

"We gotta burn him down, and quick," I yelled. "That means you're up, Allister!"

"Aww yeah!" Jason yelled and launched his Banish Undead spell. But, to my chagrin, the mob jumped to the side, and Jason's spell only landed partially. And there was no Stun.

Wayne was now getting lit up by both of the mobs that were attacking him. He could barely attack, as he kept getting hit over and over again.

This was just the first fight, and we weren't looking good. The mob Dan was kiting continued to chase him around the room, but that kept Dan's DPS entirely out of the fight, and my strikes just weren't landing the kind of damage they normally did.

"Try a Stun and then follow with a Banish Undead, Allister!"

I saw Jason cast and then curse. "Damnit! He resisted!"

My Force Multiplier would probably be enough to take these three guys down, but then I wouldn't have it for another twenty-four hours. I really didn't want to use it until it was time to face the boss, but if we couldn't beat these guys, there was no way we were getting to the Death Priest.

But before I had to make that decision Jason called out again, "I've got an idea, Alex, but if this doesn't work, I don't have any other plan."

"Do it, Allister, whatever it is!"

I saw Jason casting again and recognized the distinct glow of one of his healing spells. Wayne was low on health, and I figured his idea would come after the heal.

But that wasn't the case. The heal, as it turned out, was the idea.

The spell landed on the Moroi in front of Wayne, and it reeled back from the spell, but his hit points didn't drop at all.

Which is why I was surprised when Wayne yelled out. "Hell fuckin' yeah! Got some of my Agility back, but the Debuff isn't gone! The other guy keeps hitting me."

Wayne was right, and my attacks were landing more frequently. I also saw that the Moroi now had a debuff of his own, Holy Light.

It lasted for ten seconds, and during that time, the Moroi seemed to lose all the Agility that he had stolen from Wayne. The Moroi's leather armor only offered a low armor rating, but with that kind of Agility it likely couldn't wear anything heavier. The proc from my Dagger of Jagged Rock, which lowered a target's armor rating by 40 percent, finally landed as well when it wasn't dodging constantly. We were able to do some serious damage.

But when the Holy Light debuff ended, the Moroi went right back to tapping Wayne for his Agility. I saw Jason cast another healing spell, but this time it didn't work.

"I tried a lower level heal. Didn't take. Hold on," he said, and then cast another spell.

I saw the Holy Light debuff land on the Moroi again. And we were able to take it down.

Then we repeated the same technique on the other mob Wayne was tanking.

Now that we had a strategy, it was only a matter of controlling the debuff until we could take the Moroi down. Dan's was still almost at full health when we finally engaged it. Dan's Snare slowed the mob's movement speed but did nothing to its Agility, and it dodged most of the arrows Dan shot in its direction.

When we finally killed the last mob in the room, we let out a collective sigh. That was only the first fight in this monastery, and the mobs had only been blue. And we had almost died. We weren't in any actual danger at the time of Jason's intervention, but we wouldn't have survived without it. Unless I had used my ring.

"That was some damn good thinking, Allister," Wayne said.

"Sure was, Allisavetheday!"

"I can live with that one, Dan."

"Damn straight!" Dan exclaimed, fist bumping Jason, and we all chuckled.

"Thank goodness for the armor! I got a message that said, 'Due to your increased blessing, you have successfully casted Holy Light on the Moroi Fighter.' I don't know if that would have worked without Grumblewat's pieces. Just so you know, that's my strongest heal. I tried one that wasn't as powerful, and it didn't do anything at all," Jason said.

Jason was sitting on the floor and regenerating his mana. It was a good time for a break, and the right time to discuss our strategy. Now that we had something that worked, we had a chance.

—⁂—

The Moroi Fighters each dropped a piece of Fine Leather armor and a Fine Steel Dagger. The armor and weapons would sell for some platinum. We would restock our funds in no time.

The 10 Platinum we spent on the dyes we ended up not needing didn't feel like such a mistake now, although we couldn't have known that the front line of the King's army would move so much closer to the House Frost keep and we would only need one day of travel, not weeks of sneaking through the forest. Such was the reality of being the first players to run through these quests.

Our new strategy was working well, and we had made it through three more of the rooms. In each case, three of the Moroi fighters had come out of the other side of the room from where we entered.

The plan was pretty straight forward but did require a bit of aggro management. If we entered the room and Jason led with his Holy Light, the Moroi would aggro on him as soon as the spell landed. We learned that the hard way.

Accordingly, Wayne would need to get a few hits in, land a Taunt, and let himself get debuffed a few times before Jason could land his spell. Jason also had to wait until Wayne could gain some aggro on the second mob that Wayne tanked. Jason could only use his Holy Light on the primary mob as well. If he tried to hit the secondary mob to alleviate the debuff from that Moroi, it would attack Jason. We learned that one the hard way too.

We had to spend extra time letting Jason regen his mana after the second fight, since he had to heal Wayne, himself, and hit the Moroi with the Holy Light spell. He was going through the majority of his mana pool in the fight.

The next fight went much smoothly, and we controlled the room from the outset. All the mobs went down without any loss of aggro by Wayne.

When we exited that room, we followed a short hallway that ended up depositing us on the outside of the pyramid. Compared to the dim light of the monastery's interior, the sun from the Globi Desert almost blinded us. On the outside of the building, we followed a ledge that ran around the outside of the pyramid and ended in a set of stairs that led to the next level. At the end of those stairs was another of the pitch-black portals.

I was now traveling exclusively between rooms in my Blacksuit and I scouted ahead to the next floor. After passing through the archway, I was in another hallway that led to a room similar to the ones we had already been fighting, although it was a bit smaller. I retrieved my party and entered the new room, and three Moroi entered like usual.

The only difference was the level of the Moroi. There were now two blue and one yellow that came through the opposite side of the room. We made certain to attack the yellow first, but the fight followed the same strategy as before. The only difference was how long we had to wait for Jason to recoup his mana. The yellow mob took a bit longer than the blues had, and Jason had to expend more of his spells.

After two more rooms—and six more Moroi, two of which were yellow—we had traversed through this level of the pyramid and were deposited outside again. I followed our previous plan and went around the pyramid until I reached the next set of stairs. I went back for the team and this time had them wait at the bottom of the stairs so I wouldn't have to run all the way back around after I investigated the other side of the inky darkness.

We had continued to collect pieces of Fine Leather armor and Fine Steel daggers, and the haul would go far in fattening our purses. No matter what, this wouldn't be a total loss, regardless of what happened, but I wouldn't be happy unless we wiped the smile off that Dread Priest.

The next room we entered mimicked the first two floors, and three Moroi entered. This time, however, there were two yellows and one blue. I wasn't liking where this was going. And I didn't like the idea of Wayne having to tank the two high-level mobs at the same time and asked Dan to Snare one of the yellows.

"Resist. Resist. Landed," Dan said. And just in the nick of time. The yellow Moroi was bearing down on Dan after that second resist of his Snare. If that mob had reached Dan, it would have flayed him where he stood.

Dan was running the yellow around the room while Wayne took up his tanking duties. I hated to do it, but I was about to make a tough decision.

"Dan, after this fight, I want you to summon Broham. If that happens again, I want you to send him to attack the yellow."

"He'll die, dude," Dan said, with an obvious touch of sadness.

"Better the pet than you, buddy. Sorry."

"I understand. I'll do it, but I don't have to like it," Dan said. "Like second dates."

"What the hell is wrong with second dates?" Wayne asked.

"That's when they want to touch tongues with you. And what if they have a lumpy tongue? Is it really worth the risk? Oh no, not for me. Once bitten—or in this case, tongue molested—twice shy."

"Jesus, Dan! We really didn't need that visual. Thanks."

"Anytime, Alliweakstomach!"

I had to laugh at my teammates and especially Dan, but I didn't let it keep me from monitoring the fight closely. With one of the yellow Moroi Snared, we kept up our fighting strategy, but the fight took a while. Jason's mana was at 60 percent when we finished, far too low to go through into the next room. One mishap and he could end up burning through that much mana in a single fight. So we sat, and we waited.

It was a perfect time for Dan to taunt our Cleric some more. Dan, however, chose an entirely different topic.

"You think we'll have to take out that tower in Kich's Keep at some point?' he asked.

"Which tower?"

"The Tower, Wayne. The one that Sir Arthur told us about. The one that has all of Loust's artifacts in it and is just a wonderful piece of tasty treasure for all of his forces. The damn thing screams 'I am evil' anytime you walk next to it."

"Ahh, *that* tower. Yeah, I was thinking about that before, too. It seems logical that something like that would happen, but there haven't been any battles anywhere near Kich's Keep. The only sign of Loust was House Frost, and they wouldn't have been able to get in, I don't think. What do you think, Alex?"

So long as we weren't talking about how I knew the place is warded, I had no problem hypothesizing on the tower. "It's definitely a good theory. I've been thinking back to the rest of our playing, and I can't think of any other place that had that kind of significance, except for maybe these monasteries, and we know that Loust definitely wanted to take these over."

"Also, it's the only Tower we've seen," Dan said. Then he clarified, "I mean, the only one that sounded like it started with a capital T."

"Yup, far as I remember, that's the case," I agreed.

"So, if someone asked me to find the 'Tower' in the game, you guys would agree, that this would be the one?"

"What are you going on about, Dan? Did you get a side quest you aren't telling us about?"

"No, Baron Allisecretkeeper, you're the only one who does that."

"Damn. That was a good one. Two points for Dan," Jason said, fist bumping our Ranger. "But to answer your question, I would say yes."

I nodded my head along with Wayne. I didn't understand Dan's line of questioning, but it was a sound conclusion. Still, I wanted to know why he was asking.

It would have to wait, though, as that was the moment that Jason announced he had reached 80 percent mana and was ready to go.

The next two rooms followed the same pattern as the previous one, with two yellows and one blue. Dan had no problem with the first yellow he tried to Snare, but the second one resisted big time, and he was forced to send Broham at the Moroi Fighter.

Broham did his job and grabbed enough aggro to pull the Moroi away from Dan, giving the Ranger another opportunity to cast a Snare. Thankfully, it landed, and Dan reacquired the aggro from Broham, though it almost meant the death of Dan's pet. It was down to only 20 percent health, and Dan ordered it to sit out of the fight entirely. He didn't want to risk any chance of losing the pet, especially after it had valiantly saved Dan's life.

The end of the fight in that second room had one positive outcome, and that was Jason hitting Level 34. This wasn't the case for the rest of us, as Jason had suffered the least amount of death penalties over the course of our gaming and wasn't siphoning experience off to Broham like Dan was. It would still take some time before the rest of us hit our next level.

Once we hit the next room, we definitely knew we wanted those levels. For Jason, all the new mobs that entered were blue, meaning the ones that had been yellow were only two levels above Jason now, with the blue being only one level. That would be very crucial to Dan's ability to Snare them.

Still, getting us to our next levels would mean a lot more grinding.

We got through the room with no difficulty, but Jason's mana continued to take a hit with each fight. His level might have gone up, but it didn't change how much damage Wayne was taking.

The end of that room meant it was time to go back out to the exterior of the pyramid and climb up to the next level. From the outside, it looked like there was only one more set of interior rooms before we came to the top. I had no doubt that the Death Priest would be waiting for us there.

The guys were standing just outside the darkness, and I went through to scout the next room. I had expected to find another small room, with an exit on the other side. That wasn't the case, however. My quick glance showed me that the room in question ran the whole interior, and there was an exit to the exterior of the pyramid on the other side. There was nothing inside, and likely the mobs wouldn't spawn until we all entered, like had happened in the past.

I went back outside and told the guys what I had found. There wasn't any real choice except to walk in and assess the situation once the battle started. Wayne led the way, as he would need to be the first one to pick a target. Dan and I followed, with Jason at the rear.

As soon as Jason made it past the doorway, a large block of stone slammed down and blocked our exit. The sudden movement and subsequent crashing drew my attention, and I wasn't watching Wayne or the rest of the group.

When I turned back around, the entire room was awash in colors—greens, whites, blues, yellows, and red. And they were all over the floor. Before I could stop him, Wayne stepped on one of the green spots. A Moroi Fighter materialized out of the floor almost immediately, and Wayne stepped to the side, stepping on a blue spot in the process.

Another Moroi Fighter joined the first. This one was blue. I knew what I was looking at, and my stomach clenched up. We were dead if I didn't get this under control.

"Wayne. Stop moving!" I yelled as loud and with as much authority as I could. Wayne, to his credit, stood perfectly still and just let the Moroi beat on him.

"Walk backwards in a straight line!" I continued.

Wayne did exactly as I commanded, and the mobs stayed with him. Dan started moving to the side to get a better angle, and I yelled at him to stop as well.

"Don't bother with a Snare, Dan! Everyone just bunch up and DPS these guys to death. It's a green and a blue, so we can just muscle through."

Wayne brought the mobs to the doorway that was now blocked, and we started in on the mobs. Jason continued to use his Holy Light, and we took down the green first. It didn't last long at all.

Knowing that we would kill the blue in a short time, I gave the next set of orders. "Once this is dead, no one move. Just stay where you are."

"What's going on, Alex?"

"Let's get this down first, Wayne. I'll explain it all later. Trust me."

"I didn't hear the word 'experiment,' so I'm good," Jason said.

That got a chuckle, and the other two nodded their heads at me.

The blue Moroi Fighter died after a short time, and the guys just stood there waiting. I looted them and then turned to my team. "The room is trapped."

"Shit," Dan said. "How much of it?"

"All of it."

The three looked over from where we stood, to where the exit lay, and their faces fell.

"You can see a way through, though, right?" Wayne asked.

"You aren't hearing me. There isn't a way through. Every inch of the ground is covered in a trap, with the exception of the two places where you just stepped."

"Crap," Dan said, echoing everyone's thoughts. "And your trap detection isn't high enough to determine what is what, right?"

"Well, not exactly," I said. Everyone stood still and waited for me to continue.

Undisclosed Location

"My apologies again, Ms. Renart, on the subterfuge to get you here. I know you understand the reasoning behind it, but it can still be a pain."

"Thank you, sir. And you know you have to call me Emily," she said to the General before continuing, "I don't have too much to complain about, though. All I have to do is sit in the back of the car. Your drivers do all the work. Honestly, I took a nap."

The General and Colonel Thompson both smiled at Emily's remark.

"Well then, I consider that a valuable use of your time."

"Maybe next time add a pillow and a blanket, though. It was a long drive."

The General started laughing. Thompson was shaking his head, but his smile never left his face.

"I'm kidding, of course. But only a little. I'm easily small enough to get a full-on power nap in the back of that SUV."

"Whether you use it or not, Emily, I can guarantee you there will be a nice big fluffy blanket in the back of the next vehicle."

"Thank you, Colonel. Don't forget the pillow."

"I won't," he said, then turned to look at the General. "We've created a monster."

"And I'm happy to have her on the team. Let's get started, shall we?"

Emily nodded to the General and took on a more serious air. "I don't have much to report, General, as I haven't been given any additional accesses since our last meeting. Instead, I've been focusing on building some friendships amongst the team members."

"Good work, Emily. That type of initiative is why I never hesitated to put you on this assignment."

Emily blushed slightly at the General's words and pressed on. "I figured I might be able to get more details about the 'Tower' I heard the others mention before. I noted that one of the network guys that had mentioned the Tower before always ate his lunch alone. I asked if he wanted any company.

"He's a bit socially awkward but a nice guy. He was happy to offer the seat at his table, but he didn't really understand the concept of 'small talk.' I'd met plenty of guys like this before. You run into them all over the IT world. The quickest way to get them comfortable is to talk shop."

"Excellent observation, Emily."

"If you remember, at my last meeting, I mentioned that the network guys had introduced a 'leaky bucket' algorithm to regulate some flow of data. I'm aware of the technique but told him that I wasn't. Once I asked him what it was, it was hard to get him to stop talking."

The General smiled and nodded for her to continue.

"It was only a matter of time before I was able to ask about the Tower that they were using the leaky bucket for. It turns out that the Tower is the mechanism by which the information from the Bates Motel is transferred to and from the game, Resurgence.

"According to the tech, there is a huge amount of information pumped through the main servers at AltCon Headquarters. Every aspect of the game is housed in those servers. All the quests, the coding that delineates everything from a blade of grass to a dragon, and all the player's data. Everything, except for the specialized code that is housed at the servers in the Bates Motel. In order to incorporate the specialized code, the data has to be routed through the Motel servers and then into the game via the Tower."

"Did he say what the code was?"

"No, he didn't. I hinted around it, but he wouldn't, or couldn't, answer that question. I didn't want to overplay my hand."

"That was the right call. Please continue."

"The bottom line, as I understood it, is that the sheer amount of data being channeled through the servers tended to overload the processing point where the information was transferred back into the game—The Tower. So, they introduced a modulating leaky bucket that would continuously correct itself to optimize the amount of data transmission."

"I'm just going to admit that I barely understood half of that," the General said, smiling. "But please, continue."

Emily smiled back and said, "I know. Geek talk. Still, the picture is pretty clear. The Bates Motel servers only house a particular piece of code, one that has to be incorporated with the game but that they don't want to be associated with the main servers. So, the information from the game is sent from AltCon HQ, through the fiber line, cycled through the Motel's servers, and then sent into the game from the Motel. As far as I can tell, there's another fiber line that connects back to deliver the data into the game. I still don't know why they call it the Tower, though."

"A second fiber line?"

"Yes. That was the other thing I found out. If the information from AltCon's main servers were sent to the Motel to add the specialized code, then pumped back to AltCon's HQ for eventual transmission back into the game, then that code would undoubtedly leave traces on the main HQ servers. To avoid that, they had to add another fiber line that ran from the Motel and to a distribution node."

"I'm so lost right now," the Colonel said.

"Ha! Me too, Colonel," the General said. "Why is the Tower at the Motel then?"

"Oh! I'm sorry, General. I didn't explain that well. The Tower isn't at the Motel."

"It isn't?"

"No. The Tower seems to be a separate node to access the internet. They have huge fiber nodes at AltCon HQ that can upload and download massive amounts of data due simply to the sheer volume of data that AltCon manages. We're not talking about simple hardware, General. These are massive pieces of infrastructure. Remember, their primary business isn't Resurgence—not yet, anyway. That's why they have a dozen subterranean floors with servers at the main building.

"To get the information, and the special code, back to the players, they still have to upload the data. That happens at another node, still quite large but much smaller than what they have at their HQ. The Tower is what they call the node."

"Any idea where that is?"

"As you told me, AltCon bought a huge amount of land in this area to set up the Motel and keep it out of sight. In order to connect to the web, though, it has to be near the main internet lanes. So, I know it's close to the border of AltCon's land but not on it. Somewhere on the outskirts of the town."

"This is excellent, Emily."

"Thank you, sir. I'm afraid that's all I've got," she said. "Anything more I should be doing while I'm there?"

"Just keep on course. Maintain your friendship with the network engineer and continue to look for abnormalities. At this point, I would prefer you keep a lower profile and simply be as efficient as you've always been. Your work ethic will likely open up additional lanes of opportunity."

"Thank you, General."

With that, Emily stood up, shook the offered hands in front of her, and departed the facility.

CHAPTER 19

December 18, 2043

The guys weren't happy that I wouldn't explain right away and wanted to camp until the next day. I told them that as soon as I turned around and saw Wayne moving, I could see a sea of colors across the floor. Wayne had stepped on a green first, and that's what spawned. His next action took him to the side, and that spawned a corresponding blue mob to the blue trap. So, I was fairly sure that the colors I could see matched the level of the mobs. I told them my having the skill must have been enough.

My next idea had them suspicious, but it was because of how much it sounded like an experiment, and not because I could sense the traps accurately. They had, apparently, believed my explanation entirely.

I wanted to clear the room.

When I said that meant another, likely, 50 mobs, they blanched at me, but as I explained that I could control the mobs we got, based on the colors, they started to see the merit in my idea. The part that really sold the deal was when I noted we would all level if we stayed and did exactly as I suggested.

I didn't want to start and then have to stop in the middle for us to log off for the night, risking all the traps resetting. The guys agreed, and understood why we logged off next to the blocked doorway. That area was entirely clear of traps.

When we logged back on at ten in the morning, and we saw that the two traps we had sprung had not reset. That was a small victory but one I hadn't wanted to risk.

"How do we want to do this?" Wayne asked.

"I see a number of options," I said. "We can clear each line of traps, one at a time, and then move forward through the room that way. Another option is to focus on the easier mobs first, taking them down and then moving to the harder ones. I see some places where we would have to fight hard ones, though. We wouldn't have a choice if we want to keep them single. The final option is to go in the reverse and go after the hard ones first then just mop up the easy ones. Thoughts?"

"Let's do the easy ones first. If we do the hard ones and you guys get your levels, there's a chance that some of those white mobs become green to everyone, and we lose that experience," Jason said.

"Or we could just fight until we level up and then make a bee line through to the next door," Dan said.

"You want to give up all this easy experience? We are talking single pulls each time," Wayne said.

"I just thought it needed to be said. Make sure all the options are out on the table. No way I want to pass up all this experience for Broham!"

"I'm with Allister's idea," I said.

"Me, too," said Wayne.

"Unanimous then." Dan finished.

Next was figuring out the best way to trigger the traps. In one instance, I could do it myself, but then I would risk getting pummeled by one of the Moroi Fighters. Green or white, I wasn't a tank, and I would take a beating. This would require Jason to heal me and risk taking aggro himself.

The best way to do this was directing Wayne to each trap and having him trigger the spawn. It would be tedious at first, but it was the safest option. This close to the end, we all decided to go with safe.

Wayne started toward the traps, and I was leading him toward the first green trap. We wouldn't get any experience, but we would still get the loot. Also, we wanted to have a little room to maneuver in case we needed it. Taking out the low-level mobs was the easiest way to do this.

"I feel like I'm driving a car, blind, and you are telling me where to go," Wayne said.

"A little to your left," I said, and Wayne adjusted.

"Now a little to your right."

Wayne moved again.

"Now a little to your left."

Wayne moved again and then stopped, standing perfectly still.

"You know you're a real dick, Alex."

I laughed evilly. It was more of a cackle, really. "Sorry. Couldn't help it."

"Done having fun?" he asked, looking over his shoulder toward where he thought I was. I was actually more to his right side and wearing my Blacksuit.

"Yeah, I'm done. It's a straight line from where you are. Take small steps until you hit the spawn and then walk straight back."

Wayne shuffled forward until he activated the spawn and then took regular-sized steps back to the group. It was a green Moroi Fighter, and we got to work.

Over the next hour, we systematically cleared the room, one mob at a time. We skipped the yellows and the one red. It was easy enough to do with this many traps and the way they were aligned on the floor.

After that first hour, we had all gotten our level 34 and a few of the remaining white traps had turned green, but only a few of them. We thought about skipping all the remaining greens, if we could. We were to a point now where we wouldn't be able to hold any more loot without risking becoming encumbered.

Jason, however, changed our mind.

"It doesn't matter if we can carry the loot or not. I would prefer we clear this thing entirely, so we don't end up with all of these leftover green mobs rushing the top of the monastery in the middle of our fight with the Death Priest. That's what I would do if I was the developer."

"I agree with Allister," Wayne said.

"Yeah, I see that logic. I concur," I said.

"Alliunanimous for the win."

"Maybe we should promote Allister to leader," I said.

Jason turned and gave me one of his signature looks. He didn't have any problem seeing me in my Blacksuit with his necklace that saw through all invis. "Don't you put that curse on me. That requires even more management of Dan, and I'm already overburdened with the little I already have to do."

"You can't fool me, Alliempathy I know you care."

I broke up the banter to get back to directing Wayne to the rest of the mobs.

After another hour, all that remained were three traps. Two yellow and one red. I didn't want to fight the red.

Wayne noticed my trepidation. "I don't want to fight it either, Alex, but I think we have to. If Jason's theory is right, I don't want to be in the middle of a boss fight and another red joins in. That's not my idea of a good time."

"You want to know my idea of a good time, Wayne? Remember that elf in the tavern with the—"

"Nope. Don't want to know. And I would hate if I accidently re-layed this story to Jenny after a few drinks and it ended up getting back to Kaitlin."

"What? I was going to say the elf with the charming personality and compassion to better her fellow elf. Jeez. What kind of a letch do you think I am?"

"Does the term 'getting wasted and wenches' ring a bell, Dan?" Jason asked.

Dan held his hands to his chest and looked around like he had heard the foulest thing possible. "What a terrible thing to say. We definitely shouldn't associate with anyone so crass!"

"I've been saying the same thing for months!" Jason exclaimed.

Wayne let out a full belly laugh, and I joined him. Even Dan and Jason were smiling a bit.

This respite hadn't changed our situation, though. We still had to decide whether to face the three remaining mobs or not, and it looked like we were leaning towards doing it.

"Let's get the yellows, then. Wayne, start walking straight," I said, continuing to direct him toward the trap.

The next two mobs fell like the rest, although the fight took longer with the level being so high. I couldn't imagine how quickly a group would have wiped if they had accidently spawned the two yellows, or a yellow and a red, at the same time. Of course, they would have had to get through a whole lot more mobs than just these to get this far.

We waited until Dan and Jason were at full mana and Wayne and I had full health. Both our casters renewed whatever buffs they could give, including raising our resistances. We knew the mob was red, but we didn't know if it was a boss of some kind.

I placed Wayne directly in front of the next trap and told him he would only need to move forward to trigger the trap. Since there were no more mobs in the room, Wayne wouldn't need to back up after setting off this trap and spawning the mob.

When everyone signaled they were ready, Wayne stepped forward.

His foot landed on the trap and, like before, the mob began to materialize. The tag over its head read Raging Moroi Fighter, and his eyes were green with tinges of red. It didn't wait a moment and swung his dagger at the closest thing to him, namely Wayne.

"Shit! I just got hit with Theft of Speed. It's taken all of my Agility, and I can't move!"

Wayne hadn't only lost his Agility but all movement, to include his special skills, and looked to be rooted to the ground. Jason started casting his Holy Light spell.

Wayne yelled, trying to get Jason to stop, but it was too late. The spell landed. And the Raging Moroi took off directly for Jason. Wayne hadn't gotten enough aggro built up with his special skills disabled.

The mob was hit with the Holy Light debuff, but Wayne was still stuck. And the Moroi was almost on Jason.

From the side, a blur of fur pounced on the Moroi, driving its claws into the mob's side and latching onto its neck with its teeth. The Moroi stopped its forward movement, grabbed the dire wolf by the neck, and tore it off. He then threw the wolf to the ground and fully turned his attention on the new aggressor. The Moroi didn't hesitate, nor did it turn back to Jason. Instead, he put all his attention on the member of our party who was at the top of his aggro list. Unfortunately, in a matter of seconds, the Moroi had stabbed Broham repeatedly and thrashed him against the ground, killing him. With his death, he disappeared.

There was an audible gasp from Jason and a roar from Wayne. Those few seconds were all Wayne needed for the debuff to wear off, and he smashed his war hammer into the Raging Moroi's back, followed by a Kick and a Bash. I had no doubt he used his Taunt skill as well. The Moroi turned on Wayne and started stabbing him mercilessly with his dagger.

I hadn't engaged in the fight at all. Wayne still didn't have the kind of aggro built up that would negate a Disembowel strike if I got lucky. And with the Agility buff the Moroi could give to himself by stealing Wayne's own Stat, I wouldn't strike until Jason landed another Holy Light.

That's why I was able to see the genuine terror in Jason's eyes as he looked at where Broham had been flattened into the ground and since disappeared. He then looked toward Dan with true pity and sympathy, ashamed of what went down.

But Dan wasn't paying any attention to Jason. He only had eyes for the Moroi.

"Fucker killed my dog," I heard him whisper. "He's so dead. So very dead."

I didn't know if he meant Jason or the mob, but I got my answer when Dan finally started sending arrow after arrow into the creature. "I'm gonna send this arrow up your ass, you piece of shit! Teach you to hurt my friend!"

The Raging Moroi never landed another of the Theft of Speed debuffs. It wasn't a boss, after all, and I was guessing it was a one-time skill the mob had. It had burned it right at the beginning and would have been successful if not for Dan sacrificing his pet.

Wayne's health fell dangerously close to critical several times, but Jason didn't miss a heal. We won the fight. That one mob took 50 percent of Jason's mana.

There was no cheering when the Moroi died. I landed the killing blow, but I wasn't in a mood to celebrate. We all just looked over to Dan. Jason was the first to speak.

"I'm so sorry, Dan. That was all my fault."

Dan didn't say anything and just walked over to where Broham had fallen. There was nothing left, as Broham's body simply dematerialized when he died. He lost experience and wouldn't be able to be summoned for 24 hours, but we knew where he had fallen.

Dan took a few more moments, and then he looked toward Jason. He gave a small, sad smile and said, "He totally saved the day. You're going to owe him some power leveling after this."

"You got it, buddy. We'll take a day to get him his experience back."

Dan stood for a few more moments and then started walking toward the exit of the room.

"Let's go kill this Dick Priest. For Broham."

"You surprise me! I didn't think you would make it through the first floor of my pyramid, let alone make it all the way to the top! The wait makes what will be my undeniable victory all the sweeter. Your blood will be added to the ones before you, and our master will be one step closer to waking," the Death Priest said.

We were just past the last stair that led to the top of the pyramid and were staying still. After the last room with all the traps, I didn't want us to spring any more before I had a chance to examine the place. Nobody disagreed, and we were able to see the whole of the monastery's summit when we arrived.

The first thing I noted, and relayed to the team, was an absence of traps. I heard an audible sigh behind me. I also didn't seem to have any aggro from the boss, since I was running around the top, fairly close to him, and he wasn't lashing out at me with those swords.

The top of the monastery only held three things. The first was the Death Priest. The second was an altar of some kind. It stood about three feet off the ground, had a large top, and there were four grooves cut into the top that could channel liquid over the altar and deposit whatever the substance was, down toward the interior of the tunnel. I got close enough to examine the altar in even more detail.

Someone had desecrated it, working symbols into the original sides of the stone altar, but these were mostly gone. They looked to have been chipped away. In their places, were several symbols that I couldn't read, scrawled all over the sides of the altar and the top in some type of paint. Or it could have been blood.

The third thing I could see was a body. Or, at least, the skeleton of a body.

The skeleton had retained its armor, and the blades the person had held in their death were still dangling from its hands. It was draped over the altar, face down, and a dagger stuck out of its back.

I was pretty sure we had found Aaron Lancaster. He was another of Lady Tessa's brothers who had made it to the very end of their quest, but he had failed at the hands of the final enemy, dying with his hands still clutching his weapons. Based on the journal of Constance Lancaster, that was how Aaron would have preferred to go. I would make certain he was buried with those blades once we dispatched the priest—unless they were crazy awesome and tradeable.

None of us used blades that long except for Dan, and he almost never bothered with them. His skill at it was abysmal. So, if we couldn't trade them to someone else, they would get put in the ground with the body. We didn't need the trophies, but I wouldn't pass up loot we could give to our teammates, friends, or trade for other loot or money.

The Priest kept up with his monologue, and I was sure then that my assumption was correct about Aaron Lancaster.

"You're only the second to make it this far. The last," the priest gestured toward the body on the altar, "thought to challenge me here at the heart of my power. While his blade work was formidable, he couldn't hope to match the speed of a Death Priest of Loust, especially not a swords master such as myself."

With that, his name changed from the generic Death Priest to Maharit, Sword Master of Loust. I didn't care what his name was, he was going down just like the rest. However, I didn't have any illusions that he was going to be able to do crazy amounts of damage.

I made my way back to the guys and told them what I found. There wasn't anything in my scouting that looked like it was going to be able to help our strategy, which at this point was nothing more than "kill him before he kills us."

"He said this place was the heart of his power, so we should watch to make sure he doesn't try to use anything up here to buff himself," Jason said.

"Good call, Allister. I imagine it has to do with the altar, but it could be anything. We'll try to keep him far from the center during the fight. Maybe try to drag him back toward these stairs, Wayne."

"Forget the stairs. I'm gonna try and knock his ass off the top of the pyramid."

"Shit, I didn't think of that. Watch out for any attempt from him to do the same."

The guys all nodded. The only ones who would be close enough to suffer that type of action would be Wayne and I. Dan would be positioned far away, peppering Maharit with arrows and standing ready to grab any adds. Jason too would be away from the mob's range of striking.

"Any other ideas?" I asked.

No one responded. We were at full mana, and all our buffs were fresh. There was nothing left to do but attack.

"I'm going to Taunt him from a distance and lead with Kick and Bash before I try and swing. Hopefully, that will get me some decent aggro built up. I'm ready when you guys are."

"Let's do it."

"This one's for Broham," Wayne said. He then triggered his Taunt and ran at Maharit.

The sword master reacted to the Taunt and ran straight toward Wayne, yelling, "Die from the power of Loust!"

Maharit saw Wayne's Kick coming and moved, taking only a glancing blow off his side; however, the movement put him in direct line of

Wayne's Bash, which landed fully. Wayne's forearm impacted the side of Maharit's head, and he staggered from the blow.

"Stunned," Wayne called out. I was glad to see that Skill worked.

With the mob stunned, Wayne didn't have any problem landing a blow from his heavy war hammer, and the mob's health dropped noticeably. With his light armor, a full swing from a blunt object like Wayne's war hammer was sure to do some damage. His hammer also proc'ed, triggering the Dark Infliction that did 150 points of direct damage. Unfortunately, it didn't land at full power.

"Only 75 points of damage on Infliction. Makes sense that this guy would have a resistance to Dark magic. Looks like 50 percent."

"Means Alliwhoopass' spells should really put a hurting on him!" Dan yelled out.

"Ooh, I like that one too, Dan!"

Wayne hit with another hammer strike, and I entered the fight. I landed a critical backstab, but not a Disembowel. I was actually thankful of that, since I didn't want this guy aggroing me.

Dan saw me attack and joined into the fight. Arrows were now flying at Maharit in rapid succession.

We dropped his hit points by 10 percent pretty quickly.

And then the Stun wore off, and Maharit struck back.

I had never seen anything that looked so beautiful and so deadly at the same time.

Maharit drew his two Scimitars in one fluid motion, across his own body, and sliced them against Wayne's lower abdomen and upper torso in one go. He then brought them back around and sliced again. Wayne couldn't do anything to block any of the four strikes, and Wayne's war hammer missed entirely as Maharit slithered around the blow. There was no better way to explain it; his body looked like it was made without a skeletal structure, and he just slipped around the edge of the hammer.

At the end of the swing, he flipped the blade in his right hand into the air and drew one of the daggers from his belt. He threw it at Wayne's throat. The blade missed the mark, bouncing off Wayne's armor, but still nicked his neck.

Maharit then caught the spinning sword as it fell and continued its momentum to try and slice through Wayne's leading leg. Again, the armor held, but Wayne had no chance of dodging the blow.

But the strikes weren't glancing blows at all. "Shit, I'm bleeding!"

The bleeding debuff would drain away Wayne's hit points over time. A heal from Jason would cure the debuff, but then he wouldn't be able to hit Maharit with his own spells.

"I'm good for now. The armor is negating most of it, but I'll need a heal soon."

The damage from Dan's arrows and my daggers were doing their part, and the sword master was down another five percent. Both of my daggers also proc'ed, and I was rewarded with a 200 hit point life drain and Maharit's armor rating dropping 40 percent. He was dodging a lot of our strikes, too, but not all of them.

Maharit kept attacking, and he finally landed an Agility debuff on Wayne.

"All my Agility is gone, but I can still move. No Theft of Speed."

"I'm coming with a Holy Light, Naugha!"

Jason's spell hit, and the sword master reeled back. The debuff on Wayne was gone, and the sword master had his own debuff. It worked just like with the Moroi, so we had that going for us.

Maharit growled at Jason's spell and lowered himself, placing his swords in a new defensive position, with one pointing up and the other pointing down. He was able to parry all of Wayne's strikes that came at him and even avoid the Kick and Bash.

But he wasn't able to block any of my strikes, or Dan's for that matter. If Wayne didn't gain some aggro soon, though, it was going to switch to one of us.

Maharit was down to almost 75 percent, and I called it to the group. As a boss, he would do something at 75 percent, but we didn't know what it was.

One of Dan's arrows struck the Death Priest on his side, and the health bar dropped to 75 percent. And then Maharit reacted.

He became a swirling storm of blades. I couldn't believe that he only had two arms and two swords. His blades were everywhere, and he was spinning in a circle so fast, I could barely make out his form.

He hit with every strike, on both Wayne and me. Even more, every one of my dagger strikes was unsuccessful. To make matters worse, he didn't simply Dodge or Parry the strikes. He Riposted each one, meaning that for every dagger strike I attempted, I was rewarded with a return hit. The same happened to Wayne, although his rate of attack was way less than mine.

He was also able to hit each of Dan's arrows out of the air. He was taking no damage whatsoever, and he drained Wayne and I of our full complement of Agility, making his maneuvers even faster and more accurate. He was a wall of blades and death.

But swords couldn't stop spells. Jason's Holy Light spell landed after a short time. I was near 70 percent health, and Wayne's health had dropped about 15 percent as well. But that wasn't the worst part. The lack of successful hits, and Jason's spell, put our Cleric on the top of Maharit's aggro list.

He charged Jason.

I was thinking Jason would be sent to respawn when I saw Maharit turn and start his charge, and then the rest of us soon after, but it never came.

The sword master took two steps and then faltered as Wayne's hammer hit him in the back, and then Maharit's head snapped forward as a Bash landed in the back of his head. He stumbled, Stunned from the Bash.

"Was saving that until his Blender of Death attack ended," Wayne said.

"Blender of Death! Nice, Wayne. Trademark that shit!"

The fight regressed back to our pattern of trying to keep Wayne at the top of the aggro list while negating the Agility debuff as much as we could. Jason's mana was slowly being spent as the fight progressed, as he had to both heal Wayne and counteract the theft of Agility. Dan even started throwing his weak heals at Wayne to try and negate some of the mana Jason had to spend, but Dan's heals were not much help.

After a long while, we were about to hit 50 percent and knew another boss skill was going to be unleashed.

It was my dagger that dropped him below the 50 percent mark this time, and I stopped attacking when it happened. If I wasn't trying to land any hits, I wouldn't get hit with a Riposte, although I may take some damage from the whirling blades.

But the Blender of Death didn't come.

"Now feel the true power of Loust!" Maharit screamed and crouched down. Then he jumped, performing a back flip in midair, and angled toward the center of the platform. And the altar.

As soon as he started the jump, I swung both of my daggers, but it didn't matter. In the middle of his leap, and while he started arcing his body backwards, he twisted and slapped both of my daggers away with the flats of his blades, Parrying both strikes. Amazingly, he was able to get his foot on the head of Wayne's war hammer, as our warrior swung his weapon, and further propelled himself past me and toward the altar.

He was completing his flip, and his body was leading toward the altar. He stretched his hand out, about to hit the altar with his palm, when his body rocketed away from the center. He hit the ground and rolled across the top of the monastery. Wayne and I didn't hesitate and ran to reengage. That's when I heard Jason laughing.

"Well, shit! I should have tried that earlier! Turns out this asshat isn't a Moroi, and Banish Undead works just fine!"

Wayne slammed his war hammer into the prone figure of the sword master, followed with his aggro building skills. Once the Stun of the Banish Undead spell wore off, Maharit jumped back to his feet and was back to fighting us.

But the fight was done. It didn't matter that Maharit still had 45 percent health. We had brought out the big guns. Or, rather, the big gun.

He made another leap for the altar at 25 percent, but Jason was ready and launched him out of the air with his spell again. Jason hit him at the apex of his leap and was almost successful in executing Wayne's idea. He stopped rolling right before hitting the edge of the pyramid.

I didn't even bother with the Force Multiplier ring, since we knew we could burn this guy down with Banish Undead spells. Instead, I planned to use it after he died, so I had the full five minutes to work with for our looting.

Maharit, Sword Master of Loust, was killed by one of Dan's arrows. That wasn't by accident. We made sure the Ranger had his revenge, and he seemed pleased with the result.

As soon as the sword wielding bastard was dead, an apparition appeared near the altar. We got ready to attack, but the ghost wasn't turning to aggro on us. Instead, it walked over to the altar and shook its head.

It was translucent, but we could see that, in life it, it had worn the same type of armor as the Moroi we had fought earlier. Only this one didn't have any of the glowing green miasma coming from its eyes. And it looked sad.

It turned toward us, and a tag appeared above its head. It was a Follower of the Swift, and it started talking to us.

"I only had but a moment. My brothers had been changed, and I was the last. I stood upon this platform and took it," the apparition said. It then took from within the folds of its armor a chunk of rock.

"This was the heart of our Monastery, an item that could bestow the blessings of the monastery upon its followers. It flowed from this alter, through the monastery, and provided for all within. Now, I only pray that it can rid this place of the taint that remains." It then turned to us. "Please remove this body from the altar. I do not have the ability to do so in this form."

Wayne walked over and touched the body of Aaron Lancaster. It disappeared from the top of the stone, and Wayne walked back over to me. He then said, "Another part of the book about the king. And a map. No weapons."

I nodded, a little disappointed that we wouldn't get our hands on those swords.

The apparition then placed the rock over the altar and let go. It hung in the air and began spinning. What looked like water came forth from the rock. It rained down on the center of the altar then flowed into the grooves cut on the top. The water flowed across it before cascading down into the interior of the monastery.

After several moments, the altar changed in front of us, and the evil-looking symbols disappeared. The previous carvings returned, and I could see that they depicted men and women in various feats of agility—flipping, spinning, and fighting.

The water continued to flow for another minute until a glow came from the top of the altar and shot down through the center of the monastery. The same glow began radiating from the floor, and we walked over to the side of the pyramid. In moments, the glow had covered the entire pyramid.

"It is done. This monastery will never again house the followers of the Swift, but it will never again house the evil of Loust. You have done us a great service.

"The rock contains one last remnant of the Swift, although quite powerful. It is yours to do with as you will. The rock will also provide the bearer an endless supply of water, its original boon before it was merged with the will of the Swift ages ago."

The ghost then disappeared, and we were left with the rock spinning in place. And Maharit's corpse. It was time for some loot.

"Hitting my ring, guys. Let's get this guy looted and get out of here," I said. "But first, Dan, grab that rock. Just know that you might have to go by TheSwift instead of TheClaw from now on."

Dan laughed and grabbed the rock.

"Here it is, guys. This is awesome!"

Item	Commonality:	Weight:	Armor:	Bonus:
Essence of the Swift	Epic: One Use Only	N/A	N/A	Consumption gives the bearer an increase of 20 percent to Agility and 20 percent effectiveness to all Agility-based Skills.

"That means that your base Agility goes up 20 percent and your archery skills will go up twenty percent too!" Wayne said.

"Nope," Dan said.

"What? Nope?"

"Total Agility goes up 20 percent, including bonuses, just like your Attack, and then all my Skills go up too! This is way better!"

"Holy crap, you're going to out damage me, Dan!" I said.

"Don't take it bad, Alex. I was already looking to replace Wayne as our tank, remember? I'll just have to do it all."

"Let's just let him do all the work next time, Wayne. He can heal himself too, Allister."

"Damn. Really stuck my foot in my mouth that time, huh?"

"As if your foot ever leaves your mouth, Dan," Jason said.

Despite his earlier anger about losing Broham, Dan was all smiles now.

I still had time on the ring, so I looted the corpse of the Sword Master. It was another haul. I started feeling a little better about our chances against Supreme Overlord Riff. But only a little bit. I also knew I was going to have to deal with Dan's disbelief again.

"Here we go guys. This stuff is all pretty awesome," I said, linking the first item.

Item	Commonality:	Weight:	Armor:	Bonus:
Helm of Concentration Warrior Only	Rare: Binds on Acquisition	2.0	40	+10 Strength +10 Constitution 25 percent resistance to Stun

"Damn, Wayne! That's a nice helm. Congrats, brother," Dan said.

"Thanks, buddy. The resist to Stun will be great!"

"Here's the next one," I said and linked again.

Item	Commonality:	Weight:	Armor:	Bonus:
Leather Wrapped Leggings Brawler, Rogue Only	Rare: Binds on Acquisition	3.0	40	+10 Dexterity +10 Constitution 25 percent increase to Critical Damage

"Awesome, Alex! You better be careful to not grab my aggro, though!" Wayne said.

I looted my items and said, "Just one more piece. And I don't want to hear a word, Dan."

"No way, man. Not again!"

Item	Commonality:	Weight:	Armor:	Bonus:
Gloves of Clerical Healing Cleric Only	Legendary Clerical Healing Set Min Level: 35 Binds on Acquisition (Scalable)	3.0	40 (level 35)	+20 Wisdom +20 Constitution Effect: 20 Percent Increase to Stun Duration (level 35)

"What will that put you at when you can wear it, Allister?"

"I think all the Stats will go up to +20, and I don't know about effects. But they keep going up!"

"Congrats, Allister!" Wayne said.

"I don't know if congrats are in order. Do you realize how much the dwarves are going to drool over him now?" Wayne said.

"We don't have to tell them right away, do we Alex?"

I laughed and shook my head. "No, Allister, we don't. We can wait until the next time we see them. But you know Sharla can smell

Grumblewat armor from miles away, so I'd be careful!"

We were ready to go, but Dan noted the rock still spinning on top of the altar. I went over and laid my hands on it. It was exactly what the ghost had said, and it was called The Gift of Life. It was also tradeable. I knew exactly what I was going to do with this.

We headed to the bottom of the monastery and decided that was an appropriate place to bury Aaron Lancaster. Depositing him somewhere in the desert just didn't seem right.

Wayne laid his body on the ground, and I saw that the swords were still in his hands, crossed over his chest. As Wayne activated the prompt to bury the body, we were surrounded by a golden glow and we received the notification that our Gift of Lady Lancaster increased to +8 to all Stats and +8 to all Resistances.

Since we had played 12 hours the day before, we decided to end our session for the day at the monastery. We would start our ride back through the desert on the next day. Everyone was fine with waiting to look at the map Aaron Lancaster had on his body until the next day.

Undisclosed Location

"I figured out what the Tower is!" Dan said, as he sauntered into the conference room.

"Oh, this should be good."

Dan gave Colonel Thompson a questioning look but continued to his usual chair next to the Colonel.

The General gave Thompson a sideways glance without saying anything to the man. "Report, Mr. Hamson. What is the Tower?"

"Now don't get crazy when you hear my answer," Dan said.

"I promise to keep my emotions in check."

After several seconds of what the General figured was Dan's impression of a dramatic pause, he spoke.

"It's..." Dan held his hands up, palms facing each other, "a Tower."

The General waited several more moments before he realized Dan wasn't going to say any more. Then he chuckled.

"I totally set myself up for that one, didn't I?"

"Yup. Now we're even for the 'sweet loots' comment."

"Indeed, Dan. So, what did you find?"

Dan ran down all that he learned from Alex, from Sir Arthur Chadwick, and his own investigation. He explained the lore behind the Tower and where it was situated in the game. He then went on to explain how it was the same for him as it was for everyone else who came in contact with—or at least tried to get near—the building.

"The closer you get, the sicker you feel. I forced myself to stand right next to the thing, and I was so nauseated that I almost threw up. And I hadn't had a single thing to drink that day."

"You mean like water?" The Colonel asked.

"Who throws up from drinking water? No, I'm talking about the finest Elven Wine in the land. It's called Three Points, because after you drink enough, you will swear that all the elves have three pointy ears. It's the stuff of legend."

There was no response from the General or Thompson.

After several more moments, Dan spoke. "Right. Never again mention drinking in the game. Got it."

"See, General. He learns. Just slowly."

The General continued to look none too happy about Dan's comments but waved his hand for Dan to continue.

"I couldn't touch the place. I tried, but that feeling of sickness dropped me to my knees. And I know this doesn't make much sense to you guys, but I have some of the highest resistances to magic in all of Resurgence. If I couldn't touch it, no one could. Unless someone removes whatever spells are protecting that place, the Tower will be there forever."

"Anything else?"

"Nope, that's all I got. How are things going with Tim?"

The General gave Dan a hard stare before responding. "Don't worry about what everyone else is doing. When the time comes for the two of you to team up, I'll let you know. Until then, you should act like you have no idea what Tim is doing with us."

"Should be easy, since I have no idea what he's doing," Dan responded. "Besides, I've gotten really good at playing dumb."

The Colonel was about to respond when Dan held up a hand in his face.

"Don't take the easy ones like that, bud. It makes you look petty."

With a smile and a wink, Dan got out of his chair and headed out of the room.

Once he left, the General looked over at Thompson and raised an eyebrow.

"Sounds like the right place," the Colonel said in response to the General's unasked question. "I think we should have Emily try to find out if there is a representation of this Tower in the game. Should be an easy line of questioning for her to weave into her talks with that network engineer."

"I agree, Colonel. But the raised eyebrow wasn't about the Tower. I was wondering what you have in mind for getting back at Dan. He burned you pretty good."

Hotel Room

Terrence Jolston had arrived a half hour early for this meeting, checking in and letting his contact know which room he was in. This was the first time Jolston had ever done anything this conspiratorial. He was supposed to meet the investigator named Glenn.

Jolston did a walk-through of the room, making sure it was suitable for a discussion, then waited for Glenn to arrive. It wasn't often instructions were dictated to Jolston. In fact, the Old Man was the only person who told Jolston what to do these days. But when it came to meeting someone who was entirely off the AltCon books, Jolston was willing to take orders.

At the exact time the meeting was scheduled, there was a knock on the door. Jolston opened it and was staring at a rather unassuming man. The man didn't say anything and walked past Jolston into the room. He walked through both sides of the suite and into the bathroom before coming out and offering his hand.

"Glenn."

"Terrence Jolston."

"Figured. Let's get down to business."

Glenn was about 5'8", maybe 160 pounds. He looked to be in his early 50's with a full head of black and silver hair. He was wearing a suit that fit him properly but didn't look to be anything overly expensive, and he had no tie. His face bore the resemblance of someone from Eastern Europe.

And he had a predatory look in his eyes.

Glenn removed a notepad from the interior pocket of his suit jacket and flipped it open.

"I'm afraid I didn't earn my pay on this one," Glenn said, "not that I'm not going to take it."

"You didn't find anything?"

"Wasn't anything to find. Your two agents are definitely busy as hell. They leave their houses at the crack of dawn and are at their headquarters before most. What happens in there, I can't tell you, but it can't be too much. The first day they only stayed for 45 minutes before leaving the Bureau building, and they kept that pattern throughout."

"How did you know when they left."

Glenn gave Jolston a look and said, "I'm not paid a shit-ton for my looks, Jolston."

"Sorry," Jolston said, annoyed with this man already.

"They left," he continued, "and then traveled all over the Northern Virginia area. They stopped at several libraries. They were using the free internet systems. I've got no idea what they searched for on that first day. I just know where they went. But these guys are professional cops, not professional anything else.

"They were trying to hide what they were doing, and going to the libraries was a good idea. But then they went back to the exact same places the next day. Rookie move," Glenn said, shaking his head.

Jolston nodded but didn't say anything, not wanting to be rebuked again.

"I put some key loggers and other shit on the library computers," Glenn said. Then with a shake of his head he said, "You wouldn't believe how many people go to the library and look at porn. What the fuck are you going to do at a library with porn? It isn't like you can whip out your pud in the middle of the building.

"Anyhow they kept going back to the same libraries, and they searched for nothing but AltCon, the senior management, and the Old Man. They followed every trail they found, but they all led nowhere. There is almost no information out there on any of you, and even less on the Old Man."

"That's by design, as I'm sure you are aware. When you become a senior in the company, your internet presence becomes monitored, and anything that is even remotely outside our regulations is removed. Failure to do so is grounds for termination," Jolston said.

"I know. I was impressed the first time I heard about that."

"Thank you."

Glenn raised his eyebrows questioningly and said, "Your idea?"

Jolston nodded his head.

"I always reserve the right to change my impression of a person. You're not just a dumb suit after all."

311

"I think that's a compliment?" Jolston asked, not changing his impression of the man at all.

"'Bout the best you will get from me," Glenn answered, and then continued. "There was only one time where their search strings varied slightly. On one occasion, they searched for someone named Robert Shoal and AltCon, which led to several articles about Shoal's employment with the company, and one article about his death by tragic accident. The other time they searched for Thomas Bradshaw and AltCon. Again, there were a bunch of articles about him as the head of the Board of Directors and then the one article about the botched robbery that led to his death.

"As far as the agents themselves, there's nothing worth noting. They are both well decorated and considered highly competent agents. Both are single, no love interests, they aren't getting it on together, and their work is their life. That's the whole lot. Like I said, not much."

Glenn was right. That wasn't much. But it did tell Jolston that the Bureau was at least looking into the top tier of AltCon and using unorthodox methods to do so. They were trying to hide something.

It was even more troubling that they were looking into Bradshaw and Shoals. Jolston knew those cases were closed. And their deaths had nothing to do with the federal government and should be entirely outside the lane of the FBI.

Jolston would give the entire report to the Old Man and let him decide what the next steps, if any, should be.

With the meeting over, Jolston and Glenn said their goodbyes.

"The Old Man and I go way back. You got anything more needs doing, you know how to contact me."

With that, Glenn exited the room, and Jolston was left alone to consider what more he could need of a man like Glenn.

CHAPTER 20

December 19, 2043

"Let's get a look at that map, Wayne."

I was thinking the same thing when I logged in at the base of the monastery and had waited for the group to get online.

"Right you are, Allister. Let's take a look." I said.

"I can't open it, but it is tradeable. Alex, since you're the leader of our group, why don't you take a look at it?"

Wayne handed the item over to me, and it appeared in my inventory. I didn't have the same restriction as Wayne and popped it open. Then I shared what I found with the group.

"This isn't too bad at all. Della had said that the last location, the Monastery of Movement, was far to the east. As it turns out, it's not all that far from where we fought the House Frost traitors, only it's south of the road instead of North. That's all Forest in that region."

That made four distinct environments in which we found a monastery: tundra, swamp, desert, and now forest. The map itself didn't actually depict anything specific for the monastery's location, only a general area.

I turned the map over, and there was writing on the back.

Aaron,

I have no doubt that you will be victorious in your quest. When you are done, come to this area and find me. I know we aren't supposed to share where we are going, but Father didn't say we couldn't give a "general location." I'll be waiting for you. Together we will go find Father.

Gerald

P.S. If you find those lazy brothers of ours, bring them, too.

Well that answered where the map came from.

"Not terribly helpful, but it is a start."

"Agreed, Allister. Let's head out of here. I hope we can find the Jalusi on our way back and see if we can sell some of this armor. We are getting close to being overweight." I said.

"That gives me an idea, Alex. Be right back," Wayne said and ran into the monastery.

He came back several minutes later. "Ok, I've got all the extra armor in a pile just through that first big room and into the first chamber where we encountered Maharit the first time. We can always come back here and get the stuff if we want it."

That was a good move by Wayne, and I nodded my head in thanks. It also further added to a separate plan that I had.

I didn't want to keep hiding things from the guys, and I thought this was a good time to tell them about my plan.

"What do you guys think about us removing Chief Majid from the head of the Jalusi Tribe?"

The guys looked at me with disbelief and shook their heads.

"I know we took care of this monastery, Alex, but we couldn't hope to go against the whole tribe."

"That's not what I was thinking. Tell me how you like this?" I then detailed my plan.

It was quite simple, really. The tribe's Chief wasn't determined by their ability to fight, but their ability to better the tribe through trade. The desert glass we had collected already, and the ones we would likely collect on the ride back to Sand's Edge, would go far toward making a claim. But I also had another idea.

"The King and his army are desperate for horses. I bet I could get some kind of a deal set up in Kich's Keep between the Jalusi Tribe and the King to provide those horses for the army. In exchange, they would trade for summoned horses. Probably at a rate of four to one, or better. And the summoned horses, like ours, don't require feeding and water. Or housing of any kind.

"The King has no need for the summoned horses, as we learned, since the mages of Loust's army could cast a Banish Summoned on them and effectively take a horse right out from under a rider if they were on it. This would increase the number of horses for the Jalusi and decrease the amount of upkeep they would require."

"Oh, I like these ideas!" Jason said.

"Me too, Alex. We just need to get Mahmut alone long enough to tell him our idea," Wayne said.

"Yeah. See, that's the thing. I wasn't thinking of giving these ideas to Mahmut. I was thinking we give them to Chakib. And we tell him about all the armor that Wayne just piled up in the monastery. And then tell him where the monastery is and how to find it. That would negate the armor we are about to sell to the Chief."

"I like it!" Jason yelled.

"What if it's not enough?" Dan asked. "What if Chakib goes in there and the council decides that the amount is not enough. Chakib would be killed. I'm not good with that."

Neither was I. Nor were my teammates. We liked Chakib. But that's where phase two came into play.

"If he can get the Chief job with what we set up, great. But if he doesn't, then we have him play his trump card."

And I held out the Gift of Life, and water started pooling around my feet.

"The most valuable thing in the desert."

The trip to the Jalusi netted us several more desert glass pieces, and we held onto them to give to Chakib. We did trade the armor that we had found and made a small fortune. Despite telling us that the Tribe had no use for metal, the Chief had a huge supply of it to dole out when we presented the armor. It netted us 100 platinum, and I couldn't imagine when we would ever spend that much money.

The Chief also had to note our accomplishment in front of the council and his people. As he had sent us on this trip to restore his honor, it was mandatory that he do so. He wasn't happy about it, though, and we made the process as short as possible. The Chief was happy to be rid of us and sent Mahmut and Kalil to escort us out of his camp.

As we approached the outskirts of the camp, and we were away from any of the sentries patrolling the perimeter, I addressed Mahmut.

"Did you speak truly when you said you wished for your brother's return?"

"Indeed, Alex. I miss him greatly, and the tribe is less with him not here."

"And if he were to return, and challenge your father for the right to be Chief of the tribe, would you stand with him?"

Mahmut looked around. I imagined he was looking to make sure no one heard his response.

"I am not a member of the council, so I would have no word. But if they chose him, I would give my support," he said. But then he shook his head. "But there are none who would trade with any but my father. It would be impossible."

"You mean like clearing the monastery with just us four?" I asked, a big smile on my face. Before Mahmut could answer, I winked at him, aimed my horse away from the camp, and rode off into the desert. The guys were right next to me.

We crossed paths with several more of the Bore Worms and killed each one we encountered. We collected more of the Desert Glass before reaching Sand's Edge, bringing the total I carried to twenty pieces.

We were greeted warmly by the residents of the town and waved through the open gate. Before we could even unsummon our horses, the whole village had arrived to surround us. Leading the pack were the three councilmembers. Chakib stood just outside of his house. He smiled at us warmly but didn't join the group.

We told the council that we had completed our task and would be returning through the swamp toward Kich's Keep. I informed them that our travels would take us past Della of the Glade, and we would tell her of the warmth and friendship we had found at Sand's Edge. And of the fierce negotiation skills of their lead councilwoman. This got a loud cheer from the villagers and a slight blush from the council.

I asked if our group could speak with Chakib, and they led us over to his home. Seeing our approach, he returned to the interior of his house.

When we entered, bread and tea were already placed in front of him. This time, there was enough for all our group and the council. We shared the beverage and the food, minus any salt, and that reminded me to tell Chakib of the attempted treachery by the Chief.

He nodded his head in what looked like appreciation. "That was well played on his part. He could claim no breach of hospitality if you took the salt, since it was his son who performed the rite."

"Yes, your brother even helped us by implying the salt was not a good thing for us to take."

At the mention of his brother, Chakib went still. I had no doubt that the secret of Chakib's lineage was known to the council, but he must not have thought we would learn of it.

"Do not fear, my friend. Your secret remains safe," I said. "In fact, I have a plan you may find interesting."

I reviewed everything I told the guys while we were at the monastery. I gave him every detail I could think of. He nodded along and smiled at how I piled on one benefit after another to the tribe.

"So, that's desert glass, armor, and horses for the tribe. Plus, you will lower the amount of upkeep, since the summoned horses don't require food and water. Naturally, you will still be able to retain many of your actual horses to continue breeding. In fact, I think it would be wise to keep a number that could carry all your fighters into battle, but the ones that need to be used to transport goods or the camp could easily be of the summoned variety. What do you think?"

Chakib sat quietly for a long time. He had closed his eyes and was breathing deeply. He finally opened his eyes and looked directly into mine.

"From the moment I left my tribe, I have dreamt of the day I could return. But I would never do so without my bride. Nor could I return with the traditions we hold for women. I've seen clearly the power they can wield and how we have neglected them amongst our people.

"But I just don't know that it would be enough, Alex. The council would be hesitant to consider the kind of change I would bring with me. The tribute may not be enough. Although, with this much desert glass, this town would be free from raids for two decades. Long enough for my Father to pass and for my children to grow into strong men and women of their own."

"Who said we were having any more?" the young councilwoman asked at his side, though was smiling throughout.

"Don't tease me, woman. You're all I have," he answered with his own smile.

I didn't want to interrupt the touching moment, but I needed to get Chakib back on track.

"I thought of all this, Chakib, and that's why I asked if it would be enough. I've got one more item, and I think it could be the thing that tips any consideration in your favor. But we should go outside for this."

We left the small house and stood back in the center of the village. I took the rock from my bag and held it to my side. After only a moment, water started to pour out, turning the dirt around us to mud. There was only silence from all around me.

"It is called the Gift of Life," I said, putting the rock back in my bag, lest we all end up covered in mud. "It will never stop producing water. Ever. And I give it to you."

"That would do it, Alex. Without question. We would have water wherever we roamed, and we could even set up permanent camps with all the desert glass. These are the next steps that my people must accomplish if we ever want to be more than the nomads of the desert.

"What will this cost?" he asked.

"At some point, this war with Loust will touch all of us. When the time comes, I only ask that you fight on the side of the king. For that, I will give you all of these things to secure the chiefdom of the tribe."

"The rock alone would be enough, Alex."

"Likely. But I want you to have the rest. I want your tribe to be as strong as they can be for when the fight comes. And it will come. That I can guarantee."

"Then I accept your aid and offer mine in kind when the time comes."

I shook hands with Chakib, handed over the Gift of Life and twenty pieces of Desert Glass. There was a loud cheer that erupted from the townspeople, and Chakib grabbed his wife, spinning her around.

Before we left, I pulled Chakib aside and told him. "I will be working with the Kingdom and Della to get negotiators here to speak with you. I will also ask Della to help with the transport of the live horses through the swamp and to the king."

"They will be in my protection."

"When the time comes, Chakib, the fight may not be here in the desert, but in the heart of the kingdom. Will your men follow you? This is why I need you to keep horses for fighting."

"In this, I am your man, Alex. Call, and I will come. You have given me back my life and have bettered the Jalusi. There is nothing more honorable."

With that finished, we mounted our horses and rode off into the swamp. The next stop was another visit with Della.

⚊⚊⚊

We avoided as many fights as we could and dispatched the mobs we had to fight. We had a long road ahead of us, and I wanted to get past Della and on to Kich's Keep before the end of our day.

The small hut that housed the old Witch of the swamp came into view, and we knew Della was in residence. It no longer looked like the run-down hovel that we had first encountered. The walls were sturdy, the roof complete, and there was a small garden off to the side. Everything around the home was thriving with life. This was the benefit of the Vivre Stone.

We stopped outside the entrance of her house and called out our arrival. Della stepped through the door with a large smile on her face. She ran over and embraced all of us. She offered to host us in her home, and we happily accepted. As we sat around her small table, she brought out food and drink, and we silently shared the simple fare with her.

"So, tell me of your adventures."

It took about half an hour to go over everything that happened. I tried to make the report thorough, since we were going to need her help with Chakib. And, honestly, we knew that Della was out here on her own and that she would appreciate the company. Having a powerful spell caster happy with you was always a benefit.

She cheered when we told her our plan to supplant the Chief of the Jalusi. She had met Chakib and thought him an honorable man and a good choice.

"You four never fail to surprise me. Defeating that sword master was enough of a feat, and most would have called that a success. Not for you all. You want to turn the whole land on its head. You have my full support. Just tell me what you need of me."

I explained how I planned to set up a contract between the Kingdom and Chakib. The king desperately needed those horses, so I wouldn't find a more willing buyer. The part I needed from her was safe passage through the swamp. She promised that she would do her part.

We got ready to leave, and I asked Della for one last favor.

"At some point in the future—I have no idea when exactly—I will need the Jalusi. When that happens, can I count on you to provide this service again? I'll need safe passage for their warriors through the swamp."

"You've done more for me than any other person, save for my darling Monk, and I am forever in your debt. Though you may think our scales balanced, I still feel I owe you more. When the time comes, I'll ride at the head of the Jalusi, all the way out of this swamp!"

I embraced Della again, thanking her for everything she had done and would do. I joined my teammates on the edge of the Vivre Stone's influence, ready to head back into the swamp, when I had an idea.

"Any chance you could do the same for us now? We need to get back to Kich's Keep, and we still have a long way to go. Any time we can save running through the Swamp will be much appreciated."

"Why would we run?" Della asked and then raised her hands to the sky. She began weaving her hands in an intricate pattern and then brought them down with a flourish. A majestic beast appeared before us. It was a unicorn, the first we had seen in Resurgence.

"Say hello to Chime," she said.

I was about to ask her why Chime when the unicorn shook its head. A distinct sound of bells went off.

"Got it," I said, smiling.

"Summon your horses, Alex. We will ride together!"

Like that, we tore through the area, the Vivre Stone keeping the area around us clear. The fetid swamp was on either side of us. On two occasions, large mobs sprang at us from the swamp, but as soon as they passed the threshold of the Stone's influence, they turned from rabid beasts to timid creatures. One, a jaguar, followed alongside us. The animal never tried to attack and seemed happy to lope along.

When we approached the edge of the swamp, Della pulled her unicorn to a stop, and we all did the same. The jaguar weaved between the legs of the horses and Della's steed but was not aggressive in the least bit.

"I think I just found a new friend. He'll make another wonderful protector for the Glade. Good things happen wherever you go, Alex!"

We thanked Della again and left the swamp. The King's Road was right in front of us, and we turned West toward Kich's Keep. There was no happy banter between us. We wanted to move with as much speed as possible.

It was another hour of travel on the road before we saw the first signs of the capital, the outlying farms that helped feed the people living inside the keep. Soon after that, we started to see travelers with wagon trains, lining up to get inside the walls. They were off to the right of the road, and a separate, smaller line, was formed up on the left side for those traveling without wagons.

As players, we weren't stopped by the guards, and were waved on through. However, our horses weren't allowed inside the walls, and we had to walk from the main gate to the square with Sir Arthur.

Once we got there, it was time to decide on our next course of action. I had said repeatedly that I was going to try and set up a contact between Chakib and the Kingdom, but I hadn't said exactly how that was going to happen. The guys were curious to see what my plan was.

Unfortunately, I didn't really have one. I had an idea, one I honestly thought could possibly work, but it would require a bit of subterfuge on my part. I didn't like it, but I was back to lying to my friends.

"I've made contacts amongst the merchants, what with me being our main seller. And while I don't have the same kind of relationship with them as I did with that merchant back in Port Town that gave us our first unique quest, I think I can get them to talk to me. I just don't know how they'll react if the whole group is with me."

I figured Dan would be the first to question my logic, but I was wrong. In fact, he was the first to offer up something else for him to do.

"Works for me. I've got to go and get some wood from the Elder Elven Tree for my arrows, and Broham is owed some power leveling."

"Indeed, he is, Dan." Jason said.

"Cool. I'll go track down Jenny and our team," Wayne said.

"Never mind, Allipowerleveler, I'm gonna go see Kaitlin!"

We all laughed at Dan, and he shook his head. "Nah, I'll take care of Broham. He deserves it after saving everyone's butts in there."

Everyone went their own ways, and I headed to talk to my "merchant contacts."

———————

Waseem was already in the Stinky Pit when I arrived. He was my first choice for this but usually the last guy I wanted to talk to. He was just that smug.

"Ahh, my student returns. Have you come to thank your teacher for all I've done for you, perhaps with heaps of gold and platinum?"

"Hello to you too, Waseem. Any luck getting through wards these days?"

"Ooh. That was a good one. You're learning to fight back well, Alex."

"Thanks. And you are actually the person I was looking for. Have time to chat?"

"If it involves going after someone else's goods, then yes, I certainly do."

I shook my head at the thief and continued. "Not exactly. I need to know if you know anyone that can act as a contact for me. A merchant."

"Ah, I see! You have something that you need to get rid of. Something hot? Please tell me where you stole it from. Professional curiosity is all."

"I didn't steal anything. I want to set up a deal between the Kingdom and a nomadic tribe out in the desert, but there isn't anyone I know that could complete the task. So, with all the business you do, I figured you might know someone who could help."

Waseem stared at me for a good three seconds before bursting out in laughter. And it wasn't fake laughter, either. This was the real deal. I had said something amazingly funny. Only I had no idea what it was.

But Waseem wasn't going to make me wait long to find out.

"Oh, gods," he said wiping a tear from the side of his eye, "that was fresh, Alex. You really had me going for a second there. I thought you were serious," he said and then continued to laugh some more.

"What? Dammit, Waseem! I am serious!"

The thief stopped laughing for a moment and said, "Truly?"

"Yes!"

"That's even funnier then!" he exclaimed and started laughing even harder. I had never wanted to stab someone in the eye, and have them live afterwards, more than at that moment.

He finally calmed down enough to say, "Why on earth would you think that I would know anyone with that kind of contact? I steal things, Alex. The people I talk to take my stolen things. And then they sell them to other people who are perfectly happy to buy stolen things. Are any of them nobles? Certainly. Are any of them going to want to be introduced by my contacts? Not in a hundred years!" When he finished, he went right on back to laughing, making sure to add in, "And for a legitimate contract, no less," before the real laughter took over.

"Fine. Forget it."

Waseem finally calmed down a bit and stopped laughing. "Oh, fear not, little rogue. You came to the right place. You're just asking the wrong person."

"Dhalean?"

"What? No, of course not. The only merchants Dhalean has ever known are all dead by his blade," he said.

"You don't mean Sally?"

"Master Rogue Sally? No. But Special Advisor to the Bank Sally? Oh, most definitely yes."

Waseem sent a runner out to track down Sally and summon her to the Pit. I passed the hour before she arrived telling Waseem about my adventures with the team, the Lift I had to do in the Keep, the massive amount of Scaling I used, and the overall benefit of my Blacksuit. I also showed off my new pants, and Waseem actually whistled.

"Those are a fine addition! I'd steal those off you in a heartbeat!"

"A nicer compliment I've never heard," I said and laughed along with Waseem.

"I must say, Alex, there is something to be said for traveling in a group like yours. If your tale is true, then your entire party earned multiple items of an epic quality that no single individual could obtain. And, because of their magic qualities, they have bound themselves to you and can't be stolen. I may have to look into this in more detail."

"Having a group is good if it can work well together. My friends and I complement each other's skills. We created the group because of that. If you have too much damage and no healer, then you will lose. Too much aggression and no one to handle any extra attackers, and you will lose. It's a balance." I saw Waseem nodding along. "Also, you can't steal from them."

Waseem's nodding stopped. "Never mind then."

I had to laugh, and Waseem gave off a slight smile. Despite his last words, I could see he was thinking about it.

"I actually saw the truth of your words when we did our last night run. That was another time when we complemented each other. I recognized the benefit then and there."

I was going to comment more on that last "run," as he had called it, which was our hit on the Bank, when I heard a familiar and welcome voice behind me.

"I could have stabbed you in your kidney."

Not a welcome phrase, mind you, but a welcome voice.

I stood up and turned to find my friend and first trainer, Dhalean, standing behind me. His real name was Stan, but since we had been away from Port Town for so long, I had gotten used to thinking of him as Dhalean, the moniker he used in Kich's Keep.

"But you wouldn't have been able to steal my purse!"

That got a chortle from the small rogue. As a Halfling, he only stood a little over four feet, but he was the deadliest man with a blade in the kingdom. It just wasn't a very big blade.

"I've never been good at that Lift stuff, anyway. What brings you to the Pit."

I was about to launch into the story again but stopped when I saw the newest visitor arrive. If there was ever someone I feared for the sheer joy they took in seeing another experience pain, it would be Sally, my trainer for all things traps and wards. She was a woman of smaller stature and even looked to be motherly, but she wasn't fooling me or any of the other Rogues in the room.

"Excellent," I said. "I won't have to tell the story three times. Sally, Dhalean, please take a seat. I need your help."

I told the story yet again, this time glossing over some of the finer details. Waseem knew them from my earlier telling, but he didn't interrupt. With Sally present, I focused more on the parts concerning the Jalusi Tribe and my idea for changing the leadership of the nomadic travelers.

They all three sat in silence, Dhalean and Sally because they were digesting the information and my request for a contact, Waseem because he looked interested to see what the other two would say.

"I don't have anyone that could help ya, lad. But I do want to say that you are doing a wonderful job at manipulating this whole thing. We thought you could be a Gentleman Rogue when we first got a look at you, with your fancy talk, but we went with something that made you more rounded. I don't regret that decision, but I'm glad to see that if you ever decided to want to be a Master Rogue, that would be the direction you should take. The Gentleman Rogue is a political master from the shadows, and you are showing a talent for it with the Dwarves Under the Mountain and now the Jalusi.

"We better be careful, or we'll be looking at the new king before long."

I kept it to myself that my Lady Tessa quest might just upend the Kingdom when all was said and done.

"Thanks, Dhalean. A lot of these situations just fell into our lap, so I can't really take credit."

"Bah. To hell with that," Dhalean said. "You played each of these groups to make it work later when those opportunities presented themselves. Don't sell yourself short, boy."

I nodded my head in thanks again. "It's good to know. But for now, I'm happy to keep with what I've got." Thinking of all the things we had been through, however, reminded me of a question I wanted to ask the Rogues around me.

I relayed how Dastin Frost seemed to think that the Court of Shadows had been the one to get him out of the city once his treachery was known. I didn't think anyone in this room was stupid enough to do that, but I wanted to make sure.

"You are right there, Alex," Sally replied. "We'd heard the same, and things are in the works to make certain the perpetrators of that crime are uncovered. It will quickly become obvious that the culprits had no connection to any underground criminal organization and were actually another house. They hoped to gain greater standing in the city with House Frost gone, and they used the Kingdom focusing on House Frost and the war against Loust to undertake some rather nasty business," Sally said.

"I see I'm not the only one working in the shadows," I said with a chuckle.

"In regard to your earlier question, concerning a merchant," Sally interrupted, "I have just the person in mind. Meet me in front of the Bank in twenty minutes. I'll be there for the introduction."

"Who will I be meeting?"

"Why, the President of the Bank, of course."

Sally was true to her word, and I saw her standing in front of the Bank with a man dressed in the finest clothes I'd ever seen in game. I walked up and said hello to Sally and then extended my hand in greeting to the man. "Hello, I'm Alex, an adventurer here in Tholtos. It is a pleasure to meet you Mr..."

"Banks."

"Naturally," I said, smiling along with Sally and Mr. Banks at the unsaid joke.

"Mistress Sally here tells me she came across one of you adventurers who had quite a proposal, one that would be financially worthwhile to whomever was bold enough to undertake the prospect. Turns out, we aren't just a Bank," he said and smiled. "What have you got?"

I didn't know this man, and everything I had planned rested on the fact that whoever the merchant was had to deal with Chakib exclusively. I made that plain to Banks.

"So, if I understand this correctly, in order for you to even tell me what the deal is, I have to first swear an oath that I, or any of my associates that could be linked back to me through any number of cutouts, will only negotiate this contract with Chakib currently located at the settlement of Sand's Edge on the border of the Globi desert?"

"Exactly."

"You a Barrister?"

I laughed and shook my head no.

"Because that was a damn good, on-the-fly, oath, especially the part about the 'any number of cut-outs' part. I'm going to steal that if you don't mind?"

"Nah, I don't mind."

"Well, if your deal is anywhere near as good as your negotiating skills, I can't wait to hear this. You have my oath to the aforementioned conditions."

President Banks of the Bank has sworn an Oath to only negotiate with Chakib.

"That works for me. So, here's the deal."

I was getting really good at telling this story. For Mr. Banks, I simply explained the situation of the Jalusi, their horses, and the fact that they would trade for summoned mounts. Banks, in turn, could sell the horses to the Kingdom and undoubtedly make a hefty profit.

"I didn't include this in the Oath, but I would ask that you let the Kingdom know that the trade was done with Chakib of the Jalusi Tribe."

"Why?"

"Chakib wants to bring the tribe more into the fold of the Kingdom."

"Ah. So, an emerging market as well. I like this. I'll take the deal."

I explained that in order to get to Sand's Edge, Banks would need to travel across the swamp. He didn't seem concerned and explained that he had a contingent of warriors that would escort his merchants through and protect them from any harm.

His eyebrows lifted when I told him that wouldn't be necessary. I said that if he arrived at a predetermined location, at a preselected time, an escort would already be waiting, that would negate any concern for his merchants.

I showed him the location of Sand's Edge on a map he produced then showed him the location where Della would meet him.

"And who is this Della?"

"She is the Keeper of the Swamp. She has agreed to provide safe passage through the swamp for your initial negotiations and the eventual delivery of the horses. All will be unhindered during their voyage."

"The witch? I thought she was a legend told to children to frighten them?"

"She is no longer a witch, Mr. Banks. In fact, it would probably be worthwhile for you to make the initial journey yourself and make contact with her for the potential "enterprises" you could establish," I said. "Please treat her kindly. I count her as a close friend."

"It shall be. Now, what of your commission?"

I hadn't known that a commission was coming. I said as much.

"Ha! I was wondering why these negotiations were so much different than any other I've ever done. Usually, the person in your position spends almost the entire time haggling over the amount they will get."

I turned and looked at my Rogue trainer and asked, "Sally, as a trusted advisor to the Kingdom, what would you suggest as a fair commission?"

"Ten percent is the going rate, I believe."

"Aye, it is," Mr. Banks said. "But I would have to make the stipulation that it could only be for the horses, not for the subsequent business deals."

"Sale of the horses to the Kingdom, you mean."

"Damn! Good catch. I thought I had you there for a second," he said and laughed, reminding me of King Steelhammer's way of negotiating.

"Instead of straight platinum, I would ask that my group be given the option to select an item of equal value from your bank's personal vault."

Mr. Banks considered the request for a moment and then nodded his head. "With the only caveat being that I have a right of refusal and can revert to platinum instead."

"Agreed."

We shook hands, agreed on the time and place for the meetup with Della, and went our separate ways.

We would need to stop at Della's before heading to the next monastery.

Undisclosed Location

The General watched from his office as former Marine Corps Staff Sergeant Timothy Slokavitch sat in the conference room. The man had been led into the conference room by Colonel Thompson several minutes earlier. He sat down at the seat identified by the Colonel and hadn't asked any questions. In fact, Thompson informed the General that he hadn't asked any questions at all on the ride to the facility. He had commented on the lack of visibility from the back of the vehicle but didn't say anything more when it became obvious there wouldn't be a response to his comment.

Since arriving in the conference room, the former Marine had simply sat and waited. But the General noticed his eyes. He was taking in everything around the room. That he was assessing the situation and looking for the exits, the General had no doubt.

The Marine had waited long enough.

The General walked into the conference room and locked eyes with Tim. For a brief moment, the two assessed each other. Two predators determining who would win in a fight.

The General was first to break the eye contact and made his way to a seat. Instead of sitting at the head of the large table, where he usually held court, he sat across from Tim, and placed a folder in front of himself. He sat patiently, waiting for Tim to make the first comment. After a minute of silence, the General acquiesced and spoke first.

"Most people stand up when I enter the room."

"Was a time I would have too, General…"

"General is fine."

"Well, I'm not that guy anymore. I finished my enlistment, and I'm not on inactive reserve any longer. I'm a civilian. I stand when I choose."

"This is going to get off on the wrong foot, I fear," the General said.

"Pretty sure that happened when you put me in the back of a car with no way to see where I was going. Couldn't jump out either. I tried the doors."

"I saw that," the General said. "Car was going pretty fast."

"Didn't really know where I was going, did I," Tim responded. "If it weren't for the uniforms that let me out of the car, I probably would have tried to fight my way out of this place. Wherever it is."

"Well I'm glad you didn't."

"Yeah. So are they."

That comment left an air of tension in the room. The saying about being able to cut it with a knife would have been appropriate here. The General knew he needed to take over this conversation and get it back on track.

"Start over, then? You're in an undocumented building, owned by the Department of Defense. I'm the General that oversees this program. And you are here, Mr. Slokavitch, because I need your help."

"Just Tim is fine, General. Like I said, I'm a civilian now," Tim responded. "And I've got more questions than I just got answers for, so I'm hoping you're willing to be a bit more forthcoming."

The General stared at Tim for several more moments and then got a small smile on his face.

"Damn if I don't like you, Tim. I've got a couple of Special Forces guys here with me, but none of them have a record like yours. It's been a long time since I've been in a room with a guy who probably could fight his way out of this complex."

Tim couldn't help it and smiled a bit himself. "Well, flattery will get you only so far, General. I'm still going to need some answers. What's going on here."

The General opened the folder. It was really just for show—a way to control the flow of the meeting. The General knew all the information in the file already.

"In August, you began working for a company called AltCon. You were hired to test a video game, Resurgence. The hardware for that game introduced the most advanced form of Virtual Reality the US Government has ever heard of. The Virtual Reality Augmentation Container."

"We just call it the RAC."

"Right, the RAC. The technology of the hardware allows a person to become fully immersed in the reality provided by AltCon. Nothing before it even comes close."

"I know all this, General. I lay in my RAC every day," Tim said with a bit of annoyance. "I see you know what I'm doing, but that's not really telling me why I'm here."

The General planned to drag this out, connecting dots along the way, but that didn't seem to be Tim's style. The General decided to be blunt, instead.

"Ok. Have you noticed anything odd about the game?"

"Resurgence? No. It's hyper-realistic, but I haven't come across anything that I would consider outside of normal for a fantasy video game."

"And what about AltCon?"

"What about them? AltCon is damn near the greatest company I've ever had the opportunity to work for. If they weren't paying me to do this beta, I'd probably still do it for free. I can't say a negative thing about them."

The General wasn't surprised to hear the words coming out of Tim's mouth. It was obvious; he had been conditioned.

The General needed a person willing to help him, but Tim's conditioning could create a problem that the General couldn't overcome. Although, the General did note that Tim said he couldn't say a negative thing about the company. The General wondered if on some level he was aware of the manipulation to his subconscious thoughts.

"So, you think all of AltCon's activities have been rational?" The General asked.

"That's a strange way to word it. I think everything they've done would be considered rational to them. I suppose some might disagree."

"How do you mean that?"

"The microphones and cameras."

"The what?"

"After they put the RACs in our homes, the AltCon techs also installed mini cameras and microphones, without telling us. I imagine they did so to make sure we weren't trying to learn anything about their tech or breaking our NDAs by discussing what happened in the game."

The General looked at Tim with bewilderment. "They put these where they were easy to see?"

Tim smiled and shook his head. "Of course not," he said. "But they weren't difficult to find. Your average Tom, Dick, or Harry probably wouldn't notice them. I do protective security, though. Part of that job requires me to clear hotel rooms of threats both physical and electronic."

"Did you remove them, then?"

"Of course not, General. That would just let the company know I found them. They only put them in two places. The room holding the RAC had cameras and mics, and the living room only had mics. Instead of removing them, I told my wife that we wouldn't hold conversations in either of those rooms," Tim said with a shrug of his shoulders. "She's used to my weird requests."

That's when the General decided to lay it all out for Tim.

Starting from the beginning, the General explained that AltCon had been using the RACs to a nefarious end, breaking down the conditioning that had been going on from the outset. Without going into a huge amount of technical details, the General peeled back each layer of the AltCon onion, exposing its rotten core of manipulation.

Tim laughed when the General explained the video game debacle, wherein all the players bought outdated games that they never played. "I still haven't touched those damn things, and my wife reminds me of it constantly."

The General also shared their beliefs that AltCon had done something similar during their "Family Day" event, trying to keep spouses from impeding players' game play.

That's when Tim finally showed some emotion.

"They did what?" he said, hands balled into fists and his knuckles turning white. He growled out, "If they messed with my wife, I'll fucking end them!"

The General held his hands out in front of him in a calming gesture, hoping to subdue the man's anger. He was happy to have found Tim's trigger, though. Now he knew what buttons to push to get this man to help him, if he needed an extra push. Family was important to him.

"I can't tell you for sure, but I know that after spouses went to Family Day, they stopped complaining about the game," the General said. "I could likely prove it to you as well. You took a brain scan when you were discharged from the military. If we took another one today, I imagine it would be vastly different."

Tim silently sat at the table. He looked to be processing the information.

"What do you think of AltCon now, Tim?"

"Greatest company I've ever worked for, General."

That was exactly the phrase the General was hoping to hear.

Tim continued to stare at the officer, not saying a word, and obviously not realizing what had just come out of his mouth.

"As you can imagine, Tim, everything in this room is recorded. Both visual and audio. Please direct your attention to the monitor on the wall."

Before Tim could say anything more, the screen came to life and the last thirty seconds were replayed.

Tim sat still, mouth agape, and his eyes wide.

"No need for that brain scan, General. I'm convinced. I remember saying that but can't remember wanting to say it, if that makes sense."

"Completely, Tim."

Several more seconds passed in silence before Tim said, "How can I help?"

Inwardly, the General sighed in relief. Another asset was on the board.

"At some point in time, I have plans to take this company down, Tim. When that happens, I fear that the people playing the game could be in danger. In particular, your specific group."

"Why my group?"

"As you've seen, I have some very in-depth knowledge as to what's happening in Resurgence."

"I noticed that."

"It's because I have someone working on the inside. He's been in the beta, from the beginning, and has been reporting his findings back to us. He's far more devious than one would think, and a genius to boot."

"Alex," Tim said.

"That guy's a moron!"

The voice came from behind Tim. The former Marine had been so focused on the conversation with the General, and the scene that had played out on the monitor, that he hadn't noticed someone enter the room.

And he sure as hell didn't expect to see Dan.

"You've got to be kidding me!" Tim said and jumped out of his chair, embracing his friend. "You?"

"Who better than the dimwit that no one would expect?"

"I can't lie. That's brilliant," Tim said then turned back to the General. "So, Dan's play style and all that was all an act?"

The General shook his head and had a slight look of agony on his face. "No. I'm afraid that Dan is very much exactly like his character."

"Harsh, General."

"Although, the fire mishap was my idea," the General said, referencing the time Dan almost burnt down Jenny's apartment.

"What? Why?"

"To cement everyone's view of Mr. Hamson as the bumbling fool."

"Worked like a charm, too," Dan said.

"Can't argue there. Everyone thought Dan a bit of an idiot after that," Tim said and sat back down.

He looked back up at the monitor that had played back his conditioned response before looking at the General and Dan. "I've got to ask again, General, what do you need from me if you already have someone in the game farther along than me?"

"When this plays out, AltCon is going to look to protect their investments and remove any proof of their wrongdoing. That's when I'll need you."

"Meaning?"

"Isn't it obvious? I'll need you to keep them alive."

CHAPTER 21

December 20, 2043

The guys were happy to hear that I was successful in my efforts to secure a merchant to deal with Chakib. They were a bit surprised when I told them it was the President of the Bank. I simply offered up a wry smile, winked, and said that they obviously didn't understand how talented of a merchant I was.

"Says the guy who just said yesterday that he didn't have any good relationships with the merchants here," Dan pointed out.

"I like to undervalue my abilities. That way, when I pull something off, it looks like a miracle," I said and gave a bow.

"Alex, the Miracle Worker. I think that should be a new title," Wayne said.

"He certainly has earned it, what with all the Legendary gear we keep getting for Allioverpowered."

"You didn't seem to mind when we were power leveling Broham yesterday," Jason said.

"Oh yeah," I said, looking to change the subject. "How did that go?"

"Great!" Dan said. "We found some undead. It wasn't even a contest."

We left the town square, made our way to the gates, and got on our horses. The guys were fine with the slight detour we would need to take to talk with Della. She would likely be surprised to see us so soon.

With all our trips through the swamp, we had mastered navigating through the marshes to avoid any and all mobs. Before we knew it, we were back at Della's home and relayed our message. She was very pleased to hear that the negotiations were happening so quickly and promised to be waiting for the merchants in two days at the edge of the swamp.

I also told her that the President of the Bank would possibly be accompanying the group and that she should take the opportunity to talk with him.

"For what purpose, Alex? I have everything I need here."

"I know you've been studying the Vivre Stone. Try to find some way to increase its power. This land is full of wonders, and who knows what might make it stronger and enlarge your area of influence. The items that come from this swamp can only be collected by you, unless you want cursed goods, and that makes them some of the rarest things on the market. Use that to your advantage," I said.

"Any chance you can stay?" She asked with a smile, knowing that we couldn't.

I smiled back and told her not to worry. I had told the President to treat her fairly, as she was our friend. Those words seemed to touch her greatly and she gave me an overly large hug.

"It's been a long time since I've had someone I could truly call a friend. Thank you, Alex," she said, and then looked at the rest of my group. "Thanks to all of you."

More hugs were shared. Della was really a hugger. Must have been from all those years of not having any physical contact.

Della summoned Chime, and we jumped on our horses. She escorted us again to the edge of the swamp, and we left her with a wave.

We continued our ride toward the front of the war, and I only slowed down when I heard Dan yell out to stop.

"What's up, Dan?"

"We don't have any paperwork, Alex. And we aren't on a mission for the King. What if we get stopped by scouts again?"

I hadn't thought of that. Not to mention, I didn't think we could have gotten any since we weren't on a quest from Sir Arthur, though I bet someone amongst the rogues could have forged us some.

"Any ideas?" I asked.

"Yeah," Wayne said. "We stop being so humble. We are the 'Legends' after all. we took down the head of House Frost. And I actually think everyone knows Dan."

I had to laugh at that. Dan's antics in the taverns of Tholtos were legendary. I doubted that the NPCs knew about them though.

"So, we bluff, Naugha?"

"Nope, Allister. We just say that we are going out to rid the area of beasts and that when the King needs us, wouldn't it be better to have us near the front?"

I shrugged my shoulders at the group. I didn't have anything better, and this time, direct may be better than subterfuge.

We got to test the theory when we came over the next rise. A checkpoint had been set up by the army. This was a legit checkpoint, not some bandits trying to fool travelers and then rob them. We slowed our horses as we approached and kept our hands at our sides.

"State your business," said one of the guards. I recognized him immediately. He was the same guard that had come out of the forest and stopped us before.

"We're here to clean the latrines."

The guard took a closer look at us and started laughing. The other guards started laughing too when they recognized us and remembered the original guard's question about whether we were there to clean the shitters.

"Here to take down another house? We heard about your conquests, and we were damn proud to know that we had met the men of legend."

"No quest this time. We're heading out to clear the area of beasts, trying to stay near the front in case the King needs us. We don't have any papers, though. Will that be a problem?"

"Not anymore," he said and handed me a scroll. "Show this at the checkpoints, and it will let you through to the camp. It's moved again since last you were here. You'll have to travel a bit farther."

338

"Thank you."

"No problem. Once you get to the camp, I'm sure Major Treeswain will want to see you, though."

"Major?" I asked.

"Yup, got promoted after the last campaign to take down House Frost. Apparently, his strategy was quite good, and the King gave him a field promotion. We're all very proud of him."

I guessed that morale must be high.

The guard wasn't lying, and the distance to the camp had indeed increased. It also slowed our movement that there were now over a dozen of the checkpoints. We were forced to stop at each one and show the scroll from our guard friends. Once we were recognized, we had to wait even longer to receive all the congrats and thanks from the soldiers.

I hated when we spent almost an entire day traveling. Of course, it would have been much worse if we didn't have the horses, as this would have taken us a week to do by foot, or at least a few days on a caravan.

There were wizards that could teleport their groups to different locations as long as they had been there before and it could normally be used as a bind point. For us, that would have been Port Town, Kich's Keep, and Under the Mountain. I thought that once Chakib became Chief of the Jalusi, we would be able to get that one, too, since I figured our status with them would skyrocket. There was also the Citadel, where the dark races started, but only I had traveled there and then only to the outskirts. I had never gone in.

Still, these wizards could only transport their own group. A spell to teleport an individual to a specific point, outside of a group, had yet to be discovered.

Teleport scrolls were also an option, but we had never found one. We had only seen those handed out for the completion of quests.

The day was growing dark as we finally entered the camp. The scouts were vigilant and stopped us long before we got to the outskirts of the camp. Upon seeing our scroll and recognizing us from the feast held in our honor, we went through the same round of congratulations and thanks. We left them and made for the center of the camp at a quick clip.

Several people yelled at us to slow down, but I knew that if we took it slow, we would be overwhelmed with people wanting to thank us. I was willing to get a few clumps of dirt thrown around to avoid that fate.

We pulled up our horses right at the center tent and sent them away. The guards standing watch outside the tent knew us and saluted crisply before we walked over. We asked to be announced, and one of them entered the tent.

A moment later we were invited in.

If there was one thing we could count on, it was Treeswain and his intent focus on the campaign and all things strategy. He only took the moment to wave us over before looking back down at the map in front of him.

"Welcome, gentlemen. Your arrival was announced about an hour ago, but I imagine it took a while to get past the sentries."

"That, and everyone wanting to thank us, though we really didn't mind that part. Congratulations to you as well on your promotion."

"I got promised 37 beers," Dan said.

"Don't drink them all at once," Treeswain said with some seriousness and then winked at our Ranger. "And thank you. I used the information you provided to develop our strategy, and our losses were almost non-existent."

"Glad we could help."

"So, what brings you back? I wasn't aware of any missions that fit your specialties."

"No mission. We are looking to continue growing as adventurers. We thought there may be suitable beasts in this area for us."

"It's worth a look, but most of the animals have been wiped out by the Children of Loust's army. They eat anything."

That didn't really bother us, since we weren't looking for wildlife, but the monastery.

"We would still like to try, with your permission."

Treeswain looked at us oddly. "Permission? You four can do anything you want. We're only where we are now because of you. You have every permission you want from me."

340

Dan's eyes lit up at that line, and Treeswain recognized that look. "What did I just do?"

⸺⸺

December 21, 2043

The next morning, Dan looked completely wrecked. It wasn't any surprise, either, given his escapades the previous night. I had seen our Ranger turn it up before, but this was the first time I saw him get to 11.

And it was all thanks to his newest invention—the Cask Stand. It's basically a keg stand, only with a cask of whatever alcohol was on hand. Now, any good college student can tell you that the keg stand is a staple of universities the world over. They would also tell you that it's usually the cheapest beer one can find that goes into that keg.

Cheap beer is usually synonymous with low alcohol content, but that wasn't the case with the casks of mead that Dan used for his inaugural celebration of this juvenile pastime.

Bottom line, Dan got hammered.

And he would forever be remembered by the King's army. Songs were already being sung. The noise was killing him, with his hangover.

Our laughter wasn't helping in the least bit.

"Why won't they stop? It's not even a good song!"

That just made us laugh harder.

We left the camp and continued down the road, heading east. The actual front line was still a ways off. The main camp had been established to keep it protected from any Loust forces that pushed past our lines. I hoped the time on the road would let Dan come down from his hangover, but the constant movement of the horse didn't seem to be helping any.

We reached the front line after another hour and decided to ditch the King's Road for the forest to the south of us. If we had headed north, it would have taken us almost straight to the keep that House Frost had previously taken as their own.

If the path was clear, it would still be another two-day ride to the main fortress of Loust's army. That meant there were still ample forces ready to bear down on the king and his men.

That would be for another time, however, as we had another monastery to discover.

Treeswain had been correct in his assessment. We saw very few animals out in the forest. There were some smaller beasts, but they were all such a low level that they ran from us instead of engaging with my party.

This was good for us, though, as it allowed us to search the forest for almost the entire time we were online, practically without confrontation. We did encounter a small camp of Goblins that we dispatched, just to have something to do, but they were much lower level than we were, allowing us to take almost the entire camp at the same time. Their hits were so low, we barely saw any damage sneak through our armor. Still, we didn't want that Goblin camp to grow in strength and join Loust's army later.

We weren't just searching in a random pattern. We decided to ride to the center of the area identified on Gerald's map, then we began making larger circles from that point. It was slow going, however, as the area we were searching was almost as large as the desert. It also didn't help that the trees impeded our line of sight and our ability to travel in straight lines—or in this case, curved lines.

Despite our best attempts, our search left out chunks of unchartered territory, but not large ones. I could live with that.

The other part that made our search difficult was that we didn't know what we were looking for. We figured it had to be large, as each of the previous monasteries had been towering structures. Frustratingly, there wasn't anything that fit that bill, nor had I let the trees impede our search in this. In fact, I had used them.

Once we got to the center of the area marked, I quickly realized we wouldn't be able to see far into the woods. Instead of letting them hamper us entirely, I decided to climb to their tops.

I found the highest one in the area, and with my climbing skill, I quickly ascended the tree. It was a good hundred feet into the air, and I almost made it to the top. From my perch, I was able to see over the forest. The first thing I looked for was a structure poking out amongst the trees, but there was nothing.

The next thing I looked for was a large clearing of trees, where one of the monasteries could be. Given the sizes of the previous three, it would take a very large clearing to house one of the structures, and that should have been obvious from my vantage point.

Still there was nothing. The forest went on and on until it reached the road to the north, a range of impenetrable mountains to the south, and continued to the east for farther than I could see. There were no breaks in the trees.

This is why we were doing our systematic approach. We thought the next monastery could be underground, and we would need to find the entrance through a cave or something like that, so we methodically checked over the forest. Still, we came up empty.

When our eight hours online came to an end, no one was interested in pushing on. We hadn't gained any experience for the day and we certainly weren't going to try the monastery if we found it in the next couple hours. The decision to camp for the night was unanimous. The next day would offer a fresh start.

And, at least for Dan, he could play the whole day without a splitting headache.

FBI Forensics Center (Basement)

Bolden and Colvin sat in front of Grimes' desk. There were still heaps of papers everywhere, but there seemed to be less of it. Grimes was moving papers around his desk and looking, somewhat frantically, for something on the surface. He paused to look up from his desk and gave the two agents a brief scowl before returning to his scrambling.

The agents shared a questioning look, not understanding why Grimes would be mad at them. After a few more moments, they had their answer.

"This is your fault, you know. I cleaned up some to make the place look more hospitable, and now I can't find shit."

"Don't you put this on us, Ry. We've never asked you to move anything," Colvin said. He then smiled and said, "Besides, this is what you call hospitable?"

Grimes looked up quickly, with an even angrier look on his face, until he saw Colvin smiling. He stopped moving the papers on his desk and smiled himself. "Ok, touché. Just give me a few, and I'll find this damn folder."

"This one?" Bolden asked, holding up a manila folder that said "patent requests" on the outside.

"Yes!" Grimes said, snatched it from her hand. "Why'd you take it?"

Bolden looked a bit confused. "I didn't take it. It was sitting on this seat when we walked in."

Grimes just shook his head. "Right. I put it there so I wouldn't forget where I placed it. I'm sorry. I've been running on no sleep, lots of coffee, and more Mountain Dew than is really healthy."

The agents just smiled and nodded their heads. Grimes was known for being eccentric, but you couldn't argue with his results. The office he had tried to make "hospitable" was still layered in loose papers, with stacks rising as high as four feet. His appearance could also be off-putting to some, wearing jeans, converse, and a t-shirt of usually some band. Today was Guns N' Roses. He also had tattoos running up both arms, on the back of his hands, on his knuckles, and a rather large one on the right side of his neck.

He wasn't what you pictured when you thought "elite FBI investigator," but that's what he was. He was a master of forensic accounting and could uncover any paper trail. He had been instrumental in locating the AltCon building hidden away in the forest, and now he was holding their latest assignment, the patent search.

As soon as Annabelle and Nicodemus had finished memorizing the information provided by Director Grissten on the fiber optic line, they came to see Grimes. Only after a short explanation to Grimes, he understood what the agents wanted. He didn't hesitate to shoo them away and got to work.

"The idea of checking out their other patents was a great one. The AltCon people use certain canned language in their applications. It was pretty much across the board. I did some searches to see if I could find other instances of the same language, and I only found two. Other AltCon filings, and these," he said and passed across the folder.

Bolden took the folder back from Grimes and opened it up, looking at the first page of several included in the pile.

"Good stuff, Ry?"

"Really good stuff, Nico. Fucking awesome stuff. And devious as hell."

Bolden nodded her head in agreement. The only other applications in the folder were for patents directly related to parts for a fiber optic line. And they matched with the information that the Director had given to them.

"I take it these weren't filed by AltCon's lawyers directly?"

"Right you are, Annabelle. Check the last few pages."

Annabelle turned past several more patent forms. None of them were for the actual fiber optic line itself. Instead, they were for the individual parts. The last few pages were the articles of incorporation for a company called "FastLine."

"How did you find this company?"

"The applications have a point of contact for further questions, a landline. I searched for the billing records to the landline and got a PO Box address. I then ran queries on the PO Box and discovered it was also connected to the property tax of a physical address."

"And then you searched the address?" Bolden asked.

"Yup, but there was nothing else on it."

"So how did you learn the name?"

"Easy, Annabelle. I drove past the place. It's a small strip mall, and there's a small sign on the door that says 'FastLine,' but the doors were closed, the windows were shuttered, and there weren't any cars in front of the place."

"I love it!" Colvin said. "All this tech, and you went old school."

"Easiest ways are still usually the best."

"So FastLine is a front?" Bolden asked.

"Oh, for sure. But it doesn't stop there. Look at the last page."

Bolden continued to turn until she reached the page Grimes had noted. She could only laugh.

The form was an offer to purchase FastLine by AltCon, which had been under negotiations, but conditionally agreed upon. The date on it was two years old.

"So, AltCon owns this FastLine company?"

"Nope. And that's the brilliance of this whole thing. AltCon has to register their intent to purchase companies with the Federal Trade Commission to ensure they aren't violating any Anti-Trust laws. I have that document. But since they have been sitting in a conditional agreement between AltCon and FastLine, they haven't had to file any additional paperwork, because the sale hasn't been made final."

"Ok, I get that, but what makes it devious?"

"As soon as FastLine agreed to the conditional sale, everything made by FastLine after that agreement, including all of these patents, are considered AltCon property if the sale goes through."

"Oh wow. That is devious." Bolden said.

"Yup. And, if the military comes to the Bureau with their concerns, this should be grounds for at least a search warrant."

"Boom!" Colvin said and pumped his fist.

Grimes sat back in his chair, smiling like the Cheshire cat, and said, "Fuckin' boom, indeed."

"We'll get this to the Director. Awesome work, Ry."

"Thanks. Now, and please don't take this the wrong way, get the hell out of here so I can get some sleep!"

CHAPTER 22

December 22, 2043

Turned out the answer to the riddle wasn't going to come from below us, but rather from above.

We kept up our search the next morning. A couple more hours passed, and we still hadn't found any sign of the monastery. I was worried that we might have missed something the first go-round and would need to do the search all over again.

It was Dan's keen eye that found what we were looking for. We were in another patch of the forest, unlike any of the others that we had seen before, and were keeping our eyes peeled for any change in the ground's texture or height, a sign of some kind of underground dwelling.

We passed several trees that had bows that seemed to sag lower toward the ground than their counterparts, and Dan spotted a squirrel running from one bow to the other. If it weren't for the sag, none of us would have seen it, and we would have continued on our journey.

Dan's eyes, however, followed the progress of the squirrel. And then he stopped still in his tracks.

He was staring straight up.

And there, right in front of us, was the edge of the monastery. It wasn't in the forest. It was literally a part of the forest. The structure stretched amongst dozens of the trees. It was a bloody city in the trees.

I thought about the small tree house I had when I was a kid. I remembered thinking it was majestic as a child, but I could only laugh at the broken-down hut still in my backyard when I got older. What was in front of me now was, in fact, truly majestic.

Buried deep within the heart of the tree city was what we believed was the monastery itself. It was a three story, square structure. It was easily the largest building amongst the trees, yet it was tiny compared to the other monasteries we had found. Still, the other ones were self-contained, and this one was accompanied by a sprawling assortment of buildings and connecting bridges.

And I didn't see any way up for the group. This wouldn't be a problem for us, of course, as I could easily climb the trees then lower the rope we had used to infiltrate the House Frost keep. Getting up shouldn't be a problem.

I relayed my thoughts to the guys, and they agreed with my idea. If nothing else, I needed to scout before we went any farther. I activated my Blacksuit and made my way to the first tree I saw that was attached to one of the bridges. From there, I could climb up and begin my search. It would also be a good spot to get the guys up in the trees.

As I approached the trees, I saw that any of the paths up were yellow-hued. This meant that it was an extremely difficult climb, near impossible if not a climber at the highest levels. Once I got closer to the tree, though, I started to form my Shadows into Scalers, which would increase my climbing skill to over the maximum of 100. With the +10 bonus to my climbing from my Shadows, the routes now turned blue. Still difficult, but certainly doable with concentration.

I focused on my climbing, something I hadn't found a need to do in a while and made my way up the tree. I took it even slower than normal, because I kept an eye out for any traps or wards. There weren't any on the tree, but I did see why it was so hard to climb the massive denizen of the forest.

The bark on the outside had been shaved down then oiled in such a way that made almost the entire surface of the wood slick. These trees had been treated to keep anyone from climbing them. A first line of defense, I guessed.

Still, with my Shadows, I was able to complete the climb and was not in any real risk of falling. The bridge was about fifty feet from the top, and I knew that I could use the tree as the base of my rope. I just had to tie it around the posts drilled into the side of the tree for the bridge I was now standing on. With the width of the tree, and the spacing of the posts, it would take almost forty feet of rope to secure it. That left just enough rope to get the guys up. However, they would be sitting ducks in the open while they made the climb.

Scouting was definitely the next step before lowering any rope.

From my point on the bridge, I could go one of two ways. I decided to head further into the heart of the "city" and see if I could find any sign of what happened to this monastery. We knew Loust's army had targeted all these monasteries, and the other three had fallen, so it stood to reason that this one faced the same fate.

I crept down the bridge and made my way to the platform that connected to the bridge. There were four buildings on the platform, and they all looked like simple dwellings. There was also a small hut that was connected directly to the tree that housed this platform.

I continued my way to the platform and looked into the first hut. It was empty, and the entire contents of the hut were destroyed. It was obvious that someone had lived there, albeit someone smaller. The remnants of a broken bed and table were strewed upon the hut floor, with the legs shattered and the table ripped in half. The bed had been a simple affair, but its destruction was total. Someone, or something, had ripped through this domicile.

I didn't stop at the first house and checked the second. Or, at least, I started to look. Before I made it halfway between the first house and second, a mob stepped out from the second structure. Two more followed from the other small buildings. Finally, a fourth came from the small hut connected directly to the tree.

They were vile to look at, but it was obvious what they were. The disproportioned feet and head were a giveaway. They were, at some point, some kind of Halfling. Their size was similar to my diminutive trainer, Stan, and the smaller huts made sense, as well as the small furniture. What didn't make sense was why these ground dwellers were up in trees and why they looked so broken.

Their arms and legs looked like they had grown protrusions and their movements seemed jerky. The protrusions were oozing puss, and their faces were covered in boils. These too were either leaking puss or looked about ready to do so. Each carried a small blade at their side.

When I was finally close enough to get an even closer look, a tag appeared over their heads. It read, "Twisted Disciple of Movement," and each of them was colored red.

I slowly backed away from the group and made my way back toward where I had climbed to the bridge. There was another platform connected to the other side of the bridge, and I followed the path along to that raised area. Three more huts were visible on that platform, although these looked to be larger.

Again, upon reaching the platform, I was able to see mobs near the buildings. These also had the protrusions on their bodies and carried the same moniker, "Twisted Disciple of Movement." These mobs had started as humans. And they were still red.

If this was what the mobs on the outskirts of the monastery looked like, we had no chance of tackling this place. We would be hard pressed to take a single red mob. Three or four was absolutely out of the question.

I had seen enough and returned to the group. As soon as I reached the floor of the forest, I got the attention of the party and told them to move away from the tree city. Jason was able to see me in my Blacksuit, so he followed me as I ran away. The other two followed him.

As soon as I came out of my invisible status, the guys looked at me anxiously and waited for my report. They weren't going to like what I found.

"Impossible. No way we can do this now," I said.

I then went on to explain what I had found. I started with explaining the tree itself, and the defenses against climbing up to the bridge. I then detailed the mobs I had found, emphasizing their tags, the way their bodies had been defiled, and finally explaining their titles. Finally, I told them the worst part. They were all red.

"Shit. You're right, Alex. No way we can take that many red mobs," Wayne said.

He was always the most willing to take on a challenge and almost never admitted an inability to tackle a fight, but he was also a realist. Even he knew when we were outmatched.

"What the hell do we do know, Alex? This whole forest has been cleared out, and we haven't found a single mob that would give us experience. I hate the idea of running all over trying to find places to level up when the monastery is right here!" Dan exclaimed.

I looked around the forest for a moment, digesting Dan's words. Then, I got a really big smile on my face. That made the guys cringe a bit.

"Don't worry, I'm not going to suggest we go up in the trees," I said.

They all exhaled deep sighs.

"So, what then, Alex?"

"Well, there is a war going on."

"Back so soon?" Treeswain asked when we entered his tent. After realizing there was no way we could take the Twisted Disciples in the forest, we searched a bit more for mobs that could give us experience. There was nothing in the woods. As such, we decided to head back to the King's army and talk with Treeswain. I had a plan.

"You were as right as ever, Major. The forest is devoid of anything worth fighting. We figured if we were going to look for bigger challenges, we might as well see about helping the army too. Mind showing me where the Loust forces are and where we might have some luck?"

"You want to go past the front line and take on the Loust fighters?" he asked with some disbelief.

"Well, not all of them," I said, and that got a chuckle from Treeswain. He then waved us over to his map.

"We've been having small skirmishes all across the front. Loust's army is testing our lines, and we are doing the same. The area between our front and theirs has become a no-man's zone. Small groups, like yours, can probably move around freely. Anything larger and they would catch the notice of Loust.

"So, we've been sending small scouting parties out, and they've been doing the same. Our scouts haven't had much luck, though. Most don't make it back. That might be an area where you could try."

I looked over the map and saw the area Treeswain had indicated. It was a bit north and east from the Monastery of Movement's location. We could level up on the Loust fighters, I hoped, then move down to the tree city. The problem was how long we would have to be out here.

In order to really take on the monastery, I believed those mobs I had first encountered would need to be blue to us. As it was now, they were at least five levels above us, meaning they were at a minimum level 39. We would need to get to level 37. Again, at a minimum. That was a lot of grinding.

If we took on this task, though, we could accomplish a number of things. First, we could gain experience and loot. Second, we could hamper the efforts of the Children of Loust and have some impact at dwindling their numbers. And third, if we got close enough, we could gather the details Treeswain needed to launch a frontal assault.

We'd already taken on a few guerrilla-type tasks with the Shield of Ashtator and House Frost, and I liked our odds. My group was now comfortable with this kind of operation and were ready to agree with it.

"So, want to go ruin Loust's day?"

They all nodded.

"You know the good news, Alex?" Dan asked.

I raised an eyebrow, and he said, "That dye won't be a complete waste now. We can use it as we move in the forest and sneak up on the Loust guys."

"Well, look at you seeing the rainbow in the rain!" I said.

"Ooh, where? Pot of gold. Pot of gold! Give me your lucky charms, you wee, little bastard!"

I just shook my head and made for the exit of Treeswain's tent.

"Don't you know anything, Dan? Alex is all the lucky charm we'll ever need," Jason said.

"You got that right, Alligetallthegoodstuff!"

The guys joined me outside Treeswain's tent, and we huddled up to discuss our options.

"We don't want to try the full-frontal approach, Alex. We need to be somewhat sneaky, I think," Jason said.

"That'll be different for, Dan. He's been kicked out of two taverns for his full-frontal approach."

"That was only at one tavern, Wayne! The other one I got kicked out for suggesting I would do the same. Seems they are aware of my antics."

"Wow, Dan. You're on a tavern blacklist?"

"Only at the reputable ones, Alex. The really good ones still welcome me with open arms."

"You mean the seedy joints?" Jason corrected.

"That's what I said, Alliobviously. The good ones."

I laughed along with the guys but tried to get us back on track. "If not the direct approach, then you guys think we should try to make our way to the line itself and collect information. Try to peel off ones and twos?"

"I could see that going really bad, really quickly if they are able to call for reinforcements," Wayne said.

I had to agree with that logic and nodded my head.

"Why don't we just have Alex stand in the middle of the road?"

"Wow, so quick to sacrifice me, Dan?"

"Not at all, man. We've never encountered a single mob that can see through your invis. In fact, short of Allister, I don't know anyone that has been able to do it. And he's got an item from a super rare mob."

Jason perked up at Dan's use of his actual in game name. "Wait. Why no butchering of my name?"

"Duh. Because I'm not responding to something you said, Allisimpleminded."

"There goes the small sliver of hope I had."

"Hope, like dollar bills in a strip club, are fleeting," Dan said with a smile that just begged Jason to ask for more.

Jason didn't take the bait.

"You know," I said, "Dan's idea does have some actual merit. Maybe not standing in the middle of the road, but I can definitely scout along the path. And I can do so with almost no concern." In reality, I believed I could do so with complete impunity so long as nothing could see through my Blacksuit.

"The number of things in the game that are likely able to do that are infinitesimally small."

"Like Dan's chances with Kaitlin. Got it."

"You cut deep, Allideepcutter."

The four of us were laughing as we headed out of the camp and made our way east, back along the King's road and toward the front lines.

FBI Headquarters
December 29, 2043

The two Special Agents and FBI Director Grissten sat in the Director's office. The last time the three were in the same room, morale was not good. The Agents had hit one brick wall after another, and they were feeling lost.

That was no longer the case.

Annabelle Bolden was almost overflowing with energy, looking like she was about to jump out of her seat. Where Bolden was usually reserved, Colvin was always one to speak from his heart. And if Bolden looked energetic, Colvin was on the verge of being epileptic.

"If I don't let the two of you report soon, you may go crazy!" the Director said with as much energy as they felt. She was overjoyed to see her people this happy. It meant they had found something. Based on their demeanor, it was something really good.

Bolden led the way and broke down everything that Grimes had discovered about the patents held by FastLine, the conditional offer to buy the company by AltCon, and how that conditional offer assured that all those patents belonged to the maker of Resurgence. It wasn't uncommon for large companies to languish during potential mergers, but the act of buying a small company like FastLine usually wouldn't take two years. The length of time strongly helped their case.

Grissten listened to the whole rundown and reviewed all of the data the two Special Agents had collected. Along with Grimes, the three had been very busy. It certainly looked like they would have enough to at least approach a judge for a search warrant.

"Will this cause any problems for the bigger operation, Director?" Nico asked.

Grissten stopped perusing the papers in front of her and focused her sights on Nico. "What operation?" she asked.

Bolden and Colvin shared a look, then the lead agent spoke. "We aren't idiots, Director. It's obvious that something much larger is going on here. The fact that everything is going down on the sly, and that we can't even come close to using everything the FBI has at its disposal to work this case, tells us there's more going on than you're saying." *

"And we're fine with that," Colvin quickly added. "We just want to make sure that whatever we do next doesn't mess up the big plan."

"How so?"

"Well, if we go to a judge, there is no doubt that we are going to have to do more than provide our suspicions. We're going to need solid evidence to support our request for the simplest of search warrants. That's going to require us to put forth the Department of Defense information," Bolden said.

"And, any judge worth their salt is going to want to know how we got that information," Colvin added. "I see this unraveling really quickly."

Grissten sat back in her chair and thought about their comments. They were right about a judge wanting more information. That went without saying. Any decision to invade another's privacy, whether a person or company, required a high bar be met.

The Director knew a few judges that owed her favors, but she was hesitant to call in those markers. Any way they could avoid identifying the DoD's role in this operation was paramount.

"Do you have any ideas?" The Director asked.

Bolden and Colvin shared another look.

"I think we should go at Dr. Weiss."

"Under what context, Agent Bolden?"

"Tax evasion," she said.

"Oh. I'm listening."

Amongst all of the other documents that Grimes had found about FastLine was that the building was owned by Dr. Weiss. It was a part of a larger strip mall, but Dr. Weiss owned that particular part of the property. However, for whatever reason, he hadn't been paying his property tax on the building.

"That's a local affair, Agents. At best, a state-level problem. That's not going to pass the Federal test."

As members of a federal law enforcement agency, Bolden and Colvin were handcuffed by the type of crimes they could investigate. Property tax evasion did not fall within the wheelhouse of the FBI.

"True," Colvin said, with a wicked grin forming on his face. "And it wouldn't be within our jurisdiction at all, if Weiss lived in the same state as where his company and building were held. But the company is in one state and his residency in another. His property tax bills have to cross state lines."

"Oh, that's good!" The Director said, matching Colvin's smile.

"We can approach him under the pretense of him not paying his taxes, inform him of the penalties that could be levied against him, and note that there was a push by this administration to levy severe damages against those who were not doing their duty as American citizens."

"And if he simply offers to pay his taxes?'

"Then we will be all the happier for bringing the whole affair to a close. Of course, now that he's come under the gaze of the authorities, some additional investigation will need to be done around his company, FastLine, to ensure he is in full compliance with all tax laws there as well. But before we start any investigation, we will naturally give him the opportunity to disclose anything he wants."

"Indeed," commented Bolden, now with her own smile. "A thorough investigation of the company will have to be done. Its history, creation, and any partnerships. That will naturally require a background investigation of the man himself, of course."

"Of course," the Director said, chuckling at her devious agents.

"If we can get more out of the man, all the better. If not, we still have our original option of going for warrants."

"I like this plan of attack, Agents," Grissten said. "And well done. I look forward to your full report after the meeting."

Annabelle and Nico stood and made their way for the door. Just before they reached the exit, the Director spoke once more.

"Remember to look the part. Two top-of-the-line FBI wouldn't be sent on this type of assignment."

"Should we do our best Grimes impression?" Nico asked.

"Oh, hell no! I don't want the guy passing out in fright. Besides, where would you get all the tattoos that quickly?"

Laughter could be heard down the hall from the Director's office as Annabelle and Nico left.

CHAPTER 23

Two weeks. That's how long we were out in the woods grinding through experience. With only two breaks for Christmas and New Year's Day, we didn't miss a session.

We had to be extra careful with how we picked patrols to go after, because they were always in packs of three or four. And if there was anything higher than a blue mob, we avoided it. At first, there were many of these patrols, but as our levels got higher, we were able to take more of the patrols, which were out in abundance. Despite our need to be selective, we were able to find one fight after another.

After the two weeks, our levels increased from 34 to 37. We only took two long breaks in that time. Once when Jason and Dan had both reached level 36, so Jason could gate back to Kich's Keep and grab their new spells. Dan got an improved Snare, and Jason got an improved heal. Our fighting was slowed down until Jason could return on his horse. Another benefit was that Jason could wear his new gloves once he hit level 35.

The second was when I hit level 37. I ran back to the tree city so I could see what level the mobs were at on the platforms I had first scouted. The disappointment we felt when I saw the mobs was only half as bad as it could have been. The mobs I encountered were blue and yellow. We agreed that we had to be happy that at least they weren't all yellow.

It also meant we still needed to get the team to level 38 before we could try the monastery.

We took short breaks each night to also return to the safety of the front line. On two occasions, we rode all the way back to Treeswain's camp to sell the loot we collected. We were flush with money but didn't have anything to buy, and we were running low on the dye that we used for the Camouflage spell.

It had worked extremely well for this particular type of warfare, but it was limited in that I could only cast it once per day. We started the day by having me scout for an area where the patrols would almost overlap, stopping within sight of each other from a distance. I would place the guys at the edge of the forest, close enough that we could pounce on a patrol but still hidden from sight of the mobs.

And the mobs were the best kind for this type of spell. Each of the patrols we fought were made up entirely of humans. They could come in any type of fighter, from warriors to mages, but they didn't come with heightened senses like the elves.

That isn't to say that we fought every patrol we came across. There were those with yellow mobs, and we avoided those. At first, the yellow mobs could be humans, but as we got higher in levels, that changed. Now, without fail, the yellow mobs were always larger races. Multiple times we had seen massive Ogres that would have made Lug look small. There were also several Orcs that were accompanying the patrols.

Still, the sheer number of scouts that Loust had dispatched to this no-man's land meant that there was a steady supply of fights. We just had to find them. It would have been even faster if I could use Camouflage multiple times. With that limitation, I had to have the guys go deeper in the forest first before I could do any more scouting with my Blacksuit.

We also encountered a few of our own scouting parties that had traveled deep into the area. Twice, we saved those parties from death by the forces of Loust, and they hurried off to report their findings to Treeswain. The Major was overflowing with thanks for saving his men and the information they were able to provide. There was only one occasion where we were too late and were only able to kill the Loust patrol after the fact.

In that case, we were able to loot a "Report on Loust's Forces" that we turned in to Treeswain.

The day was coming to a close when we encountered something that we hadn't heard in weeks. It wasn't the clash of a battle. We actually heard that quite often, even if we couldn't always get to where the scrum was happening, and with the absence of any wildlife in the area, sounds traveled extremely far.

What we heard were voices. They were the distinct voices of other players.

"Shit! Stun him! Don't let him get away!"

"Thanks. I'm pretty sure I know how to do my job."

"Yeah, then why is he running in the first place? You are on crowd control!"

"Do I look like a robe?"

A "robe," was undoubtedly a reference to a caster, as the pure casters were the only class that wore a robe.

"Just shut up and kill him!"

I looked at the guys, and we all had the same stunned look on our faces. It was the Stealers. They were the top Player vs Player team in Resurgence and had won the only tournament in PvP that AltCon had put on. They were notorious for stealing people's kills and just outright killing other players. I couldn't believe they were here doing the same thing we were.

"I'm going to go see what's going on," I whispered, and waved for the guys to stay far back in the trees.

I activated my Blacksuit and crept out onto the road in the direction of the noises we had heard. I didn't have to travel far when I came across their carnage. Their rogue, Snitch, was just putting the final dagger into the back of his victim.

It was a scout from one of the King's patrols.

With the last one dead, the Stealers stopped yelling at each other.

"Good fight," their Warrior, Dredge, said. "Although that weak ass runner was a pain."

"Probably shouldn't take a four-person patrol, again. Even if we do have the element of surprise. I still can't believe these dumbasses just let us walk up on them and surround them. I figured after the first or second, 'I'm with the King,' line, they would catch on!" their Brawler, Zitt, said. "They're such morons."

"Easy experience. And the Loust guys will pay good for these," Yolo said, as he looted the bodies of the King's men. "Let's wait here for another group. I don't feel like running around."

I had seen and heard enough. These guys had betrayed the King and were fighting for Loust.

When I got back to the guys, I relayed everything I saw and heard. Wayne was pissed and wanted to rush them immediately. It was only the look on my face that kept him at bay. Wayne remembered quite vividly all of the things they had said to his girlfriend at the end of the PvP tournament, and he had been looking for an opportunity to kill each of them for a long time.

"Oh, we are going to definitely kill them. I can guarantee you that. But we can't do it like a regular group of mobs, man. We suck at PvP."

Wayne didn't want to listen to my words, but subconsciously, at least, he heard what I was saying. With arms crossed over his chest, Wayne looked at me, and said, "Fine. Then how do we do this?"

I held up my hand where I wore my Force Multiplier ring. "We cheat."

Wayne's smile got real big at that.

"Keep Dredge alive. That guy likes to talk, and I want to know what the hell is going on," I said to Wayne.

"I make no promises."

———

We moved slowly through the trees, toward where I had last seen the Stealers. We had already used our Camouflage for the day, so we weren't going to be getting any help from there. Our only advantage was that the players on the road were loud and weren't paying attention to anything but themselves.

"I'm telling you, we can do this until there isn't a bit of experience left on this road. The patrols are spread out enough that we won't get caught as long as we don't get another runner," Snitch was saying.

"You think we should hide? None of us have invis like you do."

"No, Zitt. Don't you get it? We don't need to hide. No one knows what we're doing out here. If a patrol of four comes through, all we have to do is say we are looking for Loust forces to kill and they should just move off."

"And if they don't?"

"Then we kill them," Dredge said. "Then, next time we see four we will hide."

"Worth a try," Yolo said. "How much you need until you get level 35, Dredge?"

"I'm halfway there."

I had heard enough, and so had the other guys.

We moved back, away from the road, and deeper into the forest. When we looked to be far enough away, I laid out my plan.

"We need to kill Yolo first. He's the only one that can Stun and heal. I'll go after him first. Dan, I need you to Snare Snitch so he can't go invis. Wayne will hit Dredge, and Jason will stay far enough away that he can heal. Once Snitch is Snared, start putting arrows into Zitt. As soon as you can, Snare that piece of shit Brawler too."

"They are going to converge on me, Alex."

"I know, Allister. And I'll take out whichever one is closest to you when I'm done with Yolo."

"Don't worry about Dredge. He can't do enough damage to hurt me, and I won't need a heal. Just do your best Dan impression and Kite those assholes," Wayne said.

"They're going to die fast, guys. It's just a matter of keeping Allister alive through the whole thing. That way, even if one of us does go down, Allister can resurrect us."

Everyone nodded, and we made our way back to the road. "Wait for my signal, Allister, then cast the Stun."

"What's the signal going to be?"

"Probably him screaming," I said with a smile that only Jason could see.

I activated my Force Multiplier ring and approached the group in my Blacksuit. These guys were in for a very nasty surprise.

I lined up behind Yolo, who was just standing around, waiting for the next patrol to come down the road. There was nothing left for me to do, and I stabbed out at the Paladin's back.

With my ring active, all of my core base Stats were over 100, with my Strength and Constitution close to 200, my Dexterity over 300, and my Chance at 1000. It's why we always found the best loot possible when I had the ring activated.

I hit Yolo square in his back and did a critical Disembowel. That was a base of four times my normal hit and a critical on top of that. I took 50 percent of his health in one shot, and both of my blades proc'ed. One dropped his armor rating 40 percent and the other sucked out 200 hit points.

Yolo screamed out as his health dropped dramatically, but he was a gamer and immediately turned to face his attacker. Namely, me.

I had a huge smile on my face.

"Shit, we're under attack!" he yelled.

That was the last thing he said, as Jason's Stun hit the Paladin. I took advantage of his inability to move and swung around to his back, hitting him with another backstab. That one also landed with a critical strike, taking off another chunk of his health.

The rest of my team had engaged by then, but I didn't bother to look over at the battlefield. My team was seasoned, and they didn't need any more direction from me once the plan was set. I kept all my focus on Yolo.

He tried to cast a few times, but the sheer number of strikes I was landing, and the speed at which I was hitting, was interrupting his casting. Also, almost every hit with my Blood Blade was proc'ing, so that was another 200 hit points per strike. He was dead in seconds.

With Yolo down, I surveyed the scene. Jason was running around, staying away from Zitt and Snitch, as they tried to chase him down. In any PvP situation, you took out the healer first. Like I had just done. But these two were Snared and they couldn't catch our fleeing Cleric.

Zitt was closest, so I went after him next. He fell even faster than Yolo, since Dan had been peppering him with arrows the whole time. I simply engaged my daggers, and the Blood Blade's procs drained him of all his hit points. My actual hits did a ton of damage, too.

With Zitt dead, I turned on my Rogue counterpart, Snitch. He came straight toward me, with a look of fury on his face. "You piece of shit assholes are so dead," he said.

"Couldn't have said it better," I responded and killed him quickly.

The only one left was Dredge, and he was being handled by Wayne with no problem. Our warrior had more levels, better armor, and better weapons. They had similar Skills, but Wayne would never lose in a one-on-one fight.

I decided to loot the bodies while the fight kept going. We'd never done PvP, so I had no idea what kind of loot we could get from the players.

Turned out that all we got was the money on their bodies, totaling about 50 gold, and a dull silver coin per kill. I inspected the coin in greater detail and a notification popped up:

A symbol of Loust, this coin grants entry into Loust's camps and quests from Loust's army. The coin brands you as a follower of the Children of Loust and cannot be traded or stolen. It can only be given to another follower of Loust or taken from your body. Do you wish to use this coin to change your allegiance to Loust?

There was a spot to click Accept or Deny, and I didn't hesitate to click Deny. Another prompt was displayed:

Turn in this coin to an officer of King Kameron's army to collect the bounty on Loust followers.

I collected each of the coins then turned to see Wayne continue his rampage against Dredge. The warrior was calling Wayne all kinds of names and claiming that we were a bunch of PKs for going after them. He had the audacity to say they were out here just trying to get levels.

"I should beat you to within an inch of your pitiful existence and then let the King's patrols take your head. You think we don't know what you were doing out here?" Wayne asked.

That got a reaction out of Dredge, and he stopped fighting, trying to make a run for the woods.

A Snare immediately landed on him, and his movement stopped. Knowing he wouldn't be able to run, he turned back toward Wayne and our group and took up a defensive stance. I took that time to get some info from him.

"Why kill the guards? There are plenty of Loust mobs out here. You could just as easily kill them," I said.

"Why would we want to kill Loust's forces? Loust is going to win, you idiots, and we are going to be right there to suck up all the rewards," he answered. "But don't you worry. As soon as we respawn, we are going to hunt your asses down. We are going to camp your corpses until you are back to level 19 and can't even come and get your bodies."

Technically, that was completely possible. If these PKers killed us in the open like this, and we tried to come and collect our bodies, they could just stand there and wait for us to show up. With no armor or weapons, they could kill us with little effort. Then they could just do it over and over again. Since we would lose experience with every death, it would be a matter of time before we lost level after level. If we dropped below level 20, we wouldn't have access to these zones. That's what camping a corpse was. We had little concern about that, however.

But Dredge wasn't finished.

"You have no idea how many patrols we've killed, and the awesome quests we've got from Loust. We've got titles, too. You caught us this time, but we are more than a match for you straight up. We'll have our revenge, dickheads.

"And you know what the best part is? No one will ever know it was us!" he said, laughing at us.

"I'm pretty sure those little coins from Loust are going to be more than enough to convince anyone we tell."

I watched Dredge's face really fall that time. His response was to attack again.

"I'm going to pound you into the ground, just like I did your pretty girlfriend!" he yelled.

And then he died. Wayne's patience had reached its end, and he stopped holding back. Mentioning Jenny was the last words he would utter.

I looted the body and took his Loust coin as well. I received the same prompt concerning the coin and hit Deny. I then told the guys about what I had found and what the prompt said.

"Sorry, Alex."

"Oh, I was done with that asshole, Wayne. I'm impressed you waited that long to smash his face in."

"Yeah. I was fine until he mentioned Jenny. She really hates these guys after that tournament."

"Alex," Dan said. "That ring is ridiculous. You could have taken out the whole team by yourself."

"I think you're right, Dan. But I'm not going to complain!"

That got a laugh, and we all summoned our horses. We were done hunting down Loust's patrols for now. We needed to get to Treeswain and turn in these coins.

"Let's go get a bounty!"

We entered the King's camp and made our way to Treeswain's tent. We no longer had to worry about being stopped by any of the perimeter guards, as we were well known by this point. Our success against House Frost and efforts at fighting the Loust patrols had earned us quite a bit of notoriety. Guards simply waved at us as we rode through.

Treeswain never left his tent, so we weren't surprised to find him poring over his map at the heart of his headquarters. He looked up when we entered and stopped whatever he was doing to address us.

"Welcome back to the camp. What news?"

This was the same question he asked every time we entered. The last few times when we had addressed him, I gave a report on what patrols we had faced. On the one occasion, when we had returned with the Report on Loust's Forces, we received a small bit of experience as well.

But this time was different.

I handed over the four coins that I looted from the corpses of the Stealers and waited for Treeswain's reaction.

He studied them for several moments. His demeanor worsened as each second passed. Finally, he spoke to us.

"Where did you get these?"

"Four adventurers were out on the roads, killing your patrols. We came upon them, saw them kill a patrol, and enacted the King's Vengeance. This was all that we found on the bodies."

Treeswain didn't reply. Instead, he went to the flap of his tent, poked his head out, and yelled for a runner.

Nothing more was said until the runner arrived. Treeswain gave the small guard a parcel, which I assumed had the four coins inside, and addressed the runner. "This is to go directly to the castle. It bears the mark of the greatest urgency. Do not let anyone stop you from delivering this message," he said. Then he grabbed a scroll from atop the table and handed it to the runner. "Use this to reach Kich's Keep. Go!"

The runner didn't even leave the tent, activating the teleport scroll right there and then.

I looked over at Treeswain, awaiting some kind of a reward. But none came.

Instead, he simply said, "Now, we wait."

The wait wasn't long. Five minutes later, there was a message that popped up in my view that read:

Betrayal! The lands of Tholtos have been betrayed! Citizens of the Kingdom have sided with the forces of Loust and have acted against us. But no longer! Their secret has been uncovered. Their taint will now be known across the land, and they will no longer be given free movement within the Kingdom. City guards will slay them where they stand, and they will find no respite in the cities of Tholtos. Strike them down wherever they are found!

Another message popped up after that one:

Those players who have sided with Loust are now identifiable by the forces of King Kameron. While in the lands controlled by the King, these players will be identifiable by a red aura around their bodies.

Betrayers will no longer be allowed to bind their characters to cities controlled by the King. All bind points for Betrayers have been changed to the lands controlled by the Children of Loust, and Betrayers have been teleported to those lands.

But be warned! There are no physical restrictions from Betrayers entering the Kingdom, nor will there be any identification to note a Betrayer while they are in territory controlled by Loust. However, no penalties will occur for players who attack Betrayers within the cities of the Kingdom. Indeed, a bounty has been established for any Betrayer killed by a player with proof provided to the Kingdom.

"Thank you, Alex," Treeswain said. "You and your friends have once again done a great service to the Kingdom. From this point forward, I will be able to reward you for any bounty you acquire. Here is your reward for the four bounties you have already provided and for uncovering this plot."

With that, we received a notification that we had received experience for the bounties of Dredge, Snitch, Yolo, and Zitt. And the experience was enough to get all of us to level 38.

"Thank you, Major!" I said, overjoyed at seeing the massive amount of experience we had just been rewarded.

"No, thank you," he said. "What will you do now?"

"We will rest. Tomorrow, our hunt begins again."

CHAPTER 24

January 6, 2044

Despite my words to Treeswain, we weren't heading back to the main road to look for players that wore the mantle of Betrayer. We were definitely on a hunt, though.

We arrived at the tree city after an uneventful ride through the forest. The area was still empty of mobs, and our travel was completely unimpeded. Now that we were at the city in the trees, with the platform I had previously investigated off in the short distance from us, we needed to discuss a plan.

"Kill everything," Wayne said.

I looked at him for a few moments, waiting for more. But that was the extent of Wayne's idea.

"Sounds like a good plan to me," Jason added.

I arched my eyebrows at our cleric.

"I'm not saying that I don't want a little more strategy involved, but it's a solid plan," Jason said with a smile.

"I'm totally in agreement with Wayne's plan," Dan said.

Wayne looked over at the Ranger and then back to me. "Can I change my plan?"

I had to laugh at that.

370

"It's the plan. Obviously. But I was wondering how you guys want to handle this. There are four mobs on one platform, and three on another. I would suggest we start with the three. The mobs should all be blue now, but we'll have to see when we get up there."

"Start with our usual then? Wayne takes two, and I kite another. Is the platform big enough to kite?"

"It should be. No Broham, though. I don't want to take a chance this early on something going wrong."

"Cool. Thanks for watching out for the little guy." The little guy was no longer little in the least bit and could look Dan in the eye when he put his paws on the Ranger's shoulders.

"The other platform has four mobs, though, and we won't be able to run them around like that. It's too small."

The team thought for a bit, and it was Jason who came up with an answer. "Can we use the bridges? Tag two of them with Snare and then run the other two to the first platform after we clear it? That should give us some time to work with."

It was a good plan, and I said so. There was only one concern. "If Dan has to run them back and forth along the bridge, he's going to get hit."

"I've got the hit points to take a few shots, bro. Don't worry about me. Let's do it."

We all agreed, and I headed to my Scaling tree. Like before, I was able to use my Shadows to boost my climbing skill, and I made my way up the tree. For the first time, I tried my idea at securing the climbing rope and dangled it over the bridge I stood on.

Dan, the lightest of our group, was the first to climb up to the bridge. With his natural Agility, he didn't have any problem with the climb. Once he was up, I posted him as a scout to watch the two platforms that were connected to the bridge, to make certain none of the mobs reacted to our climbing.

Jason came next. It was more of a challenge for him, and he was definitely louder in his climb. Still, he made it up, and we didn't alert any of the mobs. The three of us were braced to grab the rope and assist Wayne on his climb, but he made it up even easier than Jason, as he had a huge amount of Strength to help him with his climb.

Thankfully, the four of us made it up without alerting the mobs. Now that everyone was up top, I went and scouted the human-type mobs on the connecting platform. As we hoped, they were all blue now. Also, thankfully, there were still only three of them.

We made our way over to the platform and engaged the Twisted Disciples of Movement. Their appearance hadn't changed, and they still looked like sickly beasts. Wayne led with his war hammer, hitting one before Bashing and Kicking the second. The first one was then Taunted, and Wayne began his dance of establishing aggro on the mobs.

Likewise, Dan cast Snare on his mob and began kiting it around the platform.

"How's it looking, Wayne?" I asked.

"They're super accurate with their hits. They aren't missing at all, but they aren't hitting for much. I should be good."

"Dan?"

"Snare landed on the first try."

"Alright. Allister, give it ten more seconds and hit it with a Banish Undead. I don't think it will work, but we should at least give it a try."

"You got it, Alex."

The ten seconds ticked down, and I saw Jason cast his spell. "No good. Complete resist."

"Better to know that now than later," I said. "Engaging myself."

I jumped in to join my warrior counterpart. With both of our damage, the Twisted Disciple was going down much faster. Wayne kept aggro on the two blues in front of us, and Dan continued to kite the third around the platform.

When the first mob hit 50 percent, it surprised all of us by ceasing its attacks, jumping backwards, and yelling out, "Sacrifice!"

As one, all three on the platform, whether facing Wayne or running after Dan, stopped, took their blades and ran them down the length of their own arms, slicing through the boils and puss on their forearms.

Then, without saying anything else, they attacked again. At least, the two in front of Wayne did. The one chasing Dan didn't have any hope of catching our Ranger with the Snare still on.

I saw that the mob I was facing had a new debuff on him, simply called "Sacrifice." I didn't have any idea what it did, but it looked like the hit points on him were going down quicker.

I found out soon enough, though.

"Crap, got a DoT, Allister. Twisted Sacrifice."

"Does it say what it does, Wayne?"

"Yeah, man. It does one point of damage per second," he said, laughing. "I think I'm good."

His laughter only lasted a moment.

"Uh oh," our Warrior said.

"Baddest warrior in Resurgence says, 'Uh oh,' Alex, and I worry!" Dan said as he kept running around the platform.

"Me too, Dan. What is it, Wayne?"

"I got hit with four more Sacrifice DoTs. They stack. I'm at 5 hit points per second."

Several seconds later, and Wayne was cursing again. "Shit, shit, shit. Up to 20 hit points per second."

Thankfully, that was right about the time that we killed the first Twisted Disciple.

"Twenty-three hit points," Wayne said several seconds later. "This is kinda cool despite my getting the DoT. There is a little 'x23' next to the Twisted Sacrifice DoT. First time we've seen this mechanic in game."

I had to agree. The mobs weren't all that hard if you were close to their level, but the stackable DoT more than made up for it. If it had an unlimited stacking ability, it could take down any tank.

Jason cast a heal, and Wayne's hit points went up, then I saw them slowly start to go back down again. Not terribly fast, but that would change as the DoT stacked. Also, since this was likely to be the monastery that focused on Dexterity, the mobs were hitting often, and their proc—the DoT—was going off very frequently. It really was a perfect counter to a party of adventurers.

"There is some good news," Dan said.

"Let's hear it."

"The Sacrifice drains their own hit points, even if they don't hit anyone with the proc. I haven't been firing arrows at the one I'm kiting, and its hit points keep going down, albeit very slowly. I guess that's why it's called 'Sacrifice.'"

"Makes sense," I said, just as we killed the second mob on the platform. At first, Wayne didn't have to worry about the last one adding more DoTs to him when we attacked, as Dan had landed enough Snares to keep aggro as we chased it around the platform, hitting it in the back. Eventually, though, it turned on the Warrior and added another several of the Twisted Sacrifice on him.

When it finally died, Wayne was looking at a DoT of 34 hit points per second. And that was for a set of first-tier trash mobs. More troublesome was the fact that the DoT wasn't going away while we waited to engage the next platform.

As Wayne's hit points continued to disappear, Jason hit him with another heal.

"That took one away. I am at Twisted Sacrifice x33. Wait a few and let's see if more go away on their own or if it was because of the heal."

After 10 seconds, and another 330 hit points gone, Wayne asked for another heal.

"It's the heal. Another one gone."

"I've got crazy mana regen, Alex, but even I can cast this level heal and hope to keep a relatively high level of mana. Let me try a lower heal."

"Hold on, Allister. Let's see if Dan's heal will work."

"Good call, Alex, let me give it a shot," Dan said and cast his weak heal on Wayne.

"No luck, Alex," Wayne said.

"Oh well. It was worth a shot. We've got a safe spot here, so start with your weakest heal, Allister, and move up from there. I don't want to use a grenade when a bullet is good enough."

"That analogy seems flawed, but I get what you mean."

"Everyone's a critic," I said as I saw Jason begin to cast another spell.

"Now you know my pain, bro."

We laughed at Dan and waited while Jason went through different levels of heals.

"Another one gone."

"Ok, Naugha. That one is a mid-level. Let me cast and see if it works again."

"Yup, another one gone."

Jason began casting one heal after another. This was easily the most heals Jason had ever had to cast on our Warrior at any one time, and it was after the lowest-level mob we would face. I was seriously worried about our ability to manage our mana consumption.

Thirty heals later, and the DoT was completely gone.

"I've got a 20 percent bonus to my mana regen from the Book of Calm and a bonus to Holy Spells from my boots. It also costs me 20 percent less mana to cast heals because of my shoulders. The gloves increase my Stun, so that doesn't play in here. Overall, I think we will be ok, but only because we've been lucky with our drops."

"Understatement of the year!" Dan exclaimed.

"Well, I don't want to take too many chances. Start throwing the lower heals on Wayne when he gets a twenty stack of that DoT, as long as it stays at 1 hit point per second. If it gets more powerful, we'll have to adjust."

"Sounds good, Alex. I'll need a couple minutes to regen some mana."

Once Jason was good to go, we headed back to the first platform where we encountered the Twisted Disciples that looked human. The Halflings were on the next platform, and we were going to use the length of the bridge to our advantage. Dan would Snare the first one, drawing them all toward us. When Snare was available again, Dan would hit the second one. Then he would run the last two to the first platform, and Wayne would engage. It was up to Dan to keep the two Snared mobs busy.

The pull went off without any problems. It was a lot of mobs, but they were all blue and we had room to work with. Control of the mobs, and the fight, would mean the difference between life and death up in these trees. The worst part was knowing that if things went really bad, we didn't have anywhere to run. We had left the rope where it was, just in case we had to try and escape by climbing down, but the chances of that working for everyone were not great. If we needed the rope again, I could simply untie it and move it to the next place.

Jason decided to try and Stun the Twisted Halfling when it got to 50 percent and triggered the call for the mobs to Sacrifice. It was a smart play but didn't work. The Halfling resisted the Stun, and all of the mobs cut themselves open again. This time, they didn't all focus on the arms. They focused on wherever the boils were.

"Looks like whatever is in those protrusions is what coats their blades for the DoT," I said.

"We could try healing them at the outset, Alex. See if that gets rid of whatever is ailing them," Jason said.

"Worth a try on the next one," I agreed.

It took longer on the second group of mobs than it did on the first, simply because of the numbers. Thankfully, Jason's mana was never in any serious danger, but he was dropping lower than we were used to seeing because of the DoT.

The loot was nothing special. All of the clothing that the mobs wore had the designation of "Tattered" clothing, which meant it would sell for a few coppers at most. The blades they wielded were also worthless, as they were only "Rusty" implements. The disciples also didn't carry any money, so we left everything on the bodies. I still looted, just in case. The experience was decent, at least.

Over the course of the day, we cleared out the tree city. The outer platforms were connected by a ring of bridges that encircled the inner town. Four of the platforms—those located at the cardinal points of the compass—had bridges that connected to the next inner ring. The outer ring was made up of sixteen platforms. Once we cleared all of those, we moved in to the next ring. Unfortunately, our idea to heal the Twisted Disciples had no effect on their condition. In fact, the system notified Jason that this spell was impossible to use on this entity. It didn't cost us anything to try.

I scouted before we made our way further inward and came back with my findings: twelve platforms, again connected by bridges. Again, the platforms that were at the cardinal points had bridges that went into the next set of platforms. Another inner ring.

We started by clearing the platforms at north, south, east, and west. This gave us ample room to maneuver around the second level of the inner ring and back to the outer ring if we needed it.

We then started on the western platform and cleared to the northern platform. There was a method to this strategy.

We went to the western platform and pulled the next group of mobs to the south. When we got to the western point, Dan took his mobs for a run, dragging them to the outer ring, running them up to the northern point, bringing them down to the second ring northern location, and then running them back to our platform. This kept them going in a loop, with no chance of Dan getting hit by the mobs. Dan had been attacked on earlier kiting runs and had taken the Sacrifice DoT. It wasn't enough to do any real damage to him, but it did eat into Jason's mana when he had to heal Dan as well.

At the second tier of platforms, the Twisted Sacrifice DoT also got more powerful. Instead of one hit point per second, it was taking two hit points per second. Again, a meager amount, until it started to stack.

Unfortunately, these mobs were harder than the outer tier and therefore lived longer, having more time to inflict the DoT. Worse, however, was the fact that the heals Jason used on Wayne were no longer sufficient to clear out the DoT, and he had to go up to the next level of heals. This ate into his mana pool even more, and we had to wait longer to move from one platform to the next while he regenerated his mana.

Once we cleared the second ring of twelve platforms, I moved in to the next ring.

There were less mobs here, with only three per platform, and there were only eight platforms this time. However, the mobs were almost all yellow, with only six of the twenty-four being blue. On two of the platforms, all three mobs were yellow. We would save those for last.

Another thing that was different from the outer rings were doors that blocked the bridges from the third tier of platforms to the next ring. Those last platforms were the ones right next to the squat building where we figured the "monastery" was located.

It was getting late, and we wouldn't have time to take on the two rings remaining and whatever was in the monastery before it got too late. We decided to call it for the night. We climbed back down to the forest floor and logged off in the forest. We didn't think there would be respawn, but we weren't going to take that chance.

January 7, 2044

We were happy to find there was no respawn, and we were free to climb up into the tree city and make our way toward the third tier of rings that surrounded the building. I had changed my mind about engaging the three yellow mobs last, as one of the cardinal points was home to these mobs. I decided to engage those first. Only this time, we would run them back to one of the outer rings so Dan could use his loop trick again.

Dan led with his Snare, and all three took off for him at a flat run.

"Resist!" Dan yelled and started moving backwards as fast as he could.

Wayne grabbed two of the yellows as they were coming toward us, and they launched into their attacks on our tank. Dan cast again and thankfully the Snare landed. He took off toward the outer ring, dragging the yellow mob with him.

"Don't die, buddy!" Wayne yelled as Dan started his kiting.

"Thanks, Captain Obvious!"

Just as I had feared, these mobs were hitting even harder, and their hit points were much higher. The ones we faced now looked like Wood Elves but had the same boils and warts all over their bodies. As we were accustomed to seeing, at 50 percent the mob we were facing called for a Sacrifice.

Both of the mobs in front of us drug their blades down their chests, tearing away their cloth jerkins and slicing through the maladies afflicting their bodies. They then reengaged with our party.

"Shit, Allister! Five hit points per second!"

"I've got the next level spell already loaded, Naugha."

Several seconds later, Wayne called out heal, and Jason hit him with a spell.

"That got rid of one. I'll yell out heal when I get to twenty-five per second. Keep it as low as possible, but let me know if we need to go longer. I've got plenty of hit points."

There was a synergy between our cleric and warrior that had developed over months of playing together. I didn't see any reason to change how they complemented each other.

I decided to check on our other teammate. "How's it going, Dan?"

"I've had multiple resists on Snare. Thankfully, I'm keeping him as far away as possible. I'm not in any danger. Yet."

"We can bring him back here for Wayne to tank after the first one goes down, if you think we need it."

"I'll let you know!"

I hadn't stopped striking the first mob, and it finally went down. Wayne had called for several more heals in that time, and Jason announced his mana was at 60 percent. We turned on the second mob and noted that his health had dropped a small amount. It looked like the Sacrifice DoT was doing the same amount of damage to it, as it did to Wayne, meaning five hit points per second. Not a lot, but over time it stacked up. In a fight that went on for two minutes, it dropped 600 hit points.

The bad thing about all of them triggering sacrifice at the same time was that this second mob had a lot longer to inflict his DoTs on Wayne. The stronger DoTs didn't land as quickly as the trash mobs on the first tier, but they definitely landed with a frequency that would have dwarfed the total damage output of those on the first ring.

When the second one went down, Jason was at 40 percent mana. The last one was so pissed at Dan, there wasn't much worry that it would turn on Wayne quickly. Jason was able to regenerate some of his mana.

We finished off the last mob, with Wayne only having to tank about the last 20 percent. He accumulated a few more of the DoTs, and Jason quickly healed him when the fight was over. He was at just under 50 percent.

Technically, that would be the hardest mobs that we faced on this ring. It was a comfort to see that we could do it and that Jason still had almost half his mana. That was the discouraging part too, though. After three mobs, Jason was at less than half mana. We'd rarely faced anything short of a boss fight that affected our cleric's mana so much.

The remainder of the platforms went down quicker, except for the other one with the three yellows. In that case, Dan ended up taking some punishment when his Snares were resisted. Luckily for the Ranger, this happened before the Sacrifice was called, and he was able to heal himself with his weak heal.

When the last mob died, the door that led to the next tier of platforms opened. I ran around and confirmed that this was the case for all four of the doors. Once that confirmation was in place, I donned my Blacksuit and scouted out the last ring.

There were only four platforms. Each one had a bridge that led to the inner sanctum, where we figured the center of the monastery was held. Each platform also held only one mob. One was a human, one a Halfling, one a Wood Elf, and the last a Dark Elf. They were all yellow. Their clothing also looked a whole lot better than what we had seen on the rest of the mobs. Finally, they all carried very shiny daggers, not the rusted weapons we had seen earlier. It was easy to guess that these guys would have better armor and would hit harder. All had the boils and warts we had seen on the other mobs and were likewise still named Twisted Disciple of Movement.

We talked over our options and decided to start with the Dark Elf, partly because he was the most unknown, as none of the other mobs had been Dark Elves, and partly because we had never fought a Dark Elf before. It just seemed cool.

With only one mob, we wouldn't be using our previous strategy of having to kite any mobs. In this case, we would employ our time-tested tactics of traditional gameplay. Tank, healer, and two DPS—one up close, and one from range.

With that mindset, Wayne entered the platform first, ready to engage the Disciple, and keep him in the center. As soon as he crossed the threshold, the Dark Elf locked eyes on our Warrior.

"Have you come to free us from our blight? Do you look to end our suffering and release our champion? Such a noble cause, but unfortunately one I cannot let you accomplish. I've been imprisoned here, forced to fight. And fight I shall."

The rest of us had entered the platform but had not moved past Wayne. As the first one to enter, Wayne answered the mob.

"What of your blight?" he asked.

"Have you come to free us from our blight? Do you look to end our suffering and release our champion? Such a noble cause, but unfortunately one I cannot let you accomplish. I've been imprisoned here, forced to fight. And fight I shall."

Restoration of House Lancaster V: Cleanse the Monastery of Movement

"Crap. He's on a loop. I think you'll have to ask him, Alex."

As the leader of the group, I was the one that mobs would address. I tried to do so while keeping my invisibility going.

"What of your blight?" I asked.

The mob didn't answer.

"Well, this is the suck. Guess I'll have to drop my invis."

I stepped from out of the Shadows and asked again.

"What of your blight?" I asked again.

"Ahh, that is a sad story," he said, turning to address me. "They came like a horde. Led by a Death Priest of Loust. Their only intention, to destroy this holy place. Our Disciples had lived in harmony in the Movement for generations, yet in one day and one night, they succeeded in twisting our legacy forever. Those you have seen were cursed to become something else, the vile being you see before you.

"Our champion raged against the challenge and came to our aid. He was the true protector of this forest, and we called him friend. He slew the beasts *en masse*. Only the Death Priest remained, and in his vileness, he cast his last spell. He implanted insanity in the mind of the champion and Twisted the people of this city."

He looked down at his arms, covered in the disease we had seen on all the other Disciples, and shook his head.

"Our curse is to protect this city, sacrificing ourselves if necessary. Only the champion now protects our most holy relics, but his insanity means that he is to be locked away within this building. His release would ensure the end of our struggles. Our deaths are the only keys to opening this structure, but death is a fruit we will never taste."

"The Death Priest is dead?" I asked.

"Yes. His demise was the force that powered this evil curse."

"Then we will rid you of this task and relieve the champion of his insanity. You will finally have rest."

"A noble cause, but one I cannot allow. I apologize for taking your lives," the Dark Elf said and sprung at us.

Wayne had been waiting for this moment and met the Dark Elf with his own attack. Wayne's Bash landed squarely against the chest of the mob, and it staggered back. He followed up with a hammer strike and a Kick, solidifying his aggro on the mob.

Dan and I got in position, and Jason remained behind Wayne, ready to heal.

Wayne swung his hammer again, and the Disciple jumped backward. We weren't prepared for his next action, since the fight had just started. But we were very aware of the consequences.

The elf took his dagger and sliced it against his arm, yelling "Sacrifice!"

"Shit, already?" Jason asked, in a worried tone.

The mob launched himself back at Wayne and began cutting into our Warrior.

"It's still five hit points per second on this one, Allister, but they are landing faster."

"On it, let me know when it hits twenty-five."

"Yeah, about that, twenty-five."

"Damnit!" Jason yelled and cast a heal.

"No, good, Allister!" Wayne yelled.

"Hoped that wasn't the case! Moving to a stronger heal."

Jason casted again and Wayne acknowledged that it had worked.

If we had been facing two mobs at the same time, this would have gone quite badly, same if we had Dan out running a kite on a mob. We weren't doing either, though, so we had plenty of damage to bring this guy down fast.

The only downside was Jason burning through his mana fast. He was at 50 percent when the Dark Elf collapsed to the ground. I was sure we could do this ring, too.

But then the Disciple spoke.

"I wish it were so easy. My release will not come while my brothers live."

That's when I noticed his health bar was still there, but without any life visible. He must have only had one hit point.

And that's when we saw the timer. It was at ten minutes. And it was counting down.

"Crap! We've got to kill the other guys before the timer runs out," I said and the four of us ran to the next platform.

That fight had taken us about seven minutes, give or take. I didn't think we could make it.

We reached the next platform and Wayne immediately swung at the Halfling staring in our direction. Just like with the Dark Elf, the Halfling jumped backwards and immediately sliced himself, yelling out his sacrifice.

Jason burned through his mana again. The timer was at four minutes when we finished. The Halfling lay on the ground, not dead. He was just like the Dark Elf at the other platform. Jason was at 10 percent mana. The only way we could move forward is if he had time to regenerate some mana, or the next fight would be our last for a while.

We knew we wouldn't make it, but I had to see what happened when the timer ran out. I sent Jason back to the outer ring. I needed him to be far away from us so he could Gate away from the monastery if he needed to. I was hoping we could run back to the rope and escape the aggro zone of the mobs. But no matter what, we couldn't have a total wipe. Just to be safe, I had my Blacksuit on.

Wayne and Dan were on the bridge, right next to the open door we had run through to get to these platforms.

As the timer ran out, the Halfling popped to his feet, with full health. He looked toward Dan and Wayne and yelled out, "My brothers, to me!"

I saw the Dark Elf Disciple coming from his platform and the Human Disciple coming from another. I had no doubt the Wood Elf Disciple was doing the same.

There was no other choice. "Run!"

We got over the bridge that led from the innermost ring, and the doors slammed behind us.

"Boomerang!" I yelled. And then I saw mobs starting to spawn.

"Respawn! Make for the tree!" I yelled.

The respawn took long enough that we had enough time to get to the rope and for all of the guys to get down to the forest. I stayed up top. I had to see just how screwed we were.

And the answer? We were totally screwed. Complete respawn of the whole city.

I untied the rope and climbed back down to the forest floor. I was pissed. There was no way that we could beat this monastery. Not at this level. The mobs would have had to be green on the outer ring. And that would mean three or four more levels to grind through.

But we should have been able to beat this place. In every other monastery we faced, our levels were exactly where they should be to conquer the quest. This thing was broken.

And there was only one person who could fix it.

I needed to talk to the Wanderer, and I needed to do so without all the damn subterfuge.

It was time to have a real talk with my group.

I agonized over how to deal with this topic. I decided that I couldn't just summon the Wanderer in front of my friends and ask him to change the parameters of the quest. I was going to need to do that alone. Then, while I talked to him, I could tell him that I was done with the secrets.

I had good reason to not want to involve my friends from the outset. All of my skills as a Rogue, the secret ones at least, were contingent on the fact that no one could know about the fact that I had them. If I summoned the

Wanderer right then, it would undoubtedly lead to too many questions and could cancel out those Skills.

However, I realized just how ridiculous this was all going to sound. I was about to walk off in the woods, by myself, and ask my teammates to not follow me. I couldn't just sneak off, either, since Jason could see me just fine with his necklace.

There was no time like the present.

"Guys, I've a favor to ask," I said.

"How much you need, Alex?" Dan said.

"What?"

"You want a loan, right? That's usually how it starts. You say you have a favor to ask then tell me about how you spent all your money on the ponies. Or on a girl. Or, whatever. I then offer up whatever you need at an insanely low interest rate and a promise to help me get with Kaitlin," Dan responded. "Honestly, I've been dreaming for someone to help as a wingman!"

"For starters, Dan, I don't need any money. But thanks. Secondly, we've all been winging for you since day one. You just don't bother to listen to our advice."

"Ok. That's fair. So, what do you need, if not money?"

"I need you guys to stay here. Don't follow me. And don't ask any questions until I get back."

"Bro, if you need to go number two in the forest, no one will judge you."

I just had to laugh. Here I was seriously concerned with how this conversation would go, and Dan just brought out the humor in everything.

Once I stopped laughing, I said, "I'm serious, Dan."

"What's going on, Alex?" Wayne asked.

"I need you guys to trust me. That's all. When I get back, I'll answer whatever questions I can."

"We trust you, but I'm getting a bad feeling about this."

"I hope I still have that trust when I return, Allister. I just want you guys to know, you're the closest thing I've had to family in a long time."

None of them answered for several seconds.

And then Dan broke the silence. "Ok. Too heavy for my tastes. Just go do whatever you have to, and we will figure it out when you get back."

The other two nodded their heads but didn't say anything else.

I ran off into the forest, away from my friends, dreading what would come next.

I found a large tree that would block my view from my teammates and stopped running.

"Wanderer, I need you."

The AI walked out of the tree and looked around. After taking in his surroundings, he let off a small smile and turned to me. "The Monastery of Movement. Excellent. But you haven't begun yet. It is still fully populated."

"That's because the damn thing is broken," I said and then launched in to what happened at the monastery. I only gave the barest of details, explaining how we cleared out all of the rings then engaged the last four mobs. I explained how we had to do the whole thing in two days, due to the difficulty of regening mana after every platform. I told him about the timer, and how we were forced to run when we couldn't defeat all four in the ten-minute timer.

"Our cleric has three pieces of legendary set gear and the damn Book of Calm, and he couldn't keep up with the DoTs. There is no way we can beat this. And if the boss in the monastery is harder than the four gate keepers, there is definitely no way we can do it with a four-man group. This thing requires a raid."

"You may be right, Alex. This quest hadn't gone live, so there were likely some tweaks that needed to be made. Each of these monasteries were supposed to be completed in one full day. Although I did note that it took you two days to do the Monastery of the Swift."

"That's because we traveled across the desert for half the day before we started the last monastery. We could have done it in one day if we had started when we first logged on. This one wasn't like that."

"I understand. What would you have me do?"

"Make it a raid."

The Wanderer thought for a moment then said, "I could do that. But what would you tell your friends? They would immediately see the difference."

"That's the next thing I want to talk with you about. I'm done hiding this."

"You know how important this mission is, Alex. This isn't about a game."

"I know!" I exclaimed. "And I should have explained that to the guys long ago. Do you not think they would do everything to help? You guys picked this team specifically, and damn if you didn't make the right choice. But things are coming to a head, and I've got a real plan in place. And I'm going to need their help."

"Why then haven't you told them before?"

"Because of my Skills!" I said in exasperation. "If I tell them how this all came to pass, I'll lose my special Rogue skills. And I can't even begin to tell you how often those abilities have saved this team."

"I see," he said. "Yes. Hiding your Skills was necessary from the outset, but I don't believe we need that any longer. However, you will still need to keep your association with your trainers a secret. They are unique to you alone in this game, and bringing their attention to more players could severely impact how the moderators at AltCon see the game."

He nodded his head twice, and I received two notifications. The first one read:

Restoration of House Lancaster V: Cleanse the Monastery of Movement (12 Person Raid)

The second notification popped up after that one and read:

Quest: Secrets of the Rogue
Rogue Only
This is a solo and secret quest. Only you and your teammates may know of this quest. Informing any other individuals will immediately make the quest null and void.

"Now I must go. I've been here too long. If you need my assistance again, come to the Underground."

And with that, the Wanderer walked back into the tree. It was still cool to see him do that.

I ran back to the guys and they were all standing with their hands on their hips. They looked pissed.

"What the hell did you just do? And how the hell did you do it?" Jason asked.

I put my hands up in front of me and said, "Guys, I need to tell you a story."

Over the next half hour, I told them the whole thing. I started by explaining my run-in with a mysterious individual in the slums of Port Town and how he had given me a secret quest for rogues that specifically said I couldn't tell anyone. I told them about Simon Temple, who we had found in the sewers under the city, and how he played a part in the quest. I told them about my interaction with Simon and how that led to a secret trainer who taught me a new type of invisibility called a Blacksuit that made me invisible to almost everything.

I kept going and explained how the ultimate goal was to get to the Underground in Kich's Keep, where I was to meet with the same mysterious individual. Then I explained how everything changed at that meeting.

They didn't interrupt a single time as I went through what the Wanderer had told me, how he explained that he was the living embodiment of the AI in the game and that there was something wrong with Resurgence. I went over Robert Shoal's death, how we were specifically chosen to be a group, put together to help with uncovering the secret that likely got Shoal killed. We were to find the code, hosted in the game, and destroy it.

I told them about my other Skills: Disembowel, Scaling, Lifting, and Disassembling Wards and how those complemented the already existing Skills of Backstab, Climbing, Pickpocket, and Disarm Traps. I explained that if I had explained to them how I was able to do any of those things, it would have negated my Skills, and I would have lost them all.

I then told them about my error in the game. The one I still saw every time I logged in. And how that had been the one change the Wanderer had made to my character the first time I logged in. I explained my Chance score.

Dan whistled. "Well at least that makes more sense now. No wonder we get the best drops ever."

I nodded my head and continued. I told them how the Wanderer had made certain I got the Force Multiplier ring when it dropped, but I held up my hands and made certain they knew that was the only time that he had manipulated a roll. I explained it was because of Lady Tessa's quest, and the only way it would have spawned is if a player had a Chance of over 400.

I said that I had found the thing that the Wanderer had been searching for: the living embodiment of that code that was hosted in a mob. They all let out an audible shock when I told them that very mob was Supreme Overlord Riff Lifestealer.

Through it all, I explained that the reason I kept it all to myself was part selfish and part altruistic. The selfish part was because I didn't want to lose my Skills. The altruistic part was that I didn't want to burden the guys with the same feeling of expectation that I now felt.

"So, what changed?" Wayne asked, arms still crossed over his chest.

"I'm tired of lying to you guys!" I exclaimed. "I meant it when I said you guys are like family. And it drags on me every time that I have to. I knew I would tell you guys, that was certain, I just didn't know how or when. So, I decided to kill two birds with one stone."

"There are videos online of a guy who actually did that," Dan said.

"Focus, man!" Jason said.

"Right, sorry."

I knew I might lose my friends right here and now, but I was putting it all out there.

"I ran out to the forest and called the Wanderer. That's why I took off. I had him change my secret quest so I could only tell my teammates, instead of telling no one. And, I made him change the quest to a raid. I also told him that I was done keeping these secrets from you guys."

"You know, this would have been so much simpler if you would have told me all of this earlier," Dan said.

"Dan's right, Alex," Wayne said. "I'm not sure what to do with all of this."

"Oh, I'm all in!" Dan said.

Jason and Wayne looked over at the Ranger. Jason gave one of his signature looks, although this one was more questioning.

"Haven't you guys thought that weird things keep happening in the game? I mean, have any of you played any of those stupid games we bought? Or what about buying AltCon stock. Didn't that almost end up in a breakup between you and James, Jason?"

"Yeah, it did."

"I'm just saying, I think Alex is right. And, honestly, I don't really care that he kept the secret from us, because we now know. And it's more important that he eventually came clean on his own and not because we found out on our own. Am I right?"

"I guess so," Jason said. Then he turned to me, pointed his finger toward my chest, and said, "Look, Alex. I'm really upset with this whole thing. I'm disappointed in you for lying to us. I'm angry because you waited this long to tell this Wanderer to pack sand. And I can't help but think that if we hadn't been hit with this unpassable quest, you'd still be keeping this from us."

"No lies," I said. "If it weren't for this quest, then yeah, I would still be keeping this from you guys. Not because I don't trust you, but because I would have kept telling myself the same thing over and over. That the time just wasn't right. But I knew the time was right now."

"Seems convenient, Alex," Wayne said. He too wasn't totally convinced. And I couldn't blame either of them.

"It was. That's true. But just continuing to lie to you guys, and going back and grinding, would have saved me all of this," I answered. "Yeah, it would have taken longer, but I could have kept my secret forever. I mean it when I tell you guys that I have wanted you to know from the outset. I don't know if my word means anything, now, but I swear."

Jason and Wayne looked at each other and then they nodded to each other.

Wayne turned toward me and said, "No more secrets."

"Totally. But I'll tell you now that I can't tell you who my trainers are. The Wanderer said that any more interaction with players could alert the moderators. These mobs aren't supposed to be interacting with everyday players. I get away with it because they are rogues, after all."

"That's fine," Wayne said.

Jason nodded his head.

"Guys. I also think we need to keep this from the rest of the team. At least for now. I know we need to bring them here for this raid, but I think we should wait to tell them when the time is right," Dan said. I wasn't used to hearing him be the voice of reason.

"And when will that be?" Jason asked.

"I think we will know when the time is right," was all the Ranger said.

CHAPTER 25

"**N**ow that we have the raid, how do you guys want to do this?" Dan asked, changing the topic from my months of lying to the game at hand. Dan was really taking this better than I thought. Of the three guys in the group, he had been the one that constantly questioned our good luck and my abilities. It seemed that he just needed confirmation that his suspicions were correct, and he was ready to move on.

I prayed the other guys would be as forgiving.

Wayne looked over toward the tree city and said, "We could start clearing again. We know how to get it done and we could remove a lot of the mobs before the rest get here."

"That's true, Naugha, but the rest would lose out on a bunch of experience."

Wayne nodded his head. "It's going to take them forever to get here though."

"About the raid. We need to keep Alex's secret for now. I say we tell them that we tested the first platform since we could get up there, and then called for reinforcements when we saw how it destroyed my mana," Jason said. I was surprised he was the one to suggest it.

"Well then let's go clear the first platform. We need to sell it, after all," Wayne said.

We climbed back up and quickly dealt with the three human disciples that were on the first platform. After that we returned to the forest floor.

Wayne walked off and was probably messaging Jenny. I was about to do the same thing when Wayne came trotting back.

"Good news."

"We could use some of that," Dan said.

"Jenny and the rest are already here. They're hunting Loust patrols like we did. They can be here in no time flat."

"Awesome," Dan said. "Have you reached out to Tyke yet, Alex?"

"Nope. Doing so now."

I sent the shaman a message and waited for his reply.

"I always love getting your messages, my friend. What crazy thing have you gotten yourself into now, and how can we help?" the message read.

I replied, explaining to Tyke that we had encountered a raid, and that the rest of our group was already on the way. He, of course, was invited to join.

I also sent him the location and a reply came back quickly.

"We're headed that way already. There are a ton of players on the road, all headed toward Loust territory to try and get those bounties. You wouldn't happen to have anything to do with that, would you?"

I sent another message and told them about the Stealers and how we had sent them to respawn and had uncovered the plot by capturing their tokens.

"Yessssss! I hate those guys! We'll be there shortly. Don't start without us!"

I relayed the messages I had received from Tyke, and we waited for our larger group to arrive. It was only another twenty minutes before they came traveling through the forest.

It wasn't often we got to play with our extended group, and I always loved the comradery that instantly formed when we were together. Gary, Jenny, Kaitlin, and Tim didn't seem to notice the slight air of tension that still lingered within my group, and they embraced each of us. Kaitlin even hugged Dan.

Dan was shocked and didn't have enough time to make it awkward before she moved over to hug Jason.

That was probably a good thing.

"How's everyone doing?" Tim asked. "Haven't seen you guys since the Shield of Ashtator, but Jenny has kept us up to date on your wild adventures. I'm glad we get to join."

We shared a few of our tales, and the group was stoked to be getting to take part in one of our monastery quests.

"We've got some time before Tyke and the guys get here, and I'd rather wait to explain what we've found until they get here."

"Sounds good," Tim said. "other than gaming, how has everyone been? I mean, I already know that Wayne is whipped, but what about you three?"

"Also whipped," Jason replied. That got a laugh out of us.

The rest looked over at us. Dan looked over at Kaitlin. And then he lifted his eyebrows in a questioning manner. "I'm not against whipping. Just saying."

Kaitlin snorted, she laughed so hard.

The rest of us weren't far behind.

"I'd say everyone is doing well, Tim. Thanks for asking."

We broke down into idle banter. Jason pulled Dan to the side and whispered something in his ear. I have no idea what he said, but Dan played it cool with Kaitlin. Not pressuring her too much with his presence or his foolery. She seemed to appreciate it.

After a while, Tyke, Lug, Tammer, and Syphon arrived on the scene. There was another round of greetings and asking what everyone had been up to. Tyke couldn't help but congratulate us repeatedly for ruining the Stealers' day.

"I can only imagine how pissed they have to be now that their whole enterprise of betrayal has been uncovered. The fact that they can't go to any of the cities is just awesome."

"Well," I said, "Dredge did tell us that they had been getting lots of quests from Loust's army and that they had even gotten some titles. I do have to hand it to them. They found a way to get a lot stronger without conforming to the main story arc."

"Thanks for ruining my good mood, Alex," Tyke said.

"Don't worry, buddy. I have no doubt that we will run across those four again and we will all get a chance to enact some revenge."

"Here's to hoping," he said. "So, what do we have here?"

I launched into the story that I had concocted with the guys. We had come upon this quest to cleanse this monastery as part of a larger quest line. However, this was the first time we had encountered a raid-level fight. I told them that we had already tried the first platform, and while we had defeated the mobs, it took most of our mana to do so.

"Wow," Lug said. "Allister has a huge mana reserve. These guys must hit like tanks."

I went on to explain the Sacrifice debuff, how it took only one hit point per second, which got a laugh out of the huge ogre. However, he stopped laughing when I explained that it stacked repeatedly, leaving Wayne with a DoT of 34 hit points per second, and that it didn't wear off. The only way to get rid of it was to cast Jason's heal. I explained that Dan's hadn't worked.

"Hopefully healers like Anastasia and I can handle part of the load, but if need be, we can just heal while Allister focuses on getting rid of the DoT," Tyke said. Anastasia was Kaitlin's name in game.

Once everyone was ready, we headed back to our favorite climbing tree. The two new groups looked up to the bridge far above us and then looked around. They didn't see a way up.

"Don't worry. I've got this," I said and then cloaked myself in my Blacksuit. I ran for the tree and then began to Scale up the side. Now that I had made this climb multiple times, I knew where every handhold was and made it up to the bridge in no time. I tied off the rope like before and lowered it to the ground.

Everyone climbed up the rope, with Lug going last. There had been ample rope for the rest to climb, but Lug was dealing with the barest amount possible. We had used our own bodies to reinforce the rope's tether. Wayne was big. Lug was massive.

His body weight almost pulled us off the bridge, but we used the tree as a base, and braced ourselves against the mammoth oak. It took a while, but Lug made it up the rope. He waved his hand at us and asked to rest. His Endurance was almost completely depleted.

"Ogres don't climb. We break things until whatever is at the top comes to us."

We all laughed at that and waited for Lug to recover his Endurance. While we did, we reviewed everyone's levels. Jenny's group had just made 37, and Tyke's was almost to the same level. More of the mobs were going to be yellow to them.

"Slovak, you try to Enchant one of the adds. If it doesn't work, TC,"—I refused to call him TheClaw—"will Snare. Tammer, if Slovak lands his Enchant, you try to do the same on the other one. If it doesn't land, that'll be the one that Lug grabs. Serenity can grab the last, and she and Lug will off-tank while Naugha keeps the main target. The first one that gets to 50 percent will call for the Sacrifice, and then all of them will be trying to hit us with DoTs. The rest of us will burn down the main target. All good?"

Everyone nodded their heads.

"Normally we would have to pull these as a full group, but that's when we didn't have Sayhey and his Brawler ability to Play Dead. Before we go all buck wild, let's try to pull a single," I said. "Sayhey, you're up."

With Gary's skill of Play Dead, he could pull all the mobs at once then act like he had died. The mobs would forget that he was there and go back to their starting position. If one lingered long enough, Gary could pull it single. It was definitely worth a shot to try.

But it wasn't going to happen. We were able to see that after Gary tried a few times. The platform moved as a single mob, and they came at him at the same time. Then they retreated at the same time. It wasn't really a problem, since we already knew that our single group could handle the platforms all the way to the last ring.

"Well, it will make this more fun!" Lug said.

Gary came back to the group and apologized, but everyone assured him it wasn't because of his lack of skill. Now Gary was DPS, but I was happy to have him in that role since his damage output was insane.

"Slovak, pick a target that is blue to you. TC, target that mob and pull with an arrow. Dan, be ready to Snare. Go on TC's call."

"I really wish he would call me TheClaw," Dan said.

"Not happening!" I slightly yelled.

Dan ran out onto the bridge and fired off an arrow, and the group of four Halfling Twisted Disciples of Movement started running toward us. I saw Slovak run up and cast his spell.

"Landed!"

"You're up, Tammer," I said.

I saw Tyke's Enchanter move forward and cast.

"Resist!"

"I got it," Dan yelled, and I saw the second mob automatically slow down. The other two continued to run at us, and Lug and Wayne both stepped forward. Wayne gave Lug a fist bump and swung his war hammer at one of the mobs. Lug grabbed the next.

The enchanted mob stayed on the bridge, and Dan ran the other one around the platform. The last time we had done this, the only melee we had was Wayne and me. We were able to take down the mobs, but it took a while. Now, however, that wasn't the case. Gary and I provided pure DPS, Jenny was quite a beast herself with her sword and shield, and Syphon was able to land his own DoTs and Life Taps on the mob. Additionally, with Tammer and Tim here, we had the ability to speed up our own rate of attack and slow the mobs. Since Tim was on crowd control with Dan, Tammer handled the slows.

Bottom line, we tore through the mobs. Sure, they called for Sacrifice at 50 percent, but the mobs didn't have much time after that call to stack many of the debuffs. Oddly, I noted that even the enchanted mob was able to break out of his entranced state to cut himself before he was back to being held by Tim's magic.

When we cleared the mobs from the platform, Jason only had to heal a total of 15 Sacrifice DoTs, and all of our players were at max health thanks to the healing of Kaitlin and Tyke. We were a bit disheartened to find that only Jason and Jenny were able to get rid of the DoT. Kaitlin and Tyke's heals were ineffective. As for Jenny, it took her highest heal to clear out the Sacrifice. We knew that after the outer ring, her heals would no longer work. Besides, it took too much mana from Jenny to use that heal repeatedly.

With the speed at which we had cleared the platform, we didn't have any need to rest and regen mana. We were off to the next platform.

We mimicked our previous route and cleared out all of the outer ring platforms, taking down the sixteen mobs. The routine continued, with us clearing the next twelve platforms. During that time, Tyke's group eventually all leveled to 37. These mobs were all yellow to our fellow raid members, and it was harder for them to land their enchanter spells. Dan was still able to Snare them, and he was showing off running them around the outer ring. The enchanter Slow spells had no problem landing, though, and it greatly reduced the amount of mana Jason and our other healers had to expend. I couldn't stress how awesome it was to have four damage dealers instead of just me.

The next set of platforms, the ring of eight, came next. Our counterparts noted the closed doors, and I feigned ignorance at why they remained close. It made no difference, since we knew our goal lay on the other side of those doors. It was an accurate guess on their parts, but one that didn't take too much thought. We had come to the same conclusion.

The ring of eight was much tougher than the previous two rings, and we had to rest for a short moment between each platform. Still, it was nothing like the five to ten minutes we were forced to wait before as we relied on Jason's abilities only. The fact that we were having to rest at this point, though, definitely told me the quest had been broken to begin with and should have been a raid from the start. We were twelve against three at each platform, and we had to rest for a minute to feel comfortable with our mana. Again, I knew we didn't really need to wait that long, as we did this before with less mana, but there were appearances to keep up.

With the death of the last mob on the ring of eight, the doors opened. We approached the Dark Elf again. He was still yellow to us, but he was red to our level 37 teammates.

And like before, as soon as Wayne crossed the threshold, the Dark Elf spoke.

"Have you come to free us from our blight? Do you look to end our suffering and release our champion? Such a noble cause, but unfortunately one I cannot let you accomplish. I've been imprisoned here, forced to fight. And fight I shall."

From that point forward, we reenacted the whole scene as from before. I asked the same questions and got the same answers. At the end of the dialogue, he attacked. But this time, we were far more equipped.

The fight took a little over three minutes, and we didn't pause to contemplate the fact that the Dark Elf was still alive. As soon as the timer started, I yelled for the raid to head to the next platform. No one questioned my orders and just ran like mad for the next mob.

We did this three more times, and I noticed the timer hadn't stopped. We still had to kill the mobs! I yelled again for everyone to take off to a different platform and not to worry about aggro. Whoever got there first, hit the Disciple.

We made it with twenty-three seconds to spare. It was damn close. But thankfully, not countdown-to-the-last-five-seconds close. With the Disciples dead, we braced for the next fight. But nothing happened.

"Let me scout while everyone heals up and gets mana," I said. Then I took off toward the three-story structure sitting in the middle of the tree city. It didn't take me long to see the problem.

After my investigation, I ran back to the first Disciple we had killed, the Dark Elf. His body was still there. When I leaned down to loot his body, he only had one item on him. A key.

I checked all the other bodies and found the same thing. This made sense. When I was scouting, I had seen that each of the four sides of the structure held a place for a keyhole. We needed to use these to get inside the structure. At least, that was my belief.

I had Wayne, Lug, and Jenny take keys. I did the same. Then, with my Blacksuit still on, I went around to the opposite side of where the Dark Elf had died. I was on the platform of the Wood Elf. I then called for everyone to insert their keys and activate them at the same time.

I counted down from three. At one, we turned the keys.

There was an immediate reaction, and the building started shaking slightly.

"Alex, everyone, get back over here!" Wayne said. He was where the Dark Elf had fallen.

When I came around and joined up with the group, I saw that the door to the structure was open. It had swung inward, and I could barely see inside the structure. But what I did see made me happy and apprehensive at the same time.

Sitting on the floor was our last mob to finish the quest. Over its head was the tag Champion of Movement, and his name was red.

Even sitting, the beast made Lug look small. And when he stood, I finally saw the full extent of our foe. We were facing a Giant.

⸻⬙⬙⸻

We'd faced some pretty righteous beasts in our time. There were all the different Death Priests and the swarm of mobs we conquered to get to them. We'd beaten the trolls, and the House Frost mages, and numerous other baddies. But nothing was like this.

The giant stood over ten feet tall. It could have been closer to twelve. It had some armor on, but it barely covered its body. The giant had thick leather wrappings covering its calves and up to its knees. Its feet, however, were uncovered, and each toe on its feet looked as thick as my wrist. It wore a leather kilt of sorts that hung down to mid-thigh and covered its nether regions. I was thankful for that. I couldn't imagine the comments Dan would let out if a Giant member was flapping around while we fought. Probably something about it being just a bit smaller than his.

The giant had similar leather wrapped around its forearms, making them look like bracers, but no gloves. Only two bandoliers of leather covered the giant's torso, leaving its chest entirely bare, as were his arms save for those bracers. It also didn't wear a helmet of any kind, and we could see its face quite clearly.

There were scars running down the left side of its face, but it did not look to affect his eyesight. His facial features were akin to human.

400

No jewelry adorned its face, or hands, but he was carrying one obvious item.

A massive club was in its right hand. It reached all the way to the floor and was more than just a simple piece of wood. It was fashioned to hold multiple spikes running through the top, and each one could easily go all the way through Wayne. The smaller ones may have gotten stuck inside Lug. Either way you looked at it, not a weapon we wanted to get hit with.

The Champion of Movement wasn't moving to engage, so I had time to look around the room. I wasn't the only one doing so.

"Look at all the loot!" Tyke yelled out.

And he was right. All over the floor of the structure were piles of items, and coins. I could easily see stacks of platinum and gold. There were also chunks of metal that looked like mithral, and armor and weapons lay scattered across the ground. There was more than we could ever hope to haul off by ourselves. Unfortunately, it was all behind the giant.

The ceiling was supported by four branches of the tree that grew from out of the base of the floor. There were wards placed on all of the branches. My Skill allowed me to see the wards, but I had no idea what they did.

"Before we go in any further, let's talk strategy," I said. "To be honest, I don't really have much of a plan."

That got a laugh from everyone.

"To be expected on a first fight, Alex. Are you thinking just straight up tank?"

"Pretty much. Naugha will main tank, and Lug will be the back-up," I said, looking over to the ogre. "Use Kick and Bash, but no Taunt. If the time comes that Naugha goes down, hit it with the Taunt."

Lug nodded his head.

"Allister, Anastasia, and Tyke, set up a heal rotation. I don't want us over-healing Naugha and wasting mana."

The three nodded as well.

"Us damage dealers will do our thing, but I want you to be careful with those DoTs, Syphon. This fight could take a while, and I don't want you accidently pulling aggro. Serenity, you'll be damage for now. Do you have Lay on Hands up?"

Lay on Hands was a skill that Jenny had, which would heal her target for 75 percent of their hit points. At a higher level, we supposed, it would heal 100 percent.

"I do."

"Ok, last ditch cast if we need it. I promise Naugha will do dishes."

That got laughs from our group, but Tyke and the others looked confused.

"I don't just give away my best Skill. He gets to earn it with dish duty," Jenny explained with a smile on her face.

"Harsh penalty, Naugha," Lug said while laughing.

"Worth every penny, bro."

"That leaves our crowd control. Dan, I want you to be shooting from a distance, but be ready to Snare. Your primary duty here is to control adds if we need it. The extra damage is just a bonus."

"Got it, Alex."

"Until we get any adds that we need to deal with, I want our Enchanters hitting him with Slow. If we get any low-level adds, you can try a Charm. I wouldn't mind having one of these mobs helping us out.

"That's the best I can come up with until we see how the fight plays out. Let's stay away from those branches as well, because they look to be trapped. Time to do this!"

Everyone entered the room and approached the giant. As we got closer, he took his massive club and slammed it against the ground.

"You would defile my home! I crushed you once, you puppets of Loust, and I will do so again!"

Before I could respond that we weren't a part of Loust's army, the giant was charging.

It was comical to see Wayne slam into the giant's midsection with his overhead hammer swing and then throw a Bash into his stomach. It was even funnier to see him kick straight out and only reach the giant's leg. This thing was huge.

But the Bash worked, and the giant was stunned for a second.

That was enough time for everyone to get into position and wait to engage. Wayne needed time to establish aggro.

Wayne took another swing and cycled through his Skills again before calling us forward to attack.

"Hold off on Skill attacks until I've done another round of Skills," Wayne yelled.

His health was dropping steadily, but our healers were holding off for Jason to start the rotation.

After another several seconds, Wayne yelled, "All in!"

And with that, we attacked together. Weapons and arrows flew through the air, and I saw Slovak, Syphon, and Tammer casting their spells.

"Slow landed," Tammer and Slovak both yelled at the same time and smiled at each other.

"DoTs landing too," Syphon said.

"His skin is tough," Gary said. "I'm not doing much damage."

It was the same with me.

After about a minute, the giant had only dropped a couple of percentage points in health. Thankfully, with three healers, we weren't burning through mana. In a fight for attrition, we would win. But this was a boss, and we were sure to face special attacks as the fight went on.

After a few more seconds, the giant's health went from 97 percent to 98 percent.

"Damn, he's got crazy regen," Wayne said.

There wasn't anything to say, so we kept hitting.

Five minutes later, the boss hit 90 percent, and he screamed out, "Protect our home!"

Three mobs ran into the room, all Twisted Disciples of Movement. I had no idea where they came from, but I didn't really care. All three were green.

Dan immediately caught one with his Snare, and the two Enchanters grabbed the other two with a spell that mesmerized the mobs. They were just standing there.

"We good to Charm, Alex?" Tammer asked.

"Go for it. The more melee the better," I answered.

A few seconds later, two more mobs were attacking the giant.

The fight kept on for another minute, and it wasn't looking good. Despite having even more fighters, we weren't making a dent on the giant's hit points. In fact, it was worse than that. I had just seen his hit points go from 90 percent back up to 91.

Our healers were still fine on mana, but that wouldn't be the case forever, especially if the giant continued to heal itself. This was a losing battle at this point.

The giant kept attacking, and the Charmed mobs were standing in front of the giant, instead of behind it like the rest of the melee were. Because of where they were, they could get hit by a retaliatory strike, like a Riposte. This was the case for our two disciples, and Slovak yelled out that his was at half health.

That's when the Charmed mob jumped back from the fight and yelled out "Sacrifice!" Despite being Charmed, both mobs, and the one Snared, completed their programming and sliced into themselves.

Then the two Disciples got back in the fight, and the other one kept chasing Dan.

But then a strange thing happened. A debuff landed on the giant. And it wasn't one of ours.

"Holy Shit! They just landed the Twisted Sacrifice on the Champion!" Jenny yelled.

I saw it too, and after a few seconds, the stack was at a factor of ten.

The giant stopped attacking Wayne to turn on one of the Charmed Disciples. He yelled out, "Traitor!" and flattened the mob with his club, killing it instantly. But the stack of debuffs didn't go away. The second Disciple continued to land the DoT, and after another five stacked before the Champion killed that one with one hit too.

"One of you guys Charm that last mob and get him on the giant!" I yelled.

Tim and Tammer both cast at the same time, and I had no idea whose landed first. All I knew was that the Disciple trudged over to the giant. It was still Snared, so it moved a bit slowly. Still, once it got in range, it started stabbing the beast, and another five DoTs stacked. Then it was killed like the other two.

We had never stopped fighting, though, and I saw that with the DoT and our damage, the giant was back to losing hit points.

When the giant hit 80 percent, it repeated its call and another three Disciples entered the room. This time, I didn't hesitate and called out new instructions.

"Serenity and Sayhey, take one. Get it down to fifty percent. Tammer, Charm the other one. Dan, grab the third. When that first mob calls for Sacrifice, Slovak, Charm it and get it into the fight.

"If Tammer's gets knocked down to 50 percent first, immediately Charm the one with Serenity and Sayhey. Go!"

Everyone yelled out their acknowledgement and took to their duties. I didn't plan to wait and give the giant time to regen back toward full, because that's what it was already doing. When it hit 80 percent, the rate of regen increased again, and it negated the DoT stack it continued to hold.

Our plan worked well, and we were quickly restacking the DoT on the giant, keeping it from regening past 82 percent. The Disciples were wiped out quickly, but not before they raised their total for the DoT to forty times, meaning at least 40 hit points of damage per second.

I had been focusing on the fact that the giant called for reinforcements each time he dropped 10 percent that I totally forgot about the fact that he was a boss. When it hit 75 percent health, I was caught entirely unawares, as were all of the people within his swinging range.

Wayne and Lug dropped to 60 percent of their health. Jenny was down to 50 percent. Gary and I were looking at 30 percent. And Syphon, he was too close and got hit so hard that he lost 90 percent of his hit points.

The giant had executed a special attack when he hit 75 percent and spun his massive body around. He hit all of us that were close enough with both his club and his arm. Multiple times. What's more, his reach was so massive that his club hit one of the tree branches, activating the trap, and destroying a part of the branch and outer wall. The resulting debris buried a significant amount of the treasure, while shards of wood landed all around us. The ceiling groaned with the damage. As did our group when they saw the loot buried.

The giant immediately turned on Syphon, since he was down to only 10 percent, and a perfect target of opportunity. One flick of the giant's toe would have killed our Death caster.

Thankfully, two things happened at the same time. Syphon landed a Life Tap that took his hit points up to 50 percent, and Wayne landed a Taunt on the giant. With the caster back to half, he wasn't as much of an easy target, and the Skill to take aggro from other players and load it on to Wayne had succeeded.

No one died, but valuable mana was wasted as Jenny was forced to throw heals at all of us, including herself, while Tyke and Kaitlin also landed several heals on our raid. That could have easily have been a wipe if we hadn't had such high-level players with good gear.

But I felt better now about the fight than I had at any point since we started. We knew how to negate the giant's insane regen, and we knew how to avoid the spinning attack. We simply had to get out of range of his spinning melee AOE damage attack.

And so, the fight went. New Disciples arrived at every ten percent, but we used those to offset the giant's regen. If I had to guess, the fact that a raid was needed for this quest wasn't the only thing that needed to be tweaked about the fight. This boss would have needed way more than just twelve players if we hadn't been lucky enough to get two Enchanters in our group.

Or maybe that's how this fight was supposed to be won. You could only do it with Enchanters, and we had been lucky—again—to have two with us. It was impossible to know, but I could see the game doing something like that.

At 50 percent and 25 percent, the giant executed his spinning at-tack. And just like with the first time, the attack triggered the traps and destroyed one of the branches. The ground was now covered with remnants from the branches and the walls and almost all of the treasure we had seen when we first walked in was now buried. The only treasure remaining was the pile near the base of the last branch. That looked to be our loot if we succeeded.

The giant had just passed the 10 percent threshold, and the last of the Disciples had come out. We repeated our strategy, and the giant had a 180 hit point per second DoT on him, at least. Still, his regen had gone up each time, and the DoT only kept him at an equal footing with us.

The fight had taken forever, though, and our healers were almost out of mana. It had been a grueling affair, and easily the longest single fight we had ever faced. The Champion of Movement was no joke, indeed.

Right as the giant hit 1 percent hit points, he played his last card.

"You will never have the treasure you seek, Loust, nor will any of you leave this room alive!" he screamed and then turned from us.

With what looked like no effort, he lifted his giant club and aimed it toward the last branch in the room.

He was going to bring the whole place down on top of us. And himself.

"Launch every Stun you have!" I yelled.

And then I activated the Force Multiplier ring, my own trump card.

If the Stuns hadn't landed, I wouldn't have had the time to take him down, even with my ring, but thankfully, someone's Stun did hit, and the giant stopped in his tracks. And that was all the time I needed.

Looking like a whirlwind of blades, I launched myself into the giant's back. My Backstab landed for a critical, and my Blood Blade's Life Tap was proc'ing non-stop.

The Stun wore off before he was dead, though, and he took one more step.

And that was his last.

With a final Backstab, the giant slammed to the ground.

The entire grouped yelled out in triumph. We had done it!

I was about to run over and congratulate the group when the giant turned his head to me.

He wasn't dead!

I got ready to stab him again when he said, "You aren't of Loust. I see that now. Thank you for my release. But you must save the Guardian. She is all that remains to stop his rise."

And then he died.

A message appeared before my eyes:

Restoration of House Lancaster VI: Save the Guardian.

I looked back to the group and said, "It's done."
Then the group really stated cheering.

What remained of the giant's hoard was spread out before us. When we first entered, I had never seen so much loot in one place, and I cursed the developers for that last round with the giant. If the walls hadn't come down, and the rest of the treasure buried, it might have taken us the entire day to go through all the items we had seen when we first walked in. We did try to salvage it though! Wayne took his mining pick out and went right to the piles, hoping to remove the rubble. His face said it all, and we knew we couldn't chip away to the treasure.

As it was, this wasn't some small haul we were looking at, and I was sure everyone in our raid party of 12 was going to get at least one item. I just had to stop Wayne who seemed to be in a trance as he walked toward the pile with his arm out.

"Wayne, stop!"

Wayne pulled up short and looked back at me as I was jogging toward him. "Shit, sorry Alex," he said while blushing a bit. Everyone knew I was our looter, but something had drawn Wayne toward the pile.

One look past him, and I saw what had lured our Barbarian.

Sticking out of a pile of gold, and I really hoped we got to keep the piles of gold we did see, was a long handle made out of metal. I couldn't see what the handle was connected to, but I imagine that Wayne hoped it was a war hammer.

"I'll grab the handle first, Wayne. Don't worry."

"Thanks, Alex. I saw it sticking up like that, with the etchings on the shaft, and the pommel on the end, and it was like it was calling to me."

We both looked around after Wayne's comments, mostly to make sure Dan hadn't heard him use the word "shaft," and then smiled at each other when we realized we had done the same thing.

"I think we're in the clear. Dan's over there, busy telling Kaitlin about his heroics. Running those mobs around. Like she wasn't here to witness them."

We spared only a moment to appreciate our Ranger's efforts with Kaitlin, then I made my way to the trove of goods. We still had ample time on my ring's buff, and I was happy I didn't have to rush to get to our treasures like has happened so often in the past.

I hadn't noticed the etchings or the pommel the first time I saw the handle and paid a little more attention as I approached. Wayne was right, and I could see some type of runes etched into the metal. They were faint, but they were definitely there. The bottom of the handle, right before the pommel Wayne mentioned, was wrapped in a tight weave of what looked like leather. However, the leather looked to be brand new, and I wouldn't have been surprised to learn that the leather had been magically enchanted to not degrade—or something like that. We never got that detailed of information from the items we looted, but it made sense. And Occam's Razor is as good in virtual video games as it is in the real world. When presented with competing explanations for something, the simplest is likely the correct assumption.

When I first noted the end of the handle, and the pommel specifically, I thought it to be a simple bulb of blackened steel that would serve as a counterweight for whatever lay at the other end of the handle. As I got closer, I could tell it was in fact a gem sitting at the end. And what looked to be black in color from a distance was actually a deep blood red.

Without wasting any more time, I laid my hands on the pile of loot and was immediately blinded by all the text boxes that popped up in front of me. Before I went through each one and began informing the group, I found the one I was looking for and called out what I found.

"Hey, Lug and Naugha! I've got two items here that are Warrior only. One is a bad ass two-handed sword and the other is some crappy looking war hammer. You guys want to roll to see who gets to choose first?"

Wayne gave me an evil glare, but it was hard to keep the stern look when Lug was laughing his ass off. "You really are a dick sometimes, Alex," he said while smiling from one ogre ear to the other.

"Isn't he, though?" Wayne said as his scowl turned to just a look of contempt.

"Fine, they're both awesome. Lug, you want to stay with swords?"

"Yup."

"Mind if Naugha loots this first, as I can see he is moments away from losing his mind?"

Lug laughed again and said, "Not at all. I want to see this thing, too."

Wayne nodded his thanks to Lug and threw me a finger, but he did so with a smile and grabbed the handle sticking out of the pile of loot.

"Holy shit," was all Wayne said. Then, before anyone could ask what deserved such a response, Wayne pulled the weapon from the pile. As he pulled it up, we could all see the jewel at the bottom flash once, and the etchings along the shaft lightly lit up to match the same blood red as the jewel.

The war hammer was definitely a thing of beauty. The etchings didn't stop on the shaft and continued up to the head of the hammer and covered that portion of the weapon as well. The metal that made up the head and shaft looked lighter in color than normal steel, on par with the mithral armor Wayne would soon be wearing. I wouldn't be surprised to learn that the metal was mithral, and I made a mental note to ask Master Smith Perry the next time we were in the dwarven kingdom.

The hammer's head was a masterpiece all to itself. While cubed in shape, and more rectangular than squared, that was where it stopped in comparison to other hammers I had seen. Even the war hammer Wayne used now, the Warhammer of Darkness, was mostly just a solid piece of steel with spike protrusions on both faces of the hammer for damage increase. The head of this hammer was much different.

Only one of the faces had similar spike protrusions. This would likely be called the front of the hammer, as the other side had a spike coming out of that face. On top of that, the top of the hammer had another spike, about the same length. I imagine that if you used the top of the hammer to drive into someone's stomach, that spike would do lots of damage.

The same could be said for the spike on the secondary face of the hammer. A backswing, with that spike coming at you, would certainly signal the end to your bad day.

"Wayne, tell them the name," I said, as I had already read the name and the attributes that came with it.

"Giant's Bane." And he linked the item.

Item	Commonality	Weight	Atk Mod	Spd	Bonus
Giant's Bane Two-Handed Warhammer Large Races Only Warrior Only	Legendary: Binds on Acquisition	6.0	+40	0.5	+20 Strength +20 Constitution +20 Atk Mod to Giants Effect: Giant's Bane - +200 Damage to Giants and 50 percent chance to Stun

"I so hope this means we get to fight more giants!"

"Really? Because almost getting smashed by one wasn't enough for you, Dan?"

"You can't fool me Alliadventurous, I know you love it."

Before the two could get any further in their usual bickering, I heard Lug get Wayne's attention.

"Naugha, dude, duel me!"

Wayne looked down at the new hammer in his hands and got a big smile on his face.

"You got it, brother. Someone be ready to heal."

"Don't worry, little Barbarian, I won't go too hard on you," Lug responded while grabbing his sword. I was tempted to have him loot his prize first, the two-handed sword in the pile, but once the duel had been accepted by Wayne, there was no way these two were going to pause for anything.

An ogre was about as close as we had seen to a giant at this point, and what Wayne's hammer did to Lug was ridiculous. Thirty seconds into the fight, we saw why the hammer was called Giant's Bane.

For the briefest of moments, we all saw the blood red gem at the bottom of Wayne's new hammer brighten, then we watched as the light from the gem moved up the shaft of the hammer, illuminating the runed etching as it went, culminating at the head of the hammer. We then saw what looked like an explosion of magical energy connect with Lug's chest where the hammer hit, sending the ogre flying backwards. I won't easily forget the image of flying ogre, I knew that much.

It took Lug a few seconds to get back up, due to the fact he was also stunned from the blow. We saw Lug wave his hand back and forth a few seconds while he got up, and the duel was effectively over. Wayne put his hammer away, and Lug sheathed his sword.

"That's one duel I will happily concede, Naugha. Congrats on the hammer."

"Thanks, Lug. Although we are going to have to do this again. Just wait until you see your sword!"

⚜

I was right, and everyone got something from the pile of loot at our feet. They were all upgrades, especially for Tyke's team, but nothing as impressive as the Giant's Bane. For my part, I got an improved leather helmet that didn't add any increase to Armor but did give me a +15 to Dexterity. I was happy with the upgrade, as Dexterity was my main Stat.

Part of me was thankful that we didn't get another piece of Grumblewat's armor. I would have never heard the end of that from Dan.

Unfortunately, there were also a number of items that we couldn't use. Since they were all untradeable items, we had to just leave them there. It didn't make anyone happy, but it wasn't like we could call in anyone else to take the loot. Since they didn't take part in the battle, they wouldn't have the access to the drops anyhow.

There was also a ton of money. The game had made it easy for us. Six hundred platinum meant that every player got 50 platinum each. That was more money than anyone had seen at any one given time. Our friends were ecstatic with our find.

While the group was still together, we looked for the body of Gerald Lancaster. We searched within the structure but didn't find anything. We hadn't really searched much of the outside before the fight, and I ran back out. It took me about five minutes to find a corpse near where the Wood Elf had died.

Wayne approached the corpse and reached down to it. Like before, the body disappeared when he touched it.

"I'll bury this when we get down to the forest," Wayne said. "There was also another part of the parchment, Alex. He was also holding this map."

I took the parchment and map from Wayne and put them in my inventory. That was four pieces of the document that the father of House Lancaster had found. When all five were put together, it would reveal the information that had got the whole of House Lancaster, save for Lady Tessa, killed.

I opened the map and had to laugh. Like, a lot. Once I finally stopped laughing, I linked the map to our group and read the message on the back out loud.

Father shouldn't leave these things lying around. If you find this, my brothers, get to Father. He can't save the Guardian alone.
– Gerald

The map was a detailed sketch that labeled the location of all the monasteries, except for the Monastery of the Swift. For that one, it just showed a general area in the desert with a notation that said, "Find the Jalusi." The one place we weren't familiar with was further east and north, even more in Loust's territory. It was in a mountain range and was only labeled as "the Guardian."

"Would have been nice to have this damn thing from the beginning, huh?"

"Right you are, Dan!" I said. "But where would the fun have been in that?" I asked. Only a few chuckles came my way.

"I'm not complaining," Jason said. "If we hadn't done this on our own, we would have never met Della or Chakib!"

The rest of our raid was still around us, and they just looked on with bewilderment. As least, Tyke and his group did. I explained that this monastery was the fourth in a very long quest chain that we had been going through for months.

"So that's how you keep getting all this good gear!" Tammer exclaimed, a little miffed at our luck. "You could have told us, too, you know."

Before I could answer, Jenny was there to have my back.

"I think it's a one off, Tammer. We knew about it from the beginning and were never able to get the quest giver to spawn. We even had its exact coordinates."

"You did?" I asked, looking at Wayne.

"She threatened me, bro. Like, in real life."

We all had to laugh at the fear in our Warrior's eyes when he spoke of Jenny's promised wrath.

"Well, I guess we can forgive it then," Tammer replied, with a smile on his face now. "But we definitely want in on this Guardian fight if it's a raid!"

"Wouldn't have it any other way, brother. You guys are the only people we call."

Soon after that, everyone went their own ways, with Tyke and his group heading back toward the King's camp and Treeswain's command center.

Once they were gone, our full team had our own celebration. We were overwhelmed with joy at the number of drops we had got and the progression we had made. The decision was made right there that the celebration had to continue, but outside the game.

"I'm taking care of this next one," Dan said. "I'll have drivers come and pick everyone up. Dress casual. I'm not going to do anything ridiculous. I've learned my lesson."

That got a round of applause from all of us, and Dan even did a mock bow.

"Why the drivers?" Gary asked.

"So, we can imbibe at our leisure. If you need a driver to take you home, no problem. Otherwise, you can just crash at my place. I have ten rooms."

That got another round of clapping.

"Let's say tomorrow night. Drivers will pick you guys up at seven. No kids, though!"

"But then you don't get to come, Dan," Kaitlin said.

"Oohh! That was good, Kaitlin! Have you been getting lessons from, Alligotjokes?"

"She doesn't need any help from me, buddy. She's more than capable to knock you down," Jason said, laughing.

"And keep me down?" he asked, with a wiggle to his eyebrows.

The laughter that echoed across the platforms also looked like it was the signal to end this adventure.

"Thanks again for the invite, guys. We'll see you soon," Jenny said.

I held up my hands, though, and stopped them from going.

"There is still one more thing we need to find here. All of the monasteries have had some kind of special prize at the end. We haven't found that here yet. If this one is anything like the others we've found, it will be tied somehow to a player's Dexterity. You know about the ones we already got." They all nodded their heads.

"I wasn't worried about Tyke's group, since none of them have a Dexterity build. But that's not the case with our team. Let's go find it, and Gary and I can roll for what we find."

Our teammates all looked at each other, then Gary started shaking his head with a smile on his face. "You can't be serious, man. This is your guys' quest. I wouldn't think of rolling on that. I do want to see what you get, though!"

"Are you sure? I'm happy to roll for it. We've all gotten new gear, so it's not mine by elimination."

"Dude. It's way cool that you would even think to include us, but you definitely deserve it. You ran this whole raid and even quickly realized how to handle the giant. As raid leader, you should totally get it."

I shook my own head. "Anyone would have recognized how to do the giant. And, seriously, how many times do I have to say that I'm not the leader?"

My refusal to take on that mantle, even after all this time, made everyone chuckle.

"Let's go find it. It's yours."

We went back inside the sanctuary that had been the home of the Champion and searched around, but we didn't find anything. The area inside wasn't all that big, so most of the team went out to the platforms to search around there. Still, there was no luck.

We were back inside the building and standing near the loot. I was looking over it again but didn't see whatever the item was that I was looking for. I thought again to all the loot we lost when the walls came down, and how if we hadn't stunned the giant, he might have buried what loot we did get.

I kicked the bottom of the branch and said, "Good thing we stopped the big guy from knocking this one down too, huh? Wouldn't have got anything if he completed that swing!"

And right as I finished speaking, a hidden cubby in the bottom of the wood popped open, activated by my kick. We all just looked at each other.

"Luckiest S.O.B. alive, I tell ya," Dan said.

I was only half listening, and laughing a little, as I looked into the hideaway. Inside was a book. The Tome of Movement.

Item	Commonality:	Weight:	Armor:	Bonus:
Tome of Movement	Epic: One Use Only	N/A	N/A	Consumption gives the bearer an increase of 20 percent to Dexterity and 20 percent increase to all Critical attempts and effectiveness.

"Hot damn. I change my mind. I want to roll," Gary said.

I turned to look at the Brawler, ready to try my luck, but he was smiling from ear to ear.

"Just messing with you! Congrats, Alex!"

Everyone else cheered and added their congratulations. I thanked them and then didn't hesitate. With a click, I added the Tome of Movement's abilities to my character.

"Now we're done," I said. "Let's take tomorrow off. We deserve it!"

I heard a chorus of agreement.

We descended to the forest floor. Wayne buried the body of Gerald Lancaster, and our Gift of Lady Lancaster went up to +9 for all Stats and +9 for all Resistances.

With that done, we chose to log off right there in the forest. I decided to take a quick look at my character with my new bonuses and items before leaving.

Alex:				Resistance:	
Rogue:		Level: 38		Resistance:	
Str:	38 (+21)	Atk:	790	Fire	54
Cst:	42 (+58)	Hps:	10000	Water	54
Agi	10 (+37)	Mana:	0	Air	54
Dex:	(76 (+83)*1.2)	Armor	200	Earth	69
Wsd:	22 (+20)	Movement:	90	Holy	54
Int:	1 (+20)			Dark	54
Chn:	250 (+21)			Poison	54
				Disease	54

We were still a far way off from being able to take on Riff, but I was feeling better about our chances.

With a wave, I said, "See you all tomorrow night!"

And I left Resurgence.

CHAPTER 26

January 8, 2044

I was sitting in my living room reading a book when I heard a knock at the door. It wasn't unexpected. Tonight was the party at Dan's place, and he had promised to send drivers for all of us. I thought it was a bit of overkill, but Dan said he wanted all of us to feel like we could let loose as much as we wanted. The drivers would take us home after the party.

When I opened the door, I saw a very large man standing in front of me. He had a very close-cropped haircut and wore a tight-fitting black suit. The outfit only looked so tight because of his size. He was easily over six feet tall and well north of two hundred pounds. And he looked to be in excellent shape.

"You must be my ride," I said.

The driver nodded and motioned toward a black Cadillac parked near the curb of my home. All of the windows had a heavy layer of tint. "This way, Mr. Stanton."

"Please, just call me Alex. That's a pretty sweet ride."

The driver didn't answer and preceded me to the vehicle. He approached the rear door and opened it for me. I slid in without a word and nestled into a very spacious and comfortable back seat. I noticed there were a couple of water bottles and some food in the back. No alcohol, though. I certainly thought Dan would have provided some booze.

As the driver got into the car, I realized that I couldn't see him in the driver's seat. There was a black partition that was blocking my view from being able to see the front seat and out the windshield. I also noticed that the tint on the back windows was complete. Not only was it impossible for anyone to see in, but it was impossible for me to see out.

"What's with the windows?"

Over an internal intercom I heard the driver answer. "Mr. Hamson's idea. Wants it all to be a surprise," he said. A few seconds later, the driver muttered, "He's a little weird."

"No worries, man. I know Dan, and that's the understatement of the year. Just let me know when we get there."

"Will do, sir. There are some magazines on the door, and you can put a show on the center console. It's not a long drive, but it could get boring back there."

"Much appreciated."

I took his advice and rifled through a few of the magazines. They were all gossip rags about what celebrity was sleeping with another celebrity and the like. I normally wouldn't bother with these types of mags, but I found myself enjoying all the rumor mongering they dished out.

Sooner than I expected, the intercom clicked on again, and I heard the driver say, "We're here, Mr. Stanton. Please wait for the door to be opened."

Several seconds later, the door to the car swung open, and I saw a man standing on the other side. Behind him were bright lights and a cavernous room. I couldn't see anyone past the man, but I wasn't looking all that hard for anyone else. The man in front of me was taking up all my attention. It's quite rare that I encounter someone in a military uniform.

"Mr. Stanton, my name is Colonel Thompson. Welcome. You are the first to arrive."

"This doesn't look like a party, Colonel. Where are we going?"

"Everything will be explained in due time, Mr. Stanton. Please just continue to follow me."

It's the only line that I'd been getting out of the colonel since I got out of the car. It made me think of an NPC that was on a loop, where they say the same thing over and over again, because I wasn't asking the right question. And I had no clue what the right question was. All I knew was that I had no idea what was going on. I certainly didn't feel like I was about to be entertained.

From the moment I had stepped out of the car, in fact, it was pretty clear this wasn't some kind of twisted fantasy that Dan had come up with for a party. Not that I wouldn't put it past him. He seemed exactly like the kind of guy that would have an elaborate costume party, complete with props and actors, but not tell the guests.

Colonel Thompson wasn't the only military member I saw. The large room where the car stopped was full of them. Both men and women were going from one location to another. No one was moving with urgency, but everyone looked to have a purpose. Only the ones with guns were stationary. This was part of what made me guess this wasn't a Dan charade. Those guns looked too damn real.

I didn't have much of a choice, so I followed the colonel. The massive room had various halls that branched off from it, and it was one of these halls that we were headed to now. I took one last look around me and noted the lack of any items that could identify where I was or even what military unit this was. I figured that time might unravel this mystery, though, so I was fully compliant.

"And would you please just call me Alex. I don't know what this is, but it doesn't seem like I'm in any trouble."

"Why do you say that?" the Colonel asked.

"I'm walking freely. No handcuffs or shackles or any other non-sense like that. You don't seem the least bit concerned about me as a threat," I said. "Not that I could fight or anything, but your demeanor tells me you don't consider me a 'hostile,' if that makes sense."

"You're pretty good at reading body language, Alex," Thompson said as he continued to walk me down the hallway. It had neither windows nor doors and looked to go on forever. "How'd you learn that?"

"Selling in games. Virtual reality means that people's tells will come through when they are trying to buy stuff. Negotiating or straight lying about how much money they have. I learned to look for those things to get a better deal."

Thompson nodded his head in front of me as he walked. "Pretty impressive skill."

After a few more meters, the colonel stopped in front of a door. There were no markings on it, so I had no idea what lay beyond. When I was next to the door, he looked at me and said, "You seem like a good guy, Alex. This could have gone a lot of ways. I'm happy to see you kept your cool and didn't freak out."

"Oh, I'm freaking out, Colonel. I've just got a decent poker face, I guess."

A smile escaped his lips before he said, "Keep your cool in there as well, and everything will be fine. I'll be seeing you soon."

I walked through the door and found a large conference room. Inside was a table, big enough to sit twenty. On the wall, across from, me was a large, inactive monitor. On the walls to my left and right were maps of the world.

The only other thing in the room was a man. He was dressed in fatigues, and I noted he didn't have a name tag. Running down his chest were three black stars. I didn't know what rank that made him, but I knew he was at least a General.

"Please, Alex. Have a seat."

I walked over to the seat across from the military man and took a long look at his face. I couldn't tell his age, but he looked old, the kind of old that comes from worry, not age. His hair was cut close to the sides of his head, with nothing but grey left. I guessed that his hair had been black in his youth, though, as there were a few stray black strands in his eyebrows. His hair receded a bit, but not enough that one could call him bald.

His eyes were fierce. They were set back a bit in his skull, casting a small shadow over them, making them seem black. They were also intense, and I found it hard to look away. His jawline was strong, and his face a bit gaunt at the cheeks. His wrinkles, of which there were few, did not touch his eyes. This man did not have "laugh lines." There was no doubt in my mind that whoever this man was, he was the boss.

"You have me at a disadvantage. You know my name, but I don't know yours."

"General will be fine, Alex. It's what everyone calls me."

"A bit cliché, but fine. General it is. Would you like to tell me what I'm doing here?"

"In fact, Alex, I would."

I sat up straight and waited for him to continue.

"But first, there's another that needs to join us," he said, and reached for the intercom set into the table in front of him. "Colonel, please send him in."

The door behind Alex opened, and in walked Dan. Unlike the last time there was a party with all of the team, Dan wasn't wearing some gaudy outfit. He was outfitted with loose trousers, a short sleeve button up shirt with Hawaiian floral patterns, and sandals. He also wasn't wearing his usual smile. In fact, he looked a bit nervous.

"Hey, Alex."

"Dan. Quite the party you invited me to. Should I be asking for a lawyer here, bud? This seems more like an inquisition than a celebration."

"Nah, man," Dan said. "There's actually a lot to celebrate, but it's all a little confusing. The General here should be able to clear it up, though."

"That's right, Alex. This is a cause to celebrate, but not because of any achievement you've made in the game," the General said. "More accurately, not because of any mission you've been granted by AltCon."

The General was talking in riddles, and it was making me annoyed. I let that show on my face.

"Your real mission is what I'm talking about, Alex. The one given to you by the Wanderer."

My head turned quickly to Dan. "What the hell, man! I told you that in confidence!"

"I know! I know!" Dan exclaimed, holding his hands out in front of him. "But just hear us out. You'll see what this is all about."

I stared hard at the man I thought was my friend and looked back at the General after several more moments. "Alright. I'm listening. But if this isn't good, I'm not saying a word and getting a lawyer."

The General folded his hands in front of himself and began to tell his story to Alex. Unlike with Tim, the General started farther back, with the phone call from Robert Shoal that had been received by the technician within the Department of Defense. The General explained how Shoal's death had sparked an investigation and unearthed some concerns about what could have happened to Shoal. The decision was made to plant someone into the game.

"That person was Mr. Hamson."

"From the beginning, Dan?" I asked.

"Yeah, man. It's why I couldn't get mad at you in the forest when you told all of us about the Wanderer. I realized that you and I had been working on the same thing all this time, only from different angles. Like I said then, it's better that we come clean first rather than having everyone find out on their own."

"Mr. Hamson had his suspicions for a long time, Alex. Your ability to achieve impossible results highlighted you," the General said. "Of course, none of us even considered that the game's AI was helping you along the way."

"So why are you showing me all this now?" I asked, waving my arm around the conference room and indicating the whole secret installation.

"Because you don't have the whole story, Alex. None of us have. At least, not until now. You see, from early on, we knew what AltCon was doing. You mentioned to Dan that there was a code implanted in the game."

"That's what the Wanderer told me, yeah."

"And that makes sense with everything we know. The difference is that you knew about the code but didn't know what it was for. Here, we knew what was happening but didn't know what the code was. We knew one existed, but nothing more."

"Ok. Then what's it for?"

"Manipulation, bro," Dan said. "The assclowns at AltCon have been conditioning the players to get them to act in a certain way. We think it starts when you log in. During that process, they do something that changes the way we think. They try to make us more compliant to their requests. Do you remember the video games?"

I looked at the General and Dan, nodding my head. "Yeah, I remember that. I still can't believe you guys bought them."

"Almost everyone in the game did, Alex," the General said. "Not just your team, but all the beta testers. Dan spent a lot of time confirming that fact. The only person he came across who didn't buy the games was you. It was the same with the option to buy stock in AltCon.

"It was not a simple compulsion. Rather, a desire that had been instilled in them to do it. Until they completed the task, that desire would remain. Like with the games, after the purchase was made, they didn't have any further inclination to buy more."

"I didn't do that," I said.

"Again, you were one of the outliers. But it seemed the move to purchase the stock was a mistake. The efforts made to manipulate the players was done haphazardly and lacked the earlier finesse we had seen from AltCon's efforts."

"Wait. How can you tell? Just because of how much people wanted the stock?"

"No, Alex," the General said. "We've been monitoring Dan's brain patterns for months now. We can see the effects the conditioning is having on Dan's brain activity."

"There's activity?"

The General stopped for a moment and then burst out in laughter. "Damn, Dan! These guys are ruthless!"

But Dan wasn't paying any attention to the General. He was looking at Alex. "Really? Even now?"

I smiled for the first time since I'd arrived at this military fortress. "Couldn't pass it up, buddy. Please, General, keep going."

The General stopped laughing. "So, we looked at Dan's brain scans, and a neurological specialist was able to tell us what was happening, how the conditioning would reward Dan and the other beta testers for complying with their wishes. It's all been very subtle, but according to the specialist, the thing with the stock prices looked like a hatchet job.

"We have no idea who made the call for that particular decision, but soon after, AltCon's former Director of the Board was found dead from a failed robbery attempt."

The General paused there to let the new information sink in.

First Robert Shoal and now this director guy. "Another body added to AltCon's list, then?"

"There's no proof that they were responsible for either death, Alex, but it certainly does look suspicious."

"Yeah, it does," I agreed.

"But now we have a better picture, bro. We've known what they were doing, and to some degree, how they've been doing it, but we never understood if anything in the game was directly involved. Now we do."

"Dan is right, Alex. We've been working tirelessly to uncover this plot. There are multiple organizations tackling this problem from all directions. Your contribution is the latest, and it greatly amplifies our understanding as to what is going on in the game. Up until this point, we had come up rather empty on that front."

I looked at Dan, and he simply shrugged his shoulders. "I was paying attention to everything and asking around, you know, gathering information. But I didn't have that insider knowledge like you had."

This made me think about the past few months and the man sitting next to me. It had all been a lie, but I couldn't get too angry about that. I'd been doing my own share of lying. I just wondered if any of it were real.

"I may have hidden a lot from you guys, that's true. But my friendship for you guys was no lie. Was this all an act, man? Everything?"

Dan looked a bit ashamed and said, "A little of it, yeah. I'm nowhere near as inept as I let on, but the General wanted me to play that role to keep anyone from suspecting me. I think it annoyed him when I stayed in character all the time, though."

"You have no idea, Mr. Hamson."

I couldn't help but smile at the comment.

"And the thing at Jenny's house, that was all an act too. I never would have done something that stupid on my own," Dan said, sighing. "But it worked. You guys never let me forget it, and it probably ruined any chance I could have ever had with Kaitlin, but I knew what AltCon was doing, bro. It's a sacrifice I had to make."

"And our friendship?"

"What about our friendship? Dude, that's never been in question. I'd do anything for you guys."

I felt a sense of relief from hearing his words. Like me, he had his own agenda, but the feelings were real.

The General continued. "We still don't know why you are different, Alex, but at least we know we have one person in the game who does not seem to be affected by the conditioning. That's a good bit of information and makes me feel comfortable that AltCon can't get to everyone."

I had an idea as to what it was that blocked me from this conditioning they kept talking about—the Wanderer's intervention.

"I get an error message every time I log in," I said. "Dan, you remember that first time I logged in and was out in the middle of the forest?"

"Sure, we had to come find you and save you from the killer bunnies."

I laughed and said, "Right. Let's tell that story so it's not only Wayne who got hammered by the rabbits. Before I logged in, I had a sudden bout of claustrophobia. It had never happened to me before. I didn't know what to do, and I tried to log out. The RAC wouldn't let me, though, and I kept getting an error message. I finally calmed down, and I popped into the game where you found me.

"I found out from the Wanderer that it was that instant when he decided to change my character and gave me my bonus to Chance. Now, every time I log in, he has to tweak the process to keep my Chance score. It's a very small change that no one has ever noticed, but the same "error" message pops on my screen for the briefest of moments before I enter Resurgence. That probably messes with their conditioning."

"I'd have to consult with our specialists, but it sounds reasonable," the General said.

"I don't think the Wanderer could do that to everyone. It would tip off the AltCon people as to what is going on," I said, thinking about what had been happening to everyone I knew in the game.

I had been overwhelmed from the outset, thinking about how I would tackle this problem all by myself. When I finally told my friends about what I had been doing, an unrealized weight had lifted from my shoulders. Now that I knew I truly wasn't alone in this fight, I felt something totally different. It was hard to explain, but I think for the first time I felt like the impossible just might be attainable. But the odds were still heavily against us. I let the General know my feelings.

"I can't even begin to tell you the relief I have, General. I didn't know what this was when I got here. The whole military thing really freaked me out. But knowing that Dan and I are out there, working together, let's just say it's uplifting.

"But still, what can we do against a company like AltCon? Now that I know the full extent of this whole thing, I've got to ask. What can two guys do against a behemoth like that?"

The General smiled and shook his head at me. "Behemoth? Alex, you are sitting in a military installation. The behemoth is the Department of Defense and the power it wields. And don't forget, I told you there were other organizations on our side, and their abilities, while different, are unparalleled. I'm not going to get into who is doing what, but know that the true behemoths are on your side."

"Don't worry, bro. He never tells me who's doing what either. The General is sneaky like that. I figured you would appreciate it."

"Says the guy who's been working undercover for months."

"Well," Dan said, "I did actually tell you guys months ago what I was doing, you just didn't believe me."

"What? When?" I asked.

"In front of the Monastery of Might, when I called forth the bridge across the water. I said, and I quote, 'If I were like that all the time, none of you would believe that I wasn't really a deep cover operative.' Remember that?"

"Well, sure. But that was you being you."

"Pretty much. But you can't say I didn't tell you," he said, while smiling and holding out his hand for a fist bump.

He had me there, and I reluctantly bumped fists. Smiling, I said, "I'm just glad Jason isn't here to see this. Still, it doesn't change my earlier statement, General. The embodiment of the code in the game is about as close to an end game quest as you can get. I've got some ideas on a way to go at the code, and it's good to know that Dan will follow my ideas, but we're still just two guys."

"What makes you think there are only two of you?"

At that moment, the door opened again, and all of my friends walked through the door. Jason and Wayne were there, as were Gary, Jenny, Kaitlin, and Tim.

They stopped at the far side of the table. I stood up and was prepared to explain everything, but Jason put his hand up.

"We heard everything, Alex. I think we actually got here before you. We were in the other room with that Colonel guy, and he explained the situation. Tim, who apparently is also working with this General guy, filled us in as well."

I looked at the General and said, "Tim?"

"He was actually a later addition to the team, Alex. But he's known about AltCon's intentions for a while now."

"Something we'll be talking about later," Jenny said as she glared a bit in Tim's direction.

"Don't be too harsh. I recruited Tim for what he can do outside of the game, Jenny, not for what he can do inside."

"I don't understand," I said.

"Tim has a very unique set of skills that might be needed in the months to come," the General explained, but I still had no idea what he meant. Dan picked up on my confusion.

"Tim can beat the crap out of anyone. Probably several anyones—I mean someones. Lots of people."

"At least we know that part of Dan's personality was never an act," Tim said as he walked up to me and shook my hand. "The General asked me to come up with a plan to protect my friends and our families outside the game. That's what I'm good at."

"Anyone else in on this?" I asked, completely flabbergasted at that point, but happily returned the hand shake.

"Don't look at the rest of us," Gary said. "I can't tell you the number of times I heard someone say, 'What the hell?' in that other room. This is all a surprise to us, too."

"Yup. But we are all in, Alex. The Colonel was very convincing," Wayne said. "Also, I did not get slaughtered by bunnies. Fix that memory in your head, Dan."

Everyone let out a small laugh at that.

Kaitlin, who hadn't said a word since she entered, walked up to Dan.

"I heard everything. We're going to have a long talk, you and I," she said, planting a small kiss on his cheek. "Just know that I'm very proud of you, Dan. You are a hero in my eyes, even if you did almost burn us all down."

Dan blushed several shades of red as Kaitlin walked back over to stand with the rest.

Putting his hand on his cheek where Kaitlin kissed him, I heard him say under his breath, "So worth it. Completely and totally worth it."

The General stood from his chair after everyone had stopped talking. "I've heard time and again from Dan that you are the leader of this group, Alex, albeit somewhat reluctantly at times."

"I've never asked to be leader."

"And yet these people look to you when it comes time to formulate strategy. And I've been told from Dan that, of the eight people here, you were chosen by the Wanderer to carry his mantle. It wasn't because you were the most honorable, but because you were the likeliest to be the most cunning."

"Yeah, Wayne would have been the most honorable of us."

"And I'd have never gotten us as far as you have, bud. We've talked it over, and you're the boss. Get over it."

I couldn't help but grin and chuckle a bit at Wayne's words.

"This is your Team, Alex," the General said. "The people in this room, including myself, the Colonel, and the people in this facility. Even those outside resources I mentioned earlier. Naturally, I'll handle everything outside the game, but inside, it's going to be your call. Lean on them for the support you need, knowing that you don't need to hide anything from them any longer."

I was having a hard time controlling my emotions as I looked at every face in the room. The General was right, and I could see the trust they had in me, reflected in their faces. I couldn't mess this up.

The fact that all of these people were counting on me to make the right choices started to weigh on me, and I was feeling more than a little anxiety. This was more than just me sneaking around the woods of Resurgence, trying to level my character and complete an impossible task. I was surrounded by the full force of a government, for heaven's sake! The General must have recognized my hesitation.

"Don't think about everything, Alex. Focus on what you can control. The game."

I nodded my head in his direction, silently thanking him for the advice. But he wasn't finished.

"You said you had an idea of how to go after the code. What is it?"

I looked around the room and realized that I could finally talk about my big plan. However, I couldn't be sure it would work. There was still one step I needed to take.

"I still need to talk to the Wanderer. I've got a plan, but I need to find out if there's a way to trigger a quest. A world-wide event."

"To what end?" the General asked.

"Well, I don't know how much you know about what's going on inside the game, sir."

"Explain it as if I know nothing."

"Ok." I took a deep breath, and then started to explain my plan. "Resurgence is a fantasy-based role playing game. Inside this world, there are good guys and bad guys. Although, the term 'good guy' is a bit misleading. The King, who is in charge of the good side, sent a whole family to death just to protect a secret that could dethrone him."

"Sounds like every despot the world over," the Colonel said.

I nodded my head in agreement. "Pretty much the case. Still, the King's enemy is far worse. Think of every villain you've seen in every fantasy movie, and that's the Children of Loust."

"Loust is the bad guy?" the General asked.

"At some point, yeah. But he's been gone for a long time. The people fighting in his name now are called the Children of Loust," I explained. "And while the King may be a bastard for killing off that family, the minions under Loust's banner have slaughtered hundreds of innocents. It's no contest. The Children of Loust are the bad guys.

"As soon as we entered the game, we were informed by a system-wide message that the King and the Children of Loust were fighting it out. Loust's men wanted to destroy the kingdom and enslave everyone, and the King's army is defending the land. Classic fantasy trope."

"Agreed. Not a huge amount of originality there," the General agreed.

"No reason to tweak a formula that works well, and it has made the game quite enjoyable for us. But the adventurers—that is to say, the players—aren't a part of the army. If you take on quests from the King, you can fight for the good side and gain items and experience."

"Right. The sweet loots Dan speaks about all the time."

That got a chuckle from everyone as we saw this grizzled older warrior talk about "sweet loots."

"That's it exactly, sir. Recently, we learned that players could fight on the side of Loust as well. I have no idea what they get in return, but I imagine it is the same as what we receive fighting for the King. But the fact that the players can choose either side is what gave me this idea.

"Ever since I learned about the code, and figured out where the code was placed, I've been trying to come up with a way to storm Loust's positions and kill the mob who represents the code."

"There is an entire mob of them?"

"Sorry, sir. Game-speak. Mob means 'Moving Object.' It's what we call a beast or monster we are going to kill."

"Got it. Please continue."

"Ok. Well, if I were the programmer behind the code, I would have placed it in some random tree out in the middle of a forest. No real chance it would ever be discovered. But AltCon went in the other direction. They placed it in the most unstoppable force in the game.

The mob is called Supreme Overlord Riff Lifestealer, and it has singlehandedly wiped out entire companies of the King's army."

"Makes sense for a company of AltCon's standing to take over the highest-level creature for its own reasons. It's a direct reflection of their ego," the Colonel said. "Also, mental note, if Alex decides to ever try and take over the world through a game that requires a secret code, we burn every last tree in the forest down."

I couldn't help but laugh, as did the others, but I also shook my head at the Colonel and said, "It's hard to explain, but it's not actually a part of the game. Despite having such an impact, the Wanderer remains completely unaware of Riff's action or the story surrounding him. Honestly, it doesn't make much sense to me at all."

"As it turns out, Alex, it makes perfect sense to me," the General said, and turned to Thompson. "The game is housed on AltCon's main servers, the code is at the Motel, and it gets pumped into the ether through the separate node. I don't know how the code is stripped out of the game's primary code, though, before it gets back to AltCon's main servers. That's the only way to explain that the Wanderer isn't aware of this Riff character. Let's try to figure that part out."

The Colonel nodded his head and wrote something down on a pad of paper.

"Care to explain, General?" I asked.

"No, Alex, I don't. Remember when I said I would take care of everything outside the game? Well this is one of those times. Just know that it makes sense. Now please, continue."

"You weren't kidding, Dan. He is sneaky," I said to my friend and got a light laugh in return. "Basically, that's it. One side is fighting the other, and the players can take part on either side, which is what led me to my idea.

"Instead of me and my team trying to attack Loust's army directly, along with a few friends that we've met along the way that we trust, we get everyone involved. The fact that players can choose sides is what sold it for me. In every game that I've ever played, which follows this same story line, there is always a world-wide type of event where the players can choose a side to fight for in the 'great battle.' I plan to talk to the Wanderer, learn how to trigger the quest, and then do just that."

"And then attack the code while the rest of the beta players are taking part in the quest?"

"Essentially, General, that's it. I have a few other surprises in mind, but I'm not sure if those will pan out."

"Can you elaborate on those?" the General asked.

"No, General, I can't. Remember when you said I should take care of everything inside the game? Well this is one of those times."

I heard half of my teammates gasp behind me and the other half laugh loudly. The General just raised his eyebrows with a small smirk.

"Guess I deserved that one, huh?"

"Indeed. But don't worry, sir. I plan to make it an all-out battle. To get rid of that code, we'll need everyone.

"I'm going to start a War. A complete and total War."

Epilogue

Terrence Jolston wasn't the only person who had access to the Old Man, but there were few in AltCon who had as much. Ever since the concept of Resurgence, the RACs, and the Old Man's genius plan to use the RACs as a delivery system to encourage compliance to AltCon's wishes, Jolston had been in this office more than anyone else.

"I've read the report from Glenn," the Old Man said.

"There wasn't much to it, I'm afraid," Jolston said, "but the man seems quite capable in his duties." In truth, Jolston hadn't liked the man from the outset, but he understood the need for assets that could operate outside the official channels of AltCon.

"That he is. And his skills are far more complex than you might imagine. There have been a number of times that Glenn has come through when I've needed him. His loyalty is as hard won as yours, Terrence."

Jolston could only nod at the Old Man.

"I've asked Glenn to continue monitoring the two Agents. They remain an unknown, and I don't much like unknowns."

"I'm sure he will follow his orders dutifully."

The Old Man cackled at Jolston's words. "Oh, Terrence. That is rich. I think you would be hard pressed to find a man less likely to follow anyone's 'orders.' That man does what he likes," the Old Man said and laughed a bit more. "But have no fear; what that man likes most is the money I provide him, and he'll not fail in this simple task."

"He seemed to be a professional, sir, and I fully trust in your judgement."

"As you should, Terrence. After all, I did elevate you against all others. I think the opinion on my judgement, at least from you, should be quite secure," the Old Man responded, smiling at Jolston.

"Now, Terrence, what of our program?"

Jolston took out a tablet and began running down the recent numbers for the beta test of Resurgence. The Old Man wasn't interested in the game itself, of course, but the results of the ongoing conditioning. The numbers there were quite impressive, with more and more players falling in line with their coding.

"But we do have a resistance to the programming?"

"Yes sir, we are at 98 percent effective."

"Well within acceptable parameters. It was a mistake for anyone, especially that fool of a former director, to think that there wouldn't be outliers. Have we come up with another test for the subjects?"

The former director was Thomas Bradshaw, the man who had died at the hands of some miscreant during a botched robbery. It was Bradshaw's death that provided the opportunity for Jolston to take the position over the Board of Directors, cementing the direction of the beta.

"We are looking at ways to implement subtlety into the code, sir. At this point, we feel comfortable in the level of appreciation felt by the players for the company. When faced with a negative stimulus, directly resulting from the actions of AltCon, the players have been unable, and unwilling, to put that blame on the company. More so, even when it's quite clear, their response is to defend the company and sing its praises.

"What type of stimulus are we talking about?"

"In several instances, we have introduced bugs into the game that have negated hours, and sometimes days, of work by specific players. The result is a total loss of their promised rewards, with no ability to compensate them for their efforts. Where this should lead to a distinctly negative reaction to the company, we've seen the exact opposite. They are willing to place the blame on 'coders' whom they believe are the ones responsible for messing up the game, but they won't disparage the company."

"That is an excellent means by which to test the players, Terrence. Subtle, indeed. Perhaps I could suggest something a bit harsher, though," the Old man said.

"Of course, sir. What did you have in mind?"

The Old Man leaned back in his chair and reviewed the information in front of him. He spent several more moments doing so before nodding his head.

"A 98 percent acceptance rate is phenomenal. It's far better than anything I could have imagined. It's the only reason that I think we can try this next step. But be warned, this one needs to be corrected. It can't be like when the players lose their progress in the game."

"Yes, sir. We'll set up whatever idea you have," Jolston agreed.

"I want you to withhold their pay. But not from everyone."

"Sir?"

"Figure out those players who are living paycheck to paycheck, the ones who would be most impacted by a loss of their income. Then I want you to create a clerical error wherein they do not receive their pay."

Before Jolston could comment, the Old Man continued. "Like I said, I want you to fix this problem within enough time that they won't actually be harmed personally or have their livelihood affected. I don't want anyone losing their homes or cars. And, for the love of god, make sure no one is using that money to pay off a bookie or some other lowlife who could come looking for their money or hurt our employees. Don't lump those people in with the test group at all."

"I understand, sir. But to what end? I'm not sure I understand the desired outcome?"

The Old Man laughed again. "Not everyone is as loyal as you, Terrence. I know you would do anything for me and this company."

"Without question, sir. I'd jump in front of a moving vehicle for you," Jolston said, with absolutely no hesitation.

"That won't be necessary, I promise you. But not everyone has benefited from this company as you and your family have. When people's lives come undone, they often look for the largest entity to become their scapegoat. It's not their fault that they haven't accumulated savings or lived within their means. No, it's always the government, or some other ambiguous element that receives that blame, the great 'They' you always hear about. 'I could have done this or that, but They stopped me.' In this case, we will be that entity.

"When that happens, the first—and in this case, accurate—blame should fall on the shoulders of AltCon. That's what I want to test. When their lives are on the brink of falling to pieces, will the conditioning hold out, or will they blame this company?"

The test the Old Man was suggesting was brilliant in its simplicity. A simple clerical error, stretching out for a week, would truly test the conditioning. And in the end, there would be no overall harm to anyone, as the problem will be fixed and never repeat itself.

"It will be done, sir."

"This is one of those truly watershed moments, Terrence. Everything about this concept will be proved viable if this has the desired effect. Don't fail me on this."

"Have no fear, sir. Like in all things, you can count on me for this."

The End of Redemption

The Rise of Resurgence (Book Three)

The story will conclude in:

Retribution
The Rise of Resurgence (Book Four)

Thanks for reading!

This book was, without a doubt, the most fun I've had writing a story. From the older characters of the Dwarves and Della of the Glade, to the new environments of deserts and forests, I loved the changing environments and new characters I could weave into this story. I had originally planned a trilogy, but there were so many fun things to explore, and so much more story to tell, that I felt I would have cheated you, the reader, if I didn't complete this story with one more, full length book. The two worlds, inside and outside the game, will come crashing together in the final book of the series, Retribution, and I hope you are going to love it as much as I'm enjoying writing it!

Please leave a review!

I echo every other author out there, I know, but the reviews are so important to getting our stories noticed by Amazon. As many readers are aware, there has been a push to have GameLit as its own genre, and the more stories with large numbers of reviews, the more likely Amazon will recognize our request. And I can tell you it was the feedback from the first two books that made this third one a better story, both the positive and negative.

If you find that you enjoyed these books, and the idea of a story taking place inside an environment largely crafted from the ideas of a game, then I encourage you to check out these Facebook pages dedicated to stories of GameLit and LitRPG.

GameLit Society
LitRPG Books

The most far reaching of the LitRPG Facebook groups, with over 10,000 members, the LitRPG page hosts authors, readers, fans, and quite a few characters in their own right! If you are a fan of these works, you would do yourself a disservice to not check out the LitRPG FB page!

Acknowledgements

It goes without saying that these works couldn't be completed without the help of so many other people. Listing them below is in fact the least I can do, and I'm forever in their debt for their help along the way. I plan to keep bringing you a product that is well written and pleasing to the eye, and void of those pesky typos and grammar mistakes. None of that would be possible without these amazing folks. Thank you so much for everything!

Terisa Rupp (Alpha Reader)
Dustin Frost (Editor)
Rachael Johnston (Artist)
Maureen Cutajar (Formatter)
Stanley Justin
Daniel Hamman
Brenda B. Davis
Cecilia Foust
JD Williams
Jason Wayne Wong
Wayne Whitlock
Jason David Geer
Treb Padula